angel
Uncovered

Katie Price x

arrow books

This edition published by Arrow Books 2011

2 4 6 8 10 9 7 5 3

Copyright © Katie Price 2008; Rebecca Farnworth 2008

Katie Price and Rebecca Farnworth have asserted their right under the Copyright, Designs and Patents Act 1988 to be identified as the authors of this work.

First published in Great Britain in 2008 by Century
First published in paperback in 2009 by Arrow Books

Arrow Books
Random House, 20 Vauxhall Bridge Road,
London SW1V 2SA

www.randomhouse.co.uk

Addresses for companies within The Random House Group Limited can be found at: www.randomhouse.co.uk/offices.htm

The Random House Group Limited Reg. No. 954009

A CIP catalogue record for this book is available from the British Library

ISBN 9780099553182

Typeset by SX Composing DTP, Rayleigh, Essex

The Random House Group Limited supports The Forest Stewardship Council (FSC®), the leading international forest certification organisation. Our books carrying the FSC label are printed on FSC® certified paper. FSC is the only forest certification scheme endorsed by the leading environmental organisations, including Greenpeace. Our paper procurement policy can be found at www.randomhouse.co.uk/environment

Printed and bound in Great Britain by Clays Ltd, St Ives PLC

Chapter 1

Happy Ever After?

'She's the nation's favourite glamour girl! And last month she got married to one of our most famous footballers. She's the fabulous Angel Summer, of course, and here she is looking absolutely stunning!'

Chat-show host Robbie Johnson sounded as if he could barely contain his excitement as he introduced Angel as a guest on his TV show. As she made her way down the staircase, a bright spotlight trained on her, the audience cheering wildly before her, Angel gave a dazzling smile as if she couldn't have been happier to be there. But inside she was experiencing a toxic mix of nerves and insecurities. She hated being interviewed on TV. It made her so nervous and she was always paranoid that she'd say something that would make her look stupid. She was slightly reassured by the warm welcome the audience gave her, but only slightly. She just wanted the ordeal to be over as quickly as possible.

Robbie gave her the compulsory two kisses, while she air kissed him back.

'Well, Angel, married life certainly seems to suit you!' he gushed as she sat down on the purple velvet sofa. 'You're looking even more gorgeous than ever!' Robbie came from the interviewing school of thought that believed outrageous flattery of celebs always got the best results – something that Angel usually found quite sick-making, but today she was glad to be let off the hook. She wasn't up to an exchange with someone who wanted to discover the *real* her – she was on safe ground with Robbie.

'Thanks,' Angel replied. 'Though it's all down to good make up. You should have seen the state of me before my make-up artist got to work!'

The fact was that Angel was an incredibly beautiful woman with amazing green eyes, sculpted cheekbones, sensuous lips and flawless skin. But she was always modest about her beauty, down-playing her looks whenever she could. Now she shook back her long honey-blonde hair so that it cascaded silkily down her back and smoothed her short dress over her thighs – it really wouldn't do to flash the audience. *God, she was nervous*.

'I don't believe a word of it!' Robbie shot back. 'So, Angel, we have to start by talking about your wedding. It really was like something out of a fairy tale, wasn't it? The carriage, the horses, the castle!

Where do we begin? I guess with the dress. Was it your own design?'

As Angel replied the huge plasma screen to the side of her displayed a series of pictures from her big day. There she was getting out of the white and gold Cinderella-style carriage, pulled by six magnificent greys; there were pictures of her walking up the aisle in her breathtaking dress with its pearl-and-diamond-encrusted bodice and a huge train sweeping behind her. Then there was Cal, her gorgeous husband, sliding the glittering diamond band on to her finger, and there they were kissing after they'd been proclaimed man and wife. It really did look like they had found their happy ever after. But the reality could not have been more different and now, in the studio, it took all Angel's strength not to cry.

The bitter truth was that her wedding had been one of the worst days of her life, and she still didn't understand what had gone wrong. She was marrying Cal Bailey, the man of her dreams, the man she had been hopelessly in love with for as long as she could remember – handsome, sexy, passionate Cal Bailey who every woman on the planet with a pulse lusted after. He was all she had ever wanted and when he'd asked her to marry him it had truly been the most wonderful moment of her life. But when the day came Angel was at an all time low, depressed and wretched. In fact, she had been desperately unhappy for the last six months, ever since the birth of her beautiful and much longed for daughter, Honey.

When Angel had found out she was pregnant her reaction had been one of total joy and so had Cal's. For Angel, the discovery that she was having a daughter made the news even more precious because of what had happened in her own childhood. She had been adopted when she was two since her drug addict mother was unable to look after her. Angel longed to give her own little girl the unconditional love she had never had from her own mother. But when Honey was born Angel had been crippled with depression, felt she hadn't bonded with her daughter, and so far hadn't been able to tell anyone. Not even Cal.

She felt deeply ashamed of her inadequacy and feared that she would be seen as an unfit mother because of it, that her daughter would be taken away from her, just as she had been taken away from her own mother. No one knew that inside she felt like she was dying, that every day it was such an effort merely to get out of bed, nor that she felt like the worst mother and the most worthless person in the world.

Robbie started to ask questions about Honey. 'She's absolutely gorgeous,' Angel replied automatically.

'And you seemed to have no trouble getting your

amazing figure back, did you?' he carried on. 'What's the secret?'

Feeling too depressed to eat is a really good appetite suppressant, was the true answer. Instead Angel replied, 'I had the wedding to aim for, so I found it really easy to lose the weight. I just worked out and watched what I ate. Sorry,' she added, hearing the collective groan from women in the audience who had not found it so easy to shift the baby weight. 'I guess I was just lucky.'

'And so what's next? Are you moving to Italy to be with Cal?'

Eight months ago Cal had been bought by AC Milan from Chelsea. Angel hadn't wanted him to go. She was happy living in their new house just outside Brighton, close to her family and friends and within easy distance of her modelling work in London. But it was a fantastic opportunity for Cal and she knew she couldn't stand in his way. So far she had only spent a few days every other week there with him. Cal had accepted that she wanted to have the baby in Britain and that she needed a few months to get used to being a mother before she moved to another country. But now he was getting tired of only seeing his wife and daughter part-time and was insisting that Angel move over to Italy.

'Yes, I am,' she replied, forcing a smile. 'Can you imagine, all that shopping!' she lied. She had lost all interest in buying things for herself, but knew that as a WAG she was expected to love all things designer.

'Ooh! Cal'd better watch his credit cards!' Robbie laughed.

'Actually, I've got plenty of money of my own,' Angel replied, a little frostily. She hated people thinking that she didn't pay her way. Cal may be a millionaire, but she had done very well for herself with her lucrative modelling deals and valued her own independence.

'Of course you have,' Robbie replied a little anxiously, not wanting to upset his star guest. 'Along with your modelling, there's your lingerie and swimwear range and your perfume . . . have I missed anything out?'

Angel smiled. 'Well, there's still my mission for world domination. I haven't quite achieved that yet.'

'Oh.' Robbie looked slightly confused, he didn't do irony.

Angel took pity on him. 'There's various projects in the pipeline. One might involve a TV series in the States – that's all I can really say about it at the moment.' Just before she became pregnant she'd auditioned for a major new TV series set in LA and they were desperate to have her. But the pregnancy had put paid to that. And anyway, at the moment she didn't feel up to going to a strange place and doing something new. It was taking everything she had to hold it together.

'Well, that sounds very exciting. Good luck with it all, Angel! Give it up for Angel Summer, everyone!'

Thank God that was over.

'Darling, you were wonderful!' exclaimed Jez, her hairdresser and one of her closest friends, as she walked wearily back into the dressing room. He was thirty pretending to be twenty-four, flamboyant, camp, wickedly bitchy, obsessed with his looks but incredibly warm-hearted to his friends. Angel adored him and they'd been working together practically from the moment she became a glamour girl. 'So where do you want to go now?' he continued.

Angel looked at her friend blankly. All she wanted to do was go home, crawl into bed and sleep. The old Angel would have been up for hitting the town, having a few drinks and a laugh. But that fun-loving, happy girl was someone the new Angel didn't recognise any more.

'Oh, Jez, I'm sorry but Cal's back for a couple of days and I really want to see him.'

'Of course! I bet you're dying to see him . . . *and the rest,*' Jez said salaciously, winking at her. And Angel forced herself to smile, not wanting him to see that there was anything wrong. Not only was she depressed, Cal was being worryingly distant with her and had been for months now. However, Jez saw right through the fake smile and said, 'Is everything all right between you guys?'

Angel was about to lie that of course everything was fine but found herself saying sadly, 'I don't know, Jez, he's been really offhand with me lately.'

'Well, it can't be easy when you're living apart. And he still doesn't know whether he's been selected for the England team, does he?' Jez said sympathetically. The World Cup was just over two months away and Cal was desperate to be picked. He'd missed out on the last tournament, and if he wasn't selected now the chances were that he would be too old for the next one.

'I know, but every time I try and discuss it with him, it's like he shuts down.'

'That's Cal, isn't it? He can be the most emotionally expressive man I know – apart from me, of course! Or he can be Ice Man,' Jez replied.

And Angel wanted to add that her state of mind hadn't helped things, but didn't. Instead she changed the subject. 'Where's Gemma?' she asked wondering where her best friend and make-up artist had got to.

'You just missed her. She waited until the interview was over and then said she felt so ill she had to go home.'

'Is she okay? I didn't realise there was anything

wrong with her,' Angel replied, instantly concerned for her friend.

Jez sighed, 'Period pain.'

'Oh,' Angel said quietly. That was not good news. Gemma, who was married to Angel's brother Tony, had been trying for a baby for the last year without success. The doctors didn't appear to be taking her concern about not becoming pregnant seriously as she was only twenty-three. But Gemma was convinced that there was something wrong – her own mum had suffered a number of miscarriages – and was becoming more and more anxious and obsessed.

'I'll call her later,' Angel added, gathering her things together and wondering if her friend would want to hear from her. She and Gemma had been close since primary school and had always been there for each other. But since Angel had had Honey there had been a sense of distance between them. Angel didn't feel able to confide in Gemma about how low she felt, believing that her friend wouldn't be able to understand how she could be unhappy when she had everything Gemma longed for.

Jez kissed her goodbye and Angel walked slowly back through the long corridors of the TV studio and outside to where her car was waiting. She felt as if her body was made of lead; she could barely put her legs one in front of the other. As soon as he saw her Tel, her driver, got out of the blacked out Mercedes and opened the door for her.

'Thanks,' she said gratefully, collapsing on to the back seat and wrapping a pale pink pashmina round her shoulders. It was the end of April and the evenings were still cool.

'Radio or CD?' asked Tel.

'I don't mind, you choose,' Angel replied, unable to make even that simple choice. This was what she was like about everything at the moment. Thankfully Tel sensed her mood and just put music on quietly as he expertly negotiated the London traffic.

Angel looked out through the black-tinted glass as they drove through Shepherd's Bush. It was just after six in the evening and everyone she saw – the officer workers heading off for a quick drink, the lovers walking slowly with arms draped round each other, the mother pushing a buggy with a toddler – looked as if they had a purpose, as if they knew their place in the world, knew who they were. Only Angel felt completely lost.

I don't know who I am anymore, she thought bleakly. *What's happening to me?*

An hour and a half later Tel pulled up in her driveway. Thanking him, she got out of the car and walked towards the house. She and Cal had bought it a year ago and Angel loved it. It was a beautiful Georgian mansion in a small village ten miles outside Brighton. The house was set in over twenty acres of grounds, with stables for her horses, two fields, a pool and a beautiful land-scaped garden.

The downstairs lights were still on, she noticed, and instantly felt a knot of tension tighten in her stomach. She had hoped that Cal would already be asleep in bed when she got back as he was exhausted by his intensive training regime. She wanted to avoid any difficult conversations. She knew that he was bound to press her about when she was moving to Italy. She sighed and opened the front door.

Cal was in the living room, stretched out on the sofa, drinking beer and listening to music. He instantly leaped up when he saw her and came to embrace her.

'How did it go?'

'It was all right, I think,' she replied, shrugging her shoulders dismissively.

'I'm sure you were great,' he said supportively. 'You'll have to tape it for me when it's on.' He seemed much warmer with her than he had been last time they met; maybe he'd resolved what was tormenting him?

'It's okay, I don't expect you to watch it,' Angel replied, enjoying the feeling of his arms around her. She had missed him so much. 'Did Honey settle okay?'

'She's been a star,' Cal answered. 'Not stirred at all. I was almost hoping she would wake up, I've really missed her.'

'Well, when she wakes up at three, you're welcome to go in to her.' Angel hadn't meant it but there was an edge to her voice. For the last six months she hadn't had an uninterrupted night's sleep; maybe that was why she felt so low and exhausted all the time.

'If you were in Italy with me, I would get up in the night,' Cal replied, pulling away from her, his voice suddenly cold. 'It's not my fault you've chosen to stay over here.'

She could feel him slipping away from her again and she really didn't want this conversation right now. She was desperately worried about going to Italy – what if she continued to feel so depressed over there? And what if Cal still kept her at a distance like this? Instead of answering, Angel muttered something about needing a drink and kicked off her heels as she wandered into the kitchen.

She had just taken a large slug of white wine when Cal spoke to her from the doorway. 'We can't go on like this, Angel. Us not being together is doing my head in. I hate not seeing you and Honey for weeks at a time.'

So they were going to have this conversation again. The knot of tension tightened inside her once more. 'I know, Cal, but I'm just not sure if I'm ready to move to Italy yet. Maybe in a month?'

He sighed in exasperation. 'No, Angel, I can't do this anymore. I'm not expecting you to move over for good, but I need you to come over for at least the next two months. I need us to be together. I need us to be a proper family.'

Angel felt panic rising at the prospect, not because she didn't want to be with Cal but because she really didn't know if she could cope with such a change feeling the way she did. She was barely coping at home as it was. Tears spilled down her cheeks.

Suddenly Cal took her in his arms and his voice was warm again. 'Hey, it will be fine – more than fine. I'll make sure I spend as much time with you as possible and I'll introduce you to lots of people. I know it won't be easy for you, but I'll do everything I can to make it okay.' He gently smoothed back her hair. 'Come on, let's go to bed.'

'In a minute,' Angel said. 'You go on, I'll be up in a bit.'

'Okay, but don't be long. And by the way,' Cal murmured, kissing her and lightly running his hands down her back, 'did I mention how very sexy you look tonight?'

Angel stared into his beautiful brown eyes, made darker by desire, and felt nothing in return. *What was wrong with her? She so wanted them to be close again.*

Once Cal left the room she drained her glass

practically in one go, then poured herself another. Since Honey was born Angel's libido had hit an all time low. The baby books she'd read had said that this was likely to happen for the first few months, but after over six? Sex had always been such a strong part of her relationship with Cal, and it had always been amazing, they couldn't get enough of each other. Now Angel dreaded getting into bed with Cal, dreaded him even touching her. She'd made so many excuses – headaches, back aches, exhaustion – and Cal hadn't said anything, but she knew he was starting to wonder what the hell was going on. How the woman who once couldn't wait to tear his clothes off and tumble into bed with him had turned into this frigid stranger who hated anyone looking at her body and literally couldn't bear to be touched.

She walked upstairs and checked on her daughter in the nursery. Honey was lying on her back, blissfully asleep, arms stretched over her head, her chubby little fists clenched. Angel leaned over the cot as she did every night to check on her daughter's breathing. During the first weeks after the birth she'd been paranoid that Honey would stop breathing, and would barely sleep because she'd have to keep constantly checking. 'Sorry,' she whispered to her baby daughter now. 'Sorry for being such a bad mother.' It was what she whispered nearly every night . . .

*

Angel went slowly to the bedroom, wondering if she could get away with yet another excuse tonight. But as she opened the door Cal was already lying naked in bed and the lit candles clearly signalled that whatever she felt, he was definitely up for it.

Act, she told herself. *Just do it.* She walked to the side of the bed and said, 'Can you unzip me?'

Cal did as she asked. When she stepped out of her dress he said, 'God, your body is so beautiful.'

Angel smiled and said, 'So is yours.' And it was true, Cal had the most gorgeous, sexy body – long lean limbs, defined abs, olive skin without a single blemish – but as she looked at him, she didn't feel a trace of desire. She lay down next to him and immediately he began kissing and caressing her, slipping off her silk underwear. Cal was the most sensuous, most erotic lover she had ever been with, but now she just wanted it to be over, so she didn't have to think, didn't have to feel. But suddenly she *did* feel something; she felt anger, overwhelming anger. Why didn't he understand how she felt? Why didn't he leave her alone? She didn't want to be touched. She kissed him hard, biting his lip, digging her nails into his back. 'Go on,' she said huskily, 'fuck me.' *Then you'll have what you want, and I can go to sleep.*

And afterwards she felt even further from him than ever.

15

*

At four Honey woke up crying. Angel was wearily pushing off the duvet to go to her when Cal whispered, 'You sleep, I'll settle her.' He returned half an hour later. As he put his arms round Angel he said, 'Just think how great it will be when you're in Italy with me. I can't wait to see Honey every day. I feel like I'm really missing out at the moment. I want to be there for her always, not like my dad was with me.'

Cal's dad had walked out on him when Cal was only two and left him to be brought up by his alcoholic mum. Only his amazing talent for football had saved him, that and his close friendship with Angel's family.

For a moment she didn't reply, overcome with guilt that she was keeping Cal away from his daughter, then she said, 'We'll fly out to Italy next week, Cal.' But even as she said it she was filled with anxiety and it was a long time before Angel went back to sleep. She was obviously a terrible person, a terrible wife, a terrible mother. What was wrong with her? Why couldn't she be happy?

In the morning Cal told her to have a lie in, but even though she felt exhausted she couldn't sleep. Her mum, dad, brother Tony and Gemma were coming over for lunch, and somehow she had to face them and act like everything was okay and pretend to be excited about the move to Italy.

She pulled on her cream silk robe and wandered downstairs where Cal was feeding Honey her porridge and managing to get most of it over himself and the baby. They looked so happy together she felt another pang of guilt. She kissed her daughter's head, practically the only part of her that wasn't covered in porridge. Honey rewarded her with a gummy smile, showing off her two teeth, and banged her spoon on her highchair, splattering Angel's silk robe with porridge.

Cal laughed, then grabbed Angel by the waist and pulled her on to his lap to kiss her. 'Now you're as messy as us!

'I was going to make us scrambled eggs for breakfast,' he went on.

Angel shook her head. 'I'm not hungry and we'll be having a big lunch, won't we?'

'Are you sure? You look like you've lost weight.'

'No, I'm fine,' Angel replied a little defensively and got up, crossing her arms protectively round herself. It was true, she had been losing weight, but she had no appetite at the moment.

'I'll have to build you up with pasta then, won't I?' Cal teased her.

She shook her head. 'You're joking, aren't you? I know I've got to be ultra-slim to compete with those Italian WAGs.'

Cal smiled and kissed her. 'You don't have to

compete with anyone, you'll always be the most beautiful woman in the room.'

As he was being so loving Angel decided that now would be a good opportunity to ask him about what was worrying him. 'So, do you know when you'll hear about the England team?' She plunged straight in with the question and the change in Cal was instant, as if she had flicked an off switch.

'Middle of May,' he muttered, and avoided looking at her.

'But you're feeling positive about your chances, aren't you?' she persisted.

'My knee has been playing up lately, I've had to have extra physio, so no, I'm not feeling particularly positive,' he said quietly.

'I'm sure it will be fine,' she continued, wishing he would let her in.

'Look, can we just drop the subject?' Cal snapped. 'I don't want to talk about it. And can you get Honey dressed? I need to get on with making lunch.'

Sometimes her husband was completely unreachable and she felt like a seventeen year old again, hopelessly in love and completely unable to get through to him. It made her feel so lonely.

'That was a fantastic lunch, Cal, thanks,' said Angel's dad Frank, leaning back contentedly in his chair.

'Weren't you hungry, love?' Michelle, Angel's mum, asked her, sounding concerned.

Angel shook her head. She'd only eaten a few mouthfuls of salad and rearranged the rest of the food around her plate.

Her mother dropped her voice and said, 'You are eating properly, aren't you?'

'Yes,' Angel replied defensively, 'but I'll be modelling again soon and I don't want to look fat.'

Gemma had overheard their conversation and now joined in. 'Angel, you look slimmer than you did before you had the baby! You really need to put on some weight if anything. You don't want to end up with a scrawny body and lollipop head!'

Angel and Gemma used to have the kind of relationship where they could say absolutely anything to each other. After Cal, Gemma was the person she most trusted in the world. But right now, feeling depressed and vulnerable, Angel was furious at her comments. 'I'm not too thin,' she hissed back. 'And anyway, it's none of your business.'

She drained her wine glass to avoid looking at the hurt expression on her friend's face. To cover up how upset she was Gemma got up and helped Cal clear away the plates. Angel felt terrible, she knew she was in the wrong to snap like that, but she couldn't help it. She just wanted everyone to leave her alone. She could sense her mum looking at her anxiously before she spoke.

'Are you sure everything's all right, Angel?'

'Everything's fine, Mum,' she lied, wishing she could tell her how she really felt. Mum was probably one of the few people who would understand as she'd suffered from depression herself. But every time Angel thought of confiding in someone, the same thought stopped her. What if everyone thought she was mad, an unfit mother – just like her real mum – and that she couldn't look after her child? And that thought kept her trapped in her depression, making her feel as if there was no way out. The one hope she clung on to was that perhaps time would heal her. The trouble was it didn't seem to be doing a great job of it . . .

'Has Angel told you yet that she's coming to Italy next week? And this time she's staying at least a couple of months,' said Cal, coming back into the dining room and putting his arms round her.

'That's great news!' Frank replied. 'You two have been apart too much lately and it puts a strain on any marriage.' He smiled at Angel, obviously expecting her to say how happy she was.

It took all her energy to smile back and reply, 'Yes, it'll be good, won't it?' And then, because she couldn't bear the pretence any longer, she added, 'Actually, if it's okay with everyone, I'm going to go upstairs and start packing. I can never get anything done when it's just me and Honey.'

'Good idea, babe, and I'll go and book the tickets online right now,' Cal answered, kissing her.

Upstairs, Angel opened her wardrobe and stared blankly at the clothes inside, trying to decide what to take. But even that task defeated her and she could feel her eyes pricking with tears. How was she going to cope in Italy? And what was happening to her marriage? One minute Cal was lovely to her, the next so cold, and this was only adding to her feelings of insecurity.

She started at a gentle knock at the door. It was Gemma. 'Hi, do you want some help?' she asked, walking tentatively in.

Angel nodded then said, 'I'm really, really sorry I snapped at you, Gem, I didn't mean it.'

'It's okay,' Gemma answered.

'I think I'm just knackered, I feel so uptight at the moment,' Angel continued.

Gemma smiled at her friend. 'I'm sure all new mums feel like that. You've had some huge changes in your life – you've had a baby, stopped working, got married and Cal's been away. And I know I've been a bit crap . . .' Here Gemma's voice faltered.

'You haven't at all!' Angel exclaimed. 'I know how hard it's been for you, seeing me with Honey.'

'No, it hasn't,' Gemma assured her. 'I'm happy

21

for you, Angel. Honey is so beautiful . . . you're so lucky.'

'Yeah,' she answered sadly, 'I am lucky, aren't I?' Yet what she wanted to say was, If I am so lucky, why do I feel so bad? But as she looked at her best friend she realised that this was one thing she was not going to be able to tell her. And if she couldn't tell Gemma, who could she tell?

'Don't be nervous about going to Italy,' Gemma continued, sorting out the pile of clothes Angel had dumped on the bed. 'I reckon you'll have a great time. And it's not far away – we'll come and see you, and you can come back here as well.'

Angel frowned. 'To be honest, I'm worried about Cal. He's been so distant with me lately. I know it's because he's worried about being picked for the team, but sometimes he just won't let me in. Jez calls it his Ice Man side.'

'That's Cal, though, isn't it?' Gemma replied sympathetically. 'Mr Complicated. But that's why you love him, isn't it?'

'I suppose so,' Angel sighed, and then wanting a bit of light relief she picked up a green silk tunic dress and asked, 'Is this WAGtastic enough for Italy?'

Gemma gave it the thumbs up, then said teasingly, 'You're going to have to step your look up a gear. Can you imagine how stylish those Italian WAGs are going to be?' Gemma's eyes gleamed at the thought – she was a total fashionista.

'I'm never going to fit in, am I?' said Angel gloomily.

'You'll be fine.' Gemma shrugged away her friend's worries. 'They'll love you. Anyway it will be good training for the World Cup, and being with the British WAGS twenty-four seven.'

Angel pulled another face. 'That's if Cal even gets in the team, Gemma. Can you imagine how devastated he'll be if he doesn't?'

'I'm sure he will,' she replied. 'He's been playing well this season, hasn't he?'

'I really hope so,' Angel sighed. 'I'll even put up with being called a WAG if he does.' Although she was now labelled that by the press, it certainly was not how Angel saw herself. As far as she was concerned she was a model with her own career and money. She didn't rely on Cal to support her financially. And while Angel loved shopping as much as the next woman, she wasn't a designer label queen – she was just as happy shopping in Topshop as Prada, and frankly couldn't give a stuff about owning this season's must-have designer bag.

'And do you know if Simone will be going?' Gemma asked, picking up another dress and considering it critically for a minute before discarding it.

Simone was Cal's ex-girlfriend; he'd left her to be with Angel. Simone had been devastated by the split and had turned psycho bitch on him, hounding him with phone calls, texts and emails so that in the end Cal had to change his number. She had even thrown white paint all over his treasured Bentley. If they'd owned a pet rabbit, Angel would have been seriously worried . . . But just as Cal was about to go to the police Simone abruptly stopped harassing him, obviously realising that if word got out about how she had behaved she would never bag herself a footballer again. She and Cal came to a deal that she would never contact him again, and in return he wouldn't tell the world what a total bitch she had been. And it had worked for Simone. She had recently started going out with Jamie Gordan, an Arsenal player. He was nothing to write home about in the looks department – 'plain' was the kindest thing you could say – but he was loaded and able to keep Simone in the style which she thought she deserved.

Angel shrugged. 'If Jamie gets into the team, of course she'll come.'

'Don't worry about her, Angel. Everyone else is bound to hate her, she's so vile!'

'Unfortunately she's friends with Gabrielle Carter.' Gabrielle had stepped into Victoria Beckham's designer shoes as the new Queen of the WAGS. Her husband, Connor, was Captain of the England team.

'Ah, well, there'll be plenty of other WAGs you

can talk to,' Gemma said, trying to cheer her friend up.

Angel managed a smile. One of the only good things about feeling so depressed was that she actually didn't give a shit about any of them; nothing they could say to her would make her feel any worse than she did at the moment.

'Cal will look out for you,' Gemma reassured her. 'I know he's so pleased you and Honey are flying over to Italy. I bet you'll have a great time. And maybe when you're out there he'll feel more able to talk to you.'

'I really hope so,' Angel replied, and turned away so Gemma wouldn't see the look of sadness on her face.

Chapter 2

Italian Blues

'So, Angel, how are you enjoying Italy?'

She inwardly flinched at the question being directed at her by Flavia, the extremely beautiful and elegant wife of Enzo, one of Cal's team mates.

'It's great, though I do feel a bit homesick,' she answered in what was a massive understatement. She had been in Italy for two weeks and was utterly miserable. Her depression seemed to have worsened here and despite Cal saying he would help her settle in and spend time with her, he had been training even more intensively and she had hardly seen him. When they were together he seemed distracted, and every time Angel asked him how he was he either said he was fine or else changed the subject.

He had hired a nanny so Angel could begin to do things for herself again – such as riding or going to the gym. But seeing how easily Lucy the new nanny communicated with Honey, and how much the baby liked her, only made Angel more painfully aware of her own inadequacies as a mother. She still felt unable to confide in Cal about her failure to bond with her daughter.

'Well,' Flavia went on in her very nearly perfect English, 'you will have to come out with the other wives – we meet for lunch at least once a week and go shopping, depending on our work schedules.'

Angel's spirits plummeted still further at the thought. Lunch and shopping? She felt as if she was turning into a Stepford Wife!

Flavia smiled at Angel, showing off her perfect white teeth. But Angel wasn't at all sure how genuine that smile was. Since she and Cal had arrived at the lunch party which was being hosted by Flavia and Enzo, Angel had detected a definite undercurrent of hostility coming from Flavia. And Angel was pretty sure she knew why – Flavia fancied Cal. While her husband was busy talking to other guests, Angel caught Flavia gazing at him several times in a way that was definitely flirtatious. Whenever she talked to Cal she stood very close to him and made their conversation seem intimate and exclusive by speaking to him in Italian.

Cal had made a huge effort to learn the language and could actually speak it quite fluently. He had suggested that Angel have lessons too and she knew that she should but her heart wasn't in it right now.

Though it was a pity because if she'd had lessons she could have learned the Italian for 'Fuck off, bitch!' which was exactly what she wanted to say to swishy-haired, slinky-figured Flavia right now.

Angel sipped her champagne and looked round the vast, white, minimalist living room at the other guests. Without exception all the women were stylishly and expensively dressed, all immaculately made up, all with long glossy hair. They really were in a different league from the English WAGs. Angel couldn't imagine the sophisticated Italians hitting the fake tan, and wearing Juicy Couture trackies and Uggs. The thought made her feel even more homesick. She sighed and wished Gemma were with her – she would no doubt have been in fashionista heaven here, working out which designers the WAGs were wearing. Angel was also very aware of the other women sizing her up, and while they didn't look as if they were about to burst into a chorus of 'Who Let The Dogs Out', they didn't exactly look friendly either.

Now Cal walked back over to where Angel and Flavia were sitting, and Flavia rattled something off in Italian to him and Cal laughed. Angel narrowed her eyes; she felt well and truly sidelined. She got up from the sofa, saying, 'I'm just going to check on Honey.' The nannies were looking after the children in another room which had upset Angel. 'I thought Italians were supposed to love children,' she had whispered crossly to Cal when they arrived.

'Shh! They do. It's just that Flavia has got some very expensive things here and she doesn't want them broken.'

'Honey can't even crawl yet, what's she going to do?' Angel demanded. But Cal had told her to chill, that they wouldn't stay long. Now he grabbed her hand and pulled her back down on the sofa. 'She's fine, relax.'

'Ah, these new mothers,' Flavia said, in what seemed to Angel to be a patronising tone. 'Honey will be perfectly all right. You should enjoy the time with your husband.' As she said it she looked appraisingly at him. *Yes*, thought Angel, *she definitely fancies Cal.*

'Your husband's Italian is so good, aren't you impressed, Angel?' Flavia went on. 'Did he tell you that I taught him?'

'He did,' she lied. Cal certainly *hadn't* mentioned it, but no way did she want to give Flavia the satisfaction of knowing that. Angel glared at Cal, who shrugged and looked faintly guilty.

'He was such a model student,' sighed Flavia, twirling a strand of silky hair round a slim finger. She had clearly spotted that moment of tension between Cal and Angel and wanted to work on it. 'Very conscientious.'

Angel felt a sudden flash of hatred for her. With her long chestnut hair and slim but curvaceous figure that she was showing off to maximum advantage in a red silk dress, she reminded Angel of Cal's ex, Simone. In her current state of mind she felt insecure and, yes, there was no mistaking the hot feeling in the pit of her stomach and the desire to say something irrational – she was jealous. She hated thinking of Cal spending time alone with the gorgeous Flavia and her slinky figure.

'I'm sure Angel will soon be speaking the language too,' Cal said loyally, putting his arm round her shoulders. Angel wasn't so sure but she rewarded her husband with a kiss, which was as much for Flavia's benefit as it was for Cal's. He smiled warmly at her and Angel felt awful – she'd hardly shown him any physical affection lately. Then she glanced at Flavia, and was secretly pleased to see how pissed off she looked, though she did her best to disguise it by exclaiming, 'How wonderful to see two people who are so in love! Come on, we should have some more champagne to celebrate – Cal has his Angel!'

And she clicked her fingers at the waiters who busied themselves with opening more bottles. At that moment one of the other WAGs joined them. Cal introduced her as Alessia. She was absolutely stunning with huge velvety brown eyes, beautifully shaped lips, long jet black hair, and more than a passing resemblance to Angelina Jolie. Her beauty could have been intimidating but she was very friendly, and Angel instantly warmed to her when she announced that she had just been to check on her son and had seen Honey.

'Your daughter is adorable!' she exclaimed.

The two of them spent a few minutes happily talking babies which Angel noticed put Flavia's nose seriously out of joint.

Meeting Alessia made the lunch party a little more bearable but Angel felt self-conscious throughout it. She felt as if she was on show, and was all too aware of Flavia and her constant flirtatious glances at Cal.

By the time they drove back to their villa beside Lake Como Angel had a pounding headache from drinking so much champagne. 'You didn't tell me that Flavia taught you Italian,' she said abruptly, trying not to sound accusing but knowing that she did.

Cal concentrated on the road. 'Sorry, I thought I did.'

'So where did Mrs . . . Giordano,' Angel stumbled over the pronunciation, 'give you your lessons?'

'We'd meet after training and go to a café or for a walk, something like that,' he replied casually.

'I bet she was itching to get you back to your place on your own,' Angel said nastily. 'Get you to practise your oral work.'

Angel saw Cal's lip curl and his jaw tighten. 'We'll

talk about this later,' he said curtly. 'But there's nothing to make a big deal of.'

Still Angel couldn't let the subject lie. She waited a few minutes then blurted out, 'Well, I wonder how you'd feel if I'd been having Italian lessons from some sexy Italian man who fancies the arse off me and I just forgot to mention it!'

'I'm not discussing this in front of other people,' Cal said quietly, tilting his head back to remind Angel of Lucy, sitting with Honey behind them. 'Fine,' Angel hissed, 'we'll talk about it at the villa.' She couldn't bring herself to say 'home' because it really didn't feel like that to her.

But anger and jealousy seethed inside her, finally reaching boiling point. Back at the villa, while Lucy gave Honey her bath and put her to bed, Angel found herself hurling accusations at her husband.

'Admit it,' she cried angrily when they were in the living room with the door firmly shut, 'you're having an affair with Flavia!'

'Don't be mad, of course I'm not!' Cal exclaimed, sounding surprised and pissed off.

'Well, she definitely fancies you. I could tell just from the way she looked at you . . . the way she behaved around you. That woman could barely keep her hands off you!'

Cal shrugged. 'What's it matter anyway? I'm with you. I don't even fancy her.'

But Angel wouldn't be placated. 'What – not

even a tiny bit? I bet if she came on to you, you'd be tempted, wouldn't you?'

'Well, it might be nice to be wanted that way again, seeing as you don't seem to be interested,' he retorted. It was a fair comment on what had been happening between them in the bedroom, or rather what had *not* been happening, but Angel carried on, 'I've just had a baby! How dare you say that?'

Cal sighed and sat back on the sofa, head in his hands. 'You stop being SO unreasonable then! Stop accusing me of something I haven't done and wouldn't dream of doing.'

'Swear on our daughter's life that you haven't shagged Flavia!' Angel demanded, standing in the middle of the room, arms folded defensively around herself though inside she ached to be close to him again, to be like they used to be.

He lifted his head and looked at her, his beautiful brown eyes full of sadness. 'If that's what you want, okay, I swear on Honey's life that I haven't had an affair. Satisfied?'

Angel was just about to say yes, was even thinking about saying sorry and giving him a hug, when Cal got up abruptly and, muttering something about wanting to check on Honey, left the room.

Angel spent the rest of the night pacing moodily round the house, unable to settle. Lucy had gone out and Honey was sleeping soundly. Cal had shut himself in his study, saying he needed to work on the column that came out weekly in one of the English papers about his experiences playing for an Italian team. At one point she knocked at the door.

'D'you fancy watching a DVD with me?'

Without turning to look at her Cal shook his head and carried on typing. Angel bit her lip, she hated there to be any conflict between them. She walked over to him and slid her arms round his neck. 'Sorry,' she whispered, 'I didn't mean to say those things. I was totally out of order – I know you'd never have an affair.' Cal made as if to carry on typing but then he softened and turned to slide his arms round her and pull her on to his lap.

'And I'm sorry too,' he said, kissing her neck. 'I should have told you about the lessons with Flavia. You're right, she does seem to have a thing about me. That's why I stopped meeting her.'

'Oh? What did she do?' Angel asked, feeling another surge of anger at Flavia .

'Nothing . . . I could just tell. Anyway, can we stop talking about her now?' Cal slid his hands over Angel's body, gently caressing her skin. 'Do you remember how in our house back home we made love in every single room?' he said.

Angel did remember but was struggling now to recall exactly what it felt like to be that turned on, so full of desire that you couldn't get enough of another person.

'So how about we christen the study then?' Cal said huskily, now slipping his hands under her silk dress and along her thighs.

But Angel, not wanting to be touched, slid off his lap and knelt in front of him. 'And how about I remind you that I'm not so bad at oral work either?'

Angel slept badly that night even though for once Honey didn't wake up. She woke next day to an empty house: Cal had left for training and Lucy had left her a note saying that she had taken Honey to meet up with another nanny. Angel made herself a cup of tea but didn't feel like breakfast. She should have enjoyed having some space; up till now it seemed like the only time she got to herself was in the bath or when Honey was asleep. But she hated it. The silence and emptiness inside the house seemed to be pressing down on her.

She wandered out on to the large terrace which overlooked Lake Como, and sat down on one of the chairs to stare at the view. It was a stunning location: the glittering expanse of blue water in front of her, the rolling hills and mountains in the distance, the lush gardens and elegant pastel-coloured villas by the lake. But the beauty of the surroundings only made her feel more lonely. She felt she had to get out but she had nowhere to go, didn't know anyone.

In desperation she pulled on her riding things

and headed out for the nearby stables. To help her settle in, Cal had bought her the most beautiful chestnut mare. Riding was usually the best release for her, no matter how bleak her mood, but today not even that could lift her spirits. Instead, as she rode through fields and past rows of poplar trees, all she could think about was that she was letting Honey down by not being a good enough mother, and letting Cal down as well. And then she started obsessing about leaving her daughter in a nanny's care. What if something happened to her? Would Lucy know what to do? What if she gave Honey something to eat that she wasn't ready for and the baby choked? The *what ifs* built up into a crescendo of panic until finally Angel was incapable of thinking rationally. She found herself urging her horse into a gallop, desperate to get home and check that her daughter was safe.

She arrived back just as Cal turned into the drive, home from training. 'Can you phone Lucy?' she shouted, as soon as he opened the car door.

'Why, is there a problem?' he asked calmly.

'Please! Just call her, I need to know that Honey is okay,' Angel repeated, frustrated by his lack of urgency.

Cal got out his phone. 'I think Angel wants a word,' he said when Lucy answered, handing the phone over.

'Is Honey okay?' Angel asked urgently.

'She's great. We're just going to have a picnic with another nanny and her children, if that's okay? We'll be back at two, just in time for Honey's nap,' Lucy replied.

'That's fine, I just wanted to check,' Angel said. Feeling weak with relief, she handed the phone back to Cal.

'What was that all about?' he asked as they walked into the house.

'Nothing,' Angel mumbled, 'I just had a horrible thought when I was out riding.'

Cal laughed good-naturedly. 'Babe, you worry too much. Lucy is a fantastic nanny and Honey is having a great time with her.'

'Yeah, I expect you think she's a better mother to her than I am,' Angel said bitterly.

'Of course I don't think that!' Cal said, sounding surprised. 'You're a wonderful mother.' He sighed in exasperation as Angel kept walking, head down, eyes filling with tears. 'I thought you'd be glad that I hired a nanny. I *want* you to have some time to yourself. That doesn't make you a bad mother.'

Cal was right, it had been a lovely, considerate thing for him to do, so why did Angel feel like crying? Why did she feel that the arrival of Lucy was only going to make it harder for her to bond with her daughter? She put a hand up to her face

37

to hide the tears welling up in her eyes. 'I know, I'm sorry, I just had a funny five minutes.'

Cal walked over to her and gave her a hug. 'You need to chill out more. Anyway, I've had some good news. We should celebrate.'

Angel looked at him expectantly and he laughed and said, 'Yes, I've made the first selection for the squad.'

'Oh, Cal, that's brilliant news!' Angel exclaimed, hugging him back and trying to push the dark thoughts out of her head.

'So I was hoping we might be able to pick up from last night – I owe you one, remember?' he said, kissing her. Angel kissed him back but although she was thrilled at Cal's news, sex was the very last thing on her mind.

As they walked into the villa Angel tried to make an excuse about wanting a shower, but Cal was having none of it. He grabbed her arm and led her into the living room. 'I think that exercise did you good, you've actually got some colour in your cheeks,' he said, pulling her on to the sofa. 'And I do like a woman in jodhpurs,' he added, playfully slapping her bum. 'Very sexy indeed,' he continued, unbuttoning her shirt and caressing her breasts.

She could feel his hard on; it looked like there would be no getting out of this one.

'Room number three,' he murmured, unzipping her jodhpurs.

It was during lovemaking that Angel found it hardest to put on an act that everything was fine. Instead of being able to lose herself in her passion for Cal, and in what he was doing to her body, she felt herself getting more and more wound up. *Just get on with it!* she wanted to say as he caressed her. But Cal was a skilful lover who loved giving her pleasure – when ironically pleasure was the last thing she seemed likely to experience at the moment. So she faked it. And how bad did that make her feel? She'd never had to fake it with Cal before; plenty of times with her exes, but never with him.

'Mmm,' he said in a dreamy post-sex daze as he lay down next to her. 'See, I told you it would be good getting a nanny – when was the last time we made love in the afternoon?'

Angel sat up, clutching her shirt to her. 'I'd better get dressed, I'm sure they'll be back in a minute.'

'Relax,' Cal answered, pulling her back down. 'They won't be back for ages.' He closed his eyes and Angel studied his face. He was still the love of her life, the most handsome, sexy man she had ever known. Living in Italy had turned his olive skin a gorgeous deep rich brown. She traced her finger along the scar just below his right eyebrow, a souvenir from a nasty collision on the pitch – the one flaw in his otherwise perfect features.

Rescue me, she longed to say. *Save me from feeling like this*. He had saved her once, several years earlier, before they got together, when she was at risk of losing herself in addiction to coke. Maybe now he'd had the good news about being selected, she could confide in him. Not today, though. She wanted him to enjoy his moment.

'Flavia rang when you were at the stables,' Cal said sleepily.

'Oh?' Angel replied, suddenly on the alert. 'What did she want?'

'She invited you out to lunch tomorrow in Milan, along with some of the other wives.'

'Great,' Angel replied through gritted teeth. As far as Flavia was concerned, one meeting was more than enough.

'It would be good if you went, babe, you need to make some new friends.'

'I've got plenty of friends,' Angel snapped back, thinking longingly of Gemma and Jez back home.

'I meant over here,' Cal said patiently, as if talking to a child. 'Alessia will be there and you liked her, didn't you?'

Angel sighed; she knew Cal was only trying to help. 'Okay, I'll go.'

'Great,' he answered. 'I'll book you a driver so

you don't have to worry about finding your way there and parking.'

The next morning Angel slept in again after another sleepless night. She woke with a headache and felt lethargic, not at all in the mood for meeting the AC Milan WAGs. She wandered downstairs in her dressing gown, wanting to see Honey. Her daughter was in the playroom with Lucy, sitting in her play nest, surrounded by toys and happily chewing on a wooden train. As soon as she saw Angel she smiled, and Angel picked up her daughter and held her close, enjoying the feel of her solid little body, breathing in the wonderful scent of her hair and skin. Lucy then gave her a blow by blow account of what Honey had had for breakfast and Angel couldn't help feeling guilty that she hadn't been the one to feed her, especially when she wouldn't be giving her lunch as she was going out. She sighed and reluctantly put Honey down.

'I was going to ask if it was okay if I took Honey swimming today? One of the other nannies works for someone who has a pool and they have baby swimming lessons there,' Lucy said perkily.

'Oh.' Angel herself hadn't taken Honey swimming yet even though the villa had a pool and had wanted to be the first to do so, but it seemed unfair not to let Lucy take her. 'Okay, and maybe I'll come

41

with you next week. I've got this lunch date with some of the other wives today.'

'They're all really nice,' Lucy replied enthusiastically. She had previously worked for one of the Italian WAGs and had come highly recommended.

Great, thought Angel. One bitchy little comment about them might actually have cheered her up, but no such luck. She skipped breakfast and went back upstairs. What was she supposed to wear to lunch with the Italian WAGs? She hadn't bought any clothes for ages and many of the ones she had were slightly too big for her.

She pulled outfit after outfit from her wardrobe, holding the clothes up against herself and hating all of them. It just seemed like too much effort and no doubt she wouldn't have the right designer labels. In the end she went for a dark green silk tunic dress that set off her eyes. Most girls would have worn it with leggings, but Angel's long tanned legs were one of her best features and she kept them bare and wore a pair of delicate Jimmy Choo gold metallic sandals with a wickedly high stiletto heel. She might not bother about designer labels for her clothes, but Angel loved her designer shoes. She missed having Gemma by her side advising her on what to wear and doing her make up, and she could have done with Jez's hairdressing expertise too. Nonetheless, by the time she had finished applying her own make up she thought she would do.

*

It was a forty-minute drive into Milan from Lake Como, and as they drove into the city Angel felt her initial confidence ebb away. Usually she loved going to new places, experiencing new things, but right now as she looked out on to the chic designer shopping district, at the storefronts of Pucci, Versace, Gucci and Prada, she felt out of place. She longed for the familiar sights of home, wished she were driving to Brighton instead to meet Gemma.

She felt even less confident as she walked into the restaurant. It was Chandelier, one of Milan's hottest hang-outs. The décor was fantastically over the top and Angel felt as if she had stumbled on to a film set – there were baroque thrones, glittering candelabra, gilded tables, antiques wherever she looked, and jewel-coloured chandeliers lighting the rooms. And at every table were über-stylish diners.

Angel thought longingly of her favourite Italian restaurant in Brighton, a cosy family-run place which she'd been going to since she was a child and where she always ordered the same thing – a Tricolore salad and garlic bread to start followed by Tortelloni Aurora and then Tiramisù for dessert. Somehow she didn't think any of those would be on the menu here . . .

The maître d' addressed her in Italian at first, which of course she couldn't understand. Blushing, Angel explained that she didn't speak Italian and immediately he switched to perfect English and showed her to the table. The other wives, five in total, were already there and Angel suddenly felt very shy. Just as they had been at the party they were all immaculately dressed – their hair and make up were so perfect they looked as if they had stepped out of a magazine shoot for *Vogue*.

Flavia was the first to get up and kiss Angel on both cheeks. She had to force herself to smile in response when really she would like to have said, 'Back away from my husband, bitch!' But her smile to Alessia was genuine. The other woman greeted her warmly and after Angel had been introduced to the rest of the wives she was relieved to see that there was a space next to Alessia. At first they all made an effort to talk to Angel in English and she found herself the centre of attention as they asked her how she was settling in. Angel wished they would stop. She knew they were just being polite but it was so hard pretending that she was happy to be in Italy. Finally they ran out of small talk and switched to chattering among themselves in Italian.

Angel breathed a sigh of relief, not caring in the least that she couldn't understand a word they were saying. But Alessia carried on talking to her and guided her through the menu, asking what kinds of things she liked to eat. Angel really appreciated that. She felt like she needed an ally with women like Flavia around.

'I'm sure you feel homesick now, but trust me, it will pass. My husband played for Manchester United for two years and I had to move to England.' Alessia seemed to shiver at the thought. 'I felt very lonely at first but the other wives were very sweet and I got used to it.'

'I bet you were glad to come back to Italy, though, weren't you?' Angel asked.

Alessia nodded, then said, 'But this is what happens when you are married to a footballer. Your wishes and your career have to take – how do you say it? – a back seat? Though all of us work here – I'm a model, and Flavia has her own TV show. But when I was in Manchester I couldn't really work.'

Angel shook her head vehemently. 'That's not how I see it. I'll be here some of the time, but I also want to start working again in a month and then I'll have to travel.'

'You're a model as well, aren't you?' Alessia asked.

Angel nodded and Alessia continued, 'I can see why, you are very beautiful. Do you model like Kate Moss?'

'Not exactly,' she replied, smiling. 'I'm a glamour model, which means I mostly do lingerie and swimwear shoots.'

'And you've been photographed topless and even nude, haven't you?' Flavia put in bitchily. 'Cal told me.'

'That's right,' Angel answered curtly, and Flavia went on, 'I can't believe you still do this after you're married. Doesn't Cal mind?'

'No,' Angel replied, starting to feel wound up. 'Why should he? It's not like I'm a porn star!'

Flavia rattled something off in Italian and all the other wives laughed, except for Alessia who said, 'You are right. Your body is your own, to do with as you want. Flavia is just jealous because she doesn't have such a wonderful body as you.'

Flavia smiled nastily and said, 'Well, at least what I have is all my own.' She looked meaningfully at Angel's chest and her dislike of Flavia went up a gear. So what if she'd had a boob job? She'd never denied it. Again she was struck by the similarity between Flavia and Cal's ex Simone, who'd never missed an opportunity to slag Angel off.

As Flavia got up from the table to go to the bathroom, Alessia whispered, 'She might not have had a boob job but she's the Botox Queen around here and she has her plastic surgeon on speed dial. She's five years older than her husband and is paranoid about getting any lines – which I can sympathise with – but she just doesn't have to be so bitchy about everyone else.'

Angel was grateful for Alessia's comments. She felt far too vulnerable at the moment to deal with someone who clearly didn't like her.

Flavia ignored Angel for the rest of the meal,

something she didn't mind at all. Afterwards, all the WAGs planned to hit the designer boutiques and Alessia asked Angel along.

'Thank you but I really want to get home and see Honey. I feel like I've hardly spent any time with her lately.'

Flavia looked at Angel as if she were mad. 'But don't you have a nanny?'

'Yes, but I want to see my daughter,' Angel insisted. Also, the thought of shopping with these women was hardly her idea of fun.

'Okay.' Flavia shrugged dismissively. 'But I thought you might want to see the new Cavalli collection. Cal said you don't have many designer clothes at the moment.' And she couldn't resist giving Angel the once over, as if she wouldn't have been seen dead in what Angel was wearing.

'I'm more of a shoe girl,' she replied, not wanting to rise to Flavia's bait. She said her goodbyes and with a huge sense of relief got into the car waiting outside – spending time in Flavia's company was just like being back at school. But at least then she'd had Gemma to protect her.

Angel had really hoped that now Cal knew he had made the short list for the England squad he would open up to her again, and that in turn she would be able to confide in him. Instead, after a day of seeming happy, the shutters came down once more and when Angel asked him what was wrong, he insisted that now he had to train harder than ever. Just because he had made this first selection there was no guarantee he would make the final pick.

She hardly saw him, and all that kept her going in the week that followed was the prospect of seeing Gemma and Jez and his boyfriend Rufus, who were flying over to spend a couple of days with them. Angel found herself practically counting the hours until they arrived. She was still finding every day a struggle – her depression seemed to be getting worse, nothing made her feel better. So she was really hoping that a weekend with her friends would cheer her up.

'Darling Angel! It's so fantastic to see you, we've missed you so much,' Jez exclaimed, enveloping her in a huge hug the minute he'd dashed through Arrivals at Milan airport, closely followed by Gemma and Rufus.

'I've missed you all!' she cried, and thought Jez *really* must have missed her as usually he was strictly a double-kiss type of guy.

'Are there any paps around?' he asked hopefully, glancing about. 'I'm wearing my new Gucci shirt and Tom Ford glasses, just in case.'

'No, there aren't,' laughed Angel, taking his arm.

'Oh,' Jez replied, sounding disappointed. 'Well, maybe later, if we go out clubbing?'

'What is he like?' Rufus asked, rolling his eyes. While Jez had dressed up, Rufus, as always, was dressed down in faded jeans and a hoodie.

'A show off!' Angel exclaimed. 'Now come on, the car's outside. Let's get back to the house – Cal's making lunch and there's champagne!'

'How are you, babe?' Gemma asked her as they drove away from the airport. Angel sighed. 'I've been feeling low, but I'm sure that's just home-sickness, isn't it?' she answered, thinking privately that 'low' didn't even begin to describe it.

'I'm sure it is,' Gemma replied warmly, but Angel was aware of her best friend looking concerned as she took in Angel's slimmer than usual body. She still hadn't been eating much – she'd force herself when Cal was around, but when he wasn't she'd end up skipping meals.

'So what have you been up to?' Jez demanded. 'Come on, I want to know everything – which famous people you've met, what designer clothes you've bought, and what the Italiano WAGs are like?'

'Same old Jez,' Angel said fondly. He was obsessed with designer clothes and labels – he would have made a wonderful WAG. His hair and nails were always immaculate and recently he'd had his very own spray tan booth installed in his house, so he could keep up his perfect tan. Jez put the *high* into high maintenance. And since he'd started seeing Rufus he'd grown even more obsessed with his looks as his boyfriend was younger than him and extremely good-looking with a very fit body to go with it from his work as a personal trainer.

Her friends were very impressed with the villa and Angel tried to see it through their eyes, but to her, luxurious as it was, it just wasn't home. Cal had told her that she must make her own mark on it, put up pictures, buy some new furniture, but she didn't feel inspired to. Although the villa was built in the nineteenth century and from the outside looked like a period house with its pale yellow stucco walls and elegant shutters, inside it was ultra-modern and every room looked as if it could be in the pages of a glossy magazine. Jez adored the living room, which was decorated with stylish black-and-white-patterned sofas, sleek black coffee tables and huge glass lamps. It was stunning but Angel felt it was too perfect. She longed for her Brighton home where she could just curl up and listen to music in her cosy living room.

As soon as he saw her friends Cal was on full charm mode, pouring glasses of champagne for everyone. They drank it on the beautiful stone-paved terrace with its terracotta pots overflowing with vivid red geraniums. There were further exclamations of delight from her friends as they took in the view of the lake.

'Where's George Clooney's *palazzo*?' Jez wanted to know.

'His what?' Angel asked, looking puzzled.

'His mansion!' Jez exclaimed. 'You really must learn the language, *bella*.'

She rolled her eyes while Cal said, 'I'm sure when Angel's been here a little longer she'll be fluent.' She bit her lip in concern. Just how much longer did Cal have in mind?

'It's great you made the team, Cal,' Gemma said, sensing her friend's unease and changing the subject.

'It is, but I've still got to make the final selection,' he replied, looking serious. Angel felt herself tense up as she willed him not to go on a downer.

'Oh, but you will!' Jez exclaimed.

'I wish I could share your optimism,' Cal said dryly. 'And I don't mean to be rude, but do you actually know anything about football at all?'

'Football, no,' Jez replied. 'Footballers, yes. I know all the good-looking ones!'

And Angel breathed a sigh of relief as Cal smiled.

Her friends all made a big fuss of Honey, especially Gemma who bombarded Angel with questions about the baby's development and then spent ages playing with her and commenting on how beautiful she was. Gemma's open adoration of her daughter only made Angel feel worse. She was relieved when Jez and Rufus asked to see the infinity pool and Gemma said she would stay and help look after Honey.

'Poor Gemma,' Jez said as soon as they were out of earshot. 'She wants a baby so much.'

'I know,' Angel replied, her heart aching for her friend. 'And she'd make a much better mother than me. It's not fair, is it?'

'Angel, you're a great mother, why do you say that?' Jez stopped and looked at her in surprise.

She shrugged and said, 'Sometimes I feel a bit crap, Jez, like I'm not up to the job. And, of course, I can never say that to Gemma.'

'I'm sure you could,' Rufus said quietly. 'I think she'd understand. She's your best friend, you should tell her how you're feeling.'

Angel was stunned; she'd never heard Rufus speak so much before. He was usually painfully shy. *Hi* and *How are you?* were as far as his conversation went. Not that it mattered as Jez spoke more than enough for both of them. She appreciated his comments, but didn't know whether she would act on them.

That night Cal had arranged for them all to go to Diana Garden, an exclusive bar in Milan. While it was sweet of him, Angel would have been just as happy chilling out at the villa. But Jez was hugely excited at the prospect – the bar was frequented by AC Milan players and Jez fancied the pants off at least three of them, plus it was where the fashion elite went for their aperitifs, so Angel knew they would have to go or he would never forgive her.

She enjoyed the first part of the evening, getting ready in her bedroom with Gemma, listening to music, gossiping, trying on different outfits and letting her friend do her make up. They'd spent many nights like this in the past. But she didn't like it so much when Gemma started interrogating her about what she was eating.

'Look, Gemma, we had this conversation before. I'm eating fine, you don't need to keep going on about it,' Angel couldn't help snapping. 'You saw me at lunch. I ate most of it, didn't I?'

'Yeah, but that was just one meal. You don't look like you've been eating enough generally, that's all I'm saying.'

Angel sighed and changed the subject, 'Do you think this looks okay?' She was wearing a purple Dolce & Gabbana cocktail dress – a present from Cal – which was way more sophisticated than she would usually wear. But as she was in Italy she figured she had better raise her game.

'You look great,' Gemma replied, appraising the dress with her practised fashionista eye. 'How do I look?' She had teamed her bang-on-trend midnight blue silk tunic dress with high patent heels and wore her long shiny black hair down. She looked extremely pretty.

'You look the bollocks!' Angel exclaimed, and to stop her friend asking anymore questions, added, 'Come on. Let's go downstairs and find the boys.'

Cal and Rufus were in the living room drinking Peroni and watching the football. Angel couldn't help smiling when she saw Cal – was it possible that her husband had grown more handsome? He looked fresh from the shower, and she could smell his Dolce & Gabbana aftershave. Even after nearly four years together it was still her favourite smell.

'You girls look gorgeous!' he exclaimed when they walked in. When Angel walked over to him, he took her hand and pulled her down on the sofa next to him. 'I'm going to be fighting those Italian stallions off you in the bar.'

Angel shook her head. 'No, you won't.' She turned to Gemma and Rufus and added, 'Cal's a total babe magnet here. If I didn't trust him, I'd wonder what he got up to when I wasn't around.'

He kissed her. 'I'm a one woman man,' he whispered. 'You're all I want.'

'Get a room!' Gemma exclaimed in mock disgust. 'I hope you're not going to be so lovey-dovey all night!'

'You can talk!' Angel teased her friend back. 'How many times have you texted Tony since you've been here?'

'A few,' Gemma answered coyly, and everyone

laughed because Gemma's phone had barely left her hand.

Half an hour later, when they were all getting restless, Jez finally made his entrance. He marched to the centre of the room like a cat walk model, then stood, surveying his audience, hands on hips. 'Suit by Armani,' he declared. 'Bling by Theo Fennell. I like to wear my heart on my sleeve,' he continued, holding out his arms and showing off the white gold and diamond heart-shaped cufflinks: 'After-shave by Dior and hair by Jez Jones. Will I do?'

Cal laughed and said, 'Jez, if I wasn't a happily married straight man, I'd be tempted.'

'Be still my beating heart,' Jez replied, fluttering his eyelashes at Cal, but then sat down on Rufus's lap and gave him a kiss. They'd been a couple for four years – a record for Jez – and Angel really hoped that they'd stay together. Rufus seemed to give him the stability he needed. Before they'd got together, Jez's anecdotes about his many conquests had certainly been entertaining and often eye-opening . . . but Angel knew that deep down he craved the love and happiness he had found with Rufus.

For the first time in ages Angel was actually enjoying herself – although that might have been down to the number of champagne cocktails she'd been knocking back since they hit the bar. But she knew it wasn't just the drink that had lightened her mood, it was being with her friends again. The depression which was always with her and never seemed to lift, whatever she did, wasn't so overwhelming for once. She gossiped and giggled the night away. At one point, when everyone else was deep in conversation, Cal turned to her and said, 'You look so happy, have I got my girl back?'

'What do you mean?' Angel replied. 'I haven't been anywhere.'

'Haven't you?' he asked, a little sadly Angel thought. It was hardly the place to reveal how depressed she had been and still was, though, so she shook her head, not wanting to pursue the conversation. She was just about to give Cal a hug and suggest they should talk about it later when Flavia sidled over to their table.

She kissed Angel, murmuring how lovely it was to see her, then Cal. Angel expected her to move on but she stayed talking to him. In Italian, naturally. Finally Cal said, 'I must introduce you to our friends, Flavia, they've been dying to meet an Italian WAG.'

She gave a tinkly laugh, that irritated the hell out of Angel, and simpered, 'Of course!' While Gemma and Rufus were polite to Flavia, Jez was clearly awe-struck as she revealed that she was close friends with several top designers and he proceeded to interrogate her about them.

Traitor, Angel thought bitterly, scowling.

'Chill, babe,' Gemma said quietly, sensing her bad mood.

Angel rolled her eyes and whispered, 'I just don't like her. You watch her with Cal – she's all over him like a rash.'

Gemma was about to reply when Flavia said, 'Angel, you look gorgeous in that dress like I knew you would. I helped Cal pick it out for you.'

'Really?' she replied, looking at him with a what-the-fuck's-going-on? expression.

'I bumped into Flavia when I was shopping for something for you,' he quickly explained.

'Oh,' was all she could find to say. She wanted to go home right now, rip off the dress and never wear it again. She didn't want something Flavia had chosen – she couldn't stand the woman. Flavia was smiling at her now but Angel turned away. She was about to suggest to Gemma that they should go to the ladies' room so she could vent her anger in privacy but then Alessia turned up at their table and Angel was forced into making another set of introductions. But at least with her Angel didn't feel threatened. Alessia was as charming and friendly as she had been at lunch.

Angel soon found herself asking indiscreetly, 'Is Flavia like that with everyone's husband?' as Flavia yet again monopolised Cal's attention, speaking Italian to him and excluding everyone else.

Alessia smiled knowingly. 'Yes, she is, but I'm sure you have nothing to worry about. Cal is not going to fall for her, is he? He's just for you – I'm right, aren't I?'

'I hope so,' Angel answered, feeling miserable. *She could trust Cal, couldn't she?* And Alessia replied reassuringly, 'I'm certain it is so.'

Now that Flavia had joined her party, the night had lost some of its sparkle for Angel. She would far rather have returned to the villa and carried on talking to her friends there, besides putting some more questions to Cal about Flavia. But everyone else was having a great time and Angel didn't think she could suggest that they leave yet. So she pretended that she was having an equally good time, dancing with Jez and Gemma and drowning her anger in yet more champagne. They didn't leave the club until after three and were all quite drunk except for Cal who never lost control. His mother had been an alcoholic throughout his childhood. She only got dry when he was in his twenties, because he finally managed to persuade her to go into rehab and paid for her treatment. Maybe that was why Angel couldn't confide in him about her depression – sometimes, however much she loved him, Cal just seemed too bloody perfect. He never messed up.

Back home Angel didn't want the night to end and suggested Bailey's which everyone took her up on, except Cal who said he had to go to bed or he'd be wasted for training the next day.

'What a night!' Jez declared, lying back on the sofa. 'That was such a fantastic club, Angel. You're so lucky to be out here where everything and everyone is so glam.'

'Yes, especially the women,' Angel said bitterly, thinking of Flavia.

'Babe, you have nothing to fear from *them*,' Jez said, looking astonished. 'You are totally the fairest of them all!'

'Oh, really?' she said sceptically. 'Well, I wasn't very happy to hear that Flavia chose this dress. She fancies the arse off Cal. He's admitted it.'

'So what if she does?' Gemma put in. 'He doesn't feel the same about her, does he?'

'No,' Angel grudgingly admitted. 'It's just that she reminds me of Simone and I don't like her.'

'Forget about her,' Gemma urged her friend. 'Don't let her spoil your time here. So she fancies Cal? You know lots of women do and you've learned to accept that, just as he has to accept that loads of blokes fancy you.'

Angel sighed, not really believing that anyone could fancy her right now. 'It's just that I wanted everything to be perfect for your stay and now I feel as if she's ruined it.'

'It's only ruined if you let it be,' Gemma told her. 'Come on, what about those drinks? '

They only lasted another hour before staggering up to their beds. Cal was already asleep. Angel unzipped her dress, bunched it up and threw it into a corner – so what if it was designer and cost a fortune? She was never going to wear it again. She pulled on her silk PJs and got into bed, and even though she was angry with him she still curled round Cal, slipping one arm over him, enjoying the feeling of his sleep-warmed skin.

He wouldn't have an affair, would he? Not Cal.

She tried to push the dark thoughts away, the thoughts that tormented her, but one kept breaking through her defences, and that was that she hadn't been much of a wife to him lately. Would it really be that much of a surprise if Cal did have an affair? She held him tighter and in his sleep he took her hand. She couldn't bear to lose him. She would just have to make more of an effort to be happy. She could do that, couldn't she? She always used to be happy. Eventually she fell into a dreamless, alcohol-fuelled sleep.

But all Angel's good intentions to be more positive evaporated in the morning light as she opened her eyes and the hangover kicked in. When Cal walked in with a cup of tea for her, she found herself saying nastily, 'Don't ever let another woman choose my clothes for me again!'

'Look, I'm sorry, she just happened to be in the shop. And it really wasn't like she made out. I'd already chosen the dress, she just agreed with me,' Cal replied. 'Don't make this into something it's not, Angel.'

'Whatever,' she muttered.

'Anyway, can you listen out for Honey? She's still asleep and I've got to go to training. I'll be back just before lunch.' Angel nodded then closed her eyes and slumped back on the pillow, thinking she'd try and sleep off the pounding headache, but a few minutes later there was a knock at the door and Gemma padded in in her PJs and got into bed next to Angel.

'How are you feeling?' she asked.

'Rough,' Angel muttered and opened her eyes. 'How come you look so perky?'

'Well, I didn't drink as much as you. I've cut right down because of trying to get pregnant,' she sighed.

'I'm sure you will soon, Gemma,' Angel said sympathetically, feeling guilty all over again for not being happy when she had everything that her friend wanted.

'God, I don't know,' Gemma replied. 'I'm trying not to let it take over my life and my head, but it's hard, Angel. I want a baby so much! I look at you and Honey and I'm so happy for you, but at the same time it really hurts.'

Angel sat up and hugged her friend. 'Gemma, I just know you are going to have a baby, you've got to believe that.' She felt full of sadness for her friend. 'Come on, let's get up. Cal's gone to training and I expect Jez and Rufus could do with a cup of tea.'

The day went by way too fast for Angel's liking. She wished that her friends could stay longer but they could only have two days away. They all hung out by the pool, taking it in turns to entertain Honey who was becoming a complete water baby and adored splashing about in her bright yellow inflatable baby seat.

In the afternoon Angel took everyone on a boat trip – their villa came with its own speed boat and boatman, something that impressed Jez no end. While he interrogated the boatman about whether George Clooney was at his villa, Rufus turned to Angel and asked her if she was all right, saying hesitantly that she didn't seem her usual self. For a second she wanted to confide in him, but then the familiar feeling of shame took over and she found herself forcing a smile and replying that of course she was.

For dinner Cal had booked a table for them at a local restaurant. He offered to stay behind with Honey. Angel tried to persuade him to come but he refused.

'I know you'd really like some time on your own with them before they go and I need to have an early night tonight because of training.'

Angel's heart sank. She hated the thought of tomorrow when her friends would be flying back and she would be left behind. She tried to put on a brave face over dinner but everyone picked up on her sadness.

'You'll have to come back and see us next time,' Gemma said. 'And in a few months' time you'll be working again as well.'

'I know, it's just that I really miss you all,' Angel said, and then she couldn't stop the tears from filling her eyes.

'Book your ticket for three weeks' time,' Jez told her. 'We'll go out clubbing, hit the shops and have a proper London weekend.'

Angel sniffed. 'Yeah. Three weeks isn't that long, is it?' But in her head she dreaded the days ahead.

Cal said that she could book a driver to take her friends to the airport but Angel insisted she could drive them herself. Getting used to driving on the right and navigating her way to the airport were a good way of keeping her mind off the fact her friends were leaving, and she thought it was about time she got to grips with driving over here. Having a chauffeur on tap 24/7 had never been Angel's style.

Jez tried to keep everyone's spirits up on the journey by bitching about his ex's latest plans to redecorate the hairdressing salon they owned together. Usually they got on well as business partners but over matters of taste they parted company dramatically.

'He wants leopard-print chairs, ornate gold mirrors and *red* wallpaper!' Jez said in disgust. 'I told him it doesn't exactly scream timeless chic, does it? More like brothel!'

Angel smiled at Jez's comments, but if he'd wanted to cheer her up he only succeeded in reminding her how much she was going to miss him. She didn't think she was up to waving them off at Departures so just dropped them off at the terminal, hugging them and then driving off so she didn't have to see them leave.

Angel had hoped that she and Cal could spend the rest of the day together and that maybe she might be able to pick up on their conversation from the club, but he had an interview with a journalist in Milan about his charity. He wanted to set up a number of after-school football clubs in some of the most disadvantaged areas of the UK. It was a project really dear to his heart.

The minute she walked through the door Cal just handed her Honey, gave her a brief kiss and left, reminding her that it was Lucy's afternoon off. The moment he left Honey started crying. Angel tried everything to pacify her – picked her up and walked round the house with her; got out her toys;

changed her nappy; offered her milk. Nothing worked, she only cried harder.

After nearly two hours Angel felt at her wit's end. If she'd been back in Brighton this would have been the moment she got on the phone to her mum and begged her to come over. But, of course, here she couldn't. As Honey persisted in crying, Angel began to worry that there might be something seriously wrong. She did seem very hot. Panicking that she might have something awful like meningitis, Angel stripped off her babygro to check for any rashes which only made Honey cry more. She tried to take her temperature but couldn't because the baby wouldn't keep still for long enough.

'Oh, God, what's wrong!' Angel exclaimed. In desperation she picked up her mobile.

'Cal, Honey's really ill and won't stop crying, I think she might have meningitis!' Angel gabbled down the phone.

'Hold on,' he said, 'I'm sure she hasn't.' Calmly he went through all the symptoms with her – no, Honey didn't have a rash. No, she didn't seem floppy. No, she didn't seem sensitive to light. 'Look, Lucy said she was really overtired and needed a nap – I meant to tell you before I left but I was in such a hurry. Sorry. Just put her in her cot. She might cry for a bit but I'm sure she'll be fine.'

Almost beside herself with the stress of being alone with her screaming baby, Angel walked up to the nursery and tucked Honey up in her cot. She did cry for a further ten minutes while Angel sat outside the room but then she fell asleep. When Angel crept back in to check she was sleeping peacefully. Relieved as Angel was, she couldn't help reproaching herself. She should have known that Honey was tired. Why hadn't she?

She spent the time Honey was asleep preparing something for her tea, carefully following a recipe because she wasn't a natural cook. When Honey woke up, fortunately in a much better mood, Angel tried to give her tea but Honey wasn't having any of it. Most of the risotto that Angel had so painstakingly made ended up on the floor, on Honey or on Angel. And that was how Cal found them on his return. When he saw the state of them he burst out laughing and rushed to get the digital camera.

'Babe, you look so funny!' he said, clicking away.

Angel's white Juicy Couture tracksuit was covered in splatters of food.

'I'm glad you think it's funny,' she snapped, 'I spent ages cooking that.'

Cal took Honey's spoon and sampled the meal for himself, grimacing. He was about to say something cheeky when he caught sight of Angel's stern expression and said, 'Delicious, babe.'

'You don't mean that,' she said crossly. 'I can't get anything right at the moment – I can't work out when my daughter's tired. I can't even cook a meal that she wants to eat. I'm such a failure.' She could feel her eyes welling up with tears again.

'Don't be silly,' Cal said, enveloping her in a hug and not caring that now he too was covered in baby food. 'You've just had a bad day, that's all.'

No, that's not all, Angel wanted to say. *I've had a bad six months and I don't know why and I need you to help me.* But even having come so close, she still couldn't say it.

A week later Angel was feeling worse than ever. Cal had to go away for intensive training with the team and being alone in the house made her feel as if she was going mad. Lucy was having some days off as well, so it was just Angel and Honey. Cal was back to sounding distant on the phone, and reading between the lines she gathered that training wasn't going as well as it should and his knee was troubling him. Yet again, it didn't seem the right time to tell him how desperate she felt.

She tried to structure her days, taking her daughter swimming or walking to the nearest town and going to the shops, but the time without Cal felt very long and lonely.

One afternoon Alessia called round to see her. At first when Angel saw her car pull into the driveway she thought she wouldn't open the door. She felt very unlike her normal self, so insecure and paranoid, but in the end she let her in. Alessia looked like a supermodel, effortlessly beautiful and chic in her designer jeans and cream silk shirt. Compared to her Angel felt skanky. She hadn't washed her hair for a few days and had scraped it back into a pony tail. She wasn't wearing any make up.

'I just thought I'd call round,' Alessia said, walking in, 'I hope you don't mind? I was worried you might be feeling lonely. I know how I felt in Manchester when my husband was away training.'

'Thank you,' Angel replied, leading her through to the kitchen. 'As you can see I'm not doing too well.' And to her horror she found herself bursting into tears.

Alessia immediately took control and made Angel sit down and tell her what was wrong. She found herself giving an edited version of her feelings. Leaving out any mention of her depression she talked instead about Cal, how closed off he had become.

'Angel – all your husband will be thinking about at the moment is the World Cup. You understand that, don't you?' Alessia replied calmly.

'Of course I do!' Angel replied passionately. 'But he won't let me in and I can't bear it.'

'Your husband is a very complex man, no?' Alessia commented. 'He feels things very deeply, I can see that.'

'Sometimes I wish he wasn't,' Angel replied, trying to brush away her tears.

'Ah, but that's why you love him,' Alessia replied, echoing Gemma's words. 'He is an enigma, even after all the time you have been together.'

'What would you do?' Angel asked. She was not in the habit of trusting people she didn't know very well, but she trusted Alessia.

'You can't push someone like Cal, he will only open up to you when he is ready,' she replied. 'In the meantime you are going to have to be strong.'

Angel was in no state of mind to reflect that Alessia seemed to know an awful lot about her husband, and after her visitor had gone she had yet another phone conversation with Cal where he was offhand with her. She felt so lonely, and lost. That night as she lay in bed, unable to sleep, she realised that she couldn't cope any longer with feeling so depressed, and with Cal being so distant while she was so far from her family and friends. She had to go home. Surely then she would feel like her old self again?

Chapter 3

A Cry For Help

'It's Cal,' said her mum, holding out the phone. Angel shook her head. She didn't want to speak to him, didn't want to listen to him shouting at her for walking out on him like that. But her mum continued to hold out the phone and Angel knew she had no choice. Sighing deeply, she took the handset. Michelle picked up Honey from her highchair and tactfully left the kitchen.

'Hi,' said Angel tentatively, bracing herself for the onslaught.

'What the fuck is going on?' Cal demanded. He sounded absolutely furious.

'I come back from my trip and find that you've gone and all you've left is a scrap of paper saying "*Sorry, I had to go home.*" What kind of shit thing is that to do to me?'

'I'm really sorry, Cal, I just couldn't stay there any longer, really I couldn't. It was making me feel so unhappy. And I was worried about how it was affecting Honey.'

'Bollocks! You were only thinking of yourself. You just wanted to get back to your friends and your work, and never mind me. We're married, Angel, we're supposed to be together. You were barely out here a month, you didn't give it a chance.'

'I did, Cal, honestly, and –' she hesitated here, wondering how best to continue, '– you were distant with me as well.'

'What!' he exploded. 'I bought the villa, hired a nanny for you, bought you a new horse! What more could you want?'

'It wasn't about all those things. I need you to talk to me, to open up. I felt so lonely, Cal.'

'Yeah, well, I've got a hell of a lot on my mind at the moment, can't you understand that?'

'Of course I know that, and I want to be there for you,' she replied.

'So when are you coming back?' he demanded. 'You know I'm signed for the next two years. Do you really think our marriage can survive just seeing each other every two weeks?'

'I can't come back yet, Cal. I will soon, I promise, I just need you to give me some time,' Angel pleaded with him. Maybe now was the moment to tell him how she had been feeling? 'I'm really sorry, it's just that I've felt so down lately . . .' There, she

71

had said it. But Cal's response was not what she had hoped for.

'Yeah, well, so have I – married to someone who doesn't give a shit about me and walks out when things get slightly tough. "For better, for worse" we said, remember?'

'You make it sound like I've left you, Cal, but I haven't. I just can't stay in Italy at the moment,' she said despairingly, wishing he could understand how she felt.

'Yeah, whatever,' Cal answered, and all the fight seemed to have left him. 'I'd better go, I've got things to do.'

'Will you be able to come over soon?' she asked.

'Not for a couple of weeks. I'll speak to Lucy about her joining you in a few days,' he said abruptly.

'Okay,' she answered, feeling terrible, 'I'll call you later.'

'You can try. I might not be in,' he said. 'Give Honey a kiss for me.'

And then he was gone, and for the first time in their relationship there was no *I love you*. What had she done to their marriage? She'd told him she was down and it didn't seem to register, but then he was angry with her, so that was hardly surprising. And he was not himself either. They seemed locked in parallel worlds, not even close anymore, not the way they used to be.

*

She walked wearily into the living room where her mum and dad were looking after Honey. Both of them looked up at her expectantly and her dad said, 'Well? When are you going back?'

She shook her head. 'I can't go back at the moment, Dad.'

Frank frowned. 'I'm sure you've got your reasons but it really isn't good for your marriage to spend so much time apart. Cal needs to be with you and Honey. It isn't fair on him.'

'I know, Dad. I can't really explain how I feel. I just know I can't live in Italy at the moment. Maybe in a few months' time . . .'

'A few months!' Frank exploded. 'Well, I just hope you have a marriage to go back to. You should be with him, especially now. The World Cup means everything to him!'

That was her dad all over; everything was black and white to him. And he always tended to see Cal's side of things. Frank had been the one who had discovered Cal's talent for football as coach to the local youth team, and had put him on the path to success. Without Frank's support Cal might very well not have made it as a professional footballer – his alcoholic mother had never taken much interest in him. Frank had become a father figure to Cal, encouraging him and looking after him, inviting him into the family.

'Are you sure, love? Do you want to talk about it?' Michelle asked anxiously.

Angel shook her head, and then because she couldn't bear this conversation any longer said, 'Actually, Mum, I've got a headache. Will you look after Honey if I have a lie down?'

''Course, love,' her mum replied. Upstairs Angel curled up on her bed with Cal's towelling robe that still carried traces of his aftershave. She pressed it to her face as she wept. There was just one thought in her head. *Please don't leave me, Cal. Please.*

In the week that followed Angel felt even worse. She had assumed she would feel better when she was back in familiar surroundings. Instead her feelings of depression and inadequacy didn't let up. Her friends were all thrilled to have her back but all of them wondered why she hadn't stayed in Italy and Angel grew tired of explaining that she hadn't argued with Cal and that she'd be going back soon. Gemma was the only one she confided in about the way Cal was barely speaking to her and how difficult he had been in Italy.

Every time Angel called him – he never called her anymore – he kept the conversations short, said he was tired or busy. She knew how preoccupied he was with the World Cup, how intensively he was training, and longed to be able to give him encouragement. But he sounded so angry and hurt

74

and refused even to talk about his concerns that Angel hated herself even more for what she was doing to him. Even when he found out that he had made the final squad he still didn't seem to be happy.

'Are you sure you couldn't go back for a while?' Gemma asked when the two of them met in London for some retail therapy one Saturday. Michelle had offered to look after Honey to give her daughter a break.

Angel shook her head. 'I just can't yet, Gemma. But I'm so worried Cal's going to leave me.'

Gemma shook her head in disbelief. 'I know he's really angry with you, but he'd never, *ever* leave you!'

'Well, I know who will be made up that I'm not around – that cow Flavia,' Angel said bitterly.

'If you're that worried then get back out there!' Gemma exclaimed.

'Come on,' Angel answered, despairing of this conversation, 'I thought we were supposed to be shopping.'

'We're supposed to be getting something for you to wear for your birthday.'

Angel was twenty-three at the end of the month and had pinned all her hopes on making things right between her and Cal on the celebration. Jez had arranged for her to have her party at Sugar's, her favourite club in Mayfair. It had been the setting for many of her nights out with her friends and for several of her encounters with Cal before they were a couple. Including one memorable night – memorable for all the wrong reasons – when her boyfriend of the time spiked her drink. A very off her head Angel had tried to seduce Cal, but he'd resisted. Now she planned on sneaking somewhere private with him and re-enacting their encounter, except this time she hoped he wouldn't resist . . .

The two girls wandered round Topshop and Miss Selfridge – Angel always liked to see what was on the high street before she went to the designers. It was strange being out in London again. In Italy no one had known who she was but back in England she was a huge star and whenever people spotted her they wanted her autograph or her picture. Angel had deliberately dressed down in skinny jeans, flat pumps and a baggy white vest cinched in with a chunky gold leather belt. She'd tied her long hair back in a pony tail and put on huge shades . . . but still she was recognised. When the attention got too much, and she felt as if she couldn't escape it, Gemma suggested they get in a taxi and head up to Selfridge's. Angel was grateful for the suggestion – she wanted to have fans but at the moment was feeling way too fragile to deal with them.

*

Gemma was great to shop with as she had her finger well and truly on the fashion pulse and no trend ever passed her by. She was a good influence on Angel who, left to herself, would probably stick to jeans and short skirts. Gemma forced her to experiment, getting her out of her comfort zone.

'You look great in that!' she exclaimed as Angel emerged from a dressing room. She was wearing a short black dress with star motifs all over it.

'Really?' she asked, not at all sure.

'Absolutely. Stars are very now. But . . .' Gemma hesitated and Angel knew what was coming next '. . . you really need to put on some weight.'

Angel rolled her eyes. 'Not this again! I *am* eating,' she lied. 'I'm just not that hungry at the moment because I feel so stressed about Cal.'

She could see that Gemma wanted to say more so ended the conversation by going back into the dressing room and putting on another dress. Gemma was enthusiastic about everything she tried on and Angel tried to share her friend's excitement but her heart wasn't in it. In the past shopping for clothes with Gemma had always been a great pick-me-up. Now it felt like just another chore. The only thing that slightly buoyed her up was wanting to look good for Cal, as a way of making up for what she had put him through . . .

She ended up buying the black star dress and a short purple tiered skirt then treated Gemma to lunch at a little Italian restaurant in Soho that Cal had introduced her to and where no one ever bothered her. She even managed to eat something, but any pleasure she had taken in the day evaporated when she received a text from Cal.

'I don't believe it!' she exclaimed angrily.

'What's the matter?' Gemma asked.

Sighing, Angel handed over the phone and her friend read the text. *Angel, please contact my manager re arrangements for where you and Honey are to stay during the World Cup. It needs to be sorted asap.*

'What's the problem? Won't you just be staying with the other WAGs in some luxury hotel? What's the matter with that?'

Angel sighed, 'It's just the way Cal is speaking to me at the moment, giving me orders . . . I hate it. Of course I'm over the moon for him that he's playing in the tournament but I'm dreading staying with those women.'

'Those WAGs, you mean!' Gemma teased her, knowing how much the word wound her friend up.

Angel gave her the finger then said, 'I just don't fit in with them – all they care about are their designer outfits and their Burke bags.'

'It's Birkin actually,' Gemma corrected her, smiling.

'See!' Angel replied, and this time she was smiling as well. 'I don't even speak their language. You should be the one who goes, not me! You'd make a much better WAG. And I really don't want to see that bitch Simone.'

'It's not for long, Angel. Knowing England, they'll probably be knocked out in the first round. Maybe your mum and dad could come out with you as well?'

Angel shook her head. 'I do love them, Gemma, but you know my dad does my head in sometimes, especially where Cal is concerned.'

'Well, we'll just have to get you WAGged up then – starting from *now*. Show me your nails,' Gemma ordered.

Angel held out her hands. There was no messing with Gemma when she went off on one. When Angel modelled she always had perfect fake gel nails – short, usually with a French manicure, or painted bubble gum pink or sometimes dark red if she felt like being sophisticated. But as she wasn't working at the moment she'd ditched the fakes and her nails were in terrible shape from where she'd been biting them. Gemma pulled a face. As well as being a make-up artist she was also a trained beautician and her own nails were always perfect.

'They are minging! You'll have to make an appointment with Mum.'

Gemma's mum, Jeanie, ran a beauty salon in Brighton.

'Okay, next – hair.' Gemma looked critically at Angel.

'Now come on, Gemma, you can't knock my hair. I only had it done the other week *and* I had some highlights.' Angel was very proud of her long hair and did her best to keep it in condition. She had been platinum blonde in the past but was now a warm honey shade.

'Well, what about a change? What about getting it all cut off in a bob and having a fringe?'

'You are fucking joking, aren't you? I don't want a Lego head!' Angel was outraged by the suggestion. 'I know I'd only regret it and end up having to have extensions, and I don't want to do *that*.'

'I was only joking,' Gemma replied laughing at her friend's over-reaction. 'Okay, next – tan.' She looked critically at Angel who stuck out her tongue cheekily. Very luckily for her Angel had been blessed with skin that tanned easily to a golden-brown and only resorted to the fake variety when she had a shoot or a big event. 'Not bad, but you'll have to get yourself sprayed before you go out there and book yourself in for a couple of sessions for while you're there.'

'Isn't this supposed to be about football. Does it really matter what I look like and what I wear?' Angel shot back.

Gemma looked as if Angel had just killed a fluffy kitten with her bare hands. 'What are you talking about? Of course it matters! You're going to be in every celeb and style mag, you have got to look shit hot!'

Angel arranged her hands into the 'whatever'

gesture. It was fun bantering with Gemma like this but she knew she was going to find the endless beauty preparations a right pain in the arse.

'Clothes next. I reckon you're going to need at least three different outfits a day – one for the hotel or shopping, one for watching the match, and one for the evening. And no way can you wear the same thing twice.' Gemma was getting a glint in her eye at the prospect of yet more clothes shopping.

'Gemma,' Angel said firmly, 'I've got enough clothes. I'll maybe buy a couple of things, but that's it.'

'But you've got to have new bikinis for by the pool, yours are probably all out of date,' her friend protested.

'Gemma, I've got *ten* bikinis, I don't need anymore. I'll be spending most of the time with Honey, remember, and I always end up getting covered in food and gunk, so I'm not buying new outfits just for that.'

'Well, I'm going to look out some things for you,' Gemma replied. 'And put together some outfits. It won't be expensive stuff – just a few fashion must-haves.'

Angel sighed. Knowing Gemma, it would be futile to argue.

'You know, you really went into the wrong business when you became a beautician. You should have studied fashion.'

'Yes,' Gemma replied, 'but at least I can live my dream through you . . . *please* let me style you for the World Cup? I promise I'll make you look fab. I'll work out all your outfits for you and your accessories.'

'Oh, all right, 'Angel finally admitted defeat. It would make Gemma happy, and it would save Angel from having to waste time thinking about what to take. '*And* you can do my packing as well because isn't that what stylists are supposed to do?' she added cheekily.

'Don't push it!' Gemma warned her.

Back home Michelle was in a state of high excitement as she was convinced Honey had said 'Mummy'. 'Here's Mummy!' she announced as soon as Angel walked into the house.

'Who is it, Honey? Come on, say "Mummy" again?' Honey chewed her favourite teddy's ear and said nothing. 'I'm sure she said it,' Michelle carried on happily, 'and I'm sure she'll say it again. Isn't she clever!'

'Did she really?' Angel exclaimed, scooping up her daughter in her arms. 'We should phone Daddy to tell him what a clever girl you are.' She quickly selected Cal's number on her phone, wanting to share this news with him, but there was no answer.

She sighed. He never seemed to take her calls at the moment.

'Not there?' her mum said sympathetically. 'He's probably training.'

Angel looked at her watch. It was six o'clock in the evening. She very much doubted it. She just hoped he wasn't out with the poisonous Flavia . . .

'Do you want to stay for supper, Mum? I'm sure I've got something in the freezer I can microwave and we can watch *The X Factor*.'

'Thanks, love, but me and your dad are going out tonight, remember? It's the Football Club disco.'

'Oh.' Which meant yet another night in on her own. Angel had been spending a lot of nights like that lately and she didn't like it.

'But you and Honey will come over for lunch tomorrow, won't you?' her mum asked, picking up her bag and putting on her jacket. Angel nodded as she listlessly walked her to the front door.

'And Angel . . .' her mum hesitated, '. . . I really do need to talk to you. I'm worried about you.'

Angel frowned and was immediately on the defensive. 'I'm absolutely fine, Mum, there's nothing to worry about. You'd better go – you know how Dad hates being kept waiting.' To stop her mum saying anything else she pretended to have heard Honey crying and quickly went back inside. Clearly Michelle had seen right through her pretence that everything was okay but Angel just didn't think she could handle another confrontation.

The house seemed horribly empty. She put on an Al Green CD to fill the silence but the music just reminded her of Cal and of how much she missed him as it was one of his favourite artists. She picked up her mobile and tried his number but again it went straight to voicemail. 'Cal, it's me. Can you ring me back? I really want to talk to you. Love you.'

She gave Honey her bath and her bottle, then tucked her up in her cot and read her a story. Her daughter looked so much like Cal, having inherited his olive skin, beautiful brown eyes and jet black hair. Yet again Angel felt awful for coming home but she knew she couldn't have stayed in Italy a minute longer.

Downstairs again she went into the kitchen. She opened the freezer and aimlessly shuffled through the ready meals, but nothing appealed to her. Instead she poured herself a large glass of wine, went into the living room and switched on the TV. *The X Factor* was on. How did the contestants manage to look so happy and enthusiastic? They all seemed like aliens to her as she struggled to remember when she'd last felt happy.

She'd drunk the glass of wine before she realised it and went into the kitchen to get a refill then returned to her place on the sofa. She drank that glass quickly too, anything to block out the present, to win just a few hours' respite from the depression.

This time when she went to the kitchen she brought the bottle back.

She picked up her mobile and tried Cal again. Voicemail again. Where was he? If Cal was setting out to punish her, he was doing a very good job. Wanting reassurance she called Gemma but got her voicemail as well. She tried Jez, he too was on voicemail. She even tried a couple of her glamour girlfriends who she hadn't seen for months but there was no answer there either. She looked at her watch. Nine o'clock on a Saturday night . . . what did she expect? Everyone else was out, everyone else had a life. She finished the bottle of wine. She was drunk.

Because she'd lost so much weight lately and because she hadn't eaten since lunch her tolerance was especially low. Somehow she managed to get upstairs and check on Honey who was fast asleep, then she went back downstairs and opened another bottle. She downed two more glasses and then must have passed out. She woke at four to the sound of Honey crying. She stumbled off the sofa and staggered upstairs. Honey was red-faced and her eyes were swollen. She looked as if she'd been crying for some time. Angel picked up her daughter and cradled her in her arms. Her head was pounding and she felt sick. She couldn't believe that she'd slept through her own baby's crying. What kind of mother was she? Eventually Honey calmed down and Angel was able to put her down in her cot and go to her own bed. She couldn't get back to sleep, though. She just lay there, staring into the darkness, full of self-disgust. She was no better than her junkie mother.

Then she realised something else. She didn't know if Cal had phoned her back.

She got out of bed and as she made her way downstairs to the living room caught sight of her reflection in the large mirror on the landing wall. She was shocked by her own appearance: mascara smudged, skin blotchy, eyes bloodshot and face gaunt. *Jesus Christ, what am I doing to myself?* she thought in despair. She prayed that there would be a message from Cal, but when she checked her phone there was nothing. It was so unlike him not to have called back. He was obviously still very angry with her. *Miss you,* she texted him.

At half-twelve the following day Angel was driving to her parents' for Sunday lunch. She'd taken several paracetamol and forced down some toast but felt crap. And Cal hadn't yet called her.

Her parents still lived in the same terraced house in Brighton that Angel had grown up in. Stepping inside it was like going back in time. Very little had changed: there were still the same immaculately painted magnolia walls and cream carpets, the brown leather sofas in the living room. The only real differences were the photographs on the walls. Pictures of Angel modelling – at least the ones where she had her clothes on; pictures of her wedding day; Tony's too; and pictures of Honey – Michelle and Frank were very proud parents and grandparents.

'Did you have a bad night with Honey?' Michelle asked as soon as her daughter walked through the front door. Angel rarely wore much make up during the day – tinted moisturiser, mascara and lip gloss were usually all it took to make her look stunning. But today there was no way she could get away with so little, and she'd had to go for the full works. Apparently it hadn't worked.

'Yes,' Angel lied. 'She was up for hours.'

'You poor thing,' Michelle said sympathetically. 'Give her to me and go and see your dad. He's a bit hungover so be gentle with him. Tony and Gemma will be here in a minute.'

Angel handed Honey over to her mum and found her dad in the lounge. He was sitting in his favourite armchair, pretending to read the paper.

'Hi, Dad,' said Angel, bending down to give him a quick kiss and wincing at the whisky fumes. 'Good night, was it?'

'Bit too good,' Frank groaned. 'We were celebrating the cheque we got from Cal's charity.' Frank made his living as a builder but his passion was football and in his spare time he coached the youth team in Brighton. Angel looked blank.

'Didn't he tell you? It's very generous, means we can run extra training sessions and not have to ask parents for money which most of them can't afford anyway.'

Angel felt miserable that Cal hadn't told her. Usually they shared everything and she knew how much his charity meant to him.

'He's still angry with me,' she muttered.

Frank sighed. 'He probably feels very lonely out there. Coming home to an empty house every night is no life for him. You should be with him, love.'

This was the last thing Angel wanted to discuss. She muttered something about helping her mum in the kitchen. She felt bad enough about herself without putting up with her dad's criticism.

Honey was sitting on the kitchen floor banging loudly on several saucepans with a wooden spoon, an activity that was not likely to improve Angel's headache.

'So did she say it to you?' Michelle asked, as she checked on the roast potatoes and chicken in the oven.

'Say what?' Angel asked, flopping down in one of the kitchen chairs.

'Mummy,' Michelle answered in a tone that said, How could you not have remembered?

Angel shook her head.

'Oh, well, I'm sure she will soon.'

'Mmm,' was all Angel could manage, thinking the only thing Honey was likely to say was 'Bad Mummy. Drunk Mummy. Could do so much better Mummy.'

'Anyway,' her own mum continued, 'now perhaps we can have that talk.'

Angel's heart sank; she really couldn't hold it together if her mum started on her. She was about to reply that there was no need when she was saved by the doorbell – Tony and Gemma had arrived.

'I'll get it,' she said, instantly getting up.

She opened the door to her brother and best friend who both looked sickeningly healthy. They'd cycled up from their seafront flat – a wedding present from Gemma's parents. Tony and Gemma divided their time between Brighton and London so they could be close to Tony's work as one of the physios for Spurs. For the next half-hour Angel kept herself busy, making everyone coffee and setting the table so as to avoid that conversation with her mum and also trying not to obsess over why Cal still hadn't called her. But as soon as they sat down to lunch the questions about her husband kicked off.

'How's Cal?' Tony asked, helping himself to roast potatoes. 'I haven't heard from him all week.' He and Cal had been friends from childhood and were still close.

'Good. Very busy,' Angel answered, handing

89

Honey a breadstick to avoid looking at Tony, not wanting to let on that she hadn't heard from her husband for two days.

'Has he got the date yet for flying out to the States?' The World Cup was starting at the beginning of June and the team would be flying out early for three weeks' intensive training.

Angel shook her head. 'I don't think so.'

'Do you think Cal will be allowed to fly back for Angel's birthday?' Gemma asked, looking concerned for her friend.

Tony frowned. 'I doubt it. You'll just have to celebrate before he goes.'

Angel looked down at the table, willing herself not to cry. Naively she'd imagined that he would be able to fly back and that she could make things up to him then.

'That's a shame,' Michelle said.

'No, it's fine,' Angel said, falsely bright. 'I can't expect to have wonderful birthdays every year.'

Her birthday the year before had been amazing. Cal had booked them a surprise trip on the Orient Express. In Venice they stayed at the luxurious Gritti Palace Hotel, overlooking the Grand Canal. It had been the perfect romantic mini-break. The list of presents he'd bought her had been breathtaking, too – a diamond necklace he'd designed and had made by their favourite jeweller, a matching diamond bracelet, a set of Louis Vuitton luggage and Christian Louboutin heels. But gorgeous as they were it wasn't the expensive presents that had made the trip so special, it was spending time alone with Cal.

'Well, I'm sure he's got something special planned for you this year as well,' Michelle continued.

Angel thought she would scream if her family didn't stop going on about Cal and her birthday. She looked meaningfully at Gemma and luckily her friend understood and changed the subject.

Later as the two girls cleared the table and loaded up the dishwasher Gemma apologised for not calling Angel back the night before. 'We went to the gym and then to see a film.'

'You went to the gym on Saturday night?' Angel looked at her friend as if she'd lost the plot.

'Yeah. I've got to be in peak shape to get pregnant.'

'You're in fantastic shape!' Angel exclaimed. And it was true. Gemma was naturally petite with an enviable figure – her flat stomach alone was a thing of wonder to Angel. Put it this way, she could have given Gwen Stefani a run for her money on the abs front. But Gemma never used to bother with going to the gym and Saturday nights before this would always have been given over to cocktails and clubbing. Angel missed that Gemma.

'So what did you do last night?' her friend asked.

'Nothing really, just watched TV and had an early night.' She felt too ashamed to admit drinking the bottle of wine and passing out. 'I called you because I hadn't heard from Cal.'

'Oh, playing hard to get, is he?' Gemma asked sympathetically. 'Ring him now, I bet he'll answer. You know I love Cal but he can be a right stubborn bastard sometimes. And because he thinks you're in the wrong, he's not going to make things easy for you.'

Taking her friend's advice, Angel grabbed her mobile and went outside to the tiny patio garden to make her call. This time Cal answered. He sounded half-asleep.

'Hi,' Angel said warmly, hugely relieved that he was there. 'Didn't you get my messages?'

'Sorry, not until it was too late to call, I was out with some friends.'

'Who did you go with?' she asked, and couldn't help feeling a surge of jealousy.

'Just some of the lads from the club and their partners. And before you ask, yes Flavia was there, but so was her husband. I was the only one whose wife wasn't with him, so you can imagine how good *that* made me feel. Everyone thinks we've split up,' Cal said sarcastically.

'You did tell them that we're still together, didn't you?' Angel asked anxiously.

'You could tell them yourself if you came back here.'

'Please, Cal, not this again.'

'The trouble is, Angel, I'm getting pretty sick of it too. I don't exactly feel supported by you right now. Look, I've got to go. I'm going to Alessia and her husband's for lunch. Give Honey a kiss from me.' He sounded so cold and distant.

'She said Mummy yesterday,' Angel told him, desperate for him not to go.

'Yeah, well, remind her that she's got a daddy too, won't you?'

'You are coming over next week, aren't you?' *God, what had she done to Cal to make him sound so bitter?*

'Angel, I haven't seen my daughter for over two weeks. Of course I'm coming over.'

'Mum's offered to babysit so we could go out – maybe we could have an early celebration for my birthday as you can't make my party.'

'Maybe. I'll speak to you in the week.'

'Can't we speak tonight?'

'Maybe. I'll call if I get the chance.'

And that was it. Angel whispered 'Love you' to a disconnected line, feeling Cal slipping away from her and knowing that she was responsible. Miserably she went back into the kitchen.

'Did you speak to him then?' Gemma asked hopefully.

Angel nodded then couldn't stop the tears. 'Oh, Gemma, I think I'm losing him. He didn't even say he loved me.'

Gemma hugged her. 'Of course he loves you, he just misses you. Everything will be all right, I'm sure.'

Angel felt numb for the rest of the afternoon; too upset to keep up the pretence that she was okay any longer. Gemma and Tony left around four as they had to get back to London and Michelle insisted that Frank take Honey for a walk, leaving her and their daughter alone. Angel had run out of excuses. As soon as Frank and Honey were safely out of the house Michelle walked into the living room where Angel was sitting. She sat down on the other end of the sofa, a serious expression on her face.

'Angel, I'm going to get straight to the point. You're not right, are you? You haven't been yourself since Honey was born.' Her mum took a deep breath and Angel knew it was taking all her courage to speak out like this. Theirs had not been the closest of relationships because Michelle herself had suffered from depression and Angel had often felt that she couldn't confide in her.

Now she shook her head, but her eyes, which were filling with tears, betrayed her.

'I'm fine, Mum. I've just been tired . . . you

know, with Honey not sleeping through the night and with Cal being so stressed about the World Cup.'

'Angel,' her mum said softly, 'do you think I don't know my own daughter?'

'Oh, Mum.' She gave in to the tears now, sobbing out her hurt and shame. All her barriers were down, she couldn't pretend anymore. 'I've been feeling so low . . . as if I've been going mad. I don't think I've bonded with Honey. What's wrong with me?'

She looked up at her mum, pure anguish in her beautiful green eyes. Michelle moved next to her on the sofa and put an arm round her.

'You're not well, Angel. It's not your fault. I think you've got post-natal depression.'

'Everyone is going to think that I'm such a bad mother, that I'm like my real mum. I'm such a failure, aren't I?' she cried out.

'Angel, you are a good mother but you're ill, you need help. You will get better then,' her mother reassured her, stroking her hair as Angel wept with pain and relief that finally her secret was out.

The next few hours were like a blur. Angel felt overcome with emotion, but inside there was a spark of hope. She knew now that she wasn't mad, that she would get better. She talked to her mum for hours and by the end had agreed to see her doctor the next day. But she made Michelle promise not to tell anyone. 'I can't bother Cal with this while he's so stressed about the World Cup,' she insisted. 'I can't distract him. I've got to get through this on my own.'

Chapter 4

The Distance Between Us . . .

'Darling, welcome back to the wonderful world of work!' Jez exclaimed as Angel walked into the dressing room where he and Gemma were busy getting out the tools of their trade. It was the morning of a shoot for *Loaded*, where Angel was supposed to show that despite being a mum she was still Britain's hottest glamour girl. 'I've got you a large builder's tea, bacon sarnie, chocolate croissant and freshly squeezed orange juice. See, I remembered all your fave things.'

'Thanks, Jez, but you're not going to believe this . . . I'm not hungry,' Angel replied, flopping down on the chair in front of the mirror. Usually before a shoot she would have liked nothing better than the food Jez had bought. 'I feel too nervous to eat. Perhaps I haven't got what it takes anymore?'

She had always been confident about her modelling, a complete natural in front of the camera, but say she had lost it? She didn't take anything for granted about her life anymore, though thank God she was feeling so much better after seeing her GP and being prescribed anti-depressants. He had warned her that they weren't a quick fix and that she would need therapy as well. She didn't feel quite back to her usual self, but most of the darkness had lifted and she no longer felt imprisoned by a terrible sense of failure and anxiety. She knew there was some way to go but at least she wasn't totally alone now.

'Don't be ridiculous!' Jez declared, scandalised. 'You're going to be fantastic, especially when Gemma and I have finished with you!'

'Oh, 'course you haven't lost it, Angel,' Gemma told her, giving her a sympathetic hug. 'Come on, I'll get started.'

While Gemma applied foundation to Angel's skin, Sabrina, the magazine's stylist came into the dressing room. She and Angel had already spoken about the look of the shoot and Angel had said that she wanted to be, 'Pinked out to the max!' Sabrina had clearly taken her wishes on board because when she opened a large suitcase it was like gazing into a pink paradise. Angel smiled as Sabrina began pulling out hot pink bikinis, baby pink bras and thongs, knee-high pale pink suede boots, pink diamante sandals and armfuls of fake bling.

'What do you want to start with, Angel?' she asked.

Angel liked her; they'd worked together before and Sabrina always listened to Angel's ideas, which wasn't true of some of the stylists she'd had.

Angel considered the pile of lingerie. 'I think I'll go for the bra and thong with the suede boots and that long diamante chain.'

'How do you want your hair, darling?' Jez asked.

'Let's start with it in a really sleek pony tail,' Angel replied confidently, sure that would look good. Perhaps she hadn't lost her touch after all.

It took an hour to get her ready – both Gemma and Jez were complete perfectionists about their work and always took their time. As she watched herself being transformed into Angel the glamour model, with dark smoky eye shadow, long lashes and bubble gum pink glossed lips, she felt her old confidence return. By the time she had put on the lingerie and boots, she felt ready for action.

Sabrina handed her a white towelling robe and they all made their way to the studio where Aidan the photographer was setting up the camera and his assistant was busy arranging the lights. Angel had worked with hundreds of photographers over the last five years – some had been absolutely lovely, others total bastards. Today, thankfully, it was one of the nice ones.

Straightaway Aidan came up to her. 'I won't kiss you, I don't want to spoil Gemma's work, but it's great to see you again. How are things?'

'Great,' Angel replied, giving him a dazzling smile which she hoped would put him off asking her anymore questions. Today she just wanted to work, wanted to forget about what was going on between her and Cal, wanted to forget the depression that had been crushing her down for so long. Sabrina fussed around her, rearranging the diamante chain, adjusting straps. For the first set of photos Angel was to stand against a white background. It took several rolls of film for her to relax fully, get back the sultry, sexy, challenging stare that had always been her trademark, but after that there was no stopping her and she was back in her stride, suggesting poses, slipping her bra straps down her shoulders suggestively, leaning forward to show off her impressive cleavage, slipping her hand cheekily under the strap of the pink lace thong, as if she was about to whip it off.

'Wow, Angel that's gorgeous . . . hold it! Bit more . . . perfect!' Aidan called out instructions and encouragement while Angel focused only on the camera. It was as if she was looking at her lover, working out ways to please him, tease him, turn him on. She felt inspired for the first time in ages.

For the next series of shots Angel chose to wear hot pink French knickers, white ankle socks and sky-high pink patent shoes. Jez took her hair down and gave it that just-got-out-of-bed look while Angel posed on a luxurious sheepskin rug. She lay on her stomach, revealing a tantalising glimpse of her breasts . . . but just a glimpse. She had already said that she wasn't going to do full topless.

'Okay?' Gemma whispered to her during a quick make-up check.

Angel nodded. 'Do you think the pictures are going to be all right?'

Aidan overheard and said, 'Angel, I think this is the best shoot I've ever done with you. Really, you look amazing . . . sexier than ever.'

'So people aren't going to be looking at me and thinking, She's had a baby, what's she still modelling for?' Angel asked.

Aidan laughed, 'Just because you've had a baby, it doesn't stop you from being sexy.'

'Don't worry,' Jez called out. 'All the men who see you are still going to want to give you one. You're definitely a MILF – well, you would be to me, if I wasn't a homosexualist.'

'Cheers, Jez,' Angel replied, 'I can always rely on you to lower the tone.'

'It is my duty!' he told her.

The next two hours flew by as Angel posed in more pink lingerie, finishing the day as a sexy cheerleader in a pink satin mini-skirt and cute cropped white tee-shirt with a plunging neckline, and her hair worn in bunches. She was actually enjoying herself. It was wonderful to be working again, to be doing something she was good at, something she felt confident about. She was on a high throughout the shoot. It was only when she sat in the dressing room afterwards, taking off her make up, that she crashed. She picked up her mobile, hoping that Cal might have texted her to wish her luck for the shoot. He hadn't. Jez and Gemma were busy getting ready for a film premiere – one of their clients had got them tickets – and Angel felt just the tiniest bit jealous.

'Why don't you come too?' Jez suggested.

'Oh, I can't. I should get back to Honey.' Angel had really missed her daughter as this was practically the first day that she'd been apart from her. But she hadn't had a night out in ages and she wanted to hold on to the happiness she'd just experienced.

'Come on!' Jez urged her. 'I've just had a text from a friend saying she's got an extra ticket.'

'I'm sure your mum won't mind having Honey for the night,' Gemma put in. 'You can stay with me and go back first thing. Go on, it would do you good.'

Angel hesitated for a few more minutes then gave in. A quick call to her mum and she was ready to hit the town. Jez insisted on redoing her hair in the sleek pony tail, Gemma touched up her make up, and when Angel complained that she couldn't turn up on the red carpet in jeans and a tee-shirt, which was all she had with her, Sabrina lent her a figure-hugging white halterneck dress that showed off Angel's amazing figure. The skirt was so tight that it meant underwear was out of the question.

'You'll just have to go commando,' Gemma said when Angel tried it on and moaned about her VPL.

'Okay,' she agreed, 'but don't let any one pap me getting out of a taxi. I bloody well don't want to be plastered all over the tabs with a star over my cookie.'

'Absolutely, darling, the commando look is *so* last year,' Jez said. 'Come on, let's grab some cocktails at Jewel.'

So the group headed off for cocktails then the premiere. It was fun being on the red carpet again. Angel received lots of press attention. She'd had just enough to drink to take the edge off, so she enjoyed posing for the photographers, winking at them and signing autographs for fans. The film was hilarious and had the three of them in stitches. Then it was off to the after-film party at Funky Buddah and more cocktails.

Angel, who hadn't eaten lunch and had only had a tiny bar snack, was soon drunk. She didn't care; she was having such a good time. But then she bumped into Cal's ex-girlfriend Simone and was brought sharply back to reality.

She had walked into the Ladies' and was confronted with the sight of Simone touching up her perfect make up at the mirror. *Shit!* Angel thought, wondering if she could pretend not to have seen her. She was perfectly within her rights to ignore her as the last time they'd met Simone had called her a tart and lied about Cal wanting to see her again, never mind her weirdo stalking behaviour . . . But it was too late, Simone had clocked her.

'Oh, it's you,' she said coldly, clicking her Chanel bag shut and turning to look at Angel. As usual Simone was in head to toe designer. Angel shrugged, trying to act nonchalant, and carried on walking past Simone. Now she regretted all those cocktails – she didn't want her old enemy to see her at a disadvantage.

'Classy as ever, I see,' Simone called after her. 'You've spilt something on your dress.'

Angel checked it. Bollocks! Simone was right.

'Bacardi, was it? You always did have simple tastes, didn't you?' Simone continued nastily. Now she had walked up to Angel and was standing just a few feet away, close enough for Angel to get a blast of her expensive, heady perfume. And for her to notice that Simone had definitely had a boob job – she'd always mocked Angel for her breasts and claimed her own were perfect, but maybe they hadn't been perfect enough to attract a Premiership player. Her new boobs were at least two sizes bigger. Angel had had a boob job herself when she started modelling and could always spot them.

'And you've got new boobs, I see,' she replied, willing herself not to sway and give away the fact that she was drunk.

Simone flushed angrily under her fake tan. 'I haven't! Not every woman wants to go around looking like a plastic Barbie!'

'Fuck off, Simone, it's obvious you have. And what's the big deal? Everyone else does.' Angel was now desperate to get away from her. But Simone stepped forward, a smile on her perfectly glossed lips. 'I hear Cal's been hitting the bars in Milan. You better watch it, Angel. He cheated once; he could easily do it again.'

How did Simone know what Cal had been up to?

Angel turned away, not wanting her to see the hurt she had caused, while Simone, sensing her weakness, ruthlessly carried on her attack. 'Yeah, you know what these footballers are like. They have their needs, and if you're not around to meet them, then some other woman will. And you've seen how gorgeous those Italian WAGs are.'

Angel shook her head and muttered, 'Cal's not like that.'

'Oh, yes he is, Angel, Cal's exactly like that.' And Simone actually laughed as she turned and walked out of the Ladies'. Suddenly Angel was seized by nausea and only just made it into the cubicle before throwing up in the loo. Five cocktails and a run in with Simone was a toxic combination.

She was just trying to repair the damage to her make up when Gemma walked in. 'Oh, there you are. I wondered where you were,' she said. Angel carried on trying to wipe off the smudged mascara. 'Hey, what's the matter?' Gemma asked in concern.

'I've just seen Simone,' she replied miserably, all her enjoyment in the night out gone.

'Shit! That can't have been fun.' Gemma was fully aware of what a Number One bitch Simone was.

Just then the door opened and three young girls trooped in. Angel didn't want to reveal anything in front of them so instead said, 'Gemma, do you mind if we go home now?'

''Course, babe. I was going to suggest it anyway as I've got an early start.'

Angel had hoped to walk out of the club unobserved but the photographers were out in force and immediately started taking pictures of her. They crowded round as she got into the limo. Gemma was behind her and Jez in front and Angel sat down as carefully as she could to avoid any wardrobe malfunctions, but some cheeky paparazzo stuck his camera right into the limo and fired off a shot. Angel had a horrible feeling that he'd taken it from an angle that would reveal she'd left her knickers at home.

'Bollocks!' she exclaimed as Jez hustled the photographer away and shut the door. 'Tell me he didn't get a picture of my cookie?'

'You'll find out tomorrow,' Gemma said grimly. 'God, those guys make me sick. It's not like you were flaunting yourself. How dare they go around sticking a camera up a woman's skirt? They're all pervs.'

Angel sank back on the seat and sighed. *What a perfect end to the night.*

It wasn't until the two girls were back at Gemma's flat that she finally told her friend what Simone had said.

'Bitch!' Gemma exclaimed. 'She hasn't changed, still total poison.'

'But she's right, isn't she? Cal has been unfaithful before and who's to say that he wouldn't do it again?' Angel said anxiously. She was sobering up now, on a downer, the alcohol making her feel paranoid and on edge.

'Angel, he was unfaithful with *you* when he was with Simone, and he married *you*. Don't let that cow get to you. She's just bitter and twisted because you're with him.' Gemma stifled a yawn. 'Sorry, I'm knackered.'

'You go to bed,' Angel told her, suddenly feeling very lonely and longing to be back at her own house with Cal and Honey.

'Sure you'll be okay?'

'I'll be fine,' Angel lied, thinking that she was getting very good at saying what she didn't mean.

Eventually she went to bed around three and not for the first time she woke up crying. She'd been dreaming of Cal and in her dream she'd been in a crowded club, desperately trying to get his attention while he was surrounded by beautiful women and ignoring her. *It was just a dream,* she tried to tell herself, wiping the tears from her eyes. She got up hoping to see Gemma but she'd already left for her shoot – when she wasn't with Angel she worked with several other models and freelanced for magazines.

Angel felt exhausted and hungover but wanted to get back home and see Honey as soon as she could. She tried to ignore her headache and quickly showered and got dressed. Tel arrived to pick her up at seven.

When she got into the car he said quietly, 'Have you seen the papers yet?'

Angel shook her head. Tel sighed and handed her a pile of tabloids. She was on the front cover of one of them and on the showbiz pages of all the others. It was the shot of her sitting back in the car, a star placed strategically to cover her modesty, but revealing enough to show that she was knickerless. The headline read: *'Forgotten something, Angel?'* She stared at the picture of herself – she looked the worse for wear even though she'd repaired her make up.

Angel threw the papers on the seat next to her in disgust.

'Don't worry,' Tel told her. 'It'll be forgotten by tomorrow.'

'No, it won't,' Angel replied. 'Then it'll be in all the celeb mags. They'll get their chance to print the shot of me and of all the other celebs who've been caught out.'

Tel had bought her a croissant and latte for the journey back but she couldn't eat anything. She sipped her coffee and stared aimlessly out of the window. She just hoped Cal didn't see the papers, though she knew he was bound to find out and didn't like to imagine his reaction.

Ten minutes later her mobile rang. It was Cal, and he was furious. 'I can't believe you went out like that! What the fuck were you thinking?' Angel tried to speak but he cut across her. 'You're a mother now, Angel, do you really want our daughter seeing pictures of you like that?'

'She's six months old! I don't think she'll be that interested.' Angel tried to lighten the tone but Cal was having none of it.

'Well, I'll have the piss ripped out of me by the

lads. And those pictures will turn up on the internet. Did you think of that when you forget to put your knickers on? Of course not, because as usual you were only thinking of yourself. Did you think it would get you some good publicity, remind people who you were?'

'No! Please, Cal, stop being like this. The photographer pushed his way into the car and stuck his camera up my skirt, it's not my fault!'

'And where was Honey last night?' Cal continued shouting. 'It's bad enough I hardly get to see my daughter. Now you're abandoning her, getting caned and flashing your cunt.'

Angel winced. 'My mum had her. It was one night. I've hardly been out.'

'Well, you'd better stay in from now on! Jesus Christ, like I need this publicity before the World Cup!'

'Cal, I've said I'm sorry,' Angel pleaded. 'Please can't you forget this?'

He sighed heavily. 'Yeah, well, it wouldn't have happened if you were in Italy with me where you should be. I've got to go now. I've got training.'

''Bye then,' Angel said sadly. 'Love you.' But there was no point. Cal had already hung up.

'Not too happy, was he?' Tel said sympathetically as Angel sniffed and brushed away the tears. 'Don't worry, he'll get over it.'

'I hope so,' she replied. 'I don't know, Tel, we seem to be getting on so badly at the moment.'

'All marriages have their ups and downs,' he said. 'Trust me, it's just a bad patch.'

Angel shrugged, too emotionally drained to say anything.

It was another week before she got to see Cal, a week of worrying about what he was doing or who he might be seeing. Simone's comments had really got under her skin. 'Look! There's Daddy!' she told her daughter as they waited at the Arrivals gate at Gatwick airport for Cal. He didn't see them straight away and Angel got to observe her husband from a distance. Her heart flipped when she saw him. She'd missed him so much these past weeks. He looked gorgeous, tanned, fit – in both senses of the word. She could see other people staring at him. Then he spotted Angel, walked swiftly over and took Honey from her arms. Angel watched as he kissed his daughter and held her up in the air, making her giggle. She was delighted to see father and daughter reunited but couldn't help wondering where her hello was. Then Cal finally seemed to register her. 'Hi, thanks for meeting me,' he said formally, and kissed her lightly on the cheek. *What kind of welcome was that?* Angel thought, feeling rejected. Where was the passionate kiss she'd been anticipating?

'That's okay, we really wanted to see you. Shall I take Honey?'

'Actually, can you push the trolley then I can hold my daughter and remind her that I still exist.'

Whoah, that was harsh! Cal was obviously still furious with her. Angel trailed after him as he strode purposefully through the airport, not bothering to see if she could keep up as she struggled to negotiate the trolley through the crowds. When they got to the car, he insisted on sitting next to Honey in the back while Angel drove and talked to the baby non-stop about what they could see from the window, totally ignoring his wife.

Twenty minutes into the journey Honey fell asleep and Angel finally felt able to talk to Cal. 'Mum said she would babysit tomorrow night so we can go out. I've booked a table at Hôtel du Vin. I was thinking it could be my birthday celebration . . .' Her voice trailed off. It hardly seemed as if Cal was in the mood to celebrate anything.

'I'll see how I feel,' he answered abruptly. 'I might just want an early night; training has been so intense lately.'

'Oh,' Angel answered, seeing her plans for a romantic meal were already in ruins.

'Anyway you've got your party coming up. You can celebrate your birthday with your friends, can't you?'

'Actually I've cancelled it,' she answered.

'You didn't have to,' Cal replied, sounding surprised, 'I thought you were really looking forward to it?'

'I'm not bothered,' Angel answered, too sad to make the usual *Am I bovvered?* joke. 'Last year's was so wonderful, and I'd rather celebrate with you after the World Cup. Maybe we could go away for the weekend?'

'Maybe, I'll need to check my schedule.'

God, he sounded so distant, like he didn't care about her at all. How was she going to win him back?

As soon as they arrived at the house Cal focused all his attention on Honey and hardly said anything to Angel. She'd really made an effort for his visit, buying all his favourite food and drink. And she'd made an effort with her appearance too – she'd gone for the natural look that she knew Cal loved, but it was a natural look that required effort so she'd had a spray tan and her nails done.

For the first time in a while she'd bought some new clothes, too. She was wearing a pair of white jeans and tight white top that made the most of her figure. Round her neck she wore the stunning necklace Cal had bought her for her last birthday that spelt 'Angel' in pink diamonds. Jez had recently done her hair and she'd had more blonde highlights put in to give her a sun-kissed look. But Cal said nothing about the way she looked; in fact, he barely seemed to notice her.

Angel let it go for a couple of hours but by early-evening she was desperate to get a response from him. As she watched him bathing Honey she found herself blurting out, 'Don't you love me anymore?'

'Don't be mad!' Cal answered, finally looking at her. 'Of course I love you, I just haven't seen you lately, and I'm still fucking fuming about the fact you've abandoned me.'

'I have not!' Angel said hotly.

'Look, I'm not going to argue in front of our daughter,' he answered tersely.

'I'm not arguing,' Angel protested, but Cal shook his head, and realising she would get nowhere, she left the bathroom. He spent the next hour putting Honey to bed. Wondering what was taking so long Angel tiptoed into the nursery and discovered him sitting by Honey's cot, watching her sleep. Seeing Angel, he got up quietly and followed her out of the room.

'I've missed her so much,' he said.

'I know,' Angel replied, longing to hold him. They stood on the landing, gazing at each other, and for a minute Angel thought he might finally kiss her. But he said abruptly, 'Shall we order a pizza? I'm too knackered to cook.'

'But I was going to make something!' Angel protested. 'I bought sea bass.'

Cal laughed and it wasn't a particularly nice

laugh. 'That'll be the day! Leave the sea bass, you'll only burn it. I'll phone for pizza.'

They spent the evening in front of the TV, Cal drinking beer, Angel white wine. They sat on the sofa but whereas usually they'd be sitting close, arms round each other, Cal sat at one end and Angel at the other. She longed to talk to him but didn't know how to begin to bridge the distance between them. He was being so cold. When he wasn't watching TV he was texting, making her feel even more excluded. After he'd sent off five messages Angel asked who he was texting.

'Just Rico. I don't think you met him, he's one of my team mates. He wants some advice about a girl he's just met. D'you want some more wine?' he asked, getting up from the sofa. 'I'm having another beer.'

Angel shook her head. This was far from the evening she had planned. She'd imagined that after Honey was asleep, she'd take Cal to bed. But he didn't seem remotely interested. She looked at the coffee table where his mobile was lying and had to know for sure who he'd been texting. Quickly she picked it up and tried to access his messages, but it was password protected. That was odd; Cal had never had a password on his phone before. She felt a prickle of unease. Had he really just been texting a friend? An image of Flavia flashed up in her mind as she recalled Simone's words that if Cal had been unfaithful once, he was capable of being unfaithful again. She heard him walking back towards the living room and quickly put the phone down.

'Have you thought about what you're going to wear to the Carters' World Cup party? It's white tie and diamonds,' Cal said, flopping back down on the sofa.

As England's Captain, Connor Carter epitomised what it was to be a Premiership footballer. Young, good-looking and absolutely loaded, he was married to Gabrielle who had been a model once but had given it up when she married Connor and now dabbled in fashion design – she had her own jeans and sportswear label. Gabrielle was also something of a style icon and many WAGs and Wannabe WAGs aspired to be like her. They just didn't want to be married to a man like Connor who had been unfaithful to Gabrielle at least twice – or so the kiss and tells said. And on top of that there had been some very unsavoury rumours about what he'd got up to recently at a party, which wives and girlfriends had been banned from attending. Whatever the truth, Gabrielle had maintained a dignified silence, but was known to be extremely jealous of any woman who went near her husband.

Angel shook her head. 'No, I guess I'll ask

Gemma to help me find something.' That was the least of her worries at the moment.

'Well, you'd better get on with it. I bet all the other wives have got their outfits sorted. And I really think you need to wear a top designer. The ball is going to be on TV and the pictures will be everywhere. And please wear knickers.'

Angel hated being told what to do, always had done. She was strongly tempted to tell him so, but couldn't face the thought of another row so instead said flatly, 'What designers do you suggest?'

'I would have thought Roberto Cavalli or Valentino. Of course, if you were in Milan it would be so much easier. I could come with you and help you choose.'

'I'm perfectly capable of choosing my own dress,' she snapped, unable to stop herself. 'You don't need to treat me like a child. And don't worry, I'm not going to show you up.'

Cal yawned and stretched his arms over his head. 'Whatever.' He carried on watching TV.

Angel sat seething on the sofa for a few minutes before she was struck with a horrible thought. 'Do you think Simone will be there?'

'I expect so, but why are you so bothered? I dumped her for *you*, remember? And she knows not to come near us.'

'I'm bothered because she's a right bitch. I bumped into her the other night and she was vile to me.' Angel was about to tell him what Simone had said but Cal shrugged. 'Just ignore her, she's not important. Anyway I'm knackered, I'm going to bed.' And with that he got up, picked up his phone and left the room.

Angel felt totally powerless. She didn't know how to reach her husband. Should she tell him how depressed she'd been feeling? About how she was on medication now? She hadn't wanted to so close to the tournament, but the way things were between them, she worried she was losing him. But when she went upstairs Cal was sitting on the end of the bed, his head in his hands.

'What's wrong?' she asked, sitting down next to him and putting her arm round him.

He sighed heavily, 'I'm so worried.' He paused and Angel felt sure he was going to say that he was worried about them and their marriage, and she was about to say that she was worried too, but Cal carried on, 'I'm so worried I won't be good enough for the tournament, that my knee won't hold out and I'll let everyone down.'

He had suffered a serious knee injury a few years back on the pitch, which had been made worse later when he was attacked while trying to protect Angel in a fight. At the time it had been touch and go whether he would play again.

'Oh, Cal, I'm sure it will be fine. More than fine.

You'll be brilliant. And your knee has been okay for three years now. You're bound to be nervous because it's such a big thing, but you mustn't worry.'

Angel ached to see Cal look so stressed. She also realised there was no way she could tell him about her depression now. It wouldn't be fair when he was so anxious. Hard as it would be, she'd somehow have to keep herself together until the World Cup was over.

Cal gave a small smile, 'Yeah, I know, just pre-tournament nerves, I guess. You get to bed, I'll check on Honey.'

Angel slipped off her clothes, put on her silk camisole and lay on the bed. *I'll make love with Cal and then everything will be okay,* she told herself. *He'll stop being so distant with me.* But when he came to bed he simply gave her a quick kiss on the cheek.

'Night, Angel. I'll get up for Honey, if she wakes up.' And he turned over.

Angel switched off the light and lay there, not knowing what to do. She longed to feel Cal's arms around her. Tentatively she slipped her arm around him, feeling his warmth. He took her hand and held it as if to prevent her from touching him any further.

'See you in the morning, babe,' he said, making it quite clear sleep was the only thing on his agenda.

*

Sunday was just the same. Cal virtually ignored Angel and made no attempt to get close to her. He was flying back that night. It would be another week before they met up and that would only be for two nights – one of which would be the World Cup party – and then he'd be flying out to LA. Angel had hoped they'd spend the day together, that she might even be able to get him into bed when Honey was having her nap, but Cal told her he had arranged to take the baby to see his mum for the afternoon.

'What time is she expecting us?' Angel asked, thinking she'd visit as well even though she had a very uneasy relationship with Cal's mother. She couldn't forgive her for neglecting him when he was growing up.

'Actually I think it's best if I go on my own with Honey. You two really don't get on and I don't need the aggro right now.'

'But it's practically the only time we'll have together before you go to the States,' Angel cried despairingly.

Cal shrugged. 'You're the one who's made that happen, Angel.' His phone beeped then and he checked his texts.

'Is it your friend wanting advice again?' she asked, and couldn't help sounding snide. She was feeling really hurt by the way Cal was cutting her out.

'No, it's my agent actually, giving me the flight details.' He held up the phone so she could read the text. 'I'm going to get Honey ready to see Mum.' And he walked out of the room.

Rather than mope around the house, Angel decided to spend the afternoon riding. She could have called Gemma but knew her friend would think it strange that she wasn't with Cal. Well, it was strange, wasn't it? And upsetting. Was her husband being so distant just because of nerves? She had no way of knowing.

'That's the one!' Gemma declared as Angel emerged from the dressing room. She was trying on dresses for the World Cup Ball. So far Gemma had made her try on over twenty, all of which had seemed okay to Angel. But Gemma insisted that they didn't have the Wow! factor. Now apparently she had found it in this beautifully cut full-length red dress with the asymmetric top that showed off Angel's slender shoulders and slim figure. Angel had to admit that it was a stunning dress, she just didn't know if it was her. It seemed so sophisticated.

'Are you sure?' she asked.

'Positive,' declared Gemma, walking round Angel and checking her out.

'What about jewellery?' she asked. 'Should I get a necklace on loan?'

Gemma shook her head. 'No, let the dress make

the statement. Just wear that diamond bracelet Cal bought you last year. I think you should have your hair up too and maybe have jewelled clips, but that's it. Less is more. That way you'll stand out because I bet those other WAGs will overdo it, especially Simone who's bound to be blinged up in Chopard diamonds or whatever else she's bullied her boyfriend into buying her.'

'Okay,' Angel replied. 'Just so long as Cal likes it.' She had finally told Gemma all about their disastrous weekend.

'You're going to be the Belle of the Ball, I promise,' Gemma told her. 'And Cal will be knocked out.'

'I hope so,' Angel said sadly. Contact with her husband continued to be frustrating and brief – he'd barely called since he returned to Italy, and when he did it was only to ask about Honey. For her birthday he'd sent her favourite flowers, two dozen white roses, but he said he hadn't had time to choose her a present and he'd have to get her something after the World Cup. Angel knew that he'd been really busy but a little voice inside couldn't help reminding her that if he'd really wanted to he could have bought her something . . .

'So how do I look?' Angel asked as she walked into the living room where Cal and her parents were sitting. Even she knew that she looked good, though. Jez had styled her hair beautifully in a sleek bun; Gemma had excelled herself with the make up, giving her dramatic eyes, flawless skin, and just a hint of colour on her lips. She'd been right about the dress – it clung in all the right places, showing off Angel's figure perfectly. It was extremely sexy, but not in any way tarty.

'You look beautiful, love!' Michelle exclaimed. 'Look at Mummy, Honey, doesn't she look like a princess?'

'You look wonderful,' Frank agreed. And that just left Cal. He, of course, looked heart-stoppingly gorgeous in white tie and tails and would no doubt have every woman at the party lusting after him.

He glanced briefly in her direction. *Please say something nice,* Angel thought, not knowing if she could take anymore of his coldness. 'You look really good,' he said quietly. 'We'd better go.'

Cal barely said a word to her on the hour-long journey to the Carters' mansion in Surrey, which made Angel feel more and more unhappy and nervous. She wasn't looking forward to the ball, having to make small talk with people she didn't know, and was absolutely dreading seeing Simone again. She just didn't feel strong enough emotionally.

'Go easy on the champagne when we get there,' Cal said abruptly as the car turned into the impressive driveway leading to the Carters' mansion. There were four burly security guards at the gate, all dressed in black and wearing earpieces. They looked like ex-soldiers. The men checked the guests, making sure no paparazzi got in. Angel and Cal were approved and the car was waved through.

Angel was stung by the implication that she would drink too much. 'I wasn't planning to drink anything,' she hissed back.

'Well, you can have one glass, but just be careful is all I'm saying. You know what these events are like, with waiters coming round and filling up your glass non-stop. You don't want to end up pissed.'

'Don't worry Cal, I won't show you up if that's what you're worried about,' Angel snapped back.

He sighed, 'I'm sure you won't,' then muttered, 'Jesus, when did marriage become such hard work?' Angel had no answer to that one.

'Anyway, smile,' he said, opening the car door. 'You're on camera.'

There was a TV crew filming the guests arriving. Gabrielle and Connor had agreed to take part in a one-off documentary about their lives in the run up to the World Cup, culminating in this party. Cal took Angel's hand and they followed the procession of guests towards the marquee. She tried to take in everything so she could tell Gemma afterwards – the fairy lights sparkling in the trees, and the flickering torches that lined the path to the marquee, giving the garden an enchanted look; the women all in beautiful jewel-coloured evening dresses and the diamonds round their necks and wrists sparkling; the men all so dashing in their white tie.

Gabrielle and Connor were waiting just inside the marquee to greet their guests. Gabrielle wore a full-length white silk dress, slashed to the thigh and low-cut, with a huge diamond choker round her neck. She looked incredibly glamorous but Angel couldn't help thinking that if she was Gabrielle she would have spent the whole night worrying that her tits were going to fall out. And she couldn't help noticing that her hostess didn't look quite so good in the flesh as she did in her airbrushed photo shoots.

Connor was dressed in a white suit and was undeniably good-looking, but he was too 'done' for Angel's taste, with too much fake tan and overly styled hair. He wore way too much bling as well: diamond studs in both ears, a large diamond crucifix that would have given P. Diddy a run for his money, and diamond skull-and-crossbones cufflinks.

Both host and hostess looked pleased to see Cal. Connor shook his hand and hugged him, and Gabrielle kissed him. Angel suddenly felt shy. She'd been famous long before she got together with Cal but she had never bought into that celebrity life style where celebs only ever seemed to mix with other celebs, and had never felt particularly relaxed at big A-list events – she would rather be out having a laugh with close friends. Cal, however, was confident in any situation.

'This is my wife Angel,' he introduced her. Connor gave her a friendly smile and kissed her. *Too much aftershave*, she thought.

'It's lovely to meet you at last. I believe you know my friend Flavia?' said Gabrielle, giving her two air kisses, though Angel was aware of the other woman sizing her up and her heart sank at the mention of Flavia's name. And she didn't warm to Gabrielle Carter, Queen of the WAGs, one little bit.

'You look beautiful!' her hostess declared. 'Are you wearing Valentino?'

Angel shook her head.

'Balenciaga?'

'No, it's by an up and coming designer – Nina Rose – she has a boutique in Brighton.'

'Really? I've never heard of her.' Gabrielle arched one perfectly shaped eyebrow.

Angel was about to say that she could text her the details but Gabrielle had already moved on to the next guest, and apparently they looked beautiful too.

Posh and Becks had set the standard when it came to throwing World Cup parties and it was clear that

Gabrielle and Connor had pulled out all the stops to try and match them. They'd taken Hollywood as their theme and the marquee had been lavishly decorated like an old-fashioned Art Deco movie theatre: red velvet seats, gilded tables and pillars supporting elaborate arrangements of deep red roses and heavily scented lilies. The ceiling of the marquee was swathed in blue velvet and hung with thousands of fairy lights to look like a star-lit sky. All the waiting staff, circulating with trays of vintage champagne and delicious-looking nibbles, were dressed as movie stars or characters from films. Angel spotted a Marilyn Monroe, Charlie Chaplin, Lara Croft, Indiana Jones and Spider Man. Clearly no expense had been spared.

For the next hour she and Cal mingled with the other guests. Angel felt quite star-struck as she looked round the room and saw so many famous faces – there was Elton John and David Furnish chatting to Liz Hurley; Sharon and Kelly Osbourne; three of the boys from Take That. Daniel Craig was looking well hot to trot and Angel had a lovely moment when she remembered the scene in *Casino Royale* where he emerges from the sea in his trunks . . . And, oh my God, was that petite blonde woman in the peach silk dress really Kylie?

Cal knew practically everyone and Angel was feeling a little left out, though she tried not to show it. Also, although her medication had kicked in and she felt worlds better, she was still not quite herself. And her husband, usually so thoughtful in situations like this, and so careful to include her in conversations, hardly seemed to notice her tonight. She wished Gemma was there. Her friend would have made her laugh, would have loved seeing what everyone was wearing too. Angel left Cal deep in conversation with one of his team mates and wondered off to get herself a mineral water.

'Hiya, I'm Candy.'

Angel looked up to see a sweet-looking girl. She had blonde ringlets piled on her head and was wearing a slinky blue silk halterneck dress that matched her blue eyes perfectly. It was Candy Tyler, girlfriend of Liam Miller, the newest and youngest member of the England squad. 'I've been wanting to meet you for ages,' she said excitedly in her Manchester accent.

'Hiya,' Angel answered, shaking her hand.

'Isn't this ball amazing?' Candy said. 'I've seen so many famous people. When I went to the Ladies' and I was putting on my lip gloss, I was standing next to Dita von Teese – she's so pale, I couldn't believe it! In fact, I can't believe that I'm here!'

'It's great,' Angel replied, half wishing she shared Candy's enthusiasm.

'And I'm so looking forward to the States. I just can't wait!'

'Me either,' Angel answered, horribly aware of how insincere she sounded.

'So, have you got all your outfits planned for the trip?' Candy asked.

Angel shook her head. 'I'm not that into clothes to be honest. I mean, I like them, but I can't get that excited about them.'

Candy looked horrified and exclaimed, 'Angel, you have *got* to start planning. All the WAGs here have got theirs sorted already.'

Angel laughed. 'You'd get on well with my friend Gemma. She's been having a go at me too. In fact, I'm leaving her to choose all my clothes.'

'You'll have to come up to my house in Liverpool and I'll show you what I've got,' Candy suggested. 'I've labelled everything with the day I'm going to wear it, and worked out what accessories I'll need as well.'

'Oh, God, she's not going on about clothes again, is she?' They'd been joined by Liam her boyfriend, a cute-looking lad with short brown spiky hair and a cheeky grin. He and Candy were both twenty-one and had been childhood sweethearts since they met at school in Manchester. Liam had recently been signed to Liverpool and they both lived there now.

'And I thought it was supposed to be about football,' Angel answered.

Liam rolled his eyes and put his arm round

129

Candy. 'Yeah, well, so did I, but not Candy. You are going to come and watch the matches, aren't you, babe?'

She laughed. ''Course I am! You know I wouldn't miss them for anything.'

'Not even if Roberto Cavalli offered you and only you one of his exclusive designs at the same time as England were kicking off?'

Candy looked as if she was thinking hard. 'It would be a difficult decision, but in the end you'd understand, wouldn't you, babe?'

Angel and Liam both laughed.

'You're terrible!' he said, kissing his girlfriend. Angel felt a sudden pang watching them. They seemed so in love, just like she and Cal used to be, hardly able to keep their hands off each other, continually flirting and teasing each other. And now Cal had his back turned to her and didn't seem to care who she was talking to. Didn't seem to want her anymore. But suddenly he turned round and, seeing Angel, walked over to their group. She was glad he had joined them but the contrast between Candy and Liam and Cal and her was painful. Candy and Liam kept touching each other – he would stroke her arm, she would smooth back his hair – but it was more than a physical bond. They seemed connected, on the same wave-length, whereas she and Cal were worlds apart.

Candy knew all about Cal and Angel, having

followed their relationship in the tabloids and celebrity mags, and seemed to be in awe of them. She kept saying how stunning Angel was, how amazing their wedding had been.

'When I get married, I want a wedding just like yours,' she declared.

'Sorry,' Liam said, smiling. 'As you can see, Angel, she's your Number One fan. But, I promise, she's not a weird stalker type, I've got her under control.' It seemed strange to Angel that Candy would look up to her when she felt her marriage was in such a bad place right now.

Liam went on, 'It's good you two have met. Some of the other wives and girlfriends haven't been so friendly to Candy because she's new to the whole thing.'

'Be good for Angel too,' Cal said. 'Especially when we go to Portugal next weekend with the team.' Angel looked at him enquiringly and Cal said, rather irritably, 'I told you last month, Angel. Before we fly to the States we've got a team-building couple of days, and wives and girlfriends are coming too.'

Angel couldn't remember him mentioning it but that wasn't surprising, she hadn't exactly been with it lately. But she didn't like his tone of voice. It was as if he was ordering her, as if she had no identity of her own anymore, that she mattered only in relation to him. 'I'll have to check that I'm not working,' she replied quietly. She knew she wasn't but hated the way he just assumed she would drop everything for him.

Cal clenched his jaw. '*Everyone* is going, Angel.'

And Candy leaped in, obviously picking up on the tension, 'Angel, you've got to come, you can't leave me alone with all the other WAGs!'

'Oh, I'm sure Gabrielle would look after you,' Angel said, and even though she was angry with Cal, couldn't help smiling at Candy who was every bit as sweet as her name.

Dinner was next and Angel was really hoping that she would be on the same table as Candy and Liam but she wasn't. Instead she found herself sitting next to Gabrielle's best friend Lauren, a skinny, hard-faced blonde who'd OD-ed on the St Tropez and was naturally extremely unfriendly. After the briefest of hellos she ignored Angel completely. Cal was sitting next to his wife too but was soon deep in conversation with Lauren's boyfriend, so Angel was forced to sit in silence. The table was too big for her to be able to join in with the conversations opposite. Worse still, when she looked over at the table next to her she noticed Simone.

Angel quickly looked away, wishing they could leave. She turned to Cal, hoping to join in his conversation, but he made no attempt to include her. She sighed and stared miserably into space, hoping that she wasn't being filmed at this precise moment. She could just imagine the commentary: '*And here's an example of what a No Mates WAG looks like . . .*'

After dinner her heart sank further still when Simone sashayed over to Cal. She was wearing a gold off the shoulder evening dress and Angel had to admit she looked stunning, but there was something cold about her beauty, probably because she rarely looked happy.

'Cal, good to see you!' she exclaimed, kissing him while ignoring Angel.

'Hello, Simone,' he replied, sounding cool. 'How's it going?'

'Good. Jamie and I are getting on *so* well,' she murmured, looking all the same as if she longed to touch Cal.

'Glad it worked out for you,' he replied.

Simone lowered her voice but Angel could still hear her. 'It's not what I would have wanted, Cal, you know that.'

'Yeah, well, there's nothing more to say on that score, is there, Simone? And I don't need to remind you of our agreement, do I?'

And without waiting for an answer he took Angel's hand and said, 'Come on there's some more people I want to introduce you to.'

Simone gave the iciest of smiles as Cal and Angel walked past her and Angel heard her exclaiming, 'Lauren, so wonderful to see you!'

Angel couldn't resist turning round. She saw Simone sit down next to Lauren and start bitching right away. No wonder Lauren had ignored her, if she was such good friends with Simone. Angel squeezed Cal's hand and whispered, 'She's such a poisonous cow.'

Cal sighed, 'I know, just ignore her.'

'I will, but it's not going to be very nice in Portugal and the States. She seems to be in with all the other wives and girlfriends.'

'She's not in with all of them, Angel. Please remember we're going there for the tournament . . . the most important tournament of my career! So try and get things in perspective.' He didn't sound sympathetic at all and Angel felt riled again by his lack of understanding.

'Okay,' she said sulkily, 'I'm going to the bathroom.'

She headed to where she thought it was, weaving her way through the partygoers, some of whom were now definitely the worse for wear, and headed down one of the red velvet-lined corridors. But as she turned a corner she froze because there, leaning against one of the walls with the Marilyn Monroe waitress kneeling in front of him, was Connor. Angel was in no doubt what the waitress was doing and it didn't involve canapés . . . She quickly turned round and started walking back, praying he hadn't seen her. *God, he was vile.* But it was too late.

He called her name. 'Angel!' Reluctantly, and very slowly, she turned round. Connor shrugged as if to say, What do you expect? and buttoned up his fly. 'I'd be grateful if you didn't mention this to anyone. Maybe you and Cal fancy borrowing my yacht in the South of France sometime?' Marilyn meanwhile was nonchalantly reapplying her lipstick.

Angel shook her head. *What a creep.* 'There's no need, Connor, I won't say anything to Gabrielle.'

'Good girl.' He smiled knowingly, showing off a mouthful of bleached teeth, 'After all, you know what it's like for your secrets to come out in the press, don't you?'

When Angel was nineteen she'd had a relationship with Mickey – a boy band member. It was Mickey who got her into taking cocaine and it was Mickey who persuaded her to have a three-some. Unfortunately for Angel, the third party was a hooker who then sold her story . . .

She itched to tell Connor to fuck off. Instead she murmured, 'Like I said, I won't say anything,' then turned and walked quickly away.

'The next item is a weekend cruise on Connor and Gabrielle's luxurious yacht, fully crewed, round the South of France . . . oooh, la-la! Who's going to start the bidding at twenty-five thousand?' declared Duncan Williams, the comic and TV presenter hired by the couple to compere their charity auction. So far he'd auctioned a £750,000 diamond necklace, a white Ferrari, and a pair of diamond watches. *God knows what Connor has got up to on that yacht,* Angel thought as she took her place next to Cal, and then realised that her husband was bidding. She wanted to tell him not to then stopped herself in case the cameras were on her. Instead she had to sit there while he ended up outbidding everyone else for a fifty grand weekend on Connor's floating shag pad!

As soon as the auction finished Candy came rushing over. 'Oh, how romantic, Angel, your own personal cruise. I'd love to go on one of those!'

Angel wanted to say that she was welcome to it, but decided that sharing her discovery about Connor could wait until another day.

'Do you want a glass of champagne?' Liam asked and Angel found herself saying yes. The night was nearly over, and she could really do with a drink. Liam chatted to Cal, while Angel and Candy picked up their conversation from earlier. Angel could do with some allies when she went away with the WAGs – or hags as she was beginning to think of them. Several of them could have accessorised their outfits quite well with a pointy hat and a broom . . .

Conversation grew more difficult as the disco started up. Angel wondered if Gabrielle would actually be able to dance in her dress. It appeared not as she stayed chatting to her guests, but Connor was obviously up for it and before Angel knew what was happening he was in front of her and Cal, asking her for a dance.

Angel shook her head. *No way was she dancing with this perv!* But Cal intervened. 'Go on, Angel, you love this song.' It was Mika's 'Lollipop', a song that she had been known to dance to outrageously with Gemma. She knew it would look really rude if she turned her host down and very reluctantly followed him on to the dance floor, trying not to think about the activity she'd just seen him involved in. Unfortunately the lyrics didn't help – she knew someone had sucked his particular lollipop only too recently!

'And to think I would have given you a trip on the yacht for free!' Connor shouted at her over the music. 'Ironic, isn't it? Still, it's all for charidee.'

Angel stared at him coldly. *He was such a wanker.* 'Smile, Angel, they might be filming you,' he shouted, grabbing her by the waist and twirling her round. *God, she was going to have to disinfect this dress.*

'Cal's a very lucky man,' he said then, leaning closer to make himself heard over the music. 'I hadn't realised how stunning you were in the flesh.' His eyes slid appreciatively over her body and Angel had to fight the urge to tell him to fuck off. *God, why did he have to be the England Captain? Why couldn't it have been someone lovely like David Beckham?*

She managed to escape after one dance, but just as she was making her way back to Cal, Simone sidled in front of her. 'That was a lovely thing Cal bought at the auction, wasn't it? But then, he was always very generous, I remember.'

'Let's not pretend we have anything to say to each other, Simone. I'll keep out of your way if you keep out of mine,' Angel shot back.

Simone flicked back her hair – Angel had forgotten just how much that habit annoyed her – and hissed, 'Don't imagine that just because you've got a ring on your finger it means a damn' thing. Maybe it will be a different girl who gets to try out the yacht with Cal. Maybe an Italian with a little more class than you, although that really wouldn't be hard, would it? You've always been more chavvy than classy.'

That did it! Angel forgot her resolution not to sink to Simone's level. 'Fuck off, Simone. You don't know anything about Cal. No wonder he left you.'

'He wouldn't have left me if it hadn't been for *you*, you scheming, big-boobed bitch!' Now it was Simone's turn to lose her cool and this last comment came out as a screech.

By now the guests immediately next to them had stopped their own conversations and were openly listening to the slanging match. But just as Angel was about to retaliate, Gabrielle came marching over. 'Ladies!' she hissed. 'Can we cut the bitch fest! We're not on *Jeremy Kyle* now, are we?'

Simone was the first to regain her composure, 'I do apologise, Gabrielle.' And the two women walked swiftly away from Angel, but not before Gabrielle shot her a filthy look. *Go and ask Marilyn what she's been doing to your husband,* Angel felt like saying.

'See, it wasn't so bad, was it?' Cal said as they lay in bed later. *It was so much worse!* Angel wanted to protest, but he was going away with the England team in the morning and she couldn't bear anymore conflict between them. So instead she nodded and curled her body round his, wondering why Cal didn't seem interested in making love with her anymore. She knew she'd pushed him away enough times in the past, but now he was the one who was being distant.

'You looked beautiful tonight,' he whispered. 'I do love you, Angel. Sorry I've been so crap. I've just got so much going on in my head at the moment . . . Sorry.' And he turned away from her again.

Chapter 5

Indecent Proposal . . .

A week later Angel was settling into her luxurious suite in a five-star hotel at the exclusive Vale do Lobo resort in the Algarve, overlooking the glittering blue Mediterranean. But the stunning location meant nothing to Angel who was seriously pissed off. She had expected Cal to be there already but he'd just phoned to say he'd been delayed and wouldn't arrive until the next morning.

'God!' she exclaimed, throwing her mobile on the double bed in disgust. The only reason this trip had seemed bearable was because she'd be able to spend some time with Cal. Now she was faced with the prospect of a night out with the WAGs and their partners while she was unaccompanied.

Just then there was a knock at the door. It was Candy, looking beach fit in a turquoise bikini, a matching sarong wrapped round her waist, and turquoise-coloured sunglasses. She clearly liked to accessorise.

'Hiya, I'm just off to the beach and wondered if you wanted to come?'

'Only if you promise we don't have to sit anywhere near Simone or Gabrielle,' Angel replied grimly.

Candy laughed. 'Don't worry, I haven't seen them. I expect they're getting their hair done for tonight's party, or their tans, or their nails, or their Botox!'

Candy then spotted Honey and spent the next few minutes cooing over her. 'Angel, you really do have everything, don't you?' she said in wonder.

'D'you think so?' Angel replied, thinking, *If only she knew the truth*.

'Definitely. You're my total role model!'

'Please do yourself a favour and get another one,' Angel said quietly then changed the subject. 'Will this bikini do?' She held up a hot pink one and twirled it round her finger.

'Oh, it's gorgeous!' Candy answered. 'So girly.'

Ten minutes later Angel was ready to go. She'd tied her hair into a pony tail, put on her favourite white Chanel sunglasses and slid a pair of tiny denim shorts over her bikini. She'd slathered Honey in sun cream – much to her disgust – and dressed her in her sunsuit and hat. 'I won't stay long in case it gets too hot for the baby,' she told

Candy as they made their way to the hotel's private beach.

Angel was relieved it was private. She didn't feel like having her picture taken, and she definitely didn't want to be photographed in her bikini. It was all very well getting her kit off for glamour modelling but those were carefully thought out poses, and she'd seen too many candid pictures of celebs on the beach with their bikini bottoms disappearing up the crack of their bum or their top falling off. She was also relieved to see that her least favourite WAGs were nowhere to be seen. Probably they couldn't come out in daylight, but were staying in their coffins until sunset . . . Instead she noticed a couple of wives with young children and waved at them, and they waved back. Clearly Simone hadn't turned everyone against Angel yet. But give her time, Angel thought bitterly . . .

Despite wishing Cal could be with her, she had a good couple of hours. Honey was in a great mood and loved playing in the sand and going in the sea with her mother. When she was getting tired she let Angel put her in her buggy under the parasol and went contentedly to sleep.

'She's such a good baby!' Candy exclaimed.

'She is today,' Angel agreed. 'But, believe me, it's not always like that.'

She yawned and Candy said, 'You have a lie down if you want, Angel, I'll watch her. I've probably had enough sun for a bit.'

Angel gratefully agreed; Honey still didn't sleep through the night. She lay back on her lounger, enjoying the feeling of the sun on her skin. Maybe this trip away was just what she and Cal needed. Maybe away from home and from Italy they might actually be able to talk to each other. But she was abruptly pulled out of her musing by a very unwelcome voice.

'Cal not with you then?' It was Simone.

Angel sat up quickly, not wanting to be at a disadvantage in front of her enemy. She was wearing a white shirt dress, huge sunglasses and a large white hat. She looked cool and sophisticated and Angel suddenly felt hot and sticky and self-conscious about her body laid out on display.

'Does Jamie know how much time you spend thinking about Cal?' she said in retaliation.

Simone was about to reply, no doubt with another bitchy comment, when Candy said, 'Well, we could always ask him, he's just coming.'

All three women turned to look at Jamie. Any attraction Simone felt for him had to be entirely down to his personality and his pay packet because although Jamie was not ugly he was incredibly ordinary with pale skin, freckles and mousy hair, and a physique that was skinny and sinewy rather than muscular. If he'd been anything other than a Premiership footballer Angel doubted that Simone would have given him the time of day.

He was completely lacking the Phwarr! factor. No wonder Simone still obsessed over Cal. And he was only twenty-two, a boy compared to Cal at twenty-seven.

'Hi, Simone, aren't you going to introduce me?' Jamie said, his gaze lingering rather too long and intently on Angel's cleavage.

Simone coolly made the introductions and Jamie looked as if he wanted to stay and chat with Angel and Candy but his girlfriend dragged him away, saying that they had to meet Gabrielle and Connor. The two girls waited until they were well out of ear-shot and then burst out laughing.

'Oh my God!' Candy said. 'Did you see him staring at your tits?'

'I wondered why Simone had had a boob job, she was always so bitchy about mine,' Angel replied. 'Now I know, it was to get him interested in her!'

'She's such a cow, isn't she?' Candy commented.

Angel nodded. 'But then, the way she sees it, I stole Cal from her. And I'd be well pissed off if someone stole Cal from me and I ended up with Jamie! Can you imagine having to shag Mr No Charisma? And did you see those pimples on his back – gross!'

The two girls giggled again, and for a while Angel didn't feel so uptight about Simone. She was just a jealous cow. She couldn't hurt Angel.

*

'You promise you'll call me if she gets at all upset,' Angel said to Lucy. She had been a great choice of nanny. In her late-twenties and highly experienced with children, she had such an easygoing, cheerful nature. She was cute rather than pretty, with short black hair, and lived in combats or baggy jeans. Angel trusted her completely. She was about to go to a party, a kind of getting-to-know-you bash being thrown by the England manager, but as Angel only wanted to know Candy and Liam, she was not looking forward to it.

'We'll be fine, I promise,' Lucy reassured her. 'Just go and have a lovely time.'

'Mmm,' Angel muttered, taking one last look in the mirror. Knowing that all the other WAGs would be dressed up to within an inch of their life, she'd kept things simple but dramatic. She'd chosen a bright fuchsia dress with a ruffled hem, which Gemma had assured her was *the* colour for '08, and wore her hair in a sleek pony tail which said sophisticated rather than Croydon face lift. She made one last check on Honey who was sleeping soundly and then set off for the party.

To start the evening the guests were being treated to cocktails on the terrace overlooking the dazzling sea and glorious sunset. Angel anxiously scanned them all, looking for Candy and Liam, but there was no sign of the couple. *Damn*, she thought, *I should have arranged to meet them first.* Feeling

145

extremely self-conscious and wishing that she had Cal by her side, she made her way over to where Phil Hardcastle, the England manager, was standing, thinking that she should at least introduce herself.

Phil was in his early-fifties, his black hair flecked with grey. Once boyishly good-looking, he was aging rapidly but that seemed to be the fate of all England managers. He at least was widely respected by players and the fans alike for his tough, no nonsense approach. He was talking to Gabrielle and Connor. Angel steeled herself as she walked over to the group.

Gabrielle saw her first and Angel couldn't help being aware of the other woman measuring her up, checking out what she was wearing. The smug smile she gave told Angel the Captain's wife was not that impressed. She herself was wearing a short gold silk dress, gold designer sandals, and a gold designer bag on her shoulder. Her hair and make up were perfect. *God, it looked like hard work being her!*

Connor gave Angel a knowing smile and kissed her. *Gross*, she thought, air kissing him back.

'Angel! How lovely to see you again.' Another air kiss from Gabrielle. 'Do you know Phil?' Gabrielle took control.

'Hiya,' Angel said shyly.

'Nice to meet you, Angel,' he replied, shaking her hand. 'My daughter's a huge fan of yours.'

'Really?' Phil wasn't nearly as scary as she'd thought he would be.

'Yes. In fact, I'm going to have to ask you for your autograph, if that's okay with you?'

'No problem. I can always send her a photograph if you think she'd like one?'

'It would make her day. Now, can I get you a drink?'

As Phil busied himself with getting her a glass of champagne Angel noticed that Gabrielle looked thoroughly pissed off. Obviously she preferred to be top dog. She muttered something about having to mingle, grabbed Connor's arm and swished away.

'So do you know many people here?' Phil asked when he gave her her drink. Angel shook her head.

'Well, stick with me and I'll introduce you to some,' he said kindly. He reminded Angel a little of a younger version of her dad – the same down-to-earth attitude. 'Maybe you'd like to meet some of the more grounded wives – ones who don't think the world revolves around getting the latest designer handbag?' he said, eyes twinkling mischievously.

'Are there any?' Angel joked back.

'One or two, believe it or not. Come on.'

Ten minutes later Angel was deep in conversation with Suki and Madison. Both were in their early-thirties, married with kids, and both had their own career. Suki owned a beauty salon and

Madison was a personal trainer. They weren't anything like Gabrielle and Simone. True, like nearly all the wives and girlfriends she'd met, they were pretty, slim and well dressed – Suki had bleached blonde hair in a stylish crop and Madison had long auburn hair – but they didn't look like their designer clothes were the be all and end all to them. They were friendly and open with Angel, laughing about how crazy it was to be staying in a luxury hotel, surrounded by paparazzi.

'But I guess you're more used to the paps than we are,' Madison commented.

Angel frowned. 'I don't think I'm used to it. It still surprises me that they want to take my picture. I'm like, What's so great about me, walking down the street in jeans and tee-shirt with no make up on? Or the worst one I had was one of me stuffing my face with a sandwich. Actually, no, that wasn't the worst.' She felt embarrassed to say this. 'It was the one they took up my dress.'

'They're such shits!' Madison exclaimed sympathetically.

'Apart from *that* shot, the press want to show that you're normal, like their readers, not just a celebrity,' Suki put in.

'I *am* normal!' Angel exclaimed.

'With that body and that face? Oh, Angel, you're not!' Suki laughed. 'But I mean that in the best way.'

148

Candy then came over and introduced herself to everyone, and the four women spent a very lively half-hour gossiping over cocktails. Madison and Suki knew who everyone was as their husbands had played for England for eight years, and Angel liked them even more when they made it clear that they didn't like Gabrielle either.

'She's so fake,' Madison said quietly. 'All she cares about is being photographed with A-list stars. And she only puts up with Connor because without him she'd be nothing.'

'He's a piece of work, isn't he?' Angel said. And was almost tempted to reveal what Connor had got up to at the party, but she kept it zipped.

'I can't stand him!' Suki exclaimed. 'He is such a lech. And I don't know why he goes around acting all cocky because –' and here she lowered her voice still further '– someone with inside knowledge told me that he's not very big in *that* department.'

The women exploded into giggles and just at that moment the man himself wandered over to them. 'Glad to see you're enjoying yourself, ladies,' he said smarmily, which only made them giggle more. Angel tried to pull herself together and became aware that Connor was giving her the once over yet again.

When he was safely out of earshot, Candy said, 'Ooh, he likes you, Angel! I think you're in with a chance!'

She mimed putting her fingers down her throat.

'Getting in training for him then?' Candy continued. 'Though maybe just the one finger – the little one!'

'You are bad,' Angel shot back, but she was laughing. She stopped when she caught sight of Simone looking daggers at her and quickly turned away.

'The other person I can't stand is Simone Fraser,' she told her new friends.

'That's a shame because we're such good mates with her,' Suki replied.

Angel stared at her aghast. She was clearly going to have to revise her opinion of Suki.

'Just kidding!' Suki exclaimed. 'We hate her too – she tried it on with my husband just after she split up with Cal.'

'Thank God for that!' Angel said with feeling. 'I mean, not that she tried it on, of course.'

'I know what you mean,' Suki answered, smiling.

At dinner the women managed to stay together. Angel felt safe with them, felt she could almost be herself, they were so unpretentious and down-to-earth. Simone and Gabrielle were sitting some distance away and Angel was relieved to be spared their company. She had three allies now.

Just before dessert she decided to make a quick check on Honey. Lucy was lying on the sofa in the sitting-room of the suite reading, and told her that the baby was fast asleep, but Angel still wanted to see for herself. Lucy was right, though, Honey was out for the count. Angel was just quietly shutting the door to her suite when someone called her name. She turned round. It was Gabrielle.

'I just wondered if we could have a quiet word in my suite?'

'Why don't we talk on the way back down to dinner?' Angel replied, anxious not to spend any longer than she had to in Gabrielle's company.

She shook her head. 'It's a personal matter, Angel.'

'Okay,' she answered, extremely reluctantly. Spending any longer than was strictly necessary with the Queen of the WAGs was about as pleasurable as a full bikini wax. Gabrielle didn't say a word as they travelled up in the lift. Angel tried to guess what she wanted to say to her and could only imagine it was something to do with Simone. *God knows what lies that witch had been spinning her.*

As soon as they were in the suite, Gabrielle made a beeline for the drinks cabinet. 'I'm going to have a Southern Comfort, would you like one?'

Angel shook her head and watched as Gabrielle poured herself a very generous measure, threw in a couple of ice cubes and downed half of it in one go. Then she swirled the rest of the drink around in her glass, the ice cubes clinking. She suddenly

151

didn't seem quite so sure of herself as she said, 'Connor and I were wondering if you wanted to join us after dinner here?'

'Thanks, but I need to get back to Honey,' Angel replied, surprised by the invitation.

'It would be for a *very* exclusive party.' Gabrielle was gripping the glass hard and looking distinctly awkward.

Angel shook her head. 'Sorry, another time.'

'Just you, me and Connor,' Gabrielle continued, avoiding eye contact with her. 'It's the kind of party you've had before, I think. Connor wanted me to ask you.'

For a few seconds Angel wondered what the hell Gabrielle was on about, then realisation hit her and she burst out, 'Are you seriously asking me to have a threesome with you and your husband? Well, you can fuck right off, both of you! How dare you think I'd be up for anything like that?'

She swung round and headed for the door, not wanting to spend another second in the same room as Gabrielle. But the Queen of the WAGs moved surprisingly quickly for someone in such high heels and reached the door before her. She stood there blocking Angel's exit and said snidely, 'Oh, come off it, Angel, don't play the innocent with me. I know all about your threesome with Mickey and that hooker.'

'It was one time only in the past, when I was off

my head. I would *never* do it again,' Angel shouted back passionately.

'Well, if it's coke you need to get you in the mood, I can easily find you some,' Gabrielle persisted, clearly not used to being turned down. Angel wondered how many other women she'd propositioned for her husband.

'No fucking way! Not if you and your pervy husband were the last people on earth.' She put out her hand to open the door and Gabrielle grabbed her arm. She looked ugly with anger, her skin red and blotchy under the fake tan. 'How dare you turn us down? A slut like you! You'd better not tell anyone about this or I will do everything I can to ruin you.'

'Get out of my way, Gabrielle, you can't tell me what to do!' Angel shouted angrily, shaking her hand away and opening the door. She was about to slam it behind her when someone seized her arm. 'Hey!' she exclaimed, trying to pull away. She was being restrained by a mountain of a man, dressed entirely in black and wearing an earpiece. She recognised him as Gabrielle and Connor's bodyguard.

'Everything all right, Mrs Carter?' the bodyguard asked.

'Can you tell him to get off me?' Angel exclaimed, struggling. He was gripping her arm extremely hard.

Gabrielle gave a barely perceptible nod and the guard let her go. Angel winced as she rubbed at the red marks his fingers had left on her skin.

'I hope you'll remember what I said, Angel,' Gabrielle said coldly. Angel ignored her and headed for the lifts. Suddenly her arm was seized again by the bodyguard.

'Fuck off!' she yelled in pain and anger.

'Mrs Carter asked you a question,' the man mountain said. Angel fleetingly considered kneeing him in the nuts, but thought better of it.

'Yes, I heard her,' she hissed, 'and if you don't let go of me, right now, I'm going to scream the place down and then people will want to know why you've assaulted me.

'Let her go,' Gabrielle ordered, and the bodyguard abruptly released her. Angel swiftly walked away from the pair of them, extremely shaken by what had just happened. She was so disturbed by it that there was no way she felt up to returning to dinner. Instead she went straight back to her suite and asked Lucy to let Candy know that she felt ill. Then she curled up on the bed still fully clothed.

Despite the warm night she suddenly felt cold and shivery. The nerve of Gabrielle, thinking that she would be up for something like that! The threesome with Mickey had been one of the biggest mistakes of her life. She'd done it to please him and had had no idea that the other woman was a hooker. When she sold her story, Angel was plastered all over the tabloids and her life fell apart.

Cal had rescued her. He had never judged her for what she'd done. In fact, when they finally got together he made a point of saying that they should never get hung up about each other's past, that what had happened belonged in the past. Now she didn't know if she could tell him about Gabrielle's proposition – their marriage seemed to be so fragile nowadays, she didn't want to remind him of her past mistakes. And she couldn't possibly say anything negative about Connor in the run up to the tournament. Still, she longed for Cal now: to feel his arms round her, to know that he loved her.

But from the minute her husband walked into the hotel suite the following day, he seemed tense and on edge.

Angel threw her arms around him and kissed him. 'Cal, it's so great to see you!' He kissed her back, but it wasn't a passionate kiss.

'Do you want to go to the beach? We could take Honey in the sea . . . she loved it yesterday.' Angel was aware that she was gabbling but she so wanted a response from him, she couldn't bear his silence.

He shrugged. 'Could do. Then I'd better have a couple of hours in the gym.'

'Really? Haven't you done enough? I thought this trip was supposed to be a bit of down time?'

Cal looked annoyed. 'I've got to be at my best for the tournament, Angel, surely you understand?'

'Okay,' she said sadly, turning away and starting to gather up all the things they'd need.

At the beach Cal stripped down to his trunks and for the first time in what seemed like a very long time Angel felt a flash of desire. He was so gorgeous – with his muscular, perfectly proportioned body, just the right amount of hair on his chest and that delicious line that ran from his navel into his trunks. She remembered what it had been like wanting him so much, being so turned on by him, what it had felt like ripping off his clothes, feeling his hard cock, tasting him, touching him, fucking him; remembered how he knew exactly how to turn her on, how he gave her the best orgasms ever . . .

'Do you want some sun cream on you?' she asked.

'Yeah, thanks.' Cal lay down on his stomach and she started smoothing cream across his shoulders and back. 'You know, we could ask Lucy to take Honey for a walk this afternoon then we could spend some time together,' she murmured, imagining getting Cal back to their suite and making love with him.

'No, I told you, I've got to go to the gym.'

'Well, there are other ways of working out, aren't there?' Angel asked suggestively.

And then regretted it as Cal said abruptly, 'Maybe later. Gym first.'

God, she couldn't even seduce him anymore! Angel finished applying the sun cream and flopped back on her lounger, feeling disappointed and frustrated. The first time in months she'd felt like having sex and Cal didn't want to. What was wrong with her?

They spent the next couple of hours on the beach and Cal focused all his attention on Honey and barely spoke to Angel. She wandered down to the sea, taking pictures of him and Honey in the water – the baby in her yellow inflatable seat, laughing as Cal spun her round.

'Hey, are you feeling okay now, Angel?' It was Suki. Angel had almost forgotten that she'd pretended to be ill last night after her encounter with Gabrielle.

'Yeah, fine. I suddenly felt really sick but it didn't last long,' she lied.

'Well, you missed all the fun – Connor and Gabrielle had a blazing row and she threw a wine glass at him. He ended up in Casualty having four stitches.'

'Wow! Do you know what the argument was about?' Angel asked, suspecting it had been to do with her.

Suki shook her head. 'Probably about his womanising – he's got a terrible reputation. Phil was absolutely livid, gave Gabrielle a right dressing down. I don't think she's ever been spoken to like that in her life. Anyway the good thing is they'll be keeping a low profile for the rest of the stay.'

At that moment Cal came out of the water, holding Honey in his arms. He knew Suki and they spent a few minutes catching up. 'Do you guys fancy meeting up tonight for dinner?' she asked.

'That would be great, wouldn't it, Angel?' Cal replied.

Angel agreed, even though she would far rather have spent the evening alone with him.

She was hoping that Cal might have changed his mind about training in the gym, but as soon as they got back to the suite he was into his sports gear and trainers. 'Don't you want to have some lunch first?' she asked.

Cal shook his head. 'No, I want to get on. I'll be a couple of hours.' And then he was gone.

'What shall we have for lunch then?' Angel asked Honey who was sitting on the rug chewing on what Angel saw was Cal's mobile.

'Oh, Honey, don't do that!' she exclaimed, racing over to take the phone from her, triggering a wail of protest and tears from her daughter.

'Look, have this.' Angel tried to distract her by giving her the toy phone. But that apparently was not as good as Daddy's and she continued to cry. So

158

Angel resorted to giving her a rice cake. Suddenly Cal's phone vibrated and beeped. He had a text message.

Angel hesitated. She could take his phone down to the gym or she could see who had texted him. She had never wanted to check his texts before but right now she had the strongest feeling that she should open this message. He hadn't password protected his phone this time so she was able to access his inbox, where she discovered the message was from someone Cal had simply labelled A. Well, at least it didn't say F for Flavia. She opened the message. It was written in Italian and ended in three kisses. Suddenly it became very important for Angel to know who the message was from and what it said.

But just then the door opened and Cal walked back in. 'I forgot my phone,' he said, stopping in his tracks when he saw that Angel was holding it.

'Who's A?' she asked, trying to keep her tone casual while feeling anything but.

'Have you been looking at my messages?' he demanded. 'Christ, Angel, I would never look at your phone! Give it to me.' He held out his hand but she kept hold of the phone.

'I just wondered who would give you three kisses. Obviously not a male friend . . . and three kisses seems like a lot for a female friend to give. That's if they are just a friend?'

'Give me back my phone,' Cal repeated, his voice low and angry.

'Tell me who texted you then,' Angel persisted.

'I don't believe it! I would never question you like this.' He came right up to Angel and stood in front of her.

'Well, I'm sorry, but I'd like to know who's sending my husband texts with kisses on them.'

'A is for Allegra – she's my physiotherapist. Satisfied?'

'Very friendly for a physio,' Angel said coldly. 'I doubt my brother puts kisses on the end of texts to his clients.'

Cal sighed in exasperation. 'She's Italian. It doesn't mean anything.'

Without warning Angel threw him his phone. She just didn't know whether to believe him or not and hated feeling so insecure.

'Hey! There was no need to do that!' Cal snapped, only just managing to catch the mobile. 'I'm going back to the gym, and I hope when I've finished you'll be in a better mood.'

'Aren't you going to read your message from Allegra?' Angel said as he was walking out of the door.

'I'll read it in the gym. It'll just be some advice about my knee. You know, the knee I injured trying to protect you from some nutter. The knee that could ruin my playing career. But don't worry about that, you just carry on worrying about a stupid message you shouldn't have read anyway!'

Cal was shouting at her now and Angel was torn between wanting to retaliate by demanding how he'd feel if he found a message with three kisses on her phone and feeling sorry for him when he was obviously anxious that his knee would not hold up for the tournament. In the end sympathy won. 'Okay, I'm sorry, I shouldn't have looked. Don't worry about your knee, I'm sure it'll be fine.'

'Oh, right, and I should respect your opinion, should I? Seeing as you're such an expert in physio-therapy.' And with that Cal stormed out of the room, slamming the door behind him, which caused Honey to burst into tears again.

It took Angel a good half hour to calm her down and by the time she had they were both exhausted. Honey fell asleep in her arms and Angel gently put her on the bed and lay down beside her. What was going on with Cal? She couldn't believe how badly they were getting on. They had never quarrelled like this before. Two hours later he still hadn't returned. Angel called his mobile but he'd switched it off.

'Come on, Honey,' she said, strapping her daughter into her buggy. 'Let's go and find your daddy.' But when they got to the gym it was empty. She tried his phone again but there was still no reply. Maybe she'd missed him and he was on his way up to the suite. She was just navigating the pushchair through the gym doors when someone said, 'Here, let me hold them open for you.'

'Thank you,' she replied gratefully, then instantly wished she hadn't because the man helping her was Connor. He smiled at her in a predatory way. 'Hi, Angel, looking for someone?' She made to carry on walking and ignore him, but he positioned himself in front of the buggy so she couldn't get past.

'Cal,' Angel answered through gritted teeth.

'Pity. Thought for a minute it might have been me, that you might have reconsidered our little proposition. I was disappointed – I really thought you'd be up for it, given your track record. And, you know, if you didn't fancy the threesome, we could do a four-way. My wife has always had a bit of a thing for your husband. Or how about just the two of us? I know we could be so good together.'

Angel glared at his cocky, handsome face, his left cheekbone looking puffy from the row of recent stitches, and hissed back, 'I'll say the same thing that I said to your wife: fuck off! And don't ever come near me again or I'll go to Phil and tell him what you've been up to. I don't think he'd be impressed, do you?'

Connor smiled.

'I'm his star player, Angel. Do you really think

he'd be interested in what a glamour girl, who gets her kit off for a living, would have to say? Let's not argue, I really want us to be friends.'

But she looked right through him, and after shrugging his shoulders he stepped aside and Angel pushed the buggy past without another word.

Cal was back in the suite when she walked in. She felt so shaken up after seeing Connor that she almost wanted to tell him everything. But he was stretched out on the sofa and looked very low.

'Hiya,' he said.

'We just came to look for you,' Angel replied. 'How was your work out?'

'All right,' he said flatly.

Angel unfastened Honey from her buggy and came and sat next to him.

'I'm sure your knee will be okay,' she tried to reassure him again.

'God, I don't know, Angel.' He turned and took Honey from her for a cuddle. 'I'm sorry I snapped earlier. It's just that my knee's been hurting a lot lately and I can't help stressing about it.'

Angel wanted to carry on reassuring him, but Cal had obviously decided that was all he was going to say. He concentrated on Honey, making her giggle by playing Peek-a-Boo with her.

*

'Would you like a refill, Angel?'

Liam was passing round the champagne. Angel had already had two glasses and really should have stopped there, but she felt so miserable she needed something to pick her up. She was surrounded by happy couples and the comparison between them and her and Cal was too painful. Cal had switched to charm mode for dinner and chatted away to everyone. But he didn't talk to Angel, and whereas in the past he would have been checking every now and then to see whether she was okay, he barely looked at her tonight. It seemed to her that she might just as well not have been there. So she decided to drink.

By the time her main course arrived she was already feeling too drunk to really eat anything. She picked at her food and switched from champagne to white wine which she drank as if it was water. She was just topping up her glass again when finally Cal looked at her. He raised his eyebrows as if to say, Go easy, but Angel carried on pouring the wine, then raised her glass to him and said, 'Cheers.'

During the meal they'd stuck to an alternate boy/girl seating plan but after dinner they all swapped places and the women ended up at one end, men at the other.

'I'm really glad I've met you three,' Candy said then. 'I feel much better about going to LA now.'

Angel agreed and rather indiscreetly said, 'Just so long as we don't have to spend any time with those two witches Gabrielle and Simone. God, I can't stand them! And have you met Gabrielle's bodyguard?'

'Yeah, you mean Odd Bod or whatever his name is,' Suki replied. 'Apparently he's totally devoted to her. Some American film star was supposed to have wanted him for herself and offered him a shit load of money but he wouldn't leave Gabrielle.'

'Perhaps she pays him for other services,' Angel giggled. Unfortunately that was the other moment Cal chose to look at her. He seemed annoyed that she was being bitchy but, fuck, he didn't know the half of it.

The three other women laughed and Madison added, 'At least Simone and Gabrielle won't leave a carbon footprint after the flight over to LA – they can just go on their broomsticks!'

'Shh, ladies,' Candy said, giggling. 'They're over there.'

They all looked across the restaurant to where Simone and Jamie, Gabrielle and Connor, were being shown to their table. Both women shot poisonous looks in Angel's direction as they sat down.

'God, I'm so glad I'm not with them!' Suki declared. 'I can just imagine Gabrielle and Simone working out how many calories are in their dressing-free salad and Connor and Jamie leching after all the good-looking women in the restaurant.'

All four girls laughed loudly at this and Cal shot Angel another warning look which she once again ignored.

'You didn't have to be quite so bitchy,' he said when they returned to their suite after dinner. 'I understand your problem with Simone but Gabrielle hasn't done anything to you. She's the Captain's wife, for Christ's sake. Please be nice.'

It was on the tip of Angel's tongue to let Cal know exactly what the Captain's wife was like, not to mention the Captain, but instead she opened the mini-bar and grabbed a half-bottle of wine.

'D'you want one?' she asked, opening the wine and pouring herself a glass.

'No, thanks, and don't you think you've had enough?'

Angel was drunk enough not to care, and shook her head. 'I'm just enjoying myself, Cal.'

'Well, I'm going to check on Honey then off to bed,' he answered, going through to the side room where their daughter was sleeping. Angel took a large slug of wine for courage then walked over to the double bed. She stripped off all her clothes then lay down on her tummy and waited. It had been ages since she'd been naked in front of Cal as she'd felt so self-conscious about her body after Honey's birth.

'Cal,' she said softly when he came out of the bathroom, 'do you still want me?'

'Of course I do,' he answered, getting on to the bed. He was wearing a white towelling robe and Angel undid the belt and pulled it off him. God, she loved his body, she thought, reaching out and stroking his skin. In her head she wanted to do everything with Cal that she hadn't done for ages.

He obviously had other ideas. After caressing her for the shortest time, he entered her and then it was like he wanted to get it over and done with as quickly as possible, which was how she'd been with him lately. He had his eyes closed and didn't even look at her. It was strictly roll on, roll off sex. As Angel lay underneath him she felt she could have been anyone. Instead of bringing them closer, this felt as if they were even further apart.

Chapter 6

Footballers' Wives

Back home in Brighton Angel felt almost over-whelmed with sadness about the state of her marriage. She kept trying to tell herself that everything would be okay after the tournament, but a small voice said, What if it isn't? A few days before she was due to fly out to the States she met up with Jez and Gemma for dinner in London. Both of them were so excited about her trip – Jez had planned out a number of hairstyles he wanted her to try; Gemma had put together Angel's outfits, each one of which apparently was a fashion must-have.

Angel appreciated everything her friends had done but couldn't begin to share their enthusiasm. She was intensely nervous for Cal, who remained pessimistic about his knee holding out whenever they spoke, and hated the thought of herself being anywhere near Gabrielle and Simone. She was convinced the gruesome twosome would do all they could to make her life out there as difficult as possible.

Gemma sensed her mood and was instantly sympathetic. 'Angel, it will be fine,' she tried to reassure her. 'You're friends now with some of the other . . .' Gemma was clearly about to say 'WAGs' when Angel interrupted her. 'Please don't say that word! I think I'll scream if I hear it again! I've already had Carrie on the phone this week wanting me to do a shoot showing off my WAG – God, I can't believe I've just said it again – wardrobe!'

'And are you going to?' Gemma couldn't stop herself from sounding excited.

'No, I'm not!' Angel shot back. 'I'm not a clothes horse!'

Jez rolled his eyes. 'Angel, you just don't know what's good for you, do you? You could have done the shoot, demanded a shit load of free designer gear and kept it! And even if you didn't want it, you could have given it to your nearest and dearest. Really, darling, I think you're being a tiny bit precious.'

Angel looked at Gemma's disappointed expression and sighed. 'Sorry, Gem, I just hate feeling like the only reason people are interested in me is that I'm married to a footballer. I'm my own person. I've worked hard to make it in my career.'

At this passionate outburst Jez burst out laughing.

'Angel, I never in a million years thought I'd hear you come out with a feminist diatribe.'

'A what?' she shot back.

'Never mind.' Jez continued teasingly: 'You don't need to worry your pretty little head about stuff like that.'

'Watch it!' Angel warned. 'I could take you any time.'

'You could,' he admitted. 'But you wouldn't want to, I fight dirty.'

'And I'll forgive you for not doing the shoot, on one condition,' Gemma put in.

'Go on?'

'When you're away, you've got to promise to wear all the clothes I've got for you.' Gemma's violet eyes took on a determined glint. 'I'm going to get you in *Heat's* best dressed section if it's the last thing I do! You're going to upstage Gabrielle Carter, and show her up for the matchy-matchy, over-accessorised label whore she is!'

At the mention of Gabrielle, Angel put her head in her hands and groaned, 'Please don't say her name!' As she hadn't been able to tell Cal about Gabrielle's sordid invitation, she didn't feel that she could confide in Gemma and Jez, but suddenly she wanted to and before she could stop herself she had blurted out the truth and even dropped in catching Connor and the waitress in a compromising position at the World Cup Ball.

For a moment Jez was speechless, then he let rip. 'The fucking nerve of them! I hope you gave her what for, Angel? God, you could make life difficult for them, couldn't you? Put a word in some journalist's ear?'

'No, Jez!' Angel said warningly. 'That's exactly what I don't want to do. They'll know it's come from me. You've got to promise not to tell anyone, and that includes journalists?'

'Okay,' he replied, rather reluctantly, 'I promise. Though it would be such sweet revenge.'

'Oh, I'm sure they'll get their comeuppance. I'm not the only one they've asked by a long way, and I bet there are plenty of girls who've done the dirty with them. In time I'm sure the story will come out, I just don't want it to come from me. Yesterday Connor even had the audacity to send me this!'

Angel reached into her bag and pulled out a leather jewellery case. She opened it to reveal a dazzling diamond necklace by Chopard.

'Sweet Jesus!' Jez exclaimed, reaching for the necklace and holding it up so the diamonds sparkled seductively in the light. 'That is to die for! It must have cost a fortune.'

'What are you going to do with it?' Gemma asked.

'Send it back to him – obviously!' Angel said determinedly. 'There's no way I want anything from that bastard.'

'But it's *sooo* beautiful, and aren't diamonds a

girl's best friend?' Jez said dreamily, causing Angel to take the necklace away from him and put it straight back in its box.

'He also enclosed this note: "*Dear Angel, never say never . . . enjoy the rocks, Connor*".'

'Oh.My.God!' Gemma was outraged. 'It sounds as if he's trying to buy you now! What a skanky bastard! And who would want to have a threesome anyway?' At this Jez looked very interested in the menu and Angel rolled her eyes at her friend.

'Oh, sorry, babe, I forgot,' Gemma said hastily.

'I don't know why you've gone so quiet,' Angel said to Jez.

At this he put back his head and said to Gemma, 'All I can say is, don't knock it till you've tried it.'

Gemma's eyes widened. 'You and Rufus haven't—'

Jez cut across her. 'We're taking LBR – life before Rufus! Do you think I would share the love of my life with anyone else? They might be better in bed than me and then what would happen?'

'Surely not, Jez,' Angel said dryly. 'Because then, wouldn't the world have to stop turning and all the stars fall out of the sky?'

'Oh, shut up,' he said, all mock-petulance. 'Anyway to go back to Connor and that incident with the waitress . . . it could have been so much worse. It could have been –' he paused for dramatic effect '– a spit roast!'

'Thanks a lot, Jez!' Angel exclaimed, grimacing. 'I already have the totally unwanted image of him having a blowie, I really didn't need to add to it.'

'Well, I'm starving,' Jez replied. 'So if there aren't any further revelations about what our England Captain gets up to, shall we order? I'm guessing you won't want the roast, Angel?'

After dinner Angel felt like going on to a bar. She wouldn't be seeing her friends for over a month and wanted to spend as much time with them as possible now, but when she suggested it both Gemma and Jez made their excuses.

'I'm sorry, Angel, I haven't seen Rufus all week because of work and I promised to get back at a reasonable time,' Jez said.

'And I really need to get home,' Gemma put in. 'I'm flying to Spain in the morning for a shoot and I haven't packed yet.'

'Great,' Angel said gloomily. 'Not only have I got to face a month with the Witchy WAGs, but now my best friends are blowing me out.'

'Babe!' Jez replied. 'We're so not. And I don't mean to sound snipey but Gemma and me have both been working really hard lately – I was in the salon from half-seven this morning and I didn't finish till seven this evening, and I bet Gemma had an equally long day. Whereas you . . .'

Angel interrupted him, 'Okay, okay, I get your

point. I just had to do a quick shoot this morning. I do realise how lucky I am, Jez. I'm sorry if it sounded like I take you both for granted, I know how hard you work.'

'I wasn't having a go!' he assured her. 'Just get yourself home and have phone sex with that gorgeous husband of yours who, by the way, should so be doing an underwear campaign! He'd be perfect on a billboard in a pair of tight white briefs.' Jez's face took on an enraptured expression.

Angel knew this was a wind up. She shrugged dismissively. 'I can't see Cal ever doing anything like that. You know he hates that kind of thing. I could just about see him advertising a car or maybe sunglasses, but pants? No way!'

'Ah, well,' Jez replied. 'A man can dream.'

Outside the restaurant they said their goodbyes and while Jez hailed a taxi Gemma hugged Angel and said, 'You'll be fine out there, Angel, I'm sure.'

'Promise you'll text me every day?'

'Promise you'll call me! I want all the gossip, and detailed descriptions of all the outfits – and I mean *detailed*!'

As soon as she arrived home Angel phoned Cal. It was just after eight a.m. in California and she wanted to catch him before he started training, needing to talk to him, needing reassurance. But as he had been so often in the past months, he was distant and barely spoke to her. When Angel said she was feeling a little nervous about her stay in LA he dismissed her fears, telling her that she'd be fine, she should just see it as a holiday. *Some holiday,* Angel thought bitterly, then changed the subject. 'How's your knee?'

'Holding out,' Cal said abruptly. 'Look, I've got to go to training now. I'll speak to you later.'

'Okay, love you,' she said sadly.

'Love you too,' he replied before hanging up.

Angel sighed. Lately it had been hard to hold on to that belief.

Poolside at the Four Seasons Hotel Beverly Hills – or WAG HQ as Angel had taken to calling it – she was aware that she was the centre of attention. All the other WAGs who were sunbathing in their designer bikinis and shades were staring at her, not for what she looked like but because she was swimming and actually getting her hair wet! Hardly any of the other girls ventured into the water and if they did they kept their heads well out of it, mindful that they could not afford to have a bad hair day. Angel could almost hear the collective gasp of horror as she emerged dripping from the water and grabbed her towel. While the England team battled to stay in the tournament, around the hotel pool an even more ferocious battle was raging – the battle to be top WAG.

Angel smiled to herself as she strolled back to her clique because, yes, while the men had to be united as a team on the pitch, their wives had divided into several distinct groups. Angel was part of what she called the 'grounded WAGs', women who actually had careers outside of being a footballer's wife. They included Madison, Suki and Candy – though Candy had a foot in another camp, the Style WAGs, who rocked the latest trends. And then there was the clique centred round Queen WAG Gabrielle, including Simone and Lauren – the Wicked Witches of the WAGs or WWWs.

Since her arrival in LA two weeks ago the WWWs had given Angel the cold shoulder; she hadn't been invited to dinners that other WAGs had gone to – which was fine by her as just being in the same room as Gabrielle and Simone made her skin crawl – and they never missed an opportunity to make a snide remark, like now as she walked past them and heard Lauren say, 'Well, I expect her implants help her to float in the water. They're big enough, aren't they?'

Angel only stuck her impressive chest out still further and smiled to herself, thinking how very pissed off Gabrielle would be to know that Connor had continued to send gifts to her even though she immediately sent them all back. The diamond necklace had been followed by a white Chanel J12 watch with white diamonds, and a gold Jimmy Choo clutch bag. He must be mad, Angel thought, he couldn't seriously think that these gifts would impress her enough to consider his proposal. But then again maybe they would work with other girls . . . Thank God she had her own friends here to keep her sane.

Much to her surprise she was actually enjoying herself in LA. England were doing well so far and Cal was playing brilliantly. Angel loved the whole LA vibe, she loved the climate and the perfect blue skies but she hadn't experienced the infamous smog yet. There were exotic flowers and palm trees everywhere. She liked the way people said, 'Have a nice day.' Even if they didn't really mean it, it beat being served by someone back home who looked as if they'd rather spit in your coffee than wish you that. And whereas in the UK she often felt she stood out with her surgically enhanced figure, she fitted in perfectly here with her blonde hair and tan – in fact, when she looked around, plastic surgery seemed practically compulsory in LA. And it seemed no part of the body was off limits. Only yesterday Candy had had them all in fits when she told them about butt hole bleaching. 'Apparently lots of girls do it out here,' Candy said knowledgeably. 'It makes it look prettier, not so dark.'

'Like, who cares what it looks like?' Angel laughed.

'You're not seriously thinking of having it done, are you?' Suki asked, open-mouthed with astonishment.

'Don't be mad, of course not! But I might consider a designer vagina after I've had kids, what do you reckon?'

'Do your pelvic floor exercises and you won't need it!' Madison shot back.

Now the women were flicking through the tabloids – an activity all the WAGs engaged in as soon as they were delivered to the hotel – but whereas Angel's group took the coverage of the WAGs with a pinch of salt, Gabrielle and her clique took it very seriously indeed, wanting to know who had the most column inches devoted to them.

'Have you noticed,' Madison said, pointing to the pictures of Gabrielle, Simone and Lauren taken on a shopping trip on Rodeo Drive, 'that those three are never smiling when they're photographed? They always look so miserable, don't they? Whereas we four –' she pointed to a picture of Angel, Suki, Candy and herself outside the über-stylish Japanese restaurant Koi in Hollywood '– are smiling.'

'That's because we'd just eaten something,' Angel put in. 'Whereas those three are surviving on a lettuce leaf and a cup of hot water and lemon.'

'So now for the really important thing – who's going to come shopping with me this afternoon?' Candy asked. 'I need something for the game tomorrow.' The other three looked askance at her.

'Candy, you brought so many clothes with you!'

Suki exclaimed. 'You can't seriously need anything else?'

'Need, no. Want, yes,' Candy corrected her.

'Candy, you are turning into a such a cliché WAG,' Madison told her.

'Like, what's the problem with that?' Candy demanded, though she was smiling. 'So who's going to come with me? Will you, Angel? *Please.*'

Angel laughed. 'Okay, I'll come, but I'm bringing Honey and I want to go to Kitson's on Robertson Boulevard.'

'Ha, I knew it!' Candy said gleefully. 'You pretend not to be bothered about shopping but you love it really.'

'Actually, it's not for me, I want to get something for Cal.'

'Whatever,' Candy replied. 'I bet you'll get something for yourself too.'

England were playing Portugal the next day and the reason Angel had agreed to go shopping with Candy was to take her mind off the match. Even with Cal playing as well as he had done so far, she was anxious for him, praying that his knee would hold out . . .

'Come on, Cal!' Angel screamed from the stand, causing Gabrielle, Simone and Lauren to turn round and look down their St Tropez-ed noses at her as if she was dirt. What were they like! Angel thought. She was at a football match, how else was she going to behave? She certainly wasn't going to sit statue still like those three, more concerned with maintaining their sophisticated appearance, as if they were at a fashion show, than with whether their team did well.

Angel by contrast was concentrating all her attention on the match, willing England to win. It was their fourth match of the tournament and it had been a heart-stopping game. For a tantalising time it looked as if England were going through, with Cal scoring one of the goals, but five minutes before full-time Portugal had equalised. Neither team scored in extra time so it was penalties.

Angel felt sick with nerves. She had chewed off half of her fake nails in her anxiety. 'Oh my God!' she exclaimed, clutching Candy's arm. 'I don't know if I can bear to watch this!'

She knew that Cal would be one of the players to take a penalty. Usually he was one of the team's best penalty-takers, but she worried about the pressure on him and about his knee. Several times during the match she had seen him limping slightly. She looked at her husband, in a huddle discussing tactics with his team mates and Jack. *Please let him score*, she prayed.

And then the whistle blew. Portugal were first to take a penalty and the player easily scored. Connor Carter was next for England. He strode confidently towards the ball. At any other time Angel would have been willing him to miss, but as England's fate hung in the balance she tried not to think negative thoughts – tempting as it was. The Captain tricked the goalie into thinking he was aiming the ball left, before shooting to the right and scoring.

'Flash git!' Candy muttered so only Angel could hear. She whole-heartedly agreed though she was glad he had scored. She managed to chew off another nail while the opposition scored another penalty and then it was Cal's turn.

You can do it, Cal, she willed him on. She watched him walk up to the penalty spot, place the ball down then walk back several paces, getting ready to take the shot. And then he ran and kicked the ball. The goalkeeper flung himself towards it – and to Angel's absolute horror managed to save it. There was a deafening roar from the Portuguese supporters while the English fans sat stunned and silent.

Angel looked at Candy, her eyes wide with horror. 'Oh my God! He'll never forgive himself for this.'

Cal, his shoulders bowed, walked despondently back to his team mates who all rallied round him. Angel's heart went out to him.

'Don't worry, Angel,' Candy put in. 'Maybe the other team will miss.'

Madison was sitting on the other side and put her arm round Angel, to try and comfort her. Naturally Cal's failure also drew a reaction from Gabrielle and

Simone who turned to look at Angel as if she had somehow been responsible. Angel itched to give them the finger but resisted, knowing it wouldn't look great to have that image of herself beamed round the world. And then to her delight Portugal missed their next penalty while England scored theirs. Portugal missed again and England scored. When Portugal scored again it was all down to Liam who blasted the ball into the back of the net.

The England supporters went wild! Shouting and singing filling the stadium with what felt like a wall of sound, but though Angel joined in her heart felt heavy for Cal. She knew that, despite England's victory, he would be beating himself up over his own failure.

Phil was very strict about how long the players could see their wives and girlfriends for, and after the match they were allowed only the briefest of meetings in the lounge.

Angel bit off her last remaining nail as she waited for Cal to come up from the changing rooms, ignoring Candy's comments that her hands looked minging. She really didn't give a toss right now. Cal was the last player to enter the room. Usually so confident, he walked in like a defeated man, head bowed. Ignoring all the reassuring comments from his team mates he went over to where Angel was standing.

She immediately hugged him. 'Please don't be too hard on yourself,' she whispered.

Cal gave her the briefest of embraces and then pulled away. 'I don't want to talk about it,' he said in a voice drained of emotion.

Angel longed to reassure him but she knew what Cal was like, knew how uncompromising he could be, knew that there were places he went sometimes where she couldn't reach him. So she simply took his hand and said, 'I love you, Cal.'

His automatic 'Love you too' was so dismissive she almost wished he hadn't said it at all.

On the coach journey back to LA the other women were in high spirits, laughing and chatting. But Angel was quiet, simply gazing out of the window. She still felt concerned for her husband.

'You look thoughtful,' Madison said, sitting down next to her. 'Thinking about Cal, I expect?'

Angel nodded and bit her lip.

'He's bound to feel bad today but he'll get through it, they always do, and at least England won,' Madison continued.

'Yeah, I know. It's just, I wish I could be with Cal right now. I know what he's like, I know he'll be beating himself up about missing that penalty.'

'He'll be all right, the others will look out for him. They understand because they've all been there.'

Just then Candy popped her head over the seat in front. 'Angel, you're still going to come out tonight, aren't you?'

'I'm not sure,' she replied.

'Oh, come on. Tonight of all nights you don't want to stay in your hotel room on your own, it will do your head in. We're going to have dinner at the Ivy then check out one of the clubs,' Candy went on.

Angel wavered; she really didn't want to stay alone in her hotel suite, brooding about her husband.

'You don't think Cal will think it's really callous of me to be going out?' she asked Madison.

'No! Anyway, we're celebrating England's victory. There's no point in obsessing over one mistake.'

'You promise the WWWs won't be there?' Angel whispered.

'I doubt it,' Candy replied. 'And even if they just happened to be at the Ivy at the same time, they'd ignore us so no worries.'

'Okay.' Angel finally gave in. 'But do I have to get really dressed up?'

Candy looked at her as if she was deranged. 'Yes, obviously!'

Angel groaned. 'Can't I just wear jeans and a tee-shirt? The LA look is supposed to be much more relaxed than back home.'

'Angel, you're representing your country!' Candy teased her. 'It's got to be full on designer or you'll be publicly stripped of your WAG title.'

'I hate that expression anyway,' she grumbled. 'I'm not a WAG, I'm a human being!'

'God, Angel, you do realise that thousands of girls would give anything to be a WAG and there you are, dissing the honourable profession! I'll tell you what, I'll come to your room and help you choose what to wear. I know you've got loads of designer stuff really.'

Angel gave up; she did have designer gear with her. True to her word, Gemma had acted as her personal shopper/stylist and had pulled together a number of stunning outfits, none of which she'd worn so far even though she had promised to.

Usually Angel would have Gemma help her get ready for a big night out, especially if she was going to be photographed. However much Angel didn't want to be photographed here she knew there were bound to be paparazzi in LA just like there were in London. She realised the others would spend hours getting ready but still felt too sad about Cal to go to too much effort, so kept her own hair and make up simple.

Candy had been through her wardrobe and chosen a pink halterneck dress for her to wear but Angel wasn't in the mood for something so girly. She wanted to look more feisty. So she decided instead to wear a short black satin jumpsuit which was sexy but understated. She teamed it with a pair of black patent Jimmy Choo sandals. The only jewellery she wore was her wedding ring.

In contrast Candy, Suki and Madison were decked out in their finest designer labels – Cavalli, Prada, Chloe and Gucci – and sported a dazzling array of bling. They all looked exactly like Premiership WAGs were supposed to look.

'Why aren't you wearing the pink dress?' Candy demanded when Angel met them in the foyer.

She shrugged. 'I'm just happier in this.'

'What is it? Marc Jacobs?' Candy went on.

'House of Topshop, I believe.'

'You look amazing, Angel,' Suki told her. 'I think you make the rest of us look a bit over-WAGGed.'

They had a great time at the Ivy, sitting outside in the pretty garden with its sweet white picket fence, gossiping and star-spotting. They all tried to be subtle about it but none of them could stop doing double takes when they saw Cameron Diaz, Mischa Barton, Paris Hilton and Simon Cowell, though not together!

'So, I bet you're looking forward to seeing Cal tomorrow night?' Suki said to Angel as they waited for their main course.

She looked blank. 'What do you mean? Why would I be seeing him?'

The three other women looked at her in surprise and Suki said, 'Because Phil has given the team the night off and they can come and see us at the hotel.'

'Oh,' Angel replied, stunned that Cal hadn't told her. Maybe he didn't want to see her.

'I got a text from Reece just before I came out. I expect Cal will call you tonight. He's probably still brooding.' Madison said diplomatically.

'Probably. I don't know how he feels because he wouldn't talk about it,' Angel answered, trying not to show how upset she was.

'You know what men are like,' Madison continued. 'Just give him time, he'll be fine.'

'And shag his brains out tomorrow night!' Candy put in cheekily. 'That ought to do the trick. Men are simple creatures.'

Angel put on a smile, remembering only too clearly what had happened when she and Cal last made love. Maybe he just didn't love her anymore? Maybe that's why he had been so distant with her. Maybe he was just waiting for the right time to tell her it was over between them. The thought was unbearable to her. She knew she couldn't keep sitting at the table without speaking to him. Muttering about needing the loo, she excused herself and headed for the privacy of the bathroom.

For once Cal had answered his phone.

'Hi, its me.'

'Hi, how are you?' he said.

Ignoring his question Angel went on, 'Why didn't you tell me that you've got the night off tomorrow?'

187

'Sorry, I meant to text you.' He sounded as distant as ever.

'Cal, you do still love me, don't you?' she burst out.

'Of course I love you!' Now he did sound passionate, more like the Cal she knew.

'It's just that all the other wives knew about tomorrow night and I was the only one who didn't.'

'I'm sorry, I was going to tell you. And I am looking forward to seeing you, I really am.'

Angel wanted to say something flirtatious, like she couldn't wait to see him either or to get his kit off, but it seemed inappropriate saying something like that at the moment; there was too much distance between them. Instead she played it safe. 'I'm looking forward to seeing you too.'

She walked slowly back to the table, feeling exhausted, not so much physically as emotionally, worn out with keeping up the pretence that her marriage was the fairy tale everyone else believed it to be. Maybe she was being over-sensitive about Cal? Of course he was on edge and worried at the moment – all his life he'd dreamed of playing for England at the World Cup and he didn't want to blow it. Was that all it was then? Angel could only pray that it was, and that when the tournament was over she would get her husband back.

'All right, Angel?' Suki asked her when she re-joined the others.

She nodded. 'Yeah, I just wanted to speak to Cal, check he was okay.'

'Well, just think, this time tomorrow night you'll actually see him. I bet he'll whisk you straight off to bed!' Candy exclaimed.

Suki and Madison both seemed slightly more sensitive to Angel's mood and obviously realised something was not quite right between her and Cal. They were older than Candy and had probably experienced their share of marital ups and downs. But Candy was oblivious – she was young, wildly in love with Liam, and assumed that Angel and Cal were in the same loved up state.

'Shall I order some more wine?' Angel asked, anxious to deflect attention away from herself.

Thankfully she got through the rest of the meal without Cal's name being mentioned again, but some of the pleasure had gone out of the night for her and now all she wanted to do was get back to the hotel. She had no desire to go clubbing. But she had reckoned without the persuasive skills of Candy, who would not take no for an answer. 'We have got to go to Hyde,' she insisted. 'It's one of *the* celeb places in LA.'

Angel smiled. 'You've said that about everywhere we've been so far.'

'I know, but I really want to go there,' Candy replied. 'I read that Robbie Williams goes there sometimes, and I've loved him forever!'

Angel gave up, secretly thinking that they probably wouldn't even get into the place if they weren't on the guest list. Sure enough, when their limo pulled up outside the club on Sunset Boulevard there was a huge crowd waiting outside to get in. Completely unfazed, Candy got out of the limo and marched to the front of the queue to negotiate their entrance with a six-foot blonde with the looks and superiority of a super model who decided which of the crowd was cool enough to get in. Angel, Madison and Suki trailed behind her, like reluctant children. Angel missed the first part of the conversation and came in on Candy exclaiming, 'No fucking way! Don't you know who we are?'

Oh, no, Candy, Angel thought. *That was so not the way to do it!*

The blonde amazon rolled her eyes and blew bubble gum in Candy's face – clearly she was not from the 'Have a nice day' school.

'I don't care who you are, you're not coming in.' Her eyes flicked past Candy and settled on Angel. 'Oh, but she could.'

Angel shook her head and took Candy's arm to stop her from saying anything else. 'Let's go.' She was turning away from the club when her path was blocked by a tall, extremely good-looking blond man who bore a striking resemblance to Josh Holloway, the actor who played Sawyer in *Lost*. Angel had always secretly fancied him like mad and for a moment thought it was him. Then he spoke to her and she realised it wasn't.

'Hey, you're not leaving already, are you?' He spoke in that sexy LA drawl, staring at her with a pair of intensely blue eyes.

Angel smiled at him. 'Yes, I'm afraid we are.'

The mystery man was about to reply when they were surrounded by paparazzi snapping away at them. *How did they know she and the girls were going to be here?* Angel wondered, then realised the attention was all on Mystery Man, who raised his eyebrows at her and said, 'See you again, I hope,' before pushing his way through the paps and straight into the club.

'Whoah! He was fit!' Candy exclaimed. 'He looked just like Sawyer from *Lost*.'

'Come on, Cinderella, let's go. Don't you need your beauty sleep for seeing Liam tomorrow night?' Madison put in.

'You're right,' Candy replied. 'And of course I've got to decide what to wear . . . Though I'm well pissed off about not getting into that club. Do you think I should try again?'

'No way,' said Madison firmly, taking her arm and practically frogmarching her to the limo.

The following morning Candy and Angel were having breakfast by the pool. During their stay they'd got into the habit of ordering the most mouth-watering dishes they could and then exclaiming loudly about how delicious the food was within earshot of Gabrielle and Simone. Today they'd gone for scrambled eggs and smoked salmon.

'I still haven't seen them eat anything,' Candy whispered. 'They must be starving all the time. No wonder Gabrielle's got that miserable cow expression on her face – her body must be gagging for some carbs.'

Gabrielle and Simone lay on sun loungers opposite, flicking through magazines, but in spite of their best efforts they kept looking at the food.

'And check out the look of longing on Simone's face!' Angel whispered back. 'I bet she doesn't look like that when Jamie gets his kit off!'

Candy and Angel giggled even though they knew that they would have to pay for eating so much by doing an extra-hard session in the gym later, but it was worth it to make those two suffer.

'I love hot buttered toast so much, don't you, Angel?' Candy said loudly, shovelling a piece slathered in butter into her mouth. The sight was clearly too much for Gabrielle and Simone who leaped up from their loungers and practically ran back into the hotel.

'One nil to us, I think,' Angel declared.

Candy gave her the thumbs up then said, 'D'you have any idea who that gorgeous blond man was last night?'

'What gorgeous blond man?' Angel pretended to look puzzled when the truth was she'd had a few thoughts of her own on those lines. He really had been incredibly good-looking and not the kind of man you would easily forget.

Candy saw right through her. 'Oh, please don't be all coy with me. You know exactly who I mean!'

Angel shook her head, but she was smiling. 'Candy, I've no idea what you're talking about.'

Candy reverted to her all time favourite topic of conversation. 'So have you decided what you're going to wear tonight when you see Cal?'

Angel looked blank. 'I've no idea. Probably jeans and a vest.'

Candy rolled her eyes. 'Angel! Why don't you wear the pink halterneck dress. You look so sexy in that!'

Angel sighed, 'I guess I could.'

'And what about your hair?' Now Candy had got up from her seat and started arranging Angel's long hair, seeing what it looked like piled on top of her head.

'I'll wear it down, I suppose.'

'I've just had a great idea! Why don't you go platinum blonde again? I thought you looked incredible like that, and wouldn't it be a great surprise for Cal? You could have my appointment at Privé – it's owned by Laurent D, the guy who does Uma Thurman and Gwyneth Paltrow's hair. I thought I'd need my highlights doing again but they're fine. What do you reckon?'

'Do you boss Liam around like this?' Angel replied, smiling, though actually it wasn't a bad thought. She felt like she could do with a change. Maybe going platinum would help put a bit of va-va-voom back into her marriage. God knows, it needed it.

And so, after checking on Honey and Lucy, Angel found herself on her way to Privé Salon which was where she spent the next four hours. She felt rather guilty, knowing that Jez would be upset that she hadn't gone to him. But what the hell? This was a spur-of-the-moment decision.

By the time the hairdresser had finished, Angel was thrilled with her appearance. She always tanned easily and in the LA sun had gone a beautiful golden-brown. Combined with that, platinum hair made her look sexy and exotic. The players weren't due to arrive at the hotel until seven which still left her plenty of time to get ready and she decided to go with Candy's suggestion of the pink dress. She had even booked a table at Comme Ça, a hip brasserie on Melrose Avenue, as she didn't want to eat at the hotel surrounded by all the other footballers and their wives.

As it drew closer to seven, she felt increasingly tense – she so wanted Cal to like her new look. Candy popped round to her suite and told her she looked amazing, which boosted her confidence. But when she left Angel found herself anxiously scanning her reflection. Did she really look all right? Would Cal think she looked sexy?

When he turned up, he looked surprised rather than captivated by her hair. He kissed and hugged her briefly then said, 'I thought you preferred your hair darker.'

'I thought a change would be good. Don't you like it?' she replied, her heart sinking. He obviously wasn't impressed.

'Of course I like it. You look beautiful, you always do.'

But Angel couldn't take any comfort from this comment because although the words were what she longed to hear, the way he'd said them sounded lacklustre and routine. And the evening went downhill from there. He seemed annoyed when she told him they were going out to dinner, saying that he was tired and would rather have had room service. When they arrived at the restaurant he barely said a word. Angel did her best to try and engage him. She chatted about Honey – how much she loved going in the swimming pool, how she was starting to crawl, and what new words she'd come out with. She asked him how his knee was holding out, how he felt about the next game, but nothing she said generated anything more than a monosyllabic response.

Then she brought up the subject of the missed penalty. 'Cal you've got to stop beating yourself up about it. '

'You've got no fucking idea, have you?' he exclaimed angrily. 'Of *course* I can't stop thinking about it! What if I do it again and it costs us the next match?'

'I know you're upset but don't you think it would be a good idea to move on?' Angel tried to say calmly even though she felt terribly hurt by the way he was speaking to her. 'I'm sure Phil and the rest of the team would want you to do that.'

'Oh, yes, I forgot you were an expert in these matters,' he said nastily. 'Remind me again how many penalties you've taken?'

Hardly able to believe how cruel he was being, Angel got up from the table and practically ran to the Ladies'. She didn't want him to see her cry nor did she want anyone else in the restaurant to see her tears. Once there she bolted the cubicle door and sobbed. What had happened to the man she loved? She didn't think she could take anymore of this.

Eventually she calmed down and then had to spend the next few minutes repairing her make up. She looked in the mirror, hating her hair, hating the sexy dress. It had made no difference to anything. Clearly Cal didn't want her anymore. She understood that he was stressed, but he'd been stressed before and he'd never spoken to her like this. Feeling numb, she made her way back to the table.

'I sent your meal back to keep it warm. Why were you so long?' he asked as she sat down.

Still not trusting herself to look at him, Angel stared down at the table and muttered, 'I couldn't bear the way you were speaking to me. I know how important the tournament is to you but please don't treat me like this.'

She waited for Cal to snap back at her. Instead he reached out and took her hand. 'Angel, I am so sorry. I know I'm being a complete shit,' he said in a voice that was husky with emotion. Now she looked at him and for the first time in ages his brown eyes were warm. 'I love you, babe, you must believe that. I'm just in a really difficult place at the moment and I need you to understand.'

'I do understand!' Angel said passionately. 'But, please, share it with me.'

'I'll try,' he promised.

But back at the hotel, where Angel longed to get close to Cal, the shutters once more came down on her. When they got into bed together he made a big show of yawning and saying, 'God, I'm knackered.' He put his arm round her and she snuggled up to him, but when she started caressing his chest and running her fingers over his hard stomach, he said, 'Angel, I'm too tired. Sorry . . . maybe in the morning.' Then he switched the light off and seemed to go to sleep, leaving her feeling completely rejected. In the morning either he had forgotten what he'd said or he didn't want to because when she woke up he was already showered and dressed.

'It's okay,' he said when he saw that she was awake, 'you have a lie in and I'll take Honey down to breakfast. Do you want me to order you some room service?'

Angel shook her head, and burrowed back under the covers.

'God, Angel, you look well knackered! Cal keep you up did he?' Candy giggled as she caught up with her by the pool. The players had left just after breakfast and Angel was back to putting on a brave face and pretending that her marriage was peachy. She was glad she was wearing sun glasses and Candy couldn't see her eyes, which she knew looked sad. 'Yep, all night,' she said, which wasn't exactly a lie as she had been awake most of the time, just not engaged in the same activity as Candy. 'What about you?'

'Yep!' Candy said with relish. 'I rode him like a beast all night! I'm feeling very satisfied, if you know what I mean. It was good to have the real thing for a change. I was worried that I was getting a bit too addicted to my Rabbit.'

Angel was relieved when Suki and Madison turned up and they could change the subject.

'Hey, Angel, you're in *Grazia*,' Madison said, handing her the magazine.

'Really?' Angel replied, surprised; she didn't usually make the style mags. 'Oh, God, it's not criticising something I've worn, is it?'

'No, the opposite. It says that you looked stylish and understated and that other WAGs should take a leaf out of your book,' Madison continued.

Angel was pictured at the last England match in an Ed Hardy black tee-shirt with *Dedicated to the One I Love* written on it, huge black shades and black skinny jeans. The contrasting picture was of Gabrielle who was Gucci-ed up to her eyeballs – Gucci shades, dress, shoes and bag. The accompanying article was not complimentary and poked fun at her lack of style and the way she was far too matchy-matchy with her clothes and accessories. Gemma would be thrilled; Angel would have to call her later.

'She won't like that, will she?' Candy exclaimed.

'No,' Angel replied. 'And it gives her one more thing to hate me for.'

'Why do you think she does?' Madison asked, and Angel quickly backtracked, not wanting to reveal Gabrielle's request for a threesome.

'She hates everyone except Simone and Lauren.'

'Well, they're three of a kind, aren't they?' Candy put in.

At just that moment the WWWs appeared at the poolside.

'God, it's freaky the way they can do that!' Suki exclaimed. 'I swear they really are witches.'

Clearly Gabrielle had not taken *Grazia's* advice to dress down because she was currently sporting a zebra-print tunic with matching zebra-print sling backs. She walked over to where Angel was sitting and when she saw them all looking at *Grazia*, said scornfully, 'Enjoy your moment, Angel. I don't suppose it will be long before you're back to wearing tacky outfits and showing off your tits.'

'Leave her alone, Gabrielle. She's got more style in her little finger than you could ever have,' Candy exclaimed loyally.

'And that means so much coming from you, who never stops acting like a caned Essex girl on a night out.'

'I'm from Manchester, you div, but there's nothing wrong with Essex girls,' Candy shot back. 'Better than being a stuck up bitch like—'

Suki quickly interrupted her. 'Come on, girls, there's no need for this.'

'Gabrielle, let's go,' Simone put in. 'We've got our manicure appointments now.' But as they walked off she couldn't resist turning round and shooting Angel yet another poisonous look.

'God,' Angel groaned, 'how many more weeks of this have we got to put up with?'

'Just think of the great holiday you can have with Cal and Honey when it's all over,' Madison said sympathetically. 'And then will you be going back to Italy?'

'Oh, don't ask,' she exclaimed. 'I really don't want to live there, but I think my marriage won't survive unless I move.'

'What do you mean?' Candy was looking at her, open-mouthed with surprise, 'You and Cal have got a perfect marriage. I'm always saying to Liam that if we can be like you two then we'll be all right.'

'How ironic. I was just thinking if only Cal and I could be more like you two,' Angel replied wistfully.

It was clear that Candy wanted to continue her interrogation but Madison managed to steer the conversation away, to Angel's huge relief.

As they all walked back into the hotel later Madison hung back with Angel and said quietly, 'All marriages go through their tough times. God knows me and Reece have come close to splitting up more than once. If you ever need anyone to talk to, you can tell me and it will go no further, I promise.'

'Thanks,' Angel answered gratefully. She didn't want to confide in anyone because things between her and Cal seemed so complicated, but it was still good to know that she could.

But other people too were becoming aware that there might be problems between Angel and Cal.

When Angel was back in her suite she got a call from her agent, Carrie. Angel had something of a love-hate relationship with her. Carrie had got her some amazing work, though Gemma was always pointing out that it was due to Angel's talent and not especially to Carrie's, but she could be breath-takingly insensitive when it came to the emotional stuff.

'Angel darling, why didn't you tell me about you and Cal?' she exclaimed without even bothering to say hello when Angel answered the phone.

'Tell you about what?' she asked, a sick feeling in the pit of her stomach.

'You know – that it's make or break time,' Carrie continued, seemingly oblivious to the impact of her words.

'Says who?' Angel demanded, feeling thoroughly shaken by what she was hearing.

'Darling, I had a call from a journalist friend and it's going to be all over the tabloids tomorrow. There are pictures of you leaving a restaurant together, both looking miserable, and one of your friends is quoted as saying that you fear Cal may be unfaithful.'

It had to be Simone behind this story, and probably Gabrielle too, Angel thought bitterly.

'I just thought I'd warn you so you know to expect calls from journalists. Do you want to do a shoot off the back of the story, so you can put across your side?'

'Carrie . . .' Angel fought to control her anger but was very close to telling her agent to fuck off '. . . there *is* no story. Cal and I are getting on fine, and I'm not saying anything! England are playing again tomorrow night and the last thing I want is for him to be upset by this crap!'

'Well,' Carrie replied huffily, 'there would no doubt be a good fee and I'm sure I don't need to remind you that you haven't worked much lately. There are a lot of other glamour girls out there, Angel.'

'I am here to support my husband, Carrie. I'm not working until after the World Cup is over, and I want you to tell your journalist friend that rumours of any problems between Cal and me are absolute lies. We've never been happier.'

*

Angel might have sounded confident but that was very far from how she felt and for the rest of the day she was thoroughly miserable. She couldn't get hold of Cal and had to leave a message about the story, but when they finally spoke in the evening he didn't even seem concerned about it.

'Come on, Angel, you know the papers are always printing crap. How many times have you read about a celebrity couple whose marriage is supposed to be breaking up just because they're seen looking moody on a night out? It's bollocks, just forget about it, I have.'

'But what about that friend who's quoted as saying that I'm worried about you being unfaithful?'

'What about it? There is no such friend, we both know that. And you're not worried, are you?'

Angel hesitated. The fact was that Simone had sown a nasty seed of doubt in her mind all those months ago, and that combined with Cal's touchiness about her looking at his text message had left her feeling insecure. But the night before his big match was no time for her to express these feelings.

She sighed. 'No, I know it's lies.'

'Good.' Cal sounded relieved. 'Why don't you go and see Suki and the others?'

But Angel didn't take his advice and spent the rest of the night alone; she just couldn't bear to have everyone feel sorry for her, and didn't think she could hold it together if they started to ask too many questions.

Chapter 7

A Night to Remember . . .

'Go on, Cal!' Angel screamed out, not caring how she looked if the cameras were trained on her. It was the last two minutes of the nail-biting match between England and Germany, and so far the score stood at 1-1. Cal had the ball but as he wove his way past a defender, was viciously tackled and fell to the ground clutching his knee.

'Oh, God, no!' Angel exclaimed, and Candy put her arm round her sympathetically. The next few minutes were agony for Angel as Cal remained lying down and the physio rushed over to him. This could be the end of her husband's World Cup dreams. But then he was getting up, and though he moved a little gingerly at first he seemed fine.

Because of the foul England were awarded a free kick. Reece, Madison's husband, looked as if he was going to take it but at the last second swapped with Cal. Angel thought she couldn't take anymore tension, but to her delight and that of every other English fan the line of defenders failed to head the ball away, the goalkeeper dived for it but missed . . . it was a goal! The stadium erupted into cheers, shouts and singing from the fans. Angel whooped with delight and hugged Candy and Suki and Madison, tears in her eyes because she was so proud of Cal. He had won the match for England!

More than anything Angel wanted to see him, but the players had to have a debrief and instead the women headed back to the hotel. 'We have *so* got to celebrate tonight!' Candy exclaimed as they got on to the coach.

'Too right we have!' Madison replied. 'I was totally convinced it was going to go to penalties again and we'd lose. Oh, not because of Cal,' she put in hastily, seeing Angel's expression, 'but because we usually do when it comes to penalties! Oops! I suppose as a WAG I really shouldn't say such disloyal things.'

Angel laughed. 'I'm just so relieved that Cal scored. I thought when he went down that was it.'

'So come on, now to the important thing – where are we going to go?' Suki put in.

But suddenly Gabrielle was standing up and addressing everyone on the coach, 'As the Captain's wife I'd like to invite all of you for cocktails to celebrate our boys' success.'

There were cheers from most of the women on the coach except Angel's group.

'I guess it would look really bad if we didn't go, wouldn't it?' she muttered, and reluctantly the others agreed, though Candy added, 'We'll have cocktails first and *then* go out.'

Back at the hotel Angel spent some time with her daughter, then took a long shower, wrapped herself in the white hotel robe and went round to Candy's room. She had insisted the two of them should get ready together.

She'd already opened the champagne when Angel knocked at the door. 'Get your arse over here, girl, and have a drink,' she exclaimed, handing Angel a glass. 'Now what are you going to wear?'

'Well, I was going to go for my white skinny jeans and a white sequined vest,' Angel said, holding up the clothes for Candy's inspection.

'Angel! They're very nice but we're celebrating. You've got to wear something fabulous.'

'Okay, will this do?' She picked up her second choice, a short black dress with a plunging neckline and bejewelled hem and straps.

'So much better!' Candy exclaimed. 'You could wear it with your hair up and your Christian Louboutins.' *God, her resemblance to Gemma really was uncanny*. Angel took a long sip of champagne for confidence, slipped off her robe and put on the dress. It looked amazing but Angel worried it was too revealing – lots of leg and cleavage were on show and she felt as if she was hardly wearing anything.

'You don't think I'm showing off too much, do you?' she asked anxiously.

'Angel – have you ever thought that in six years' time you'll be thirty? You've got it, girl, flaunt it!'

'You really are as bossy as my friend Gemma!' Angel grumbled. 'And thirty isn't the end of the world.'

'All I'm saying is, make the most of what you've got now because you don't want to be mutton, do you?' Candy said darkly.

The two girls spent the next half an hour doing their hair and make up and finishing the bottle of champagne so that by the time they arrived at Gabrielle's cocktail party in the hotel they were already feeling merry – no bad thing, Angel thought, as it took the edge off seeing the witches.

Gabrielle was coolly polite as she greeted them. 'I've had the barman invent a cocktail especially to celebrate and everyone's got to have one.'

Angel would have preferred to stick to champagne but didn't want to have another run in with Gabrielle so she took one of the red cocktails from the tray the waiter offered her. The two girls were just sipping their drinks and looking out for Suki and Madison when Simone sidled up to them.

'I saw that story in the press, Angel. I did warn you about Cal, didn't I? How are you holding up?' she asked in a falsely sympathetic voice.

'The story was bollocks,' Angel shot back. 'So don't worry yourself about Cal and me, we've got a rock solid marriage.'

Simone smirked. 'If you say so.' She wandered over to Gabrielle.

'What story?' Candy asked, and Angel quickly filled her in.

'God, are you okay about it, Angel?'

She shrugged. 'I have to be until after the tournament at least. Anyway, I'm not giving that bitch the satisfaction of knowing how upset I am. But come on, let's not talk about it – Suki and Madison are over there.'

In spite of Gabrielle and Simone, Angel enjoyed the cocktail party. With the exception of those two, all the other WAGs she met were nice to her and everyone wanted to congratulate her on Cal's winning goal. Angel drank more than she had in ages but she felt happily merry and was looking forward to a night out with her friends. It seemed that most of the other WAGs had the same idea and after an hour of cocktails everyone deserted the hotel. None of Angel's group felt like dinner yet so they decided to go to a bar first. But not just any old bar – they headed for Bar Marmont at the legendary hotel the Château Marmont on Sunset Boulevard.

'Wow! It looks just like a castle!' Candy exclaimed as the limo drove them up the hill to the impressive building.

Madison laughed. 'That's because it is one! It was modelled on a French château and it is *the* place to stay and to be seen – it always has been. It opened in 1929 and stars like Errol Flynn and Greta Garbo were regular guests.'

The three girls looked at Madison in surprise. 'How do you know all this?' Angel asked.

She gave them a mock-serious look. 'Because, like, I actually read my guidebook – and *Heat*, of course. All the stars stay here. I'm just really hoping we might see Leonardo DiCaprio as he comes here as well. I love him . . . even though I know I'm too old.'

'It's not that you're too old,' Suki replied. 'It's . . . how can I put this delicately? It's more, lovely as you are, babe, you're no supermodel.'

Madison sighed theatrically. 'I am in my head, and I could be for him!'

Angel was still smiling as they walked into the bar. She tried to be discreet but couldn't help scanning the elegant room with its red velvet sofas and ornate mirrors on the elaborately plastered walls to see if she could spot anyone famous. There were lots of 'beautiful' people sipping cocktails and looking über-cool but she didn't notice any stars. She did, however, notice the gorgeous blond guy she'd seen outside Hyde and he smiled at her in recognition. Angel quickly looked away – she didn't want him to think that she'd been eyeing him up.

'Champagne or cocktails?' Suki asked as they were shown to a table.

'It's got to be Cristal,' Madison exclaimed. 'We're WAGs, what else are we going to drink!' Even Angel laughed. Tonight she was celebrating her husband's success, she could let the WAG comment go. As soon as the champagne arrived they all toasted the boys again on their success.

'You must be so made up for Cal,' Candy said.

'God, yes!' Angel replied. 'I'm so proud of him!'

'Wow! Check out that table of good-looking lads,' Madison whispered. 'Six o'clock . . . but don't make it obvious you're looking!' She giggled as everyone turned round to ogle with zero subtlety. The four men, including the good-looking blond guy, saw them and raised their glasses. Angel found herself once more staring at the tall blond man who really was gorgeous.

Candy nudged her. 'Look, it's that sexy man from the other night!'

'Shh!' Angel told her, feeling slightly guilty for checking him out.

'They're just a bit of eye candy, Angel!' Madison told her.

She shrugged. 'Oh, I know. It's just I know how I'd feel if it was Cal looking at some girl in a bar.'

'Well, there's no marriage vow that says you can't look,' Madison continued. *And she was right, wasn't she?* But Angel still felt guilty and a pang of longing for Cal.

Just then a waiter appeared at their table and said discreetly, 'The gentlemen over there would like you to have this bottle of champagne, and they asked if you would like to join them.'

'Should we know who they are?' Madison asked.

The waiter allowed himself a small smile. 'They're very well known over here, ma'am – they're baseball players for the Los Angeles Dodgers.'

'And that's good, is it?' Madison continued.

'Oh, yes, they're like your Premiership footballers.'

'What do you reckon, girls?' Candy asked. 'I'm up for it.'

Angel's first reaction was to say no, but not wanting to look like a total killjoy she reluctantly agreed.

Madison led the way over to the table, with Angel trailing behind, and the next few minutes were taken up by introductions. She found herself sitting next to the good-looking blond who she discovered was called Ethan.

'I hoped I would see you again,' he told her and Angel just smiled, not wanting to admit that she had felt the same. He was a complete charmer and made it his mission to draw her into conversation.

He loved the fact that she was called Angel and that she was now in the City of Angels. 'You belong here,' he told her. 'It must be your destiny.' It didn't take her long to realise that Ethan liked her – a lot. He simply couldn't keep his eyes off her. 'I see you're married,' he said playfully, gesturing at the blingtastic diamond band on Angel's left hand. 'But you hate your husband, right? I can just tell you're looking for someone else.'

He stared at her with his intensely blue eyes in a way that probably would have melted the heart and knickers of any other woman, but Angel just laughed and said, 'You're wide of the mark. I love my husband.'

Ethan groaned theatrically and put his head in his hands. 'Just shoot me now! I can't believe I finally see the girl of my dreams and you're married . . . this just can't be!'

Everyone round the table laughed at him, and one of his friends, Logan, a tall, handsome African-American drawled, 'At last Ethan meets a girl he can't have. It'll be good for you, bro. You'll learn how it feels to be like the rest of us.'

As they bantered and teased each other, Angel found herself relaxing and enjoying herself. And even though she wouldn't have admitted it to *anyone*, she couldn't deny that she was attracted to Ethan. If she hadn't been married then she surely would have been tempted . . . But as it was she could bask in his admiration. It felt good to be told by a handsome man how beautiful she was, when for the last few months Cal hadn't seemed to notice her. Once Ethan realised he had no chance, he started talking generally to her about her life and in turn she asked him about himself. Conversation flowed easily between them and she found herself warming to him even more.

'So how come you're not with someone special?' she asked boldly.

'Seriously?' Ethan shrugged. 'I haven't met the right girl.'

'He's a sex addict!' one of his team mates shouted over the table and Ethan immediately challenged him to an arm wrestle. Watching the two men lock forearms, Angel couldn't help staring at Ethan's muscular tanned arms. And found herself imagining what the rest of his body would be like . . . She quickly looked away, trying to compose herself. *Get a grip! I'm married to the man I love!*

The group then decided to go on to Tropicana at the Roosevelt Hotel, another über-A-list haunt that had Candy practically jumping up and down with excitement. Angel tried to protest that she needed to get back to the hotel but no one would let her.

And after she'd checked that Lucy was okay to keep baby-sitting Honey, she agreed. Ethan managed to ensure that he was sitting next to her again in the limo. 'Don't feel you have to stay with me there,' she teased him. 'I don't want to cramp your style. There are probably loads of pretty girls there who'll want to be with you.'

'Loads,' he agreed. 'But not *the one*.' Then gave her that look – half longing, half pure lust – which had Angel pretending to look at her watch so she could hide just how attractive she found him. *God, he was hot!*

As Angel's group was ushered through the hotel and outside to the bar with its sultry lounge feel, wrapped around the iconic swimming pool with its David Hockney mural and surrounded by palm trees, they attracted a lot of attention. These men were big stars and Angel was aware of many girls' heads turning to check out Ethan. Once they were installed at a table there was more vintage champagne but Angel switched to mineral water. She was already pleasantly drunk and wanted to keep a clear head. To feel slightly out of control around someone as devastatingly handsome and flirtatious as Ethan was definitely not a good idea.

He tried to persuade her to have champagne but gave up when he saw how determined she was. They continued their conversation, Ethan still

flirting with her and Angel laughing off his attention, which was not to say that she didn't enjoy it.
Without her really being aware of it she had spent
most of the night chatting to him while her friends
talked to his team mates.

'Dance with me, Angel.' Ethan stood up and held
out his hand, clearly expecting her to take him up
on the offer, but Angel shook her head. 'I'm going
to stay here. You go, you can't disappoint the
ladies.'

Ethan looked torn. 'Okay, but you will dance
with me eventually, I know it.'

As he turned and walked towards the dance area
Angel watched him, enjoying the view of his tall
lean figure and broad shoulders for a few seconds,
smiling to herself as she imagined all the women
vying for his attention. Then she turned back to the
group.

Logan raised his eyebrows at her and said, 'Well,
I hope you realise, Angel, that you have one of the
most eligible bachelors in the States in the palm of
your hand.'

She laughed dismissively. 'Oh, come on! I bet
he's like that with all the women, giving them the
chat about how they're *the one*?'

Logan shook his head. 'No way, never. He's
always the one being pursued. I have never seen
him look at anyone or talk to another woman the
way he has with you tonight.'

Angel tried to laugh off the comments but actually she couldn't help feeling flattered or ignore the fact that her heart was beating just that little bit faster. She found herself scanning the club, wanting to see what Ethan was doing and who he was with. When she couldn't see him she decided to take a trip to the bathroom. She told herself that this was purely to prove that he would have moved on by now and forgotten all about her.

As she walked through the bar she noticed him sitting at a table in the corner surrounded by stunning LA girls. One gorgeous model type was even sitting on his knee, her arms wrapped possessively round his neck. *Ha, I knew it!* she thought. As she walked past, Angel couldn't resist blowing him a kiss. *Logan was clearly taking the piss, she'd meant nothing to Ethan.* She checked her make up in the mirror and was pleased to see that she still looked good, then she texted Cal again. She'd sent him several messages but heard nothing back. She hoped that meant he was out celebrating and having a good time, not that he was deliberately ignoring her.

As she left the bathroom Ethan was waiting for her, just outside.

'Are you missing me then? I know you deliber-ately walked past just to torture me,' he said.

Angel smiled and shook her head. Now Ethan moved closer to her, so that she was forced to move back against the wall and he was leaning over her – his strong arms to either side. There was something predatory about the move but also something exciting. She could smell his aftershave, a musky heady smell, and suddenly she wanted nothing more than to kiss this gorgeous man. Her head said no, but her treacherous body said something entirely different . . .

She turned away, anything to avoid those blue eyes, and said coolly, as if she wasn't having to fight a battle inside, as if she wasn't aware that her breasts were almost touching him, 'You were having a great time. I just needed to go to the bathroom.'

'Whatever you say, Angel,' Ethan replied huskily, in a way which indicated he didn't believe a word.

To break the sexual tension between them she quickly said, 'I'd really like a drink now, will you get me one?' Anything to get him to move away from her, she didn't think she could take being this close to him. At any minute her resolve to keep him at a distance could go up in flames.

Reluctantly he stepped back then said, 'I'm bored of this place. Why don't you and your friends come over to my beach house?' As if sensing that she was about to say no, he said, 'Come on, it's the least you can do, to mend my broken heart.'

What the hell? she thought. *Just one drink, then I'll go and never see him again.*

*

Since becoming famous and being with Cal, Angel had grown used to luxurious surroundings, to the finest restaurants and high-end hotels, but still Ethan's Santa Monica beach house took her breath away. For one thing there was the sheer size of it. Never mind house – mansion would have been a more accurate description. When they arrived the door was opened by a butler who showed them through to a vast living room which looked out on to the ocean. There more champagne was opened.

'Okay, who's for the hot tub?' Ethan said.

Angel looked at her friends – no way was she up for that. She might have guessed this would happen. Ethan and his friends probably thought their luck was in with the four of them coming back here. She looked meaningfully at the others who all looked as taken aback as she did.

Ethan saw their looks and laughed. 'I promise, it's nothing like you're thinking! If you follow Jose, he will show you to a dressing room where there is a selection of swimsuits at your disposal. We're talking hanging out in the hot tub, not an orgy . . . we had one of those last night! Besides, we know all you lovely ladies are spoken for.'

The girls burst out laughing and Angel, feeling reassured, said cheekily, 'Just how often do you have lady callers here? No, don't answer. I can imagine.'

*

'Oh my God! It's just like being in *Pretty Woman!*' Candy squealed excitedly, seeing the rows of brand new bikinis and costumes hanging in the wardrobe Jose had just opened in the upstairs dressing room.

'Meaning what exactly – we're hookers and Ethan is Richard Gere?' Angel said dryly, while secretly being as impressed as Candy was by the array of swimwear on display. She stood back, watching her friends picking out designer bikinis – Candy a pink one, Suki a black one and Madison a silver one. But tempting as the bikinis were she had something different in mind for herself and chose a red halterneck swimsuit.

'Angel, I can't believe you've chosen the most boring costume here!' Candy exclaimed in outrage. 'What about this gold one?' she cried, waving the skimpy two piece in front of Angel. 'It would look totally stunning on you.'

'It would barely cover my arse,' she shot back, and Madison said, 'Angel knows that Ethan is dying to see her in a teeny tiny bikini so she's going to keep him guessing about that gorgeous body of hers. You know what they say about treating them mean to keep them keen!'

'Madison!' Angel said in mock outrage. 'I don't know what you're talking about. Ethan's not interested in me!'

The three other girls collapsed in fits of giggles while Angel smiled, but she couldn't help feeling a

pang of guilt even though she hadn't done anything to feel guilty about, had she?

'Angel, that man's got it *so* bad for you,' Suki said,
slipping into her own bikini and checking out her
appearance in the floor-to-ceiling mirror. 'Just
enjoy tonight. You've done nothing to be worried
about, we're just having a laugh.'

But was that all she was doing? She was very attracted
to Ethan and this unsettled and excited her in
equal measure.

The others all changed more quickly than her.
Angel took her time, checking out her appearance
in the mirror. While the costume did cover her
more than a bikini, it was cut to show off her figure
to its best advantage, so there was plenty of cleavage
on show and most of her back. But the look was
sexy and not tarty, she thought. Then, furious with
herself for even caring how she looked, she
wrapped herself in a large fluffy white towel and
went downstairs.

Outside the others were already in the huge hot
tub, drinking yet more champagne, chatting and
laughing with the boys, but there was no sign of
Ethan. She walked past them, ignoring their
appeals for her to come in, and headed to the pool.
The turquoise water shimmered in the subtle
underwater lighting. It looked so inviting. She felt
like she needed to clear her head, remind herself of
who she was.

She quickly slipped off the towel, walked to the edge of the pool and dived in. The water was colder than she'd been expecting and she started swimming in an effortless front crawl to keep warm. She swam several lengths before she became aware of someone standing by the pool. It was Ethan. She swam to the side, smoothing back her hair and wiping the water from her eyes.

'I might have guessed you'd be a fantastic swimmer,' he said. 'Do you want to warm up in the hot tub?'

Angel laughed. 'That line sounds *so* corny, I bet you say that to all the girls?'

He shook his head. 'I can't win with you, can I?'

'No. But I will go in the hot tub, I'm bloody freezing!'

But if she was hoping for safety in numbers she was in for a surprise as the others had moved back inside the house. Angel was tempted to join them but then reasoned she was only *sitting* in a hot tub with Ethan. Once she was immersed in the pleasantly hot bubbling water, she couldn't resist looking at him as he took off his robe and climbed in after her. There was no getting away from it – he had a beautiful body with golden-brown skin and well-defined abs. He was bigger built than Cal. Bigger in all departments? she found herself wondering. *Shut up*! she told herself sternly. *I love my husband. I love everything about my husband, including his perfectly sized* – her thoughts were interrupted by Ethan.

'Would it be okay if I sat over here?' He indicated the opposite side of the tub. She nodded.

'So did I mention how sexy you look in that costume? But you know that, right? You must get compliments from men all the time.'

Angel smiled. 'I'm married, remember, so no, I don't.'

'Stop reminding me of that fact. You're tormenting me!'

'You can handle it,' Angel replied. 'You'll have forgotten all about me in the morning.'

Ethan frowned. 'Well, I hope your husband realises that he's one lucky guy to have you.'

Suddenly Angel's mood changed and any flirtatious thoughts she'd been having about Ethan vanished as she thought of the distance that had developed between her and Cal. She felt a lump rise in her throat and her eyes fill with tears. 'Actually things aren't great between us at the moment. I don't know if he even loves me anymore,' she said sadly.

'I'm sure he does,' Ethan said softly.

'It's all my fault. Since I had the baby I know I've pushed him away. I've not been there for him. I wouldn't blame him.' Suddenly the words that Angel had been holding back for so long came tumbling out and she couldn't stop herself. 'I've been so depressed. No one except my mum knows – I'm getting better now but I'm afraid I've lost Cal because of it.' *This was insane, what was she doing, confiding in a total stranger about her innermost feelings?* But she couldn't stop. The tears were streaming down her face.

Ethan moved next to her, put his arm round her.

'Hey, it's okay,' he said gently.

'It's not okay, Ethan. Everyone thinks I've got the perfect life and the perfect marriage, but I haven't – it's such a mess!'

Angel was so upset she didn't even care that he had his arm round her and they were sitting practically naked in a hot tub. There was a pause as if Ethan was considering his reply, then he said, 'Much as it's against my own interests to see you happily married, you've got to tell your husband how you've been feeling.'

'There's no way I can at the moment, he's got to focus on the tournament,' Angel replied.

'Well, as soon as it's finished, you must. And you've got nothing to be ashamed of, Angel. My sister suffered from depression a couple of years ago after her son was born, and she's doing great now. It's just an illness, it doesn't mean you're a bad person.'

'I bet no one's ever behaved like this with you before, have they?' she asked, struggling to regain her composure.

Ethan smiled. 'No one's come close.' He gazed at her then seemed to pull himself together. He took his arm off her shoulders and moved away from her. 'Can I get you another drink? Maybe some brandy?'

'No, I'm fine,' Angel replied, half relieved, half disappointed that he'd moved away.

'It's no problem, I'll just buzz Jose.'

And she watched in astonishment as he pressed a button by the hot tub.

'My God, you're so flash!' she exclaimed, wanting to forget her emotional outburst as Jose appeared seconds later ready to take the order.

Ethan shrugged. 'Not really. You should see some of the other players' pads. This is modest compared to theirs.'

'Oh, come on!' Angel protested. 'This is one of the most amazing . . . no, hang on . . . this is *the* most amazing house I have ever been in.'

'I'm glad you like it,' Ethan said softly. 'You'd be welcome here any time.'

Angel smiled. She was saved from having to answer by the reappearance of Jose with their drinks. She sipped her brandy and tried to avoid looking at Ethan. The fact that he'd just shown himself to be so sympathetic only made him more dangerous.

'Look over there,' he told her, pointing out to sea. 'Sunrise.'

Angel turned and saw the first barely there pink rays emerging in the sky. 'Beautiful.' Then she allowed herself to look back at Ethan, who was staring straight at her.

'Yes, you are.'

She shook her head. 'Don't say that, it's not true. And I know I look rough now, after crying and making a complete fool of myself.'

'Come on,' he said, standing up and holding out his hand. 'Let's go watch the sunrise on the beach.'

As they walked on the sand barefoot, Angel shivered despite the towelling robe Ethan had lent her. He moved closer and put his arm round her. She automatically moved away. 'Look, I'm only warming you up,' he said. 'I promise that's all. You've made it clear what your feelings are and I respect that.'

Angel relaxed and they carried on walking. The wide sandy beach was deserted, the sea calm, barely any waves rippling the surface. The sun was rising now, a ball of orange fire over the sea. It was a new day. They both stopped and watched. Then Angel found herself drawn to stare at Ethan. He looked breathtakingly handsome in the morning light.

'So is this what you do with all the women who come back?' she asked, trying to be light-hearted and break the spell, to stop herself obsessing over him. 'I'm guessing champagne, hot tub, sex and a walk on the beach?'

Ethan grimaced. 'Right activities, wrong order.'

'Okay, sex, champagne, hot tub and walk?'

'I'd have them in any order you want.' And now Ethan was gazing at her and he was leaning down and his lips were on hers, and they were kissing, a hard, deep kiss, and she couldn't deny that she wanted him . . . But then reality hit her. *What the hell was she doing?* She pulled away and ran back along the beach, ignoring him calling out her name, back to the house, back to safety.

Everyone was in the dining room eating the breakfast Jose and his staff had just rustled up for them when Angel came racing in, out of breath, feeling almost hysterical.

'Are you okay?' Candy asked. 'Do you want something to eat?'

Angel shook her head. 'I'm going to get changed and then I must go.'

She turned and ran upstairs to the dressing room where she quickly pulled off the costume and put on her dress. *What had she been thinking? She had to get back to the hotel, back to Honey, back to her life. She was married; this whole night had been madness.* But all the time her mind was racing along those lines she was remembering that kiss.

Downstairs Ethan hadn't joined the others at the dining table. Angel sat next to Candy and poured herself a cup of tea. She was freezing now. Then she felt warm material sliding over her shoulders.

She turned and there was Ethan, gently wrapping a gold pashmina round her. She opened her mouth to speak but he said, 'Jose will drive you back when you're ready. I have to go now, I have a plane to catch.' Then he bent down and whispered so that only she could hear, 'I hope I see you again, Angel.'

Then everyone was thanking him and saying their goodbyes. Angel watched him walk out of the room. In the doorway he turned for a moment and their eyes locked. Then he gave a last smile and was gone.

'That was a totally awesome night!' Candy said, giving a huge yawn as she collapsed on to the back seat of the limo.

'It was quite a night,' Angel agreed quietly, still feeling totally shaken up by her outburst and by what had followed. 'I've said that any time the guys are over in England with their girlfriends they're welcome to come and stay at mine and Liam's,' Candy continued.

Oh, God, Angel thought, not knowing if she could handle seeing Ethan *ever* again. For the rest of the journey back to the hotel the girls were quiet. Everyone was exhausted. All Angel wanted to do was crawl into bed. She felt like she'd been on an emotional roller-coaster – the high of Cal's winning goal, the breakdown in front of Ethan, and then that kiss – she felt all over the place. She was the last to get out of the limo and as she did so Jose pressed a card into her hand. 'Mr Taylor wanted you to have this, ma'am.'

For a moment Angel hesitated, knowing it was Ethan's number. It would be better never to see or speak to him again, but then she found herself saying, 'Thank you,' and slipping the card into her bag.

It was seven a.m. by the time they arrived back at the hotel. Angel hoped they would be able to sneak into the hotel unobserved but as soon as they stepped out of the car they were surrounded by paps clicking away. *Great, this was all she needed, to be photographed looking like a complete wreck.* Keeping their heads down, the girls ran past the photographers and into the lobby but as they did so one pap shouted out: 'Good night, was it, girls? Do your husbands know you've just spent the night with the LA Dodgers?'

Angel felt like she'd been punched in the stomach. *How did they know?*

'Shut up!' Madison shouted back furiously. 'We went to a club, that's all.'

'And on to Ethan Taylor's pad, didn't you? What did you do all night then, fill them in about the beautiful game? He's got quite a reputation.'

Candy was about to retaliate this time but Angel grabbed her arm and whispered, 'Just leave it, it's worse if you answer back.'

Safely inside the lobby the girls said their goodbyes and Angel made her way wearily to her suite.
Honey had just woken up and even though Angel
was absolutely wiped out she made herself stay up
and have breakfast with her daughter. Just being
with her, watching Honey's delight as she crammed
strawberries into her mouth and squashed them on
the table of her highchair, made some of Angel's
anxiety about last night subside. It was just a kiss,
that had been all. And after the tournament she
would confide in Cal about how bad she'd been
feeling.

After breakfast she played with Honey until total
exhaustion won and she was forced to admit defeat
and go to bed. 'I'll just have a couple of hours'
sleep, then I'll take over. It's not fair to leave you in
charge all this time,' she told the nanny.

'No worries,' Lucy said breezily. 'You deserved to
let your hair down last night. Stay in bed as long as
you want. Honey and I are fine, aren't we?' And she
swept Honey up in her arms and made her giggle.

'Thanks, Lucy, I really appreciate that.'

Just before she went to sleep Angel checked her
messages. There was still nothing from Cal. She
sighed and then texted him: *Hope you had a good
celebration last night, you deserve it. Love you x*. And
then something made her open her bag and reach
for the card Jose had given her. It had Ethan's
phone numbers on it. She turned it over and there

was a handwritten note from Ethan: *'If you ever need me, I'll always be here for you . . . I'll never forget you x.'*

Angel tried to ignore the tingle of excitement that the thought of Ethan provoked and slipped the card into the back pocket of her bag. She wasn't quite strong enough to throw it away. She curled up under the duvet. She'd see Cal soon and then she'd try and put things right between them. That was all that mattered.

Chapter 8

The Fall Out

Angel was woken by her mobile ringing. Feeling completely disorientated she fumbled for it on the bedside cabinet. 'Hello,' she said groggily, still half asleep.

'You'd better have a fucking good explanation for last night.' It was Cal and his voice was like ice.

'What are you talking about?' Angel sat up in bed.

'You spending the night with Ethan Taylor! What the fuck's going on?' he shouted.

'Please, Cal, calm down. It's not what you think. I went out with the girls last night and we did meet some baseball players but it was completely innocent, we just had a laugh with them.'

'I can't do this over the phone, I'm coming to see you. Jesus Christ, I can't *believe* you would do this to me! There are apparently pictures of you getting into a car with Taylor and you look totally pissed!'

'Please, Cal, you're making this out to be something it's not – talk to Reece and to Liam – I bet they're not reacting like this.'

'That's because their wives haven't been photographed leaving Taylor's house first thing in the morning!'

'But they were with me as well!' Angel protested.

'Yeah, right, I'll see you later.' Cal ended the call.

Angel sat there for a few minutes, too stunned to think straight. It was obvious that the press had been following them last night and had come up with their own explanation for what had happened. Apart from the kiss, she hadn't done anything wrong. But, oh God, what about the kiss? Could anyone have seen them? Why had she done it? To risk her whole marriage for a kiss with a stranger . . . what had possessed her? She looked at her watch. It was eleven, she'd been asleep for three hours. She was desperate to talk to the other girls, find out what their husbands had said to them. She quickly showered and got dressed, then raced round to Madison's suite.

She had to knock loudly for a good few minutes before Madison opened the door in her PJs, looking bleary-eyed with sleep.

'Can I come in? I really need to talk to you,' Angel said urgently.

''Course, babe, what's happened?'

After Angel had filled her in, trying as hard as she

could not to cry, Madison exclaimed, 'Bollocks!' and rifled through her bag for her mobile. 'I've got a message from Reece.' She quickly read it then said, 'Well, he knows we went out last night and met up with some lads but he's not bothered. I'll call him now and tell him to have a word with Cal. He just needs to calm down. The press took that picture to make it look like you were on your own just to get a better story. Cal will understand, I'm sure.'

'Shall I go while you speak to him?' Angel asked anxiously.

'No, stay here. I'm going to make you a cup of tea after I've spoken to Reece, you look terrible.'

'I'll make the tea,' Angel insisted but her hands were shaking so much she couldn't even work out how to switch the kettle on. Madison put her arm round her and gently steered her back to the sofa then made the call.

Angel hugged her knees to her; she wanted to make herself as small as possible, as if somehow that would make everything all right again. Madison talked to her husband. Clearly he thought her drinking with a group of lads was no big deal. On the contrary, he seemed impressed that his wife had met such famous sportsmen.

'So will you tell Cal to chill out? Angel didn't go to Ethan Taylor's house on her own, we were all with her, all the time.' She listened to her husband's reply and said, 'Okay, babes, love you loads too.'

Then she turned to Angel. 'It's done, he's going to speak to Cal. Reece'll get him to calm down, don't worry.'

'Thanks so much, Madison,' Angel said gratefully. Half of her longed to confide in her friend about what she'd told Ethan about her marriage and about the kiss, but the other half thought she'd already given far too much away. She wanted to go and find Honey but Madison insisted she have a cup of tea first and she put three sugars in it.

'Cal is just wound up because of the tournament. I bet he'll call you in a bit to apologise.'

Angel nodded and sipped her tea, but she doubted it. Cal could be very stubborn.

'Shall we go in the water again, Honey?' Angel asked her daughter as they hung out by the pool. She'd left several messages for Cal but his phone had been switched off. Madison assured her that Reece had spoken to him and told him what had happened and that he'd seemed cool with it. But because she hadn't spoken to him herself, Angel had a niggling feeling of unease that things still weren't right.

She and Honey were just playing in the shallow end of the pool when Simone sauntered by, looking overdressed for the poolside in a white trouser suit.

'Good night was it, Angel? I hear you got on very

well with Ethan Taylor. Apparently he goes for blonde slutty types so you must have been right up his street.'

Angel was tempted to tell her to fuck off but as her daughter was by her side she restrained herself, muttering, 'You don't know what you're talking about, as usual.'

'Well, Cal can't have been too pleased to discover that his wife had been flirting . . . and who knows what else?'

'Cal was fine about it because he knows there's nothing to be upset about,' Angel said through gritted teeth. *God, she loathed Simone.*

'Well, why don't we ask him?' Simone continued.

'What are you talking about?' Angel said angrily, seriously losing her cool with the woman. But when she turned round, to her astonishment she saw Cal. He was marching towards her, wearing a dark suit, dark glasses and a furious expression.

'Oh, hi, Cal.' Simone simpered. 'We were just talking about you.'

He grimaced and said, 'If you'll excuse me, Simone, I need to see my wife.'

'Of course, Cal, I understand you must have things to discuss,' she said slyly, sauntering off.

'What are you doing here?' Angel asked.

'Get out of the pool and come upstairs,' Cal said in a low voice, without even bothering to say hello to her. 'Lucy will be here in a minute to take Honey.'

'Hang on a minute, Cal,' Angel replied angrily, 'you can't order me around like this! What's the matter with you?' All the WAGs round the pool were riveted by this scene and practically licking their lips in anticipation of more.

'I am not going to discuss this in public, so will you get out of the pool and come upstairs?' he insisted.

Very reluctantly Angel picked up Honey and climbed out of the water. By now Lucy had turned up and, after Cal had hugged and kissed his daughter, he handed Honey to the nanny. Angel slowly picked up her robe and put it on, hating that Cal was telling her what to do and aware that every single WAG's eye was trained beadily on the two of them.

She waited until they were in the hotel foyer and then tried to speak to him again. 'What's going on?'

But Cal shook his head and muttered, 'I'm not saying anything until we get to our suite.'

As they travelled up in the lift together Angel looked at him but he still had his dark glasses on and she couldn't see his eyes. She lightly touched his arm and said, 'Your goal was amazing, I'm so proud of you.'

Cal flinched at her touch and said, 'I wish I could say the same about you.'

The lift doors opened and he stepped out and

walked swiftly to their suite while Angel trailed along behind him, reeling inside at the cruelty of his words. Ahead Cal flung open the door and by the time Angel caught up with him had taken off his dark glasses and was standing in the centre of the room with his arms folded. She shut the door and stared back at him.

'I want to know exactly what happened last night between you and Ethan Taylor,' he said coldly.

'What do you think happened?' Angel challenged him. 'I can't believe how quick you are to assume that I've done something wrong. Do you seriously think I shagged him? Because if you do this marriage is pretty much over, wouldn't you say?' The words were pouring out of Angel. She wasn't able to think straight, she felt so hurt by Cal's treatment of her.

'I want to know what happened,' he repeated.

Angel sighed. 'I know Reece has already told you.'

'I want to hear it from you,' Cal repeated. 'Do you know how humiliated I feel? Everyone thinks you spent the night with some baseball player.'

'I was out with Madison, Suki and Candy and we met up with these four players from the LA Dodgers. We were having a laugh, celebrating the England win,' Angel said wearily.

'Couldn't you just have celebrated with the girls?'

Angel rolled her eyes. 'They asked us to join

them for a drink, that's all! Then we went to a club, then on to Ethan's beach house for a few more drinks, had breakfast, came home, the end.' She walked over to Cal and reached out to touch him. 'Please don't be like this.'

'And I suppose you'd love it if I went off with four gorgeous women and spent the night getting pissed with them? You're a mother now, did you think about that? And you're my wife! I don't expect you to behave like some slapper on a hen night.'

'Fuck off, Cal!' Angel shouted. 'I did *not* behave like a slapper! Ask anyone who was there. And how dare you bring up Honey? I knew she was safe with Lucy.'

She couldn't believe he was being like this. He was never usually so jealous. *God, did he know about the kiss? Should she tell him? Confess that she had made one stupid mistake?*

'I don't know *what* to think,' Cal shouted back. 'You've been so different lately – never wanting to make love, leaving me in Italy when I really could have done with you there. Sometimes I think you don't love me anymore.'

'Cal, how can you say that!' Angel exclaimed, rushing over to him. '*You're* the one who's turned away from *me*. I know things haven't been easy between us . . .' And she knew that this was the time she had to tell him the truth about her feelings. 'I haven't been well. I didn't want to tell you because of the tournament.'

She stood there looking at him, waiting for him to react, to show sympathy, but he kept his arms folded and still looked angry.

'What do you mean? You seem fine,' Cal shot back at her. 'You're well enough to go out partying, aren't you? Well enough to flirt and Christ knows what else with another man.'

Angel sighed despairingly. He was not making this easy for her. 'Actually, I've been depressed since Honey was born.'

'What do you mean – depressed? You've got everything you could possibly want.' Cal was shaking his head in denial. Angel couldn't believe how hard he was being. She tried again.

'I've been ill. I went to see the doctor and he says I've got post-natal depression. Please understand, I'm not making this up, I'm on medication.'

He shook his head again. 'I don't believe you're loading this on me now! I've got the quarter final tomorrow.' And he went and slumped down on the sofa, head in his hands.

Angel stood rooted to the spot for a few seconds, completely stunned by this reaction, by his total lack of sympathy. Then she went and sat on the opposite end of the sofa. Somehow she had to get through to him.

'Please don't be like this, Cal. I didn't want to tell

you now but I had to, surely you can see that?'
She was pleading with him and couldn't help
comparing Ethan's sympathetic reaction to Cal's.
Her own husband didn't seem to give a shit about
her.

'Angel, I can't deal with this right now,' he
replied, his head still in his hands. 'You really pick
your moments, don't you?'

She was about to reply that she'd had no choice
when Cal's mobile rang. He groaned. 'I'd better get
this in case it's Phil. He's bound to be furious that
I've come here.'

Within seconds of taking the call his face
hardened. 'What do you mean?' he shouted down
the phone. 'Are you absolutely certain?' He threw
down his phone and turned to Angel. 'So when
were you going to tell me about kissing Ethan . . .
and the rest?' He was furious, spitting out the
words, leaning over her as she cowered back into
the sofa – she had never seen Cal this angry
before.

'And before you try and talk your way out of it, a
pap got a picture of you both! Jesus, this just gets
worse!'

'I'm not going to deny it, I'm really sorry,' Angel
said quietly. 'But it was only a kiss, it didn't mean
anything. I was upset and—'

'What else did you do?' Cal snapped

She shook her head and whispered, 'Nothing.'

241

'I don't believe you. You screwed him, didn't you? All this talk about post-natal depression is just to throw me off the scent. You haven't got it. You're just lying . . .'

'Cal, please, I made a mistake and I'm really sorry. But you have to believe me that nothing else happened, nothing at all. I swear.' She went to touch his arm but he leaped off the sofa, shouting, 'Don't fucking touch me! I trusted you and you've betrayed me.'

'I know how you must feel but please don't say that,' Angel begged him. She couldn't believe that this was happening. She had thought that by being honest with him about her feelings everything would be put right between them. Instead, she had ruined their lives.

Cal was pacing the room again, struggling to contain his anger. 'I want you to go home tonight. I want you away from the tournament. I don't want to see you until it's finished. I'm going to call my agent and get him to book a flight back for you, Honey and Lucy. I can't be near you at the moment.'

'Oh, Cal, can't we work this out? *Please*. I don't want to fly home without you,' Angel cried out.

'You've got to. The story about you and Ethan will be in tomorrow's press and it would be best for everyone if you weren't around. You've done enough damage.'

And before Angel had chance to plead with him again to change his mind, he'd marched towards the door, pausing there to say, 'I can't believe what's happened to our marriage.'

And then he left her. For a few minutes Angel just sat there, completely shell-shocked, until the full force of her husband's words hit her and she collapsed sobbing on to the sofa.

She lost all track of time. She felt as if her heart was being torn apart. She was losing Cal, the love of her life, and she couldn't bear it. Angel gradually became aware of a gentle knocking at the door. She ignored it at first but then she heard Madison call her name and somehow found the strength to drag herself over to the door.

'Angel, I've just seen Cal. Are you all right, babe?' Madison said, looking shocked at the state of her.

'No, I'm not,' she sobbed. 'Cal's going to leave me, and all because I was so stupid! I kissed Ethan and I shouldn't have and now I've ruined everything.'

'Oh, babe,' Madison sighed, hugging her. 'You made a mistake. Cal will come round, I know he will, it's just his pride won't let him at the moment.'

'He wants me to go home, Madison. It's like he wants to cut me out of his life.'

'He doesn't, he's just hurt and angry. I know you two can work this out. Just do as he says for now and then when the tournament's over you can talk calmly.'

Angel very much doubted it, but she nodded and let Madison organise the packing. She felt too drained to do anything herself. Cal returned to the room briefly with the flight details but he refused to talk to Angel, handing the documents to Madison instead and asking if she would see that they all got to the airport safely. And then he was gone.

The rest of the day and the flight home passed in a blur for Angel. Madison insisted on her taking some Valium to get her through the trip home and Angel slept most of the way while Lucy looked after Honey. There had been no press at LAX airport but at Gatwick they were out in force, shouting and jostling and pushing to get their shots of Angel. As soon as she walked through Arrivals, pushing Honey in her buggy, she was surrounded. Flashes were going off right in her face and in Honey's.

'What's going on, Angel?' 'Have you split with Cal then?' 'Tell us about Ethan Taylor,' came the shouts.

Honey was terrified. She was crying but the paps didn't seem to give a shit that they were upsetting a child. Angel struggled past the cameras to lift her daughter from her pushchair and try and shield her face. And then, thank God, she saw Ray, the guy who looked after security for her and Cal. With two of his security guards he was muscling his way to the front, pushing the photographers out of the way to clear a path for Angel, Lucy and Honey.

'I heard about what happened,' Ray said in his gruff Brighton accent. 'And I thought you might appreciate a bit of help.'

'Thanks,' Angel said gratefully, cradling her daughter in her arms. She just wanted to get away from here, away from the cameras flashing in her face, away from the questions.

'Your mum and dad wanted to come too but I said it would be better if they met you at home,' Ray said as he escorted her through the airport.

In the hours that had passed since her argument with Cal, all Angel had been able to think about was her husband, but now she suddenly realised that everyone she knew was going to have an opinion on what had happened. There was going to be no escape for her.

The next week was the worst of Angel's life. The press were camped outside her house and she couldn't go anywhere without being followed. Cal still wouldn't speak to her. England were knocked out of the tournament, but instead of returning home like the rest of the team, Cal texted her to say that he had some things to sort out in Italy.

Ethan tried to contact her via her agent to check that she was okay – the American press had also got hold of the story because he was such a huge star. But Angel couldn't bring herself to speak to him or anyone for that matter. She was devastated – convinced that her marriage was over.

Only her love for Honey got her out of bed every morning, otherwise she would just have lain there all day. Her mum and dad were constant visitors, trying to cheer her up and tell her that everything would be all right. She had been wrong to think they would take Cal's side. Even her dad, who could be judgemental, told her that Cal would see sense in a while. Angel could have done with Gemma's advice, but she was in Dubai on a shoot and barely had time to speak to her on the phone. And even though Angel had been to the doctor's and he had diagnosed her with post-natal depression she started to doubt herself, to wonder whether Cal was right, that she had been making it up. Perhaps, after all, she was just a really bad person?

She stopped taking her medication and felt herself sliding once more back into depression. It was strange but she almost welcomed it, thinking that she deserved to feel like this. At night when she was on her own she would be gripped with the darkest, most deeply negative thoughts, and obsess about how she must be a bad mother, a worthless person, and now a terrible wife.

By the weekend Angel was feeling more and

more desperate. She arranged for Lucy to take Honey out for the day, needing to be on her own. As soon as they'd left she tried phoning Cal again, and for the first time in nearly a week he answered.

'Thank God!' she exclaimed at the sound of his voice. 'I've been calling you all week.'

'I know,' he replied coldly. 'I didn't phone you back because I had nothing to say to you.'

'Please, Cal, come home and we can talk. I want to explain about my illness, I want you to understand.'

'What's there to understand? You had a baby, felt your life had changed, were a bit dissatisfied, couldn't cope with the fact I was facing the biggest challenge of my playing career so you went off and shagged some baseball player. It's game over, Angel.'

'Cal, I can't believe that you're saying these things, they're just not true! I have been ill and I did not sleep with Ethan – I would never be unfaithful.' Angel's eyes were blurring with tears, she was so wounded by his words.

'Whatever,' he said wearily.

'Please come home,' Angel begged him. 'Please, I love you, don't leave me.'

'I just don't know anymore, Angel, I really don't,' was Cal's answer before he hung up.

Angel let her mobile slip from her hand to the floor as she got up and blindly walked from room to room, saying to herself again and again, 'It's over, I've lost him.' By the time she walked into the bathroom she was sobbing hysterically. She couldn't imagine life without Cal, she just couldn't. In a daze she opened the bathroom cabinet and picked up the bottle of strong painkillers Cal kept for the times when his knee was bothering him. She unscrewed the lid and stared at the white tablets – at last, something to take the pain away. She had wrecked her marriage, she was a terrible mother, both Cal and Honey would be better off without her . . .

'Angel, can you hear me, love? Please wake up, Angel.' From a distance she could hear her mum's voice calling her. Michelle sounded desperately worried. Angel tried to reply but she was locked in a deep, deep dream. She couldn't wake up. Her mum called her again. This time her voice seemed closer. With what felt like an immense effort, Angel half opened her eyes.

'Angel! Are you okay?'

She gingerly turned her head and tried to speak but her throat was so sore she could only croak, 'Mum, where am I? Where's Honey?' Her head was pounding and her stomach hurt as if she'd been punched.

Her mum gripped her hand tightly and was clearly trying to fight back tears. 'You're in hospital, love. You took an overdose. But you're going to be all right, we're all going to help you get better.'

Angel shook her head and whispered, 'I'm such a failure, Mum. Everything's gone wrong. Maybe it would have been better if you hadn't found me.'

'Don't say that!' Her mother looked distraught, her usually pretty features tense with anxiety.

'Cal thinks I've made up the depression. He doesn't love me anymore, Mum.' Realisation of what she'd done was coming back to her, and the physical pain was nothing to remembering that Cal didn't want her anymore. The tears streamed down her cheeks.

'That's not true! He loves you and he believes you. He's at the airport now waiting for a flight home. I'm going to ring him.' Michelle dialled Cal's number from the hospital phone by Angel's bed; she spoke briefly to him and then handed the receiver over, saying that she would be back in a few minutes.

'Angel, are you all right?' Cal sounded frantic with worry.

'I'm sorry,' she whispered back.

'Oh, my God, Angel, you've got nothing to be sorry for! It's me who's sorry, for not believing you. I was so jealous and stupid and I nearly lost you because of it. Can you ever forgive me?'

'So you're not going to leave me?' she asked tentatively.

'Angel, I'm on my way back to you and I'm going to do whatever it takes to help you get better. Nothing else matters to me. Nothing. I love you.'

'Love you too,' Angel replied, and for the first time in what seemed like a very long time she felt the beginning of something like hope.

Chapter 9

Playing Away

Six months later – New Year's Eve

'D'you want some more champagne?' Cal asked, sitting up in bed and reaching for the bottle.

'No!' Angel exclaimed, grabbing his arm, and pulling him back down beside her. 'I want more of you!'

Cal laughed as he took her in his arms again. 'This is more knackering than a match!'

'Are you turning me down then?' she demanded, running her hands over his hard, muscular body.

'Never,' he said huskily, kissing first her neck then the rest of her body, delicious sweet kisses that melted her . . .

Finally she and Cal were back to where they had been before post-natal depression had nearly destroyed Angel and her marriage. It hadn't been a quick fix – she'd been having therapy and was still taking medication. Even now she had times when she felt low, and others when she was almost crippled with guilt about her daughter and those early months of her life when Angel felt she hadn't bonded with her as she should. But those times were getting fewer, the more she felt like her old self. From the moment Cal had flown back from Milan to be at her side he'd taken her illness seriously and never brought up the Ethan incident again, telling her that he understood it had been a one off mistake because she had been ill. And he stopped being so distant with her, telling her that it had only been the pressure of the World Cup that had made him so withdrawn and that was over now.

She had also confided in him about Connor's threesome proposition and his pursuit of her. Connor had continued to send her gifts even though Angel had sent everything back. Cal had been absolutely furious to hear of it and had threatened to confront Connor. Tempting as that prospect had been, Angel had begged him not to. And anyway she had been right to think she only had to wait: the Carters did get their comeuppance in the press when a lapdancer who had taken them up on their offer sold her story. It had filled the tabloids for most of the autumn as so many other women had come out of the woodwork with further sleazy revelations. There were even rumours about the wife of another England player who had been propositioned by the Carters. Angel didn't think anything of it, though; she hadn't said anything to the press and Jez promised her he hadn't. The chances were Gabrielle had pimped for Connor many times in the past, desperate to hang on to her husband whatever the cost. The pair of them had got what they deserved as far as Angel was concerned.

Now, as she lay in Cal's arms, after an afternoon of making love, she thought she was a very lucky girl indeed. Cal had whisked her away to Venice for a romantic weekend – just the two of them, to celebrate New Year. He'd booked them into the luxurious five-star Gritti Palace Hotel, where they'd spent her birthday two years earlier, in a fabulous suite overlooking the Grand Canal with an amazing view of the city. So far they'd spent most of the time in bed, but Angel wasn't complaining . . . It was as if they both wanted to make up for lost time, and she couldn't get enough of her gorgeous, sexy husband nor he of her.

'Do you want to go out for dinner tonight?' Cal asked her.

Suddenly Angel realised she was starving. They'd only had breakfast and it was now around seven in the evening.

'We could have room service here or we could go out. I've booked us a table at a restaurant nearby.

253

It's supposed to be very good. And we could start off with Bellinis at Harry's Bar, if you like?'

Angel stretched out in bed, looking round their suite with its beautiful antique furniture, the cream and gold silk curtains, the elaborately carved and gilded bed head, that made her feel like a princess. It was very tempting to stay in. But then she thought of the effort Cal had gone to in choosing the restaurant and said, 'We'll go out as you've booked it,' kissing him and thinking what a sweet and generous husband she had.

Outside the temperature was only just above freezing and she was grateful for her full-length black sheepskin coat and hat.

'You look like a sexy Bond girl. It makes me wonder what you've got on under that coat,' Cal said cheekily, putting his arm round her as the two of them strolled through the narrow streets, crossing over the canals by elegant stone bridges.

Angel laughed. 'Thermal underwear – I wish!'

Cal kissed her and murmured, 'I have ways of warming you up.'

'Later,' she told him, kissing him back. 'I'm going to faint if I don't eat something soon.'

The restaurant was as fantastic as Cal had promised, the food delicious. Angel had never had to worry about her weight. She tended to eat what she wanted and work out to compensate. None of that dressing-free salad, egg whites and green tea regime for her! She ordered scallops to start with followed by lobster risotto, and ate the lot.

'I'm stuffed!' she declared at the end of her main course.

'You've got to have dessert,' Cal told her.

Angel groaned, 'No way, I can't eat anything else!'

'Go on, I'll share one with you.'

'Okay,' she replied. 'But you've got to eat most of it, and you'd better love me when I'm fat!'

Cal smiled at her. 'I'll always love you and you'll never be fat.'

'But if I was?' she teased him back.

'I'd make you work out more,' Cal replied, and they both laughed. She could still remember what it felt like when he was so angry with her in America. Now all she wanted to do was to bask in the warmth of his love. They drank more wine and Angel allowed Cal to choose a dessert. She didn't pay much attention when the waiter placed it before her as she had no intention of eating it. It was some kind of fancy chocolate torte with a white chocolate rose on top. She pushed the plate towards Cal.

'Go on, you have it, I really can't eat anymore.'

'Aren't you at least going to have the rose? You love white chocolate,' Cal said.

'Have you turned into one of those weird pervs

who feed up their women so much that they can't move?' Angel demanded.

'The rose,' Cal insisted.

She reached out and plucked the chocolate flower from the torte . . . then she froze because nestling inside the chocolate petals was a dazzling diamond eternity ring. She picked it up and as she did so the diamonds sparkled as they caught the light.

'Oh.My.God!' she exclaimed, totally enchanted by the gift.

'You like it?' Cal asked. 'There's an inscription inside.'

She read, '*Angel, you are my world, I am nothing without you. Yours forever, Cal x.*'

'It's stunning,' she whispered as he took the ring from her and slipped it on to her finger.

'I want us to renew our vows, Angel. I want to make up to you for everything I put you through in the summer. So will you?'

Angel looked at her husband whose eyes were full of tears. 'Oh, Cal, yes! Yes!' And she leaned across the table and kissed him passionately, not caring about the raised eyebrows of the other diners.

Back home in England they decided to renew their vows as soon as possible and settled on 31 January. They could have waited until later in the year but neither of them wanted to. It had to be as soon as possible. 'I want to put the bad times behind us,' Cal told her and Angel couldn't have agreed more. Neither of them wanted a big event – it was just to be family and very close friends with no more than thirty guests, in contrast to their wedding day when they'd had over two hundred.

Angel was so happy. It felt as if she and Cal had been given a second chance once the dark cloud of her depression had well and truly lifted. She could get on with her life. Now, when she woke up in the morning, the day felt like a gift, full of possibilities. So different from the way she had felt six months ago.

'You've got mail,' said Cal, wandering into the living room where Angel was playing with Honey. There were just three weeks to go until their big day and she was about to drive to London for her dress fitting so was enjoying some quality time with her daughter. Cal handed over the post and Angel casually flicked through the pile of letters, seeing if anything looked interesting.

Her attention was taken by a hot pink envelope – probably an invitation to some event or other. She ripped it open. Inside was a postcard, and written in elaborate gold writing the words: '*Angel . . . or should I say bitch, whore, tart? One day, very soon, you are going to pay.*'

'That's nice,' she said sarcastically, showing the card to Cal. 'I like that they've used my favourite colour, don't you?'

Cal frowned. He hated it when Angel received threatening letters, which she had several times in the past. She was about to tear it up when he stopped her.

'Give it to me. I'll put it in my office, and if you get anymore we should go to the police.'

'If you like,' she replied. 'It'll just be some jealous nutter, don't worry about it. I don't.'

And with that she kissed her husband and daughter goodbye and headed out of the door. The contents of the letter were already forgotten as she thought of the day ahead, and wondered how the dress she was having made for her vows would have turned out. She wanted something simple and understated in complete contrast to her full on wedding dress, and just hoped the designer would have worked her magic.

'What do you think?' Angel asked Gemma, turning round and studying herself in the mirror of the boutique. The dress was an exquisitely elegant ivory silk gown, off the shoulder, and fitted to display Angel's sensational curves.

'I think it's stunning!' Gemma exclaimed, walking round her friend and checking out the dress from every angle.

'You do think Cal will like it, don't you?' Angel asked.

'Definitely. It's going to knock him out. Especially as I reckon he thinks you're going to wear pink!'

'Ha!' Angel replied. 'Serve him right for thinking I'm predictable. Do you know what he's going to wear?'

Gemma shook her head. 'And even if I did, I wouldn't tell you, it would so ruin the surprise.'

Conversation was then restricted as the designer expertly checked the fit of the dress. Angel stared at her reflection. *Gemma was right, Cal would like this dress, wouldn't he?*

After the fitting the girls headed for Patisserie Valerie in the heart of Soho, for a gossip and a hot chocolate. Angel surveyed the cream on top of hers and frowned. 'Oops, maybe I should have skipped this! That dress is very clingy, isn't it?'

Gemma rolled her eyes. 'You're so jammy, you never put on weight.'

'I don't know about that,' Angel answered, scooping out the cream from the top of her drink with a spoon and then eating it. 'I'll do extra sit ups to make up for it.' She looked up at her friend and smiled. 'I'm so excited about doing our vows again, Gemma, even more excited than I was for my wedding day.'

She paused and then said reflectively, 'I think it's

because I feel so good now and I was so depressed back then. But I'm back to my old self, aren't I, Gem?'

Her friend smiled back. 'Yes, you are.' And then her face fell. 'But I still feel so guilty that I didn't pick up on your depression. You must promise me that if you ever feel like that again, you'll tell me? We've never had secrets from each other before.'

'I know, Gem, and I never want it to happen again either.'

'And now I have got a secret to tell you!' Gemma said, her eyes shining.

Angel stared at her, willing her to say the words, and was thrilled when Gemma went on to say, 'Yes, I'm pregnant!' Her face looked radiant with happiness, though she quickly added, 'It's very early days. I don't want to tell anyone else, not even Jez.'

Angel jumped out of her chair and hugged Gemma. 'I'm so happy for you, Gem! That's the best news ever!' Then she asked, 'Can I tell Cal? You know that he wouldn't tell anyone else.'

Gemma nodded and Angel hugged her friend again.

By the time she arrived back home, Cal was busy giving Honey her tea. Angel took a few seconds to stand in the doorway and watch the domestic scene playing out in front of her. Cal was chatting away to

Honey, giving funny names to the food on her plate to encourage her to eat it. He was such a good dad and Honey was being so adorable. Angel felt a wave of happiness go through her then. She was so lucky to have Cal and Honey, so totally blessed. She raced over to where they were sitting, showering kisses on both of them.

'Hey, what's all this?' Cal asked, putting his arms round her waist and pulling her on to his lap. 'I think Mummy missed us, Honey.'

She grinned and took the chance to throw a broccoli floret on the floor. Good call, Angel thought, loathing broccoli herself.

'I did miss you both,' she said, putting her arms round Cal and kissing him. 'Very much.'

'Good,' he replied, kissing her back. Then he turned to their daughter and said, 'Okay, Honey, finish up then we'll watch *In the Night Garden*. After that it's bath, story and bed. I need to spend some grown-up time with Mummy.'

Later that night as the couple lay in bed, entwined in each other's arms after their grown-up time, Angel murmured, 'I'm so happy, Cal. I can't wait to renew our vows.'

'Me either,' he agreed, raising her hand to his lips and kissing it.

'And Gemma told me some fantastic news as well,' Angel exclaimed. 'She's pregnant!'

'That's great! And maybe,' here Cal paused, 'in a

couple of years, we can think about having another baby? What do you say? I don't want to put any pressure on you but I'd love us to have another child. You and Honey are the best things that have ever happened to me.'

'You just want a son!' Angel teased him. 'A mini footballing you!'

Cal grinned. 'I wouldn't mind what we had. And anyway, if we had another girl, we could just try for a boy for our third.'

'I'm sure in a couple of years I'll be ready, but just for now I want to enjoy our little family as it is. I feel like we've been through so much,' she replied, snuggling against him.

And although the thought of having another child made her anxious because she felt she'd only just got over her post-natal depression, it excited her too, the thought of her life and Cal's carried into the future by their children.

'Are you sure I look okay?' Angel asked anxiously, facing her two friends. Gemma, Jez and she were installed in the bridal suite and Angel was just hours away from renewing her vows with Cal.

'You look beautiful,' Gemma reassured her. 'Really beautiful.'

The dress was as stunning as Angel had hoped. She wore no jewellery with it apart from her rings and a pair of diamond earrings. Gemma had done her make up as natural-looking as possible and Jez had styled her hair in an elegant French pleat that showed off Angel's graceful neck and shoulders.

'You look like Venus!' he declared. 'Only way slimmer, of course!'

'And you're sure Cal will like the dress?' Angel asked, for what must have been the tenth time already that day. She so wanted to impress him. Today was so special to her, she felt as if they were giving themselves to each other all over again. This was a fresh start for their marriage and she didn't want anything to go wrong.

'Oh.My.God!' Jez exclaimed. 'He is going to fall in love with you all over again, I guarantee it.'

'That's what I want!' she replied.

'We should have a glass of champagne. We've got time before you say "I do" again,' Jez added, reaching for a bottle of chilled Cristal.

Angel and Cal had chosen to renew their vows at a small stately home deep in the Sussex country-side. They had wanted to keep it a secret from the press – neither of them wanted to do a deal with a magazine and sell pictures of their special day. But unfortunately the press had got wind of it, and inevitably the couple had been forced to take security measures. Now, in the bridal suite, Jez poured the three of them a glass of champagne and he and Gemma toasted Angel.

'How are you feeling?' Gemma asked her friend.

'Amazing!' Angel told her. 'It's like me and Cal have been given a second chance. We've been through so much and we're still together. I just want to get up that aisle and tell him how much I love him! Because I really do, I love him so much!'

Both Gemma and Jez smiled at Angel's smiling, radiant face, and Jez said, 'I'm so pleased it's worked out for you both, babe.'

'So am I,' Gemma added, hugging Angel.

Just then there was a knock at the door and then Angel's mum walked in, holding Honey's hand. The little girl toddled unsteadily next to her, looking a total sweetie in a pale pink velvet dress with a wreath of pink roses on her head, black hair falling in shiny ringlets to her shoulders.

Straightaway Angel went over to her daughter and swept her up in her arms. 'Oh, Honey, you look so beautiful!' she cried. 'My little princess!'

Honey beamed, putting her arms round Angel's neck, and said, 'Mama lovee!' which was her way of saying 'lovely'.

'Thanks for getting her ready, Mum,' Angel said, turning to Michelle.

'It was a pleasure. We've had fun, haven't we, Honey? I just wanted to show you what she looked like. We'll see you downstairs.'

Angel put her daughter down and watched her toddle out of the room. When the door had closed behind them she exclaimed, 'I'm filling up now, just seeing Honey! Can you imagine what I'll be like during the ceremony? Promise me that mascara is waterproof, Gem?'

'And I never thought I would say this, Angel, but for the first time ever you've been upstaged by another girl – your daughter!' Jez declared. 'Did you see her working the room? She is going to be a stunner!'

'Well, so long as it's my daughter, I don't mind,' Angel replied. 'She can outshine me all she likes.'

Just then her phone vibrated with a text message. She wandered over to the dressing table and casually picked it up. It was from a withheld number which instantly made her wary as she was careful about who she gave her phone number to. But she opened it anyway.

In that moment everything changed for Angel. Shock pulsed through her as she read, *Do you know what your husband did last summer? Or rather, who he did?*

'Oh my God!' she exclaimed, her throat dry, her stomach in free fall. 'Do you think this is a wind up?' With trembling hands she handed her phone to Gemma.

Gemma and Jez read the message together. 'It's bound to be someone taking the piss,' Jez replied, trying to sound reassuring. But the words were barely out of his mouth before the phone vibrated again with another message.

'*You* see what it says,' Angel told her friends, full of apprehension. She watched them access the message. Both of them looked horrified.

'What is it?' she asked, her sense of foreboding intensifying. Her friends were silent, looking anywhere but at her or the phone screen. It must be something really bad.

'*Please*, someone, tell me what it is?' Angel cried.

Very reluctantly Gemma handed over the phone. It took Angel a few seconds to register what she was seeing, she was so shocked. It was a picture of Cal and Alessia – the beautiful Italian who had been friendly to her when she visited Italy. In fact, the one friend she thought she had made out there.

The couple were kissing in the street, and it was definitely not the kind of kiss you would give a friend. Cal had his arms round her waist; she had hers round his neck, their bodies pressed tight together.

Angel thought she was going to be sick. She put her hand over her mouth as she gagged and raced to the bathroom where she threw up the champagne she'd just drunk.

Gemma and Jez followed her in. 'Maybe it's not how it looks,' Jez said tentatively.

'Or maybe someone's faked the picture?' Gemma added. Both her friends were very obviously trying to come up with innocent explanations, but there was only one person who could reassure her on that score.

'I've got to speak to Cal,' Angel replied as she walked back into the bedroom and reached once more for her phone.

Five minutes later Cal was at the door and Gemma and Jez tactfully left the couple alone.

'What's wrong?' he asked as Angel let him in. He seemed worried. Or was that guilt she could see in his eyes? Angel could hardly bring herself to speak, so she simply handed him the phone, saying, 'Please tell me this isn't true?'

Cal looked as if he'd been turned to stone as he saw the picture. He looked at her, his eyes full of pain. 'I'm so sorry, Angel,' he whispered.

'So it's true then?' she said, her voice breaking with emotion. She felt as if everything she had ever believed in had been turned inside out and upside down. 'You had an affair with her? Last summer, when I was ill?'

Cal hung his head and said again, 'Not an affair, but I was unfaithful. I'm so sorry, Angel.'

Suddenly she felt as if she couldn't breathe. She caught sight of herself in the mirror in the beautiful silk dress. She was wearing a lie – this whole day was a lie. How could she renew her vows with a man who could do this to her?

'Sorry?' she shouted back. 'You shagged

267

someone else and you're *sorry*? Is that going to make everything all right? You lied to me, Cal, betrayed me, tried to make out that *I* was the one who had cheated . . . and all the time it was you!'

The shouting had turned to screaming now.

'Please, Angel, we can get through this,' he begged her.

'What! In a minute I suppose you're going to tell me it didn't mean anything?' Angel shouted back. And then she flew at him, pummelling his chest with her fists. 'How could you do this?' Tears were streaming down her face as he grabbed her wrists, trying to restrain her.

'How could you do this to me? To us? To our family?' Angel repeated, sobbing.

'It was madness, I know,' he said quietly. 'There is no excuse, but I suppose I felt rejected because you wouldn't stay in Italy. I wasn't even sure you wanted me anymore.'

'We're married, Cal,' she said through her tears. 'We promised to stay with each other forever, to be faithful to each other *forever*.'

'I know,' he replied. 'I made a mistake, it will never happen again.'

'How many times did you sleep with her?' Angel couldn't bring herself to say Alessia's name. She was prising Cal's fingers away from her wrists as she spoke, not wanting him to touch her.

'Don't let's do this,' he implored her. 'It's not going to make things any better.'

'I want to know how many?' Angel repeated, red hot anger and jealousy taking her over. 'How many times did you shag that Italian whore who pretended to be my friend?'

Cal hung his head and mumbled, 'It was just once. I didn't know what I was doing, Angel, I swear.'

'Your dick did, though, I bet?' she spat back. 'You bastard, I hate you!'

'I know you're angry but you don't mean that. We can get through this, we're a strong couple. We love each other.'

'Do we? And that's what you do when you love someone, is it? Shag someone else?'

'Please stop saying that. I love you, Angel.' Cal moved closer to her, but she took a step backwards.

'You'd better cancel today,' she said flatly, numb with shock.

'No way! We need to do this even more now. I need to tell you how much I love you. This is our fresh start,' he said passionately.

Angel felt as if her heart was breaking as she whispered, 'No, it's not, Cal. I can't renew our vows, not now I know what you've done. I don't know if I can even be married to you anymore.'

Cal continued to plead with her, telling her over and over how sorry he was, how he had never meant to hurt her. Angel looked at him, the man she had loved for so long, the man she thought she would be with forever, now the man who had lied to and betrayed her. How could she ever trust him again?

'Please, Cal,' she said wearily, cutting across his pleas, 'just go and sort out today. You owe me that, don't you?'

Finally her words seemed to sink in and reluctantly he agreed. 'What are you going to do?' he asked as he stood in the doorway.

Work out how to go on living without you, Angel thought, looking at the man who had become a stranger to her. She shrugged. 'I don't know, Cal.'

As soon as he left she collapsed to her knees, sobbing, tearing at the beautiful dress she was wearing, desperate to get it off. She ripped it in her haste to unfasten it, not caring. She couldn't bear to wear it another second. Then she picked up her bouquet of white roses and systematically shredded the petals, letting them fall, crushed and broken, to the floor.

The rest of the day passed in a blur of misery. All Angel wanted was to be left alone to sort out her head, which was in a mess. There were so many conflicting emotions coursing through her. She felt angry, jealous, betrayed, but above all hurt that Cal could have been unfaithful. She wanted to lock herself in her room but there were so many things to be done – telling her mum and dad, then her close friends. Everyone was shocked and wanted to know what she was going to do next. All Angel could say was that she didn't know.

'I'll do whatever it takes to make you realise that I love you,' Cal was saying. He was leaving for Italy the next day. Angel had spent the last few days in what seemed like a pit of despair. She was trying to carry on as normal but inside she wanted to scream at Cal for what he had done to her, wanted to hurt him like he had hurt her. Now the two of them were sitting in the living room. Honey was asleep, and the idea was that they should talk, calmly and in a civilised way, about what they should do.

But Angel was feeling anything but calm and civilised. Cal had suggested counselling but she was too angry and too hurt even to consider it. Whatever Cal suggested, she snapped back, wanting to be snide, wanting to make him suffer. But even as she hated him, she ached for him.

'I don't know what it will take,' she said flatly, hunched up on a chair opposite him, biting her nails.

'I could try and get a transfer from Italy,' he continued. 'But you know I'm locked into this three-year contract so it might be difficult.'

'Whatever,' she muttered. 'That's what you say. I expect you want to carry on seeing your whore.'

Cal gave a heavy sigh. 'Angel! We're not seeing each other. I haven't seen Alessia for over six months. She's not interested in me either. She's married as well, remember?'

'Neither of you remembered that fact when you jumped into bed together,' Angel said bitterly. 'And she obviously wanted me to find out or why send the picture?'

Another sigh from Cal. 'She didn't send you the text and I don't know who sent the picture. It's not a number I recognise. The question is, who took it?'

'*That's* the question?' Angel shouted back. 'You shag someone else and *that's* the question? For all I know you could have put her up to it. Maybe you just want rid of me.'

'Here's my phone, check all the messages. I've nothing to hide from you.' He held up his BlackBerry for her to take. But Angel sprang up from her chair and stood in front of him with her arms crossed. 'I'm not interested in looking at your fucking phone! I can't be with you at the moment, Cal. I'm so angry, I feel like you've destroyed everything.'

She was crying again – lately it seemed like all she did was get angry, scream at Cal, then cry.

He got up and went to try and embrace her, but she shook her head. 'I just can't be with you.'

'Then have some time to yourself,' Cal said softly. 'Have all the time you want, but know that I am here, that I love you. Don't let one mistake destroy us. *Please*, Angel.'

Without saying anything else she left the room and walked wearily upstairs to her bedroom. She felt as if something inside her had been broken. She paced aimlessly round the room for a few minutes then lay down on the bed. She had insisted that they sleep in separate rooms since the bombshell. She couldn't imagine sharing a bed with him again, let alone making love, but the bed seemed unbearably empty without him . . .

273

Chapter 10

Life Goes On . . .

'So how are you really?' Gemma asked Angel as the two girls met up for a drink at Hôtel du Vin in Brighton – or rather Angel was drinking while Gemma was sipping mineral water. It was the first time Angel had been out in two weeks. She'd been going completely stir crazy at home.

She grimaced and said, 'I feel devastated, Gem, don't know what I'm doing. One minute I think I hate Cal and never want to see him again, the next I think I can't live without him and I should just forgive and forget. What do you think I should do?'

Gemma sighed. 'I really don't know, babe. Only you know what's right for you. I know how terrible I'd feel if Tony had . . .' Gemma paused, sensitive to her friend's feelings, searching for the right words.

'Fucked someone else,' Angel said bluntly.

Gemma winced. 'God, Gem, every time I think about it, think about them together, think about him touching her, I feel as if I'm going mad! And he swears it only happened once but I just don't know if I believe him.' She put her head in her hands as if she could somehow erase the images that haunted her.

'Maybe you do need to talk to somebody – a counsellor?' Gemma replied.

Angel shook her head. 'I've talked about it to my therapist, but I hate doing it. It makes me feel like it's my problem, and it's not, it's Cal's.'

'And you haven't had any negative thoughts, have you?' Gemma asked tentatively.

'You mean, have I felt like topping myself?' Angel replied grimly. 'No, I promise I haven't. Mum's been staying with me anyway, to make sure I don't do anything stupid. But I wouldn't, Gemma.'

'So what have you told Cal?'

'He's supposed to be flying back on Sunday so we can talk – again. He phones and texts me every day, keeps telling me how much he loves me, that he's sorry. But I just don't know if I can ever forgive him for this.' Angel felt tears welling up in her eyes; Cal's infidelity had left her reeling. She put her head down, paranoid that other people in the bar would see her looking upset. No one, apart from her family and close friends, knew about Cal's betrayal. The cancellation of the wedding vows had been excused by the lie that Cal and Angel were suffering from food poisoning.

'I think it's just going to take time, isn't it? I know what Cal did was totally out of order, but don't you think you can get through this? I don't believe you two could actually split up.'

'I know, Gem, but *I* can't believe he slept with someone else! Anyway, *please* let's change the subject, I feel as if I can never escape from it and it's doing my head in. How are you feeling? You look really well.'

Gemma looked prettier than her friend had ever seen her. She'd had a brightness to her eyes ever since she had found out she was pregnant.

'I feel really well. I know it's still really early but I'm so excited! Worried as well, though,' she replied, 'because of all those miscarriages Mum had. I don't know if I could bear it if that happened to me.'

'I'm sure it will be fine, Gem,' Angel tried to reassure her.

But Gemma shook her head. 'Like you, I don't know if it will be fine, but I'm hopeful. Perhaps that's all you need to have, Angel, some hope.'

She managed a small smile for her friend, which didn't reach her eyes, then said, 'What I need is another cocktail.'

*

'So, Angel, how are you, darling? Looking lovely and slim but a bit pale. Time for some St Tropez? Or get Cal to whisk you and the *bambina* off somewhere hot. And are those dark circles under your eyes? Get some Touche Eclat on them, darling, *tout de suite*! That food poisoning must have really taken it out of you.'

It was Carrie her agent in full flow – talking at her, as usual. Angel had come up to the London office to discuss her work schedule. Trust Carrie to comment on the fact that she wasn't looking her best.

'Don't worry,' she replied, 'I'll get a spray tan if it makes you happy.'

'Not *me*, darling, the clients. Pale might cut it in *Vogue* but we're talking lads' mags, aren't we? What they want is bronzed tits and ass. Right?'

Angel shrugged by way of an answer. Carrie stared at her computer screen and slowly prodded her keyboard, her long fake red nails making speed out of the question.

'Okay then, so this is what we've got coming up for you – shoots for *FHM, Loaded, Esquire;* interviews and shoots for *Cosmo, New Woman* and *Marie Claire*. I've also put a call in to Ashton Walker, the American photographer you said you wanted to shoot your calendar, so I'll let you know when that is – probably in a month or so. It will be in the States, of course. And here are the invitations for events.' She pushed over a huge pile of envelopes for Angel. 'Plus you and Cal have been asked to present something at the National TV Awards. Are you up for it? It would be good to get the two of you to do something together. I'm sure there are plenty of career possibilities for the pair of you.'

Angel had not told Carrie about Cal's affair. She never confided in her about anything personal, their relationship was strictly business.

'I'll mention it to him, but you know what he's like about things like this. He usually only does that kind of thing for charity events.'

Carrie curled her lip. She was not known for her charitable impulses. 'Well, if you can persuade him, all I'm saying is that it might be good for both your careers. Cal can't play football forever, and you can't be a glamour girl forever either.'

Carrie managed a smile, a difficult manoeuvre for her as she'd had shed loads of Botox and collagen pumped into her face. Angel preferred it when she didn't smile. And God, talk about mutton dressed as lamb – there she was in skintight white skinny jeans, sky-high black patent leather ankle boots, and a tight black jersey top worn with no bra. She looked like one of the Fem-bots in *Austin Powers* – any minute now Angel expected her rigidly pert boobs to fire a missile!

Angel had nothing against surgery, having had a boob job herself early on in her career, but some people could take it to extremes and Carrie was one of them. She was definitely in her mid-fifties but tried to look as if she was in her early-thirties. God knows what she would be like when she was seventy. Small children would probably run from her screaming, scarred for life by the sight of her nip and tucked face . . .

'But just so you know, Carrie, I don't want to work more than four days of any week, so don't book me solid. I want to spend as much time with Honey as I can.'

'Haven't you got a nanny?' Carrie enquired.

'Yes, but I want to see my daughter.'

'Mmm,' was the only response from Carrie. She didn't have any children of her own and didn't understand why anyone would want to.

'Don't worry, you'll still get your money. I've got lots of ideas for things I want to do, including another perfume,' Angel said, wondering for the millionth time why she stayed with Carrie. *Because she's a great agent,* her head told her, *it's just unfortunate she's such a bitch.*

At the mention of money Carrie seemed to perk up visibly, it was almost as if she could smell it in the room. 'Good, we'll talk about that next time.' She looked at her watch. 'Now, I think you're due at a shoot and I've got an appointment with my nutritionist.'

She stood up and gave her client the obligatory

two kisses and Angel left, wondering what exactly
Carrie found to talk about to her nutritionist as she
had only ever seen her eat salad.

Angel's shoot was to promote her new lingerie
range, something she should have been excited
about, but all the way through the day she had to
force herself to smile. Getting the perfect pose for a
shot usually came completely naturally to her, she
would instinctively know what to do, but today
she felt as if her limbs were made of wood. 'I'm
being crap!' she exclaimed to Jez and Gemma
during one of the make up and hair changes.

'Of course you're not!' Jez exclaimed loyally. But
neither he nor Gemma looked entirely convinced
by his words.

'You're just having a bit of an off day,' Gemma
said, 'but the pictures will look great, you know they
always do.'

'Yes,' Angel replied bitterly, 'airbrushing helps.
Do you think it can make me look happy?'

Her phone beeped with a text message. It was
from Candy. The two girls had met up a few times
since the World Cup and had become good friends,
though Angel didn't feel able to confide in her
about Cal's affair. They weren't that close yet. The
message was to invite her to Candy's hen weekend
– she was marrying Liam in May.

Angel really didn't know if she was up to going;

the thought of having to pretend her own marriage was fine was just too unbearable. She groaned as she read through all the details – a night at the dogs, dinner, a club, overnight at a London hotel, then another day of pampering beauty treatments – meaning two days of acting for Angel.

'Do you think I have to go?' she asked, showing Gemma the message, and frowned when her friend nodded.

'Bollocks!' Angel exclaimed. 'I'm really happy for her and Liam but I just don't know if I can be around happy couples at the moment.'

Jez and Gemma exchanged a meaningful look which Angel picked up on instantly. 'What is it?' she asked.

'Nothing,' Jez said, a little too hurriedly.

'Jez – tell me,' Angel ordered, standing up and playfully grabbing her friend's arm. 'I can always tell when you're lying because you're the worst bloody liar in the world!'

'No, it's nothing,' he repeated, but wouldn't look Angel in the eye.

'Right! That's it, I'm going to mess up your hair unless you tell me.' And she reached out and started ruffling Jez's painstakingly styled hair.

'No, not the hair!' he cried, trying to wriggle away from her.

'Well, tell me then!' she ordered again, continuing to mess with it.

281

'Rufus asked Jez to marry him at the weekend,' Gemma said quietly.

'What!' Angel exclaimed. 'Oh my God, that is amazing news!'

'Yes,' Jez replied, smoothing his hair. 'He's going to make an honest man of me at last.'

Angel hugged her friend. 'I am so pleased for you both!' she said. 'We have *so* got to celebrate tonight. Let me take you both out for champagne. And you, Gemma, and let's get Tony along as well.'

'Are you sure?' Jez asked. 'I didn't want to tell you because of . . .' Even the usually plain-speaking Jez obviously couldn't bring himself to mention Cal's infidelity.

'Jez, please let's celebrate! You're one of my best friends and I don't want what's happened between Cal and me to ruin everything in my life.'

Angel looked at him, tears shining in her beautiful green eyes . . . tears of happiness for her friend, and tears of sadness for her own broken marriage. She was genuinely thrilled for Jez. She knew how much he loved Rufus even though he tried to downplay his emotions. His news buoyed her up for the rest of the shoot and some of her old confidence and sparkle returned when she posed. She could see the relief on the faces of the photographer and the marketing people. She'd been right in her assessment of her earlier poses – they had clearly been crap.

*

'I want to propose a toast to Jez and Rufus!' Angel declared, holding up her glass of Cristal. They were sitting in the Purple Bar in the plush Sanderson Hotel and Angel had insisted on paying for everything.

'To Jez and Rufus,' Gemma and Tony echoed, and everyone clinked glasses.

'I want to hear all about the proposal now,' Angel said, feeling pleasantly drunk. She was about to remind them of Cal's amazing proposal to her at Gemma and Tony's wedding, during his best man's speech, then she remembered how things were between them. The momentary sadness she felt must have shown on her face because Rufus replied, 'Oh, no, it's not that exciting.'

'I don't believe you and I want to hear all about it, every detail – really I do. Go on, Jez, I know you've been dying to tell me.'

He took a deep breath. 'Well, it was Sunday morning and to be honest I was in a bit of a grump. We didn't have any plans and it was raining and I hate rainy Sundays. Anyway Rufus tells me to put on something nice and that he's taking me out for lunch. I was just expecting a pub lunch somewhere, but no, he tells me he's booked us in at Scott's and I've been wanting to go there for ages!'

'Straightaway he wanted to know what it was for,'

Rufus managed to get a word in. 'And I said it was just to make up for forgetting his birthday.'

Jez frowned momentarily and the whole table took a minute to remember the fall out from Rufus forgetting that birthday. The tears and tantrums that had followed . . . how Jez was convinced Rufus was going to leave him . . . how nothing Rufus did for at least a month – the flowers, champagne, the gifts – did anything to dampen Jez's fury.

'So I thought nothing of it,' he continued while Angel smiled. Jez's birthday had been over six months ago and clearly he was *never* going to forget Rufus's slip up. 'I'm wearing my gorgeous Vivienne Westwood suit, the restaurant is lovely, the food divine, and at the end of the meal Rufus says he has something for me. I'm thinking, Is it a late birthday present? Some bijou little trinket? No, he hands me a fortune cookie and has one himself.

'To be honest I really wasn't interested in eating as I'd had enough and you know how I watch what I eat. And I always get such crap fortunes out of those cookies. I think the last one I had was something like, *"The world may be your oyster but it doesn't mean you're going to get the pearl"* – clearly so not true.'

'Jez!' Angel ordered in frustration, 'Get on with it!'

'Anyway Rufus comes over all dominant and

insists that I open it. He opens his first and pulls out a slip of paper which says, "*I hope the answer is yes.*" I still don't get it so just to keep him happy I crack mine open . . . and, fuck me, there's a ring inside! I look at Rufus and he says, "Is the answer yes?"'

'It was an incredible moment,' Rufus put in. 'For once Jez was totally speechless.'

Everyone laughed at that and then Jez said, 'So I shouted, "Abso-fucking-lutely!" And snogged the face off him!'

'So let's see the ring then,' Angel demanded.

Jez held out his hand, showing off a simple platinum band with a single diamond. It wasn't the usual kind of jewellery he wore, but Angel guessed that was all Rufus could afford on his salary as a personal trainer.

'Very stylish,' she said, trying to be diplomatic.

Jez vehemently shook his head. 'Forget about being nice. We've had the ring conversation and Rufus is cool about me taking this back and getting another one.'

Rufus nodded and rolled his eyes. 'Yes, I'm cool with it.'

'Here's a picture of the one I want,' Jez continued, getting out a photograph of a blingtastic diamond. 'I think you'll agree that's more up my street, isn't it?'

Angel could only nod in agreement. 'Okay, so now you have to tell us about the wedding.'

For the second time that day Jez and Gemma exchanged meaningful glances.

'It's *okay*,' she insisted, 'I'm fine about this, really.'

'Obviously I wanted something very low key and understated,' Jez joked – and the whole table erupted into laughter.

'You're right, I want the works!' he said, and launched into a blow by blow account of his dream wedding day.

Angel smiled away and nodded, but every word he said awoke painful memories for her – her own hopes of renewing her wedding vows and the dream day that was shattered. At the end of his wedding plan which included a stately home, an Arabian Nights theme and a honeymoon in Morocco, she said, 'So I hope I'm going to be your best woman?'

Jez sniffed, 'Well, even though I wasn't *yours* –' Gemma had been Angel's best woman at her wedding, with Tony as best man '– yes, you are!'

'Fantastic!' Angel exclaimed. 'That means I get to make a really embarrassing speech.'

'No way!' he shot back. 'I want my wedding day to be classy all the way.'

'So who are you going to have as your best man?' she asked.

A third meaningful glance between Jez and Gemma left Angel with a sick feeling in the pit of her stomach.

'We wanted to ask Cal, if that's okay with you?' Jez said quietly.

'Oh,' Angel replied, feeling at a loss to know what else to say.

'But if you really don't want us to, then we won't,' Rufus put in.

She shook her head. 'No, of course I wouldn't stop you from asking him.'

'And who knows?' her brother put in, always the sensible, calm one. 'Maybe by then you guys will have sorted things out between you.'

'Maybe,' Angel replied, trying to blink back the tears. She picked up the empty bottle of champagne to divert everyone's attention away from her and held it up. 'Shall we get some more?'

But just as she was looking round the bar for their waiter she noticed a familiar couple sitting at one of the other tables. It was Connor and Gabrielle. Angel shuddered inside – they were the last people she wanted to see, now or at any other time. Gabrielle had a face like thunder when she noticed Angel but Connor smiled straight at her and then, to her horror, he got up and started walking towards her.

'Pervert alert,' muttered Gemma when she saw him.

'Maybe he's going to proposition all of us for a gang bang!' Jez added cheekily.

'Shh!' Angel warned, steeling herself for his approach.

'Hi, Angel, looking beautiful as ever.'

Connor was standing by her chair and she was forced to acknowledge him. She made as if to stand, but he bent down so that his face was just a few inches from hers and Angel winced as she caught a waft of his over-powering aftershave. He kissed her on the cheek and she had to fight an impulse to wipe clean her skin.

'Why did you send all those gifts back?' he said quietly. 'I really wanted you to have them. It was my way of saying sorry.'

He was staring right at her, and instead of his usual cocky expression, Angel was unsettled to find that he had a look of what she could only describe as longing on his face.

She was about to reply when Gabrielle appeared beside him. 'Connor, we've got to go.' Her voice was like ice and she totally blanked Angel.

Very reluctantly he stood up, but before he followed Gabrielle, who had already marched out of the bar, he said, 'I really need to see you, Angel. Here's my number, please call me.' He slipped a card into her hand then left.

Angel's friends were staring at her in shocked silence. Jez was the first to speak.

'I think the England Captain may well have become your Number One fan, darling.'

'Oh, God,' she groaned, putting her head in her hands. 'Someone please pour me another drink.'

Angel didn't get back home until four but she wasn't tired. Connor and his infatuation with her seemed the least of her problems now. She thought about Jez and Rufus, and about how much in love they were, and was so happy for them. But a small voice inside her said, *What about me? Am I ever going to be happy again?*

She went into the lounge, walked over to the mantelpiece and picked up one of the photographs displayed there. It was of her and Cal, taken when they were in the garden one summer day having a barbecue with their friends.

Cal had his arms round Angel and they were both laughing. She'd been five months pregnant with Honey at the time, and she and Cal had just found out that she was having a girl and were both so incredibly happy at the news. Angel had felt truly blessed. Now, less than two years later, she felt as if her life was in ruins. She gazed at the picture of Cal – his handsome face so familiar and precious to her. 'How could you do this to me?' she said out loud.

She put the picture back face down then went round the room putting all the pictures of the two of them face down – she couldn't bear to look at him. And suddenly the anger she felt about what he'd done boiled up in her again. She knew she should go to bed but instead she poured herself a large Bailey's to numb the pain. The hurt was so intense it was almost physical – she felt as if she was being torn apart inside, piece by piece. 'How could you do this to me?' she said again. Then drained the glass and poured herself another . . .

She was woken the next day by the ringing of her mobile. Blearily she reached for it, checking to see who was calling. It was Carrie. No way was she up to speaking to her so early in the morning with a stonking hangover; Angel switched the phone off. Then somehow she managed to get up, all the while berating herself for having drunk so much. She pulled on her silk robe and staggered downstairs to the kitchen where Lucy was getting Honey ready to go out. 'Morning!' the nanny said brightly. Too brightly for Angel in her current delicate state.

'Morning,' she mumbled back, and bent down to pick up her daughter and give her a hug.

'I'm just going to take Honey to her singing group. Do you want us to get you anything?' Lucy continued.

'No, I'll just have some Paracetamol,' Angel replied, walking over to the medicine cupboard.

'Oh, there aren't any, I'm afraid. Cal took them last time he was here,' Lucy said, sounding embarrassed. 'He was worried about leaving them . . .' Her voice trailed off.

'It's okay, Lucy, I may be angry with him but I'm not suicidal. So could you get me some when you go out? Because I don't think Infant Calpol is going to cure a hangover, is it?'

After Lucy and Honey had left, Angel sat down at the kitchen table. She felt like shit and hated herself for having drunk so much. She knew from her drug addiction a few years ago that getting off her head didn't solve anything and since then had vowed never to let herself get out of control. The house phone rang and she let it go on the ansaphone. It was Carrie, babbling something about Angel calling her back urgently. *Oh, God, what did she want now?*

Angel forced herself to get up and call her agent. Two hours later she was sitting in Jeanie's beauty salon in the Brighton Lanes, getting her nails done. It turned out Carrie's message *was* urgent. Angel had to fly to LA the following day for the calendar shoot as that was the only time the photographer had space in his diary for the next six months.

Fortunately her hair still looked good from her last appointment with Jez. Angel tried not to think about the fact that it had been done for the day when she was supposed to be renewing her vows. She was certainly slim enough for the shoot since lately she'd hardly eaten anything, but her nails looked like shit as she'd chewed them off, and she could do with some colour – luckily Jeanie had fitted her in for a nail appointment and a spray tan. Now they were both sitting at the nail booth as Jeanie got to work on her hands and she was telling Angel off for not looking after them. 'Honestly, I've only just done them!' she said jokingly. 'It's not as if you work down a mine! I've never known anyone to trash their nails the way you do!'

'God, I can see where your daughter gets her bossy streak from,' Angel answered, but she didn't mind. She'd known Gemma's mum all her life and felt like she was part of her family. So much so that Jeanie was one of the few people who knew about Cal.

'Gemma'll be sorry she can't come to the States with you,' she continued, filing away at Angel's nails, 'but she's got a job on that she can't cancel.'

'I know it's very short notice but I do wish she was coming. I hate doing modelling jobs without her as my make-up artist. I never trust anyone else the way I trust Gem.'

'You'll be fine,' Jeanie replied, used to Angel's insecurity. 'So, how are you feeling?'

She shrugged and said bleakly, 'I feel awful, Jeanie. This is just the worst thing ever. I never in a million years thought Cal would be unfaithful to me. I feel so betrayed.'

'I know, babe,' Jeanie said sympathetically, 'but can I give you some advice? Don't let this break up your marriage. I know you feel like it's the end of the world, but it doesn't have to be.' She sighed and continued, 'I'll let you into a secret, if you promise not to tell Gemma?'

Angel nodded, wondering what Jeanie could have kept from her daughter – they usually told each other everything. Jeanie continued, 'I'm telling you this because I think it might help you with your situation. You see, I know exactly what you're going through.'

Angel looked at her in astonishment. 'Bill had an affair?'

Jeanie shook her head. 'No, it was me. *I* had an affair before Gemma was born. It was at the time when I was getting over another miscarriage. Bill was so wrapped up with his business and I was feeling so low . . . It's not an excuse for what I did, and I'm not proud of myself, but I met someone else and it just sort of happened. Anyway, after a month I knew I'd made a terrible mistake and ended the affair, but Bill found out. He was so angry and upset that I was sure he was going to leave me, but he didn't. It was really, really hard but we worked through it.

'It would be easy for you to leave Cal now and everyone would understand; no one would blame you. You would have to be really strong to stay and work things out . . . but you've always been a fighter, Angel. If anyone can save their marriage, you can. I just know that you and Cal are meant to be together.'

Was she strong enough to save her marriage? The trouble was Angel didn't feel strong anymore, she felt crushed by what Cal had done.

Chapter 11

Beautiful Stranger

Angel sat cross-legged on the bed in her LA hotel suite. Spread out in front of her lay her mobile phone, the card Ethan Taylor had given her all those months ago, and her laptop. Her dilemma was: should she ring Ethan? She hadn't spoken to him since last summer and had ignored the messages he had left with her agent. But now she was back in his city she was intrigued by the prospect of seeing him again. *He won't even remember who I am*, she tried to tell herself. But she was on her own in LA, not knowing what the state of her marriage was or even if she had one anymore. She felt so lonely . . . more lonely than she'd ever been before.

She reached for her laptop and Googled Ethan. Recently he'd been the face and body of an underwear campaign. And what a body – it was even better than she remembered it in the hot tub. *Seriously sexy,* she thought as she clicked through the

295

images of him, pausing at one which had him lying on a bed, a beautiful young model straddling him. *I wouldn't mind doing that* . . . Angel found herself thinking, against her better judgement.

Then she quickly closed down the window, feeling almost guilty that she'd been eyeing up another man in cyberspace. She checked her emails next. She had a message from Cal, another one telling her how much he loved her and saying that he hoped the shoot had gone well. Seeing his name aroused a sudden burst of anger in her and she reached for her mobile, biting her lip and hesitating for a few seconds before keying in Ethan's number.

What the hell? She had nothing to lose, did she? And simply phoning another man didn't begin to compare with what Cal had done to her. Ethan's phone went straight to voicemail. *No surprise there,* Angel thought. She left a short message, trying to sound as confident and casual as possible, as if it was perfectly natural for her to be phoning him after so many months. Then she took a shower. She'd been shooting pictures for her calendar all day and still felt jet-lagged. On her return from the bathroom she couldn't resist picking up her phone. There was another message from Cal but nothing from Ethan. *See,* she told herself, *I knew he wouldn't call.*

Wearily she pulled on her silk pyjamas and climbed into bed. She should really phone Cal but she didn't feel like it. They were still in this horrible limbo where Angel didn't know what she wanted to do. *Let him wonder what I'm up to for a change . . .*

She didn't know how long she'd been asleep when the ringing of her mobile woke her. She reached for the phone, worrying in case it was a call from Lucy back home about Honey, but an unknown number flashed across the screen. 'Hello,' she said sleepily.

'Is that *the* Angel Summer?' said a man with a sexy American accent. It was Ethan.

'It might be,' she replied, suddenly feeling wide awake.

'This is Ethan Taylor. But you know that, right, seeing as how you called me? Lucky I'm not like you – I actually return calls. God, you like to keep a man waiting, don't you? How many months ago was it since I saw you?'

'I'm not sure . . . about seven?'

'It was nine months, three days and seven hours,' he replied.

'Oh, and I'm supposed to think it's cute that you remembered and not at all freaky?' Angel was sitting up in bed now, smiling.

'You think it's cute,' Ethan said confidently. 'So . . . you want to meet up?'

'Yeah, if you're not otherwise engaged with all your lady friends,' she teased him.

'No, now that I know you're in town, I've given

them the week off,' Ethan shot back. 'So how about dinner? I could do Wednesday night, and if you let me know what hotel you're staying at, I'll get my driver to come by and pick you up.'

'Hold on!' Angel said. 'You mean dinner at a restaurant, right? Not dinner at your shag pad!'

'Angel, you're wounding my feelings. Of course I mean dinner at a restaurant. We can go to Spago.'

'Great!' she exclaimed. 'Can you really get a table there?' It was one of *the* places to eat in LA, where lots of celebs dined.

'Yes, I can get a table there,' Ethan said dryly. 'I'm famous out here, remember? I play this game with a stick that's real popular.'

'Oh, yeah, I remember. It's a bit like rounders, isn't it?' she teased him.

'There's way more to it than that, and if you're not careful I'll make you come to one of our home games and test you on the rules,' Ethan bantered back.

The rest of their conversation was taken up with arranging a time to meet. When the call ended Angel snuggled down in bed, still smiling to herself. She couldn't help feeling a little excited about the prospect of seeing him again. And, after all, it was just for dinner . . .

'Okay, Angel, now I want you lying on the sand, sideways to the camera but looking right at it.'

Ashton the photographer was calling out instructions to her as he clicked away on the beach shoot. Obediently Angel lay down and gazed provocatively at the camera. She was wearing a tiny gold bikini, her hair was deliberately tousled, her make up had been kept natural and sun-kissed. This was sexy beach babe Angel. She'd already been photographed emerging from the sea in the iconic Ursula Andress white bikini pose.

'Great . . . that's fantastic!' Ashton exclaimed clicking away. Angel tried to focus on the pose and giving the camera the smouldering-eyed stare to the max, ignoring the unpleasant sensation of cold wet sand on her body and the curious stares from other people on the beach. And she tried not to think about the next shot that involved her being completely naked and photographed from behind as she sauntered towards the sea. She just prayed there were no English paps around to get a cameraful . . .

Eventually Ashton was happy and Angel was free to get up. The stylist and make-up artist fussed over her, removing the sand from her body with mineral water, re-tousling her hair and touching up her make up.

Angel scanned the beach anxiously. It was still early-morning and there weren't too many people around, she supposed, but it wasn't exactly private. She slipped on a white towelling robe and took off the gold bikini. As she walked towards the sea, she called out to Ashton, 'I'm not doing this for long, so make sure you get the shot quickly!'

'I will,' he assured her.

Angel took off the robe and handed it to the stylist. She shivered and put one arm across her breasts, then turned and smiled playfully at the camera while Ashton shouted out encouragement as he clicked away.

'Hurry up!' Angel called back after he'd taken a roll of film. 'I'm freezing my tits off here!'

'Great ass!' a familiar voice called out.

Shit! That voice sounded just like Ethan's . . . She craned her neck round. *Shit! It was Ethan. What the fuck was he doing here?*

'Don't come any closer!' Angel ordered, trying to cover as much of her body as she could with her arms.

'Don't worry, I won't. I'm just enjoying the view.'

'You cheeky bastard!' she shot back.

'Sorry, Angel, can you just give me the smile for a few more minutes then I promise I'm done,' Ashton interjected.

Angel did her best to pull herself together and pose with her best sultry smile.

'Oh, yeah, baby! That's the one,' Ethan called out.

Angel ignored him and then, thank God, Ashton said he had the shot and the stylist quickly handed Angel her robe.

Once she'd put the garment on, and done the belt up tightly for good measure, she marched up the beach to where Ethan was standing, chatting to Ashton. His blond hair was shorter now which looked even sexier and she'd forgotten how blue his eyes were, but she wasn't going to be side-tracked by that. She went straight on to the attack. Without even saying hello, she folded her arms across her chest and launched in with, 'How did you know I'd be here?'

Ethan gestured to Ashton. 'He's an old friend of mine and just happened to say that he was photographing a gorgeous British model. I instantly thought of you. I promise I only took a little peek. The rest of the time my eyes were trained on the horizon, cross my heart. I was thinking serious thoughts about the economy and nothing at all about a certain model's beautiful *derrière*.'

Angel playfully swiped a punch at his arm. 'I really don't know if I can go to dinner with you tomorrow night now.'

'Well, actually, I was hoping you might spend the rest of the day with me. Ashton told me you had the afternoon off. I thought we could drive further along the beach and hang out.'

'I'm not sure,' Angel replied, thinking it was arrogant of him to imagine she wouldn't have plans of her own, even though she didn't.

'Well, while you're thinking about it, how about a kiss hello?'

Angel swished back her long hair while Ethan ducked his head down to kiss her on the cheek. In spite of feeling wrong-footed by his unexpected appearance at her shoot, she couldn't help experiencing a flash of attraction. He was *fit*. Just then, Ethan was surrounded by a gaggle of female fans all clamouring for his autograph and wanting to have pictures taken of themselves with him. He certainly wanted to please his fans, Angel noticed, as he patiently posed and signed away.

While he was otherwise engaged Ashton sidled up to her. 'I hope you didn't mind me telling Ethan? I had no idea he was actually going to turn up.'

Angel shrugged. 'It's fine, I'm not going to go all diva-ish on you.'

Ashton looked relieved. 'Thanks. And I have to say, he seems seriously taken with you. I've known him for years and I've never heard him sound so into a woman he's just met.'

'I thought he quickly got *into* most women he met?' Angel replied teasingly. 'I know about his reputation, Ashton, and I'm only going out for dinner with him. I'm married, remember?'

'Okay, I'm sure you know what you're doing,' he replied tactfully.

'What's she doing?' said Ethan, rejoining them.

'Nothing, we're just discussing work,' Angel replied, not wanting to inflate his ego any further by letting on they were talking about him.

Ashton left the two of them together while he and his assistant packed up the photographic equipment.

'You're not really mad at me, are you?' Ethan asked. Angel stared back into his wickedly gorgeous blue eyes and shook her head.

'So will you spend the afternoon with me?' he asked hopefully.

'Okay, but I need to get dressed now,' she said sternly.

'I'll leave you to it – my car's just over there.' He pointed over at the road to a silver Porsche Cayenne. 'I'll wait for you. And, I promise, no peeking!'

He blew her a kiss, waved goodbye to Ashton and headed for the road, leaving Angel looking at his retreating figure and thinking that his arse wasn't bad either . . .

In spite of herself and in spite of everything she'd been through lately, or maybe because of it, Angel had a great time with Ethan that afternoon. Although she'd only met him once before, she found him incredibly easy to talk to. Her natural inclination was to be quite shy with people until she really got to know them and felt that she could trust them, but with Ethan she felt an instant connection.

So when he asked her how she was feeling, she was able to talk openly about her depression and how she'd got through it.

'And I haven't said thank you, have I?' she said, coming to the end of her story.

'For what?' he asked.

'For talking to me about it and helping me to see that it was just an illness.' Angel left out Cal's furious reaction and her own suicide attempt.

'I'm just happy that you're okay now, Angel,' Ethan said softly. 'You are okay, aren't you?' he added.

'Oh, I'm totally fine now,' she replied breezily, feeling that she had revealed enough about herself, and then changed the subject by saying, 'Isn't Santa Monica beach where they filmed *Baywatch*? I used to love that programme when I was little, I always wanted to be like Pamela Anderson'.

'You're way better looking than her,' Ethan replied, and Angel found herself blushing at the compliment.

He drove them to a quieter part of the beach. It was a beautiful location: an expanse of white sand fringed by palm trees. Angel had imagined them lounging on the beach, maybe going for a walk, and was completely taken aback when Ethan unloaded two surfboards from the roof of the car and handed her a wet suit.

'You're joking!' she exclaimed when he told her he was going to teach her to surf.

'Nope, I remember you're a really good swimmer. Just think how proud you'll be when you go home and tell everyone that you can surf,' he replied.

Angel shook her head stubbornly. 'I'm never going to be able to do it.'

'Have faith,' he told her, 'I'm a great teacher.'

Even though Angel kept protesting that she would be rubbish, she still wriggled into the wet suit. The truth was she loved a challenge. And she had actually surfed before, several times in fact, so she was hardly a novice. But she thought it would be fun to tease Ethan and pretend that she couldn't and it would serve Ethan right for thinking a Brit girl couldn't surf.

Once they were both in the water, she allowed him to take her through the basics – how to lie on her board and paddle and ride the waves. She made Ethan show her several times how to surf the waves, acting like a complete novice. Then, tentatively, she got on the board herself and body surfed a wave.

Ethan sweetly called out encouragement, telling her how great she was doing, and Angel did her best not to smirk because she'd found it so easy. She body surfed a couple more waves then completely shocked Ethan by standing up and surfing the

305

wave. She was being all cocky and was set to give him the finger halfway through when she lost her balance and tumbled inelegantly off the board. He quickly swam after her and grabbed her round her waist.

'You really are a great teacher!' she said, all mock innocence.

'And you're such a liar, making out you hadn't surfed before!' Ethan exclaimed, lifting her up and then hurling her into the sea. Angel screamed in protest, while secretly admiring his strength. She went under and emerged spluttering from the salt water, but still laughing.

'Okay, you think you're so good, then we're going to go up a level. I want to see some serious surfing,' Ethan ordered her, and for the next hour he worked with her to improve her technique. Grudgingly Angel had to admit he was a great teacher and a fantastic surfer. She really enjoyed herself. It had been ages since she had done anything as fun as this. But finally she had to plead with him to stop, genuinely worn out by her exertions. Even with a wet suit on she was starting to feel cold.

'Shall I unzip you?' Ethan asked as they stood on the shore. Angel nodded, thinking it all felt a little too intimate now. She'd preferred being in the water with him. Being alone on the beach felt more dangerous.

'I'm freezing,' she exclaimed, and Ethan handed her a towel which she gratefully wrapped round her to dry off before she quickly pulled on her jeans and white cotton sweater over her bikini. Just because Ethan had practically seen her naked didn't mean she didn't feel self-conscious wearing a bikini in front of him. 'God, I must look a wreck!' she exclaimed, running her fingers through her wet salty hair and flopping down on to the picnic blanket.

'No, you look beautiful – all healthy and fresh. You look good with make up, but better without it,' he said, gazing at her.

'Oh, *perlease!*' Angel shot back. 'That is just the worst line. And I bet you say it to all the girls.'

Ethan shook his head. 'I know you want to see me as some kind of player, but where you're concerned I'm not.'

Feeling both unsettled and flattered by his attention, Angel just shrugged and changed the subject. 'I'm starving, can we get something to eat?'

'I've brought a picnic for us,' he told her.

'Don't tell me you made it?' Angel teased him.

'Okay, my housekeeper did, but doesn't the thought count?' Ethan replied. 'I suppose your husband is a really good cook?'

For a few seconds Angel was jolted back to reality at the thought of Cal. *No*, she told herself, *I'm not going to think about him*. 'He's a great cook,' she said brightly, then changed the subject. 'So can we eat this amazing picnic that your housekeeper has made?'

Ethan smiled at her. 'Yes, help yourself.' And he opened the hamper to reveal a delicious feast of antipasta, filled baguettes and fruit salad.

Angel had every intention of picking at the food in a ladylike, I hardly eat a thing fashion, but found she was so hungry after an afternoon spent surfing that she stuffed her face.

'How refreshing to meet a girl who actually eats something!' Ethan said, watching Angel biting heartily into a mozzarella, tomato and pesto baguette. 'Most of the girls I know would have taken one look at that picnic and run off screaming, terrified they would get fat just by looking at a piece of bread.'

When Angel had finished her mouthful she replied, 'Yeah, well, I'm not most girls and I've just spent the last hour in the water. I deserve some carbs!'

After the picnic Ethan suggested a walk along the beach. It was getting cooler now and Angel felt cold again. Ethan noticed her shivering and handed her his leather biker's jacket.

'No, I'm fine,' she protested.

'Have it,' he insisted, putting it over her shoulders.

She was grateful but couldn't blank out the memory of Cal giving her his jacket to wear several years ago. At the time she had thought it such a romantic gesture. Now, wanting to banish any such thoughts, she quickly ran to the waterline. There was going to be a beautiful sunset. The sky was turning vivid shades of orange and pink, the sun a huge flaming disc sinking towards the ocean.

'Come on,' she shouted back to Ethan, jogging by the sea. 'Or has all that surfing worn you out?'

By way of answer he ran quickly towards her. 'Take a hell of a lot more than that to tire me out, baby,' he said when he caught up, 'I've got the most amazing stamina.'

'Oh yeah baby, I bet you have,' she replied sarcastically, falling back into a walk. They strolled along the beach, watching the sun set. She'd really enjoyed being with him – the conversation had flowed so easily and she had found herself warming to him even more. The flirtatious banter between them was fun too, but more than that she was intrigued by him when every now and then he said something that revealed hidden depths to his character. But he was right, Angel did want to see him as just a playboy. That way she wouldn't have to risk taking him seriously.

'Well,' Ethan said, looking at his watch, 'I'm going to have to drive you back now.'

'Another date?' Angel asked.

'So you agree, *this* was a date?' he replied, smiling.

'Of course not!' she replied hotly. 'We're just friends.'

'Umm, if you say so,' Ethan answered. 'But in answer to your question, I am seeing another woman tonight . . .' He paused and Angel put an *I told you so* look on her face. 'My grandmother,' he continued.

Angel laughed. 'Yeah, right, is that what you call all those lovely ladies who can't get enough of you!'

'No, seriously, I'm taking my grandmother to a show tonight.'

Angel shook her head, not believing a word of it.

'Come with us then and you can see for yourself,' he continued.

Angel hesitated. She was sure he didn't really want her to come, and that he had a hot date, but maybe she'd call his bluff. 'Okay then.'

But Ethan looked pleased by her acceptance. 'Fine. I'll drop you off at the hotel and then get the limo to pick you up later. The show starts at eight so there'll be time to have a drink first and meet my grandmother.'

'Oh, yeah,' Angel replied cheekily, 'I can't wait to meet Granny!'

Three hours later she was forced to eat her words when she was introduced to Loretta, a well-preserved, well-dressed woman in her late-seventies. She was completely charming and a real character. She had been a successful actress and still had the occasional film role. Angel discovered that Ethan regularly took her out since her husband had died a couple of years ago.

And there I was, wanting to write him off as a shallow player, Angel thought, impressed by Ethan's kindness to his grandmother. Not only was he gorgeous-looking, he was actually coming across as a really nice guy. Damn! She didn't need this complication, she wanted everything to be black and white, wanted Ethan to be a good-looking flirt and nothing more, didn't she?

Loretta clearly adored her grandson but was also wise to his ways and spent the meal after the show teasing him about his love life. 'I keep wondering when he's going to settle down, Angel. Don't you think he's old enough? He's going to be thirty next year,' she said, putting Angel on the spot.

'Are you sure he's the settling down type?' she replied, trying to keep things light.

'Oh, yes, no doubt about that, he'd love to have kids,' Loretta continued. And then to Angel's horror said, 'What a pity you're married, you'd be perfect for Ethan. He wouldn't be able to run rings round you like he does all his other women. And I can tell that he really likes you.'

Angel couldn't look at Ethan, aware that she was

blushing furiously. It was one thing to be told by Ethan's friends that he had a thing about her, quite another to be told that by his grandmother.

Fortunately Ethan rescued her. 'I quite like her, Loretta, but her surfing would need to improve and she'd have to learn the rules of baseball. She didn't even know what a home run was!'

Now Angel raised her eyes to look at him. He was smiling and gazing right at her. She tried to hide the confusion she felt by sipping her champagne. She realised that if she didn't take care, she was in danger from those knowing blue eyes of his, but she couldn't deny the attraction . . .

At the end of the evening, against her better judgement, she agreed to have dinner with him again the following night. *It's just a bit of fun,* she told herself as she lay down in bed. But a small voice inside her asked, *What if there's more to it than that? What if I really like him?*

She spent the next day shooting the rest of the pictures for her calendar. This time the location was a studio and in contrast to the natural look of the beach shots, now she needed to be in full siren mode – red lipstick, smoky eyes, and wearing an array of sexy black and pink lingerie and stockings. But as she posed away so confidently, inside her head was in a whirl as she tried to work out what she should do about seeing Ethan tonight. A dinner date seemed like a step beyond friendship and did she really want to take it? She knew he liked her and it would be easy to take things further but was that really a good idea?

It was all so confusing. She wished Gemma was with her, she could have done with her clear-headed advice. If Cal hadn't been unfaithful, never in a million years would she be in the position of going out for dinner with Ethan. She would have felt as if she was betraying her husband, even if absolutely nothing happened.

By the time she returned to her hotel she was seriously having second thoughts about seeing Ethan again. Cal had phoned her. He sounded so happy to talk to her, so pleased that her shoot had gone well, she couldn't help feeling guilty that she was going out for dinner with another man. She had wanted to torment Cal, tell him that she was seeing someone who wanted her, but suddenly she found that she couldn't. Quite why that was she didn't know, it would have been one small way of punishing him for what he'd done, and God knows he deserved it . . .

Angel checked her appearance in the mirror. She was wearing a short gold sequined dress with thin straps which she teamed with her favourite Louboutins and a cropped black leather jacket. The dress didn't flaunt too much cleavage but there was no disguising Angel's stunning figure – curvaceous but slim. Because she didn't want Ethan to think she was trying too hard, she'd kept her make up to the minimum – just tinted moisturiser, mascara and lip gloss – and she wore her hair down. She anxiously looked at her watch. Just ten minutes before he was due to arrive, too late to cancel. She sighed and looked through the pictures of Cal she had on her phone, as if they would tell her what to do for the best. As she gazed at him she wondered whether he'd had second thoughts before his night with Alessia? Had he thought of his wife at all? And imagining that he hadn't, she snapped her phone shut. *Oh, Cal, why did you do it?* she thought for the millionth time.

She paced up and down her suite, wishing she knew what to do for the best. She felt completely at sea. At precisely eight thirty Ethan called to let her know that he had arrived. She grabbed her bag and quickly left the room before she could change her mind.

Ethan was waiting for her in the hotel lobby. He was wearing a beautifully cut midnight blue suit that accentuated his blue eyes, and a white shirt. He looked seriously sexy.

'Wow,' he said when he saw her, 'you look gorgeous.' And as he kissed her he added, 'But you knew that, right?'

Angel shrugged off his compliments. 'I'll do.' As they were driven to the restaurant in Ethan's limo the two of them once more fell easily into conversation, though Angel kept having to remind him to stop being quite so flirtatious. 'We're having dinner as friends,' she chided him when he paid her yet another compliment. 'I'm married, remember?'

'Oh, I know,' he replied. 'It's just not something I *like* to remember.'

When they walked into the restaurant Angel was aware of women turning their heads to get a better view of Ethan, and she couldn't blame them. He was easily the most handsome man there. He was also perfect company – witty, charming, entertaining, and those blue eyes were always looking at her . . . If Angel had been single she would have been more than tempted. Well, to be honest she probably would have skipped dinner and taken him straight back to her hotel . . . but as she chatted to him she felt full of conflicting emotions. Unconsciously she twisted her wedding ring round and round on her finger. Half of her didn't want to be here at all, wanted to be with Cal, but the other was drawn to Ethan . . .

'You don't have to keep touching your wedding ring!' he exclaimed, catching her fiddling with it again. 'I haven't forgotten and I haven't done anything I shouldn't have, have I?' At this he leaned back in his chair and stared boldly at her, his long legs brushing against hers.

'Though I have to say, if you were my wife, I wouldn't like the thought of you going out with someone like me. Not one little bit. So how is your marriage really, Angel?'

'My marriage is great, thanks,' she replied, though she knew her voice sounded brittle and false. 'And I don't see what the big deal is about having dinner with you. We're just friends.'

'The big deal is that you know I don't just have friendly feelings for you, Angel.' Now he leaned closer and his playful, flirtatious manner was replaced by something altogether more serious.

'I want you so badly,' he said huskily. 'I haven't been able to get you out of my head since we met. Yes, I've gone out with other women, beautiful women, but none of them has come close to you. I can't stop thinking about you, Angel.'

She couldn't help feeling flattered by his words and stared back at him. She took another sip of champagne to give her confidence as a thought started to take shape in her mind. Maybe this was what she needed to do, to make herself forget about Cal's betrayal. She couldn't yet say 'forgive', and maybe she never would. But she would go back to Ethan's beach house and she'd make love with him . . . no, have sex with him. It would be a one night stand, nothing more. Then she and Cal would be even and she could let go of the hurt and anger that had been poisoning her.

To test her resolve she leaned forward and kissed him, expecting to feel nothing, but Ethan returned it, a hard, sexy kiss that felt so good.

Angel pulled away. It felt as if the rest of the room was out of focus. Then she murmured, 'So what will it take to make you feel better?'

'More than a kiss, sweet as that was,' he replied, gazing at her with undisguised desire. By now Angel was feeling butterflies of excitement, nervousness and, she had to admit it – lust. She hesitated for a moment longer before whispering, 'Okay, let's go.'

As Ethan settled the bill, turning down Angel's request that she pay half, she drained her glass of champagne and tried not to think about what she was going to do. They walked swiftly out of the restaurant and darted into the waiting limo, both anxious to avoid any lurking paparazzi. Angel was imagining that they would play it cool until they arrived at his house but Ethan had other ideas. After speaking briefly to his driver, who discreetly closed the tinted-glass panel separating the front and back seats, he pulled Angel on to his lap and began kissing her.

It was a kiss that was gentle at first and then became deeper and more passionate, becoming the kind of kiss that led only one way . . . At first she lost herself in the kiss, was turned on by his hands caressing her body, wanting him to touch her breasts, wanting him to slide his hands along her thighs and go further still . . . She could feel his hard cock against her. *Go on*, her body seemed to be telling her, *this is easy, you can fuck him and then walk away*.

She caressed Ethan's body, slipped her hands under his shirt, felt his firm muscular chest, unbuttoned his shirt, kissed his neck . . . slipped her hands under the waistband of his boxers. He groaned with pleasure and kissed her more hungrily, caressing her through her silk briefs, turning her on. He had all the right moves. She closed her eyes as his caresses brought waves of pleasure pulsing through her, bit his lip, slipped down the straps of her dress so he could touch her breasts . . .

Go on, she thought again. *This will make everything better, everything right again.*

But then she opened her eyes and everything felt wrong. Suddenly she was pulling away, moving to the opposite side of the seat, fumbling with her straps, rearranging her dress. She couldn't do this. She didn't want to betray Cal and she knew that if she had sex with Ethan now she would have destroyed something. Things wouldn't be the same again, this wouldn't make anything right. She belonged to Cal and he belonged to her – that's what made sense of her world, wasn't it? It was Cal she wanted to be making love to her, not this beautiful stranger.

'Hey, what's the matter?' Ethan asked her.

Angel felt so ashamed she could hardly look at him. *He didn't deserve this. What had she been thinking of? How could she ever have imagined that she could have a one night stand? She'd never had one in her life.*

'I'm sorry, I can't do this, Ethan,' she said breathlessly. 'Please just let me out of the car.'

He looked taken aback – he was obviously not used to rejection. For a minute Angel panicked that he might try and force her, the way Jackson Black, a Hollywood actor, had tried with her a few years earlier.

'Come back to the house, Angel, we can talk,' Ethan replied, quick to regain his composure. 'Don't go. There's a connection between us, you can't deny it. I know you want me too.'

Angel shook her head. 'I'm so sorry, I shouldn't have led you on. I'm married and I love my husband, in spite of how it must look to you.'

There was a pause while Ethan looked at her. The desire in his eyes had been replaced by a look of hurt and wounded pride.

'Is that really what you want?' he asked quietly.

'Yes,' Angel whispered. 'It really is.'

He pressed the intercom button and murmured to the driver who pulled over. Ethan opened the door.

'I'm getting out here. The driver will take you to your hotel. Goodbye, Angel.'

She was about to repeat that she was sorry, but he had already slammed the door shut and was walking away into the night.

Back in her hotel room Angel pulled off her dress and stepped into the shower, standing under it for ages, letting the hot water pour over her body as if she could wash away the memory of tonight, wash away the memory of Ethan's hands and lips on her skin. Then and only then was she ready to make the call to her husband.

'It's me,' she said. 'I'm flying over to Italy tomorrow. I want to see you.' She paused then added, 'I want us to be together.'

Chapter 12

For Better, For Worse

As soon as Cal saw his wife at Milan airport the
following evening he ran towards her, took her in
his arms and said in a voice full of emotion, 'I swear,
I will never let you down again, Angel.'

'Shush.' She put her finger against his lips. 'No
more apologies.' And then she kissed him.

Back at the villa Angel took Cal's hand and led
him up to the bedroom. They held each other tight
for a few minutes as if they couldn't bear to let each
other go again, then they were kissing and tearing
off each other's clothes, falling on to the bed in a
tangle of limbs, and all Angel could think was that
she wanted Cal, wanted him more than anything
else, wanted to feel him inside her, to feel close to
him again. Their lovemaking was intense, violent
almost – as if they were both erasing the past. With
every thrust of Cal's body driving into hers, she
arched her back and tilted her hips towards him.

'Fuck me harder,' she urged him. Then she was on top of him, straddling him. 'You're mine,' she told him, leaning forward so that her breasts were tantalisingly close to his lips.

'Yes, I'm yours,' he replied, kissing her nipples, caressing her with his hand, so that they came together in a fever of desire, possession and love.

They spent the next day rediscovering each other's bodies, their passion made all the more intense because they had so nearly lost each other. But close as they were again, there were moments during their lovemaking when Angel thought of Cal with Alessia; thought of his hands on her body and hers on his; thought of him fucking her . . . and she felt pain then, white hot pain that shot through her, making her want to hurt Cal. She dug her nails into his back, raked them across his skin, leaving angry red marks on him. It was as though she was marking her territory, saying, You belong to me. Finally they lay entwined in each other's arms, exhausted from their spent passion.

'I've spoken to my agent about a transfer back to an English club,' Cal told her, gently smoothing back her hair. 'And he's working on it. Hopefully in a few months I'll be back in England.'

Angel hated the prospect of Cal remaining in Italy, even for a short time, hated him being anywhere near *that woman*. She gave a heartfelt sigh.

'I really wish you didn't have to be here. Do you promise you won't see her?' She still couldn't bring herself to say Alessia's name.

'I think her husband is on the transfer list. There's talk of a bid for him from Real Madrid. And, no, I won't see her, I swear.'

'And you promise no one else knows?'

'Alessia promised me that she'd told no one,' he replied, and Angel winced to hear him say that name.

'But someone knows, don't they?' Angel said. 'The person who sent that picture.' And she shivered in spite of his arms around her. Someone out there wanted to hurt her and Cal. The question was, who?

'It seems exactly the kind of thing that Simone would do,' she said thoughtfully.

Cal shook his head. 'She hasn't contacted me since she agreed not to, and I've not seen her in Italy. Anyway, why would she do something like this? She's got a new boyfriend.'

'Because she's still in love with you!' Angel exclaimed. 'And she's just using her boyfriend for his money and lifestyle, isn't that obvious?'

'Oh, come on, even she's not that much of a bitch.' One of Cal's most lovely and at the same time most annoying traits was that he always looked for the good in people, even in Simone who had behaved so appallingly after they broke

323

up. 'I know she went all mentalist on us but she did apologise.'

'And that makes it okay, does it?' Angel replied, thinking, *God, men are naïve*.

'Let's not talk about Simone,' he answered, and seeing that Angel was going to say something else, kissed her to silence anymore questions. But that didn't stop her wondering who had taken that picture and what they had hoped to achieve by it. Nothing good, that was for sure.

In the weeks that followed Angel did her best to put the past behind her; she knew she had to learn to have faith in Cal again, but there were dark times when she was wracked by doubts, tormented to think that he might be seeing Alessia again. Deep down she knew she would never be able to trust him one hundred per cent again and that hurt so much because she always had before. The belief that he would always be faithful to her had been one of the cornerstones of their marriage. So now that had been taken away, everything seemed less certain, more fragile somehow. But everyone she was close to told her that she had definitely made the right decision in giving Cal a second chance . . . she just hoped they were right.

As for Ethan, Angel was mortified about the way she had treated him. She sent him a text apologising again for her behaviour, but he didn't reply. She didn't blame him. She just wanted to forget what had happened, but couldn't help hoping that he didn't think too badly of her . . .

Cal brought up the subject of them renewing their vows again but Angel wasn't ready. 'Maybe in a year or two,' she told him. The pain he had inflicted on her with his infidelity was still too raw. When Cal saw that there was no persuading her he dropped the subject. As if he had something to prove he had a pair of angel wings tattooed on his shoulders. 'See, you are always with me,' he told her when he showed them to her.

'I thought I was here,' she replied, reaching out and touching his chest, so that she could feel his heart beating.

'You are,' he replied. 'Always.'

Just not for one night last summer, she wanted to say. But she didn't. She wanted to move on as much as Cal did.

'Do I look okay?' Angel asked, giving her make up a quick check in the mirror.

'Beautiful, of course,' Cal replied.

The pair of them were on their way to co-present an award at the National TV Awards. When Angel had asked her husband if he wanted to take part she was certain he would refuse because it was so hard for him to get time off from training. Instead he had surprised her by agreeing. 'We should do more things together,' he'd told her. 'We spend too much time apart as it is.'

When they emerged from their car the couple attracted a huge amount of attention on the red carpet – the paps all frantically taking pictures of them, vying with each other to interview the gorgeous couple. Cal smiled away for the camera – another first as he usually looked moody – even kissing Angel when one of the paps asked him to. *We must look like the perfect celebrity match,* Angel thought, and couldn't help a pang of sadness. *If only they knew . . .*

The guests were treated to champagne cocktails before the awards began and Cal and Angel were quickly swept up by people who wanted to talk to them – or rather to Cal. After his winning goal in a crucial World Cup match, he'd become something of a hero to many people, including some very A-list actors and actresses. Angel found herself left on the sidelines and smiled as she watched her handsome husband chat politely, every now and then looking over and catching her eye as if to say, *What is all this?*

Angel was so proud of him. She had never been the kind of person who expected to be the centre of attention, and she enjoyed watching him shine. But suddenly she caught a glimpse of an all-too-familiar and unwelcome figure making its way through the crowd towards Cal. It was Simone. A feeling of dread crept over Angel. *God, that woman made her skin crawl.*

Dressed in an extremely revealing black silk dress, Simone stood a few feet away and gazed longingly at Cal. *Shit!* Angel thought. She should have realised that Simone would be here, even though she hadn't worked for at least six months after her contract had been terminated on *Hollyoaks*. She watched as Simone began inching towards Cal but before she got the chance to greet him, Cal ended his conversation and rejoined Angel.

'Get me out of here!' he whispered in her ear, draping his arm possessively round her. 'I don't want to make small talk with anyone else for a while!'

Over his shoulder Angel saw Simone freeze as she took in the fact that Cal was with his wife. She appeared completely shell-shocked to see them together; then the shock turned to a look of pure hatred.

'Don't look now,' Angel warned, 'but Simone is behind you.'

'God, that's all we need,' he groaned. 'Come on, let's move away.'

They wove their way through the crowd and then thankfully it was time to take their place backstage. Jez and Gemma were waiting in the dressing room to do last-minute touches to Cal and

Angel's appearance. It was a relief to see their friendly faces. For some reason Angel felt shaken after seeing Simone. She was used to the other woman directing looks of pure loathing at her, but there had been something about the expression on her face this time that had unsettled Angel. Simone had looked almost mad with hatred . . . or maybe Angel was imagining things and Simone had just overdone it on the Botox.

'Guess who we've just seen?' she said grimly, sitting down and letting Gemma check over her make up – putting on a little powder to take away any shine, reapplying her lipstick.

Jez immediately reeled off a list of stars. 'I *wish*,' Angel replied. 'But it was Simone, one of the Wicked Witches of the WAGs.'

Both Gemma and Jez grimaced in sympathy. 'Oh well,' Jez said breezily, 'at least you haven't got to present her with an award. That really would be disturbing. Now, Cal, can I just have a look at your hair?'

Cal scowled at Jez. He hated anyone fiddling with his jet black hair which was cut very close to his head. 'A little bit of gel to give it some depth?' Jez suggested, advancing on him.

'Step away from the hair!' Cal warned. 'It looks fine like it is.' And he glanced in the mirror and simply ran his fingers through it. 'There, see, perfect.'

Jez tossed back his head theatrically and stamped his foot in annoyance. He was always trying to get his hands on Cal's hair. 'Thank God your wife's not as difficult as you!' he exclaimed, turning his attention instead to Angel and ensuring her long honey-blonde hair looked sleek. Meanwhile she was checking her script – she had hardly anything to say but was paranoid about getting the words wrong. Public speaking was not one of her skills. 'Can't I just stand next to you and smile?' she said to Cal. 'I'm really nervous!'

'You'll be fine,' he reassured her, not in the least bothered himself about the prospect of standing up in front of such a large audience and being filmed.

Angel's nervousness increased as the awards ceremony began and the four of them watched the show on the TV monitor in the dressing room. Jez entertained them all with his outrageous bitching about what everyone was wearing and how they all looked, who'd lost weight, who'd put it on, who was shagging who.

'Oh.My.God!' he exclaimed, pointing out a soap-star actress in a silver mini-dress with a plunging neckline. 'She looks as if she's wrapped in BacoFoil!'

'Are you sure you aren't related to Perez Hilton?' Angel demanded, making everyone laugh. Then she and Cal got their five-minute call and had to make their way to the stage.

Cal held her hand tightly as they walked along the corridor and all the time while they waited to go on. As the music struck up to signal the couple's entrance onstage Angel felt butterflies fluttering madly inside her and was terrified that she was going to trip as they walked down the stairs. Why were there always stairs at awards ceremonies? Was it just in the hope that some celeb would fall over and make a tit of themselves so everyone could laugh? *Please let it not be me*, she thought as she tried to walk as elegantly as possible down the steps.

The host, Robbie Johnson, was waiting at the bottom to embrace the couple. The audience were cheering and whistling but for a second Angel imagined Simone in the crowd, sitting there like a vengeful spider, full of poison, willing Angel to fuck up.

'So, Cal,' Robbie said cheekily, 'you've got something that we've all been dying to see. Any chance you could give us a preview?' For a second Cal's hand went to his belt as if he was going to unbuckle it – to wolf whistles from the crowd. *What was he doing?* Angel wondered in amazement. They hadn't planned this. Then Cal swiftly shrugged off his jacket and shirt, showing off his new tats, posing away while the crowd showed their appreciation by whistling and cheering at the sight of his gorgeous, olive-skinned, muscular body. Angel stood by laughing, her nerves forgotten. *This was so unlike Cal!*

'Whatever happened to Mr Too Cool for School?' Robbie demanded.

Cal shrugged as he straightened his clothes. 'He's realised that life's too short and how much he loves his wife.' If anyone else had come out with a line like that no doubt the audience would have been pulling faces and reaching for their sick bags, but because Cal was such a hero and considered to be so cool, the general feeling was, *How sweet.* Then he kissed Angel which had the crowd cheering again. 'Watch the make up!' she joked, but she was deeply touched that he was being so open about his feelings.

The pair of them then read out the nominations. Angel, word perfect, announced the most popular actor to be David Tennant, did the obligatory kiss, kiss, and then walked offstage to more cheers and whoops of delight.

'You're full of surprises at the moment,' she said to Cal later that night, after the awards had finished and they were at the after-show party.

'It's true what I said on stage,' he replied, looking at her, his expression serious. 'I love you so much, Angel.' And he drew her towards him and kissed her. For the first time in ages Angel actually felt happy. *I think we're going to be all right*, she thought.

But it was a moment that didn't last. Cal's attention was claimed by yet another of his admirers. As Angel was standing beside him, glancing at the crush of partygoers, Simone sidled up next to her. Angel's heart sank. There was going to be no escape from her this time.

'Hi, Angel. I did enjoy your little show on stage, it was so lovely,' she said, slurring her words slightly. 'Though let's face it, public speaking isn't your strongest point, is it? It's that Brighton accent. Makes you sound so – how can I put this? – common.'

Angel turned to face her, trying to keep her expression as neutral as possible. Simone's make up was still perfect but her eyes looked glassy and she kept sniffing. Angel hadn't had her down as a coke head, but maybe she needed the drugs to cope with life with Jamie.

'And that show of togetherness was so unexpected,' Simone continued. 'Especially with Cal playing away and everything.'

For a second Angel stared at her in disbelief. *Did she know then? Was she behind that photograph? Or was she throwing out accusations just to get a reaction?* A chill ran through Angel because if Simone did know that Cal had had an affair, she sure as hell wasn't likely to keep it a secret.

Somehow Angel managed to compose herself and reply as calmly as she could, 'I don't know what you mean, Simone, but I do feel really sorry for you if you have to obsess about my relationship. Your own not fulfilling enough then?'

Simone looked furious.

'You bitch!' she sneered, the mask of politeness slipping. 'You stole him from me and one day you're going to pay!'

'Ever thought of taking a role in panto?' Angel shot back. 'You'd make the perfect Wicked Stepmother.'

'And who do you think you are!' Simone spat back. 'Snow fucking White?'

Angel shrugged. 'Well, I guess we all know which one of us would be the fairest of them all if we looked in the mirror, don't we?'

Simone turned almost aubergine with rage.

'You'd better wake up, Princess! Your Prince has been shagging around – whatever he might say now.'

And with that she left, pushing her way through the partygoers, leaving Angel reeling. It seemed to her that Simone must know about Cal's affair, and the thought of her knowing something as damaging as that was horrifying. Just as she thought things couldn't get any worse, she turned round and walked straight into Connor and Gabrielle.

Angel nodded in acknowledgement and made as if to walk past them but Connor said, 'Angel!

Good to see you. I thought you did really well onstage.'

She was forced to look at him, and tried to work out if he was taking the piss. But as he had done before Connor seemed sincere. *Oh, God,* she thought despairingly, *I preferred it when he was a cocky git.'*

'Thanks,' she muttered, while Gabrielle held tightly on to her husband's arm and looked as if she could cheerfully have stabbed Angel with her Yves Saint Laurent Tribute heels.

'Gabrielle and I were wondering if you and Cal wanted to meet up for dinner sometime,' Connor continued, oblivious to the look of distaste on his wife's face.

'Well, Cal's not around much at the moment,' Angel replied, hoping that would be enough to put him off.

But Connor wasn't going to give in so easily. 'If you give me your mobile number I can text some dates.'

Angel was all set to give him a wrong number, then reasoned that she may as well give him the right one so that when he texted her, she could text him back, telling him to leave her alone. Only when Connor had double-checked the number was she finally free to go and quickly made her way back to Cal.

'Can we go now?' she whispered, putting her arm through his.

'You look pale, is something the matter?' he asked.

'I'll tell you when we're out of here,' she replied, desperate to get as far away as possible from Simone, Connor and Gabrielle.

Later, when the pair of them were in bed, she finally told Cal what Simone had said – she hadn't wanted to tell him on the journey home, fearing their driver might overhear. But once again he shrugged off her worries that Simone knew about Alessia.

'She's just being spiteful, she doesn't know anything,' he said, clearly anxious to change the subject. 'If she did, do you really think she'd have been able to keep it to herself?'

'Maybe she was waiting to see what would happen once I knew about it – maybe she thought we would split up if I found out? She looked shocked when she saw us together.' Angel's mind was racing. She still felt deeply disturbed by her encounter with Simone. She curled round Cal. Since she had seen Simone she'd felt unusually cold and shivery. *Perhaps the Wicked Witch had put a spell on her?*

Cal sighed. 'Angel, she always looks like that whenever we see her. She's just a bitter woman. Forget about her. She's nothing to us.'

Angel didn't mention Connor's dinner invitation,

deciding that she would nip that in the bud as soon as he texted her.

The next morning all the papers carried coverage of the awards night with the pictures of Cal revealing his tattoos featuring in nearly all of them. There were also pictures of Angel and him posing on the red carpet and looking like the ultimate loved up celebrity couple. The headlines were all about how happy they still were. Cal smiled ruefully when he saw all the coverage but Angel felt less than pleased. It was too soon after the recent bombshell for her to feel wholly comfortable. The press were making out that they were the perfect couple when she knew they were not. It felt as if they were being set up for a fall . . .

Cal was flying back to Italy that night which cast a shadow over the rest of the day for Angel. She didn't want him to go, and couldn't go with him either as she had several shoots that week. They spent the day in Brighton. It was early-April and a beautiful day – the sun was shining and the sky was a clear blue, not a cloud to be seen in it. They strolled along the seafront, pushing Honey in her buggy, then had lunch in Angel's favourite Italian restaurant. Honey was on top form. She was a year and a half now, and laughed and babbled contentedly throughout the meal. Cal was being so lovely as well.

I'm right to have stayed, Angel thought to herself, watching her husband and daughter together. *And maybe one day I'll even be able to completely forgive him for what he did.*

Cal caught her looking at him. 'Why so serious, babe?' he asked.

'I don't want you to go,' Angel said, and suddenly her eyes were full of tears.

'Hey!' he exclaimed, reaching out and taking her hand. 'I'll be back next week – and then maybe the following week you and Honey could come out with me?'

Angel nodded and brushed away her tears, but she couldn't brush away the feeling of sadness within her so easily. They spent the afternoon wandering around the shops, Cal spoiling both his girls with presents – a cute toy dog for Honey and a red Louis Vuitton scarf for Angel.

Connor sent a text saying that he would love to meet up with her to apologise properly for his behaviour. Without letting on to Cal, she texted him back telling him that she wasn't interested and he was never to contact her again.

Back home she gave Honey her tea while Cal quickly packed. At six it was time for Angel to drive him to Gatwick – her mum had come over to the house to baby-sit Honey as it was Lucy's day off.

When it was time to say goodbye, Angel felt

337

very emotional. She watched Cal go through to Departures, waiting until she could no longer see him.

It was just a twenty-minute drive or so from the airport to her house along the motorway, a route Angel was very familiar with, so she didn't worry unduly when the sky darkened and it began to rain – a downpour that quickly turned torrential. She immediately reduced her speed and moved to the inside lane. The heavy rain forced her to slow right down to thirty.

She was so busy concentrating on the road ahead that at first she didn't notice the car behind her, but suddenly she was almost dazzled by headlights which shone at full beam into her mirror. They were dangerously close, she realised.

'Back off!' she shouted out, panicking. *What the hell were they playing at?*

The car – some kind of huge 4x4 – continued to crawl closer to her, forcing Angel to increase her speed. But the conditions on the road were treacherous and she was terrified of skidding out of control. Desperate to get away, she moved to the middle lane, thinking that the other car would stay on the inside, but to her horror it pulled out behind her.

'Shit!' Angel exclaimed, not liking this one little bit. Could it be a pap following her? Surely they wouldn't be driving so dangerously? Or could it be a fan? God, perhaps she shouldn't have driven her pink VW Beetle – Cal was always going on at her, saying it made her too recognisable. The rain lashed against the windscreen. Angel increased her speed slightly, the car behind did the same – it was no more than six feet away now. She was terrified that it was going to go into the back of her. Usually she'd have had her hands-free mobile kit with her but she'd left it in their other car and her mobile was in her bag on the back seat.

Frantically she looked ahead, trying to see through the rain if there was a turn off she could take. She was now doing sixty and the car behind showed no sign of pulling back – the faster she went, the faster it went, like some terrifying game of cat and mouse. The ordeal carried on for about three miles, with Angel thinking that at any minute the car behind was going to crash into her, then, thank God, she saw a turn off. She made it look as if she was continuing straight on and then, at the last possible second, swerved sharply on to the slip road. To her intense relief the driver behind didn't react quickly enough to follow her.

Thankfully there was a service station nearby and Angel pulled into it. She was shaking so much that for a few minutes she couldn't get out of the car. She tried to calm down, taking deep breaths, all the while anxiously scanning the car park for the

4×4. Then she ran through the rain into the bright lights and warmth of the service area. Costa Coffee had never looked so welcoming before.

She sat down at one of the small tables and scrabbled through her bag for her phone to call Ray, her security guy. She quickly told him what had happened and he promised to come and pick her up as soon as possible with one of his lads to drive her car back. He advised her to call the police but she insisted she would wait until she was back home – not wanting to draw even more attention to herself.

She was desperate to phone Cal but his plane would only just have taken off; she thought of calling her mum and dad, but didn't want to worry them. She felt deeply shaken by what had happened so got up and bought herself a cup of tea, conscious all the time of the people around her. She was aware of quite a few curious looks from people who obviously recognised her, but luckily no one came over. Angel felt far too jumpy to be surrounded by strangers. As she sat down with her tea, she kept looking round the service area. *What if the person in the car had realised where she was and followed her?* She felt horribly exposed, sitting where she was. *Nothing's going to happen here,* she tried to tell herself. *There are CCTV cameras everywhere. No one would do anything here.*

After she had finished her drink she wandered

round the shops, picking up magazines and aimlessly flicking through them, anything to distract her, but kept continually looking over her shoulder. At one point someone tapped her on the shoulder and asked for her autograph. It nearly gave her a heart attack. After about twenty minutes her phone rang – it was Ray, to let her know he had arrived. It was such a relief to see his familiar face when they met up that Angel almost burst into tears.

'Are you all right?' he asked.

She'd known Ray for years. Before he'd gone into security he had worked with her dad so he was someone she trusted completely.

'Not really,' she said, shaking her head. 'Can we just get out of here?'

Back home, the first thing Angel did was to pick up her daughter and cuddle her close while Ray and her mum insisted that she call the police.

'D'you really think I need to?' she asked. 'Nothing actually happened, and I can't even give them the registration or make of the car.'

'You must report it,' Ray replied, looking serious. 'And I don't think you should drive the Beetle for a while. Stick to using the Merc, it's more anonymous.'

Just then the doorbell went. He said he would answer it and Angel went into the living room to call the police. They promised to send an officer round to the house to take a statement in the next couple of hours. In a way she felt reassured that they weren't rushing straight round, it made her feel as if the incident hadn't been too serious and maybe she was overreacting. That was until she walked back into the kitchen and discovered Ray and her mum staring in disbelief and shock at a huge wreath of lilies.

'What the hell's that!' Angel exclaimed.

'I've no idea. It was delivered by a florist while you were on the phone,' Ray told her, looking worried.

Angel marched over to the arrangement, reaching for the small hot pink envelope attached to it. She ripped it open. Inside was a single piece of pink paper with the words '*R.I.P. Angel*' written on it.

'How sick is that!' she said, showing Ray and her mum the note, but she sounded braver than she felt. Wanting to get rid of the poisonous little message, she went to throw it in the bin, but Ray stopped her. 'The police should look at that.'

'Do you think it's connected with that car?' Angel asked anxiously.

He shrugged. 'I don't know, but I don't like this, Angel. I'm going to phone up some of my lads. Get them to come over and check round the property. Has anyone else come to the house?' he asked Michelle, who shook her head.

Angel shivered, suddenly feeling cold.

'Ray, will you go and check upstairs?' she asked, picking up Honey again and giving her a cuddle, more for her own benefit than for her daughter's. And then she made sure all the blinds were pulled down in the kitchen. She didn't like the idea of anyone being able to look in even though that was unlikely as the grounds were surrounded by a high fence, topped with wire and CCTV cameras. Both she and her mum jumped when Angel's mobile rang.

'It's Dad,' Angel said.

'Oh, thank God! Are you all right?' She had never heard her dad sound so upset before.

'I'm fine, Dad,' Angel replied, wondering what had got him so worried. And then he revealed in a voice that almost shook with emotion that he'd just received an anonymous call, saying that she had been killed in a car crash.

Angel felt her knees give way and then collapsed on to a chair. Now she was scared, really scared.

'I don't know what's going on, Dad, but I think you'd better come over.'

Twenty minutes later Frank arrived looking serious and, after hugging his daughter, insisted on having a long conversation with Ray in the living room. Angel tried to get hold of Cal but his phone was still switched off. She told herself to be rational and reasonable, that his flight probably hadn't yet landed, but she was desperate for reassurance.

Then a couple more of Ray's security guards turned up, reassuringly huge and looking as if they'd be a match for anyone. They checked over the entire house and grounds but there were no signs of any intruder.

A young male PC arrived to take a statement from her and Angel ended up telling them about Simone's stalker-type behaviour when Cal had left her. The young officer dutifully wrote down what she told him but Angel couldn't help feeling that he was sceptical about it. It didn't help that Cal had never pressed charges against Simone. Maybe the policeman thought she was making it all up. *God, this was like a nightmare.*

Her mum and dad insisted on staying the night, and Michelle busied herself with making endless cups of tea and toast for everyone. Even though she'd had nothing since lunch Angel couldn't eat anything, though. The thought that someone wanted to hurt her was just too scary . . .

Finally Cal phoned. He was shocked to find out what had been going on and pleaded with her to come over to Italy without delay so that he could look after her.

'I'll be fine, Cal,' she told him, trying to put on a brave face. 'I've got two shoots this week that I don't want to cancel, plus it's Candy's hen weekend. Why should I let some nutter dictate how I live my life? Ray's going to be with me and Honey, I promise.'

She sounded much more confident than she felt and that night as she curled up alone in bed, even knowing that there were people close by, she didn't feel safe. Images of that terrifying drive kept flashing through her mind. What if the other car had driven into her? Who was out there, wishing her harm? A small voice inside said there was probably only one person who fitted the bill and that was Simone. Angel had voiced her concerns again to Cal but he still thought it unlikely his ex could have been involved in something like this. Angel wasn't convinced, though, remembering all too clearly that look of hatred on Simone's face at the party. Frankly, she'd looked capable of anything . . .

But over the next couple of days there were no more disturbing events and the police reported that Simone had been at Sandy Lane in Barbados with her boyfriend when Angel contacted them. The police seemed certain that it had been someone playing a sick joke on Angel, just after some publicity. But she wasn't taking any chances and asked Ray to be Honey's full-time security guard for the time being, and to provide guards for her whenever she went out.

Nights were the worst. She had trouble sleeping – several times she ended up curled on her duvet beside her daughter's cot, wanting to be sure that she was safe.

*

'God, Angel, your life is just like a film!' Jez told her as he arranged her hair for a lads' mag shoot she was doing.

'I could do without the drama,' she said grimly.

'I know, babe, but so long as you keep your security with you, I'm sure everything will be fine,' he said breezily. Indeed Jez was rather enjoying the novelty of Angel having two pumped up security guards with her and had been flirting outrageously with them all morning. Maybe she should try and be like him, and not take it all so seriously, but then he didn't have a daughter to worry about. At the thought of Honey, Angel reached for her mobile and phoned Lucy for the third time that morning to check on her daughter.

'All okay?' Gemma asked when Angel finished the call.

'Yes, fine, thanks, Gem,' Angel replied, then lowered her voice so Jez couldn't hear. 'Are you all right? You look a bit pale.' By now Gemma was nearly twelve weeks pregnant.

'Yes, I just feel really knackered at the moment,' her friend replied. 'I've got my twelve-week scan next week so I'll feel better when I've had that. I want to know that everything is all right.'

'I'm sure it will be,' Angel replied, wanting to reassure her and suddenly feeling guilty for being so caught up in her own worries that she'd neglected to think of her friend's. 'Listen, don't worry about staying till the end of the shoot, I'm sure I can fix my make up if I need to. You go home and rest, I don't want you to overdo it.'

'Thanks, Angel,' Gemma said, managing a smile.

'What are you two gossiping about?' Jez demanded from the other side of the room.

'Oh, just about this weekend. I've got Candy's hen night and I'm not really looking forward to it,' Angel quickly lied.

'You'd better not be this negative about my . . . umm, I'm still not sure what to call it. I'm not a hen, and I don't see myself as a stag . . . what about my cock weekend?' he replied.

'So long as you mean of the feathered variety,' Angel said dryly. 'And of course your – whatever you want to call it – will be one of *the* events of my social calendar.'

'Just one of them?' he spluttered.

'I was teasing. It will be *the* event, of course,' she assured him

'That's more like it!' Jez answered. 'And just go and enjoy Candy's party, it's bound to be fun.'

Chapter 13

The Truth Will Out . . .

'It's like WAGs Reunited!' Candy exclaimed
delightedly as she welcomed Angel into her hotel
suite at the Berkeley Hotel in Knightsbridge. She
was dressed head to toe in Chloe and looked pretty
and fresh-faced. Inside the luxurious suite Suki and
Madison were already installed on huge sofas,
drinking champagne. They looked equally pleased
to see Angel. They were less dressed up than
Candy, both in jeans which Angel was relieved
about as clothes were the last thing on her mind at
the moment. She was casual in a denim mini, black
Uggs, and a baby pink cashmere sweater.

'This is my second hen weekend!' Candy declared,
pouring Angel a glass of champagne. 'I've already
had one in Manchester with my mates up there,
which was dead wild, but I thought it would be nice
to see you guys down in London for a proper girls'
night in. I'm all clubbed out, to be honest.'

She seemed very excited that they were all together again.

Angel smiled. She'd forgotten how sweet Candy was – sweet by name, sweet by nature. She'd not been looking forward to this weekend as last week had been so stressful, but now she was with her friends it actually was a relief to be able to forget her problems, especially since Candy had downsized her hen night plans. Now they were just going to have one night spent chilling out, drinking champagne and ordering room service, and then having beauty treatments the following day. Honey was safe with Angel's mum and dad, and after a week of sleepless nights spent worrying about whoever was trying to upset her, Angel could finally relax.

The girls immediately launched into a gossip and giggle fest which was exactly what Angel needed. She felt some of the tension leave her. Candy and Liam's wedding was only a month away and she was in full pre-wedding meltdown, giving everyone a blow by blow account of how preparations were progressing. And she had so many questions for the other girls – from what presents she should give the bridesmaids to what 'something blue' she should have?

'What did you have?' she asked Angel. 'I was thinking of a blue thong but I worry it will show under my dress . . . and who wants VPL on their wedding day!'

'I had a blue ribbon sewn into the hem of my dress,' Angel told her, and Candy sighed, 'Your day looked so perfect.'

'Actually it wasn't,' Angel admitted. 'Because I had such bad post-natal depression. But I'm sure yours will be,' she added hastily, not wanting to rain on Candy's parade. She'd already told the girls something of what she had been through, but none of them knew about Cal's affair which was the way Angel planned to keep it.

'But you're okay now, aren't you?' Candy asked anxiously. 'And you and Cal are getting on great – I saw the pictures of you at the TV awards and you looked so in love! And I can't believe he had those tattoos done for you – it was so sweet!'

'Everything's good,' Angel replied, and not wanting the spotlight turned on her, asked after Suki and Madison's children. More champagne flowed, then over dinner, which they had in the suite, Candy asked another question that unsettled Angel.

'So, do you ever hear from that gorgeous baseball player?'

'God, yes!' Madison echoed. 'He was hot!'

'He was well buff!' put in Suki.

Angel tried to shrug the comments off. 'No, we're not in touch. He left a couple of messages after that story about us spending the night at his house broke, but I didn't call him back.'

Angel didn't like lying but she really didn't want to 'fess up to what had actually happened and how she had behaved like such a tease. But she obviously wasn't such a good liar as she'd hoped. She found herself blushing furiously – something Candy was quick to point out.

'You're bright red, Angel!' she exclaimed. 'I bet you still fantasise about him, don't you? All those long lonely nights when Cal's in Italy . . . don't tell me you don't think about those blue eyes and that sexy body?'

Angel shook her head. 'I really don't, I promise.' Another lie. She'd dreamed of Ethan several times, dreamed of being back in the car with him, only in her dreams she didn't push him away . . .

'Who's your fantasy?' She turned to Madison who revealed she still carried a torch for Leonardo DiCaprio and Suki confessed to fancying José Mourinho.

'How gutted was I that he turned down the England job?'

'You and most of the female population!' Madison shot back.

At first Candy refused to admit that she fantasised about anyone other than her fiancé, but under closer questioning confessed to Matt Damon. 'Though, actually, if I didn't know you so well, Angel, I'd probably have to say Cal because he's well fit. But I promise I don't,' she added quickly.

351

Angel laughed. 'It's okay, I take that as a compliment.' Though she couldn't help thinking of someone else who no doubt fantasised about Cal non-stop – Simone – and that was not such a pleasant thought.

Just then there was a knock on the door of the hotel suite. 'Don't tell me!' Candy exclaimed. 'You guys have booked me a stripper! I already had one last week, and I hope this one's better or should I say bigger – the other one had a dick the size of a party sausage. It was so disappointing!'

She leaped up from the sofa and ran to open the door while Suki, Madison and Angel all looked at each other blankly.

'Did you book a stripper?' Madison mouthed to Angel, who shook her head.

By now Candy had opened the door where she was presented with a large gold box in the shape of a heart. 'This looks interesting!' she exclaimed, then added after reading the gold label, 'Oh, it's for you, Angel,' and handed over the box.

'Really?' she said in surprise. 'But I wasn't expecting anything.'

'Maybe it's from Cal?' Madison put in. Suddenly Angel had a very bad feeling about this box. What if it contained another nasty surprise from her stalker?

'I don't want to open it,' she said quietly, putting it down on the sofa beside her and quickly filling the others in on her terrifying experience in the car and the wreath of lilies that had been delivered.

'Why don't you phone Cal and see if it is from him?' Suki suggested – ever practical. A phone call later and Angel's anxiety levels were sky-high when Cal confirmed he hadn't sent her anything.

'Oh my God!' Candy exclaimed hysterically, leaping up from the sofa. 'I've just had a terrible thought – say it's a bomb!'

'Of course it's not a bomb!' Madison insisted, rolling her eyes at Candy's over-the-top reaction.

'I'm sure you're right but I think we should get the police to check it out, given what's been happening to Angel,' Suki said reasonably.

'Oh, for God's sake!' Angel exclaimed. 'I'm sick of this person messing with my head. I'm just going to open it and be done with it.' And before any of the others could stop her she had pulled open the box. Inside was a photograph of Cal and her on their wedding day, except that Angel's face had been carefully cut out of the photograph. It looked very sinister.

'That is *so* creepy!' Candy exclaimed, looking over her shoulder. 'It's just the kind of thing serial killers do . . .'

'*Candy!*' Madison exclaimed sharply.

'Sorry!' she replied, shamefaced. 'I didn't mean it, I've just watched too many horror films. I'm sure it's nothing like that.'

'Well, I don't exactly think the person who sent me this wishes me well, do you?' Angel said, sounding way more confident than she felt. There was a small pink envelope with the photograph, exactly the same as the one which had accompanied the lilies, and suddenly she realised she'd seen an envelope like that before – on some hate mail she'd been sent several months ago. With trembling fingers Angel ripped open the envelope and drew out the matching pink card.

'Not long now before everyone knows the truth about your marriage, Angel.'

'What does that mean?' Candy demanded.

'Well, I'm going to phone reception and get them to call the police,' Suki said, taking control and picking up the phone. The mood of the evening had completely changed now. All the girls were subdued, their earlier carefree laughter forgotten as they rallied round Angel and insisted on giving her a brandy. She couldn't think straight until she had called her parents and checked that Honey was okay.

'Someone must have followed me,' she said, fear taking over. 'They must have followed me from home and seen where I was staying. How else would they know?'

'Try not to worry,' Madison said, sitting down next to Angel and putting an arm round her. 'The police will be here soon and they'll know what to do.'

'Why is this happening to me?' Angel said in despair, her beautiful green eyes wide with fear, her face drained of colour.

'Do you have any idea who could want to upset you like this?' Suki asked.

'The only person I can think of is Simone – she hates me. I mean, *really* hates me.'

'She's such a bitch!' Candy put in. 'No wonder Jamie left her.'

'Did he?' Angel asked. 'When did that happen?'

'A couple of weeks ago, I think,' Candy went on. 'I read it in one of the mags.'

'God, that can't have pleased her,' Angel said. 'I wonder if it tipped her over the edge.'

'We don't know it's her,' Madison said reasonably.

'And that makes me feel so much better!' Angel retorted. 'That there could be someone else out there who hates me just as much! I'm sorry,' she quickly added, 'I didn't mean to snap like that, it's just that I'm really frightened. I thought I was safe here, but I'm not, am I?' She got up and paced around the room, coming to rest by the window which overlooked Hyde Park. The city lights looked so pretty but Angel couldn't help wondering who was out there, wanting to hurt her . . .

The young female detective who arrived an hour later questioned her at length about recent events and once again Angel brought up Simone's name and the detective promised to follow it up. It was only as an afterthought that Angel decided to mention Connor and Gabrielle as being two other people with a possible grudge against her – though she could tell that the detective didn't believe her.

'So you feel that because Gabrielle asked you to take part in a threesome with her husband, she might be involved in this?' the policewoman had asked, her raised eyebrows and sceptical expression showing that she had her doubts.

'Look, I know it sounds really far-fetched,' Angel replied, 'and I know he's the England Captain, but they were both pissed off with me, that's all. And then a story came out about what they got up to and maybe they think it had something to do with me. Plus Connor has been sending me gifts and texts. I think he's got a bit of a thing about me.'

'And do you often get these kinds of propositions?' the detective asked. Which told Angel everything she needed to know: the woman clearly didn't believe her and thought she was some kind of attention-seeking slapper.

Angel clenched her fists, trying to keep her cool. 'No, I do not! Someone is trying to hurt me. Don't you think you should be trying to find out who they are, rather than sitting there and judging me!'

God, and to think she had been glad when she was introduced to a female detective! Maybe a man would have been more sympathetic after all.

Things became rather terse between Angel and the detective after that. She only noted down a few more details and then left, promising to keep Angel informed of any developments. As soon as she'd gone Angel phoned Cal who did his best to reassure her that everything would be okay.

'I think whoever is behind all this is going to go to the press about you and Alessia,' she said, wincing as she forced herself to say the name.

'You don't know that,' he replied. 'Try not to worry about it.'

Angel knew that there was very little Cal could say but all the same she was exasperated by his attitude – he was the one who had got them into this situation in the first place!

'Fucking hell, Cal!' she shouted back. 'How can I not worry about it? I don't want the world to know what happened, can't you understand that? It's private and I don't want everyone picking over it – wondering about the state of our marriage.'

'I know, I know,' he sighed wearily. 'But what else can I say?'

'Nothing,' Angel replied. 'There's nothing you can say.'

'I love you,' was his answer, 'and I'm sorry you're having to go through this.'

'So am I,' Angel replied bleakly, then added, 'Love you too.'

She tried to regain her composure for a few minutes before she rejoined her friends. She didn't want them to see her looking upset and couldn't deal with anymore questions. Half of her wanted to stay in her own suite where she could be alone, but she forced herself to go and join the others.

'I'm so sorry, Candy,' she said as soon as she did. 'I've completely ruined your night.'

'Don't be silly, Angel! It's not your fault. And anyway, the night's not over yet. I've ordered hot chocolates all round and we've got a whole box of treats to share, plus some chick flicks.' Angel glanced over at the pink box Candy gestured to that was overflowing with popcorn, chocolate bars and Maltesers.

'Have something sweet,' Suki urged. 'It will make you feel better.'

Angel shook her head. 'I'm not hungry anymore.'

'God, I just knew you wouldn't eat under stress!' Madison said. 'If it was me, I would have demolished everything in minutes!'

Angel sat back on the sofa, hugging her knees. 'Hot chocolate sounds good, though.'

'So did the detective give you any idea how soon they'll find whoever is behind all this?' Suki asked.

'No,' Angel replied grimly. 'And she didn't seem too concerned about it all.'

'And you really don't know who it could be?' Candy asked. 'I suppose it's very A-list, though, isn't it? To have your own stalker?'

'It's one trend I'm sure Angel could do without,' Madison said, giving Candy another stern look.

'Sorry! I wasn't thinking.'

'It's okay,' Angel replied. 'Let's just watch a DVD.' But while the others got stuck into *Holiday* she just sat there quietly, brooding about the threat contained in the note. Although she was famous and had made her name by modelling, at heart she was a deeply private person and the thought of everyone finding out that Cal had been unfaithful to her was almost unbearable. It would mean the spotlight being turned full beam on to their marriage. She just didn't know if she could cope with that.

Angel barely slept that night, tormented with anxiety about what was going to happen – the worst thing was feeling so powerless, feeling that someone else was going to decide her fate. As soon as she got up, skipping breakfast in her haste to get home, she made her apologies to Candy and left. She was in no mood to lie around all day being pampered. She felt too tense, too on edge, and with a horrible sense of foreboding. Every time she got a text message she dreaded opening it in case it was from the stalker again or else a journalist. At least Gemma and Tony were round at her parents' for Sunday lunch so she was able to talk to her best friend.

'Cal thinks it was someone playing a sick joke,' Angel told her. 'And that's what the police seem to think as well. What do you reckon, Gemma? I keep thinking of Simone.'

'But the police said she was out of the country,' Gemma reminded her.

'That doesn't stop her organising it,' Angel said darkly. 'But maybe it could have been Gabrielle?' Gemma was the only person besides the detective and Cal whom she had told about the tacky invitation.

'But why would she? It's too late now anyway, the press already knows about their pervy little games,' Gemma said.

'God, I don't know!' Angel exclaimed, getting up from her chair and pacing round her mum's tiny but immaculate kitchen. She was unable to sit still for even a few minutes.

'Why don't we go for a walk with Honey?' Gemma suggested, quick to pick up on Angel's mood.

But she shook her head. 'I just don't want to be out with Honey at the moment. I don't feel safe, Gem, I keep thinking that someone is watching me.'

She shivered and hugged herself. 'And every time my phone goes I think it's going to be a journalist telling me they know about Cal's affair. It's doing my head in!' She sighed then said, 'I'm going to have some more wine, can I get you something?' She opened the fridge and took out a bottle of Pinot Grigio.

'Just water, thanks. And try not to worry – maybe it won't come out. Cal is really popular with the public, and sometimes the press don't print stories even when they have them if the person is popular.'

Angel laughed harshly. 'I don't believe that for a second! I bet they're all dying to see us fall.' Almost immediately her eyes filled with tears and she turned back to Gemma. 'I just can't bear the idea of people knowing about him. It will be like me finding out all over again but a million times worse, because can't you just imagine how the press will drool over all the details? If this gets out it will be with us forever, and I just don't know if I'm strong enough to deal with that.'

'Angel, you are a strong person – you can deal with it,' Gemma said determinedly. 'And if you don't, then you are letting whoever is doing all this win.'

But despite her friend's fighting talk, tears continued to rain down Angel's cheeks.

*

361

Around three o'clock in the afternoon there was a knock at the door. To Angel's relief it was Cal. As soon as he saw her he took her in his arms and held her tight.

'I got the first flight back that I could and I've managed to get next week off. I'm so sorry this is happening, but it will be all right, I promise. We'll find out who's behind it.'

For a precious few minutes while she clung to Cal Angel felt as if the events of the past week had been a bad dream. Cal was right wasn't he? They could get through this.

After catching up with her parents and with Gemma and Tony, Cal insisted that they all go out for a walk by the sea, telling Angel he didn't want either her or Honey to be cooped up inside any longer. With Cal by her side, she finally felt safe again. And it was good to be out in the fresh air. She'd been spending far too much time inside lately and it wasn't healthy for her or her daughter. It was a beautiful afternoon in early-May – one of Angel's favourite months because everything seemed full of promise with the summer to look forward to.

They drove into Brighton then walked along the promenade towards Hove, enjoying the sea air and the blue sky, the cries of the gulls as they wheeled overhead. It was a typical Brighton Sunday afternoon by the sea, with families out for walks, couples strolling hand in hand, groups of friends laughing about the night before, and rollerbladers weaving about among the walkers. Everything seemed so normal, but every now and then Angel found herself looking over her shoulder, checking no one was following them . . .

That night Michelle offered to baby-sit, allowing Angel and Cal to go out for dinner with Gemma and Tony. At a restaurant which overlooked the sea the four friends caught up with each other's news and Angel realised how much she had missed nights like this. With Cal away in Italy there had been too few of them recently. In the past the four of them had gone out together at least once a week; now it felt like they barely saw each other. Angel couldn't help thinking back to those days before she'd had post-natal depression, before Cal had strayed . . . how carefree and happy her life had seemed then.

'How are Jez's wedding plans going?' Cal asked, pulling her back to the present and causing both her and Gemma to roll their eyes.

'Let's just say, full on,' Gemma replied. 'Anyone would think he was getting married next week rather than in three months' time. I just hope he hasn't driven Rufus away by then. I tell you, that man has the patience of a saint. I don't know how he puts up with Jez.'

'True love,' Tony put in. 'Just like you and me.'

'In your dreams, babe,' Gemma shot back. 'I'm just with you until something better comes along!'

'Likewise,' Tony replied.

Cal and Angel laughed at the pair of them. They were always underplaying their feelings for each other but as far as Angel was concerned they were fooling no one – she knew how much they loved each other. She looked out of the window at the silvery reflection of the moon on the inky black sea. It was a still night so there were barely any waves, the water rippling gently on the shore.

Cal took her hand and said quietly, 'You okay?'

She turned her head and nodded. 'We'll be all right, won't we, Cal?'

'Of course we will,' he said determinedly, putting his arm round her and pulling her close to him. 'More than all right, I promise.' Then he whispered, 'Love you.'

'Love you too,' she answered, leaning her head on his shoulder, praying that he was right.

But what she had no way of knowing was that this was the calm before the storm and that after tonight nothing would be the same for her and Cal ever again . . .

They were driving home when Angel got the text. The moment she saw that it had come from a withheld number she knew it was not going to be good news. With a sick feeling of dread she opened the message: *Tomorrow everyone will know what your husband did last summer. Enjoy reading all about it.*

This was it then, the moment she had feared.

'Who's the text from?' Cal asked, glancing at her anxiously.

'It's from the stalker. They've gone to the press.' Angel's voice cracked with emotion.

Immediately Cal pulled over and took her hand. 'I know it's going to be hard for you, Angel, but we can get through this. Come to Italy with me, we'll sit it out there. If we don't say anything and don't react, the press will soon get tired of the story,' he said urgently, trying to get some reaction from her. Angel was staring out of the window and into the darkness, feeling completely numb.

'It's always going to be out there now, everyone is going to know,' she whispered.

Cal put his arm round her. 'Please, Angel, we can get through this,' he repeated.

But Angel wasn't so sure.

When they arrived back at the house her sense of foreboding intensified when she saw to her horror that the press were already camped outside. There was a scrum of at least fifty of them swarming about in front of the gate, all jostling to get a shot of the couple.

'Oh my God!' she exclaimed.

As soon as the pack saw their car, the shouts started up. *'Angel, what do you think about Cal's affair?'*

'Are you going to stand by him?' 'Cal, what have you got to say for yourself?'

Angel sank down in her seat, pulling her pashmina over the lower part of her face. She desperately didn't want them to get a picture of her. Cal stared stonily ahead. He had to open his window to key in the entry code to the gate and the photographers tried to get a shot then – some actually thrusting their lenses through the open window while he tried to push them away. The gate opened and Cal put his foot down and screeched through. The photographers knew better than to pursue them inside. Neither Angel nor Cal spoke as he pulled in as close to the house as he could and the two of them ran inside. But even when they had closed the front door and she knew no one could see them there was no real escape because they could still hear the shouts outside. Angel felt completely trapped. The wolves were at their door.

'England Ace beds Italian Beauty!' & *'Cal's Italian Job!'* screamed the headlines on the paper with the exclusive – the front page dominated by that picture of Cal and Alessia embracing. Words and picture swam in front of Angel's eyes. It was like finding out about his betrayal all over again. She felt completely contaminated as she feverishly read the article. Alessia had not spoken to the press

which should have been a small comfort but in place of lurid details from her, a 'friend' of hers was quoted describing the couple's encounter: how they couldn't keep their eyes off each other in public, how Alessia had confided what a fantastic lover Cal had been, how Cal had told her that he and Angel were having problems, how he was sick of his wife's glamour modelling.

'It's not true,' Cal told her after he'd quickly read the story, 'I never spoke about you to Alessia. I don't know where the hell they got that from.'

He angrily paced round the room. Lucy had taken Honey to the playroom and was doing some painting with her so it was just Cal and Angel in the kitchen, locked in their own private hell. Or so it seemed to Angel.

'You slept with her. That much is true, isn't it?' she said bitterly, and Cal could only hang his head.

'Please, Angel, let's not go through all that again,' he replied. He looked pale with exhaustion; neither of them had slept. He walked over to Angel and tried to put his arm round her, but she angrily pushed him away.

'How do you think this makes me feel?' she shouted, sweeping the papers from the table. 'Everyone knows now. I feel so humiliated!'

'Please keep your voice down. We don't want to upset Honey,' Cal tried to calm her.

'Oh, shut up!' Angel shouted back. 'It was you not keeping your dick in your pants that got us here.'

And with that she ran out of the room and upstairs where she lay curled up on their bed, sobbing. It was as if their reconciliation had never happened. She felt as hurt and betrayed as she had when she'd first found out about Cal's infidelity, tormented by thoughts of him and Alessia together, raw with pain that he had been unfaithful. She was desperate to talk to Gemma, to get some perspective on this, some reassurance from her friend. She felt so lost, so alone. But Gemma's phone went straight to voicemail and Angel really didn't feel like speaking to anyone else.

After a couple of hours she had calmed herself enough to go back downstairs. Cal was in his study, on the phone to his agent, and Lucy was giving Honey her lunch. Cal had told her what had happened and Angel couldn't help feeling awkward with the nanny. Lucy was doing her best not to show it, but clearly she too felt embarrassed.

Angel bent down and kissed her daughter then said to Lucy, 'I'm sorry, I think we're going to have to stay in at least for today, but tomorrow I want you to carry on as normal and take Honey to her singing group. I'll get one of Ray's lads to go with you so the press won't bother you.'

At this Lucy looked even more embarrassed. 'I should tell you, Angel, that they've already contacted me and been offering me money to do an interview with them.'

Angel was horrified. 'What about?'

'They want to interview me about your marriage. Don't worry,' the girl added hastily, 'I've said no way. I mean, I signed the confidentiality agreement with you when you hired me, but even if I hadn't I would never do something like that.'

The vultures were clearly circling, wanting to pick away even more at Angel's life with Cal.

'Oh my God!' she exclaimed. 'Have they offered you lots of money?'

Lucy nodded. 'Don't worry, Angel, I'm not going to do it. And anyway, I've got nothing bad to say.'

'I'm really sorry that you've been dragged into all this,' she continued, bending down and giving Honey a hug to hide the fact that her eyes were full of tears at this new humiliation.

'Don't worry,' Lucy reassured her. 'The press will be around for a week or so and then it will all blow over, you'll see.'

Miserably Angel nodded then wandered into Cal's study. He'd finished speaking to his agent and was sitting at his desk, head in his hands. He looked up when she walked in. 'Hey,' he said. 'Did you manage to get some sleep?'

She shook her head and quickly told him what Lucy had said. He clenched his jaw. 'Bastards,' he muttered. 'We've got to be strong, babe, and expect things like this. They're probably going to be phoning all our friends and acquaintances to try and dig up some fresh dirt.'

'There's nothing else I should know, is there, Cal?' Angel asked, sick with apprehension. *What if he had been seeing someone else?*

'Of course not!' he exclaimed. 'You've got to believe me.' He got up and hugged her.

'I want to,' she whispered, 'I really do.'

Angel spent the rest of the day phoning her family and friends to warn them about the press, but she still couldn't get hold of Gemma which puzzled her as usually her friend was quick to return her calls. Everyone was sympathetic, said all the right things and promised that they wouldn't talk to any journalists – everyone except Carrie who asked Angel if she wanted to tell her story. Apparently Carrie had already received some very lucrative offers.

'There's nothing to say!' Angel had snapped at her agent. 'I'm not making any comment on this. So drop it!' And wanted to add, *or I'll drop you*. Really, this might be the time to get a different agent; she didn't think she could cope with Carrie's greed and insensitivity much longer. She treated Angel as if she were a commodity for sale to the highest bidder.

By the early-evening she was so exhausted that

all she could do was curl up on the sofa with Honey and watch *Postman Pat*, promising her daughter that she would do some proper playing with her tomorrow. Outside it was a warm evening, the garden had never looked more beautiful, but there was no way Angel wanted to go out there and risk being photographed or shouted at by the press. Cal made supper for the three of them but she wasn't hungry, even though she'd eaten nothing. Ray and his lads had been patrolling the grounds throughout the day but outside the gates the press were still waiting, still hoping they were going to get something else . . .

That night Cal tried to hold her in his arms but Angel pulled free of his embrace even though usually she loved sleeping like that. 'I'm too hot,' she lied, needing her space, still angry with him for the hurt he had caused her.

'It will be all right, Angel,' he told her again. 'I promise.'

She didn't reply; she couldn't share Cal's certainty. After yet another sleepless night she really needed to talk to Gemma and was feeling extremely upset that she hadn't heard from her. *Where was her best friend when she needed her?* She texted Gemma and tried her number again but there was no reply. She ended up leaving a rather hurt message. Half an hour later Tony called her and then Angel discovered the shocking reason why Gemma hadn't returned her calls. She'd been in hospital, after suffering a miscarriage.

'Tony, I'm so sorry!' Angel exclaimed, devastated for her friend and her brother. Apparently Gemma had had some bleeding a few days earlier and when she had her scan they'd discovered that the baby had died. 'Can I come and see her?' Angel asked, desperate to console her friend.

'I'm sure she'd like that but she's very upset,' Tony replied.

'I'm going to come straight over,' Angel promised. Though as soon as she put the phone down, she remembered her own situation. 'Shit!' she exclaimed. *How the hell was she going to get to Gemma's flat without the press knowing?* In the end Ray drove her there with several press cars and motorbikes in hot pursuit.

'You really would have thought they'd have something better to do,' Angel said bitterly as the pack followed them. Fortunately Gemma and Tony lived in a block of flats on the sea front with a private underground garage. There was no way the press could follow them in or even park outside. Telling Ray she would call him in a few hours, Angel made her way upstairs, wondering what on earth she could say to comfort her friend.

Her brother answered the door; he looked done in, with dark shadows under his eyes. 'I'm so sorry,

Tony,' she said, in a voice full of emotion, giving him a hug.

'Yeah,' he replied wearily. 'Go through, Gemma's in the lounge. I'm going to leave you two to talk. I think she could do with it.'

Gemma was curled up on the sofa in her PJs, clutching a hot water bottle to her tummy. Her usually pretty face looked white with grief and exhaustion and her eyes were puffy and red-rimmed from crying. Immediately Angel rushed over and hugged her friend. Gemma didn't hug her back.

'I'm so sorry, Gem,' Angel said, her own eyes filling with tears at the sight of her friend looking so low.

'The doctors don't know why it happened,' Gemma said flatly. 'They say miscarriages are very common – one in four pregnancies ends in one. Did you know that?' She sounded numb with shock and Angel's heart ached for her.

She shook her head. 'No, I didn't know that. Did they suggest that you talk to someone, maybe have some counselling?'

'I think they gave Tony a number but I don't see what good it would do. I've just got to accept it, haven't I?'

'Oh Gem, I don't know what to say. Can I get you anything? A cup of tea or something? You look really pale.'

'That's because my baby's just been scraped . . . sorry, "removed" . . . from me,' Gemma said bitterly. Then her face crumpled and she started to sob, harsh, loud sobs that convulsed her.

Angel hugged her again. 'It'll be all right, Gemma, I'm sure you'll be able to have another baby.'

'I wanted *this* baby,' she wept.

For a few minutes Angel just held her friend. She wished more than anything that Gemma hadn't had to go through this. She remembered so clearly the look of excitement on her friend's face when she had first told Angel that she was pregnant. Then Gemma pulled away.

'Anyway,' she said, sniffing and trying to brush away her tears, 'what's been going on with you? Is everything okay? Tony said you'd been trying to get hold of me.'

Angel sighed. 'Compared to what you've been through, it's nothing. It's just that the press have got hold of the story about Cal last summer . . .' Her voice trailed off. She really didn't want to talk about it now.

'That's awful,' Gemma said. 'How are you both doing?'

'We're okay,' Angel lied, then got up and said briskly, to disguise the emotion she felt. 'Now look, I'm going to make you some tea and Tony said you hadn't eaten so I'm going to make some toast as well – even I can't mess up making toast.'

Tony was in the kitchen when she walked in. 'How did Gem seem?' he asked anxiously.

'She's very upset, isn't she?'

'I know. She's thinking of her mum and all those miscarriages she had.' Tony looked shattered. He was like her dad in that he rarely showed his feelings but Angel knew him well enough to know how upset he must be as well.

'And how are you?' she asked.

'I'm okay, just sad and worried about Gem. I hated her having to go through the operation. She was so brave about it.'

Angel reached out and squeezed her brother's hand. 'I'm sure you'll be able to have another baby.'

'I hope so,' he said quietly. Then added, 'I was talking to Cal when you were with Gemma. It's shit that it's all come out in the press.'

'It seems stupid to be upset about something like that with what you two have got to go through,' Angel said passionately, 'but I wish they hadn't found out, Tony.'

And then it was his turn to comfort his sister, giving her a hug and telling her that everything would be okay. Angel thought she might scream if anyone else said that to her.

As Ray drove her back home, after she'd spent the morning with Gemma, Angel made a decision. She wasn't going to live like a prisoner just because the press had got hold of the story. She was determined to carry on as normal and somehow, as Cal had said, ride out the storm.

But in the week that followed it wasn't easy. Whoever had tipped off the press in the first place kept up their hate campaign. For two days they sent Angel texts – the first asked nastily if she had enjoyed reading all about her husband, then there were others suggesting it was her fault that Cal had played away, culminating in the ominous message: *Are you sure your husband has told you the whole truth? Get ready to find out what he's really like*.

When she told Cal, he swore again that there had been no one else. Angel ended up changing her phone number. The press pursued her wherever she went and on several occasions when she was out with Honey, her daughter became terrified as photographers swarmed round the car, shouting out and thrusting their cameras at Angel and Honey, jostling to get their shot.

'Get away from my daughter!' Angel shouted at the pack, while Ray and the other guards muscled their way through.

Cal was given the week off by his manager and accompanied Angel to London when she had shoots to do, both of them wanting to present a united front, but the constant press attention wore them down, left them both feeling on edge, especially Angel.

Everywhere the couple went she felt that people were staring at them, in particular at her, wondering about their marriage, wondering no doubt if Cal's infidelity was a one off. It made her feel paranoid. And still the press couldn't seem to get enough of the story – one tabloid even had a poll on whether Angel should stick with Cal or dump him; there were items about it on breakfast TV, phone-ins on whether marriages could survive adultery; even columnists in the broadsheets – who Angel thought really should have known better – waded in with their own views about the marriage. And throughout all this neither Angel nor Cal said anything to the press.

Angel tried to put on a brave face as she worked, but it wasn't easy and she missed having Gemma with her. Although Cal couldn't have been more loving and more attentive to her during this time, she still felt incredibly angry and hurt by what he had done. He had been her hero for so long, she had put him on a pedestal, and now she was starting to realise that he was as fallible as anyone else.

By Friday Angel was sick of putting on an act. Cal was due to play in an England friendly against France the following day and wanted her to go to the game.

'Cal, I really don't want to, surely you understand that?' she said, shocked that he would expect her to attend after what had happened.

'I know it's a big ask,' he replied, 'but I could really do with you being there and it would help put an end to all the speculation in the press.'

The two of them were in the kitchen and he was cooking dinner but Angel had suddenly lost her appetite.

'Cal, I just don't know if I can do it. This week has been a total nightmare,' she said, willing her husband to see her point of view. She couldn't help thinking that he was being selfish.

As if to contradict her, Cal gently took her in his arms. 'I would really appreciate you being there, babe, and it's not like you'll be on your own – Madison will be there, along with Suki and Candy. They'll look out for you.'

Angel gave a heavy sigh. 'Okay, if it really means that much to you, but don't expect me to spend long in the players' lounge afterwards. And I'm *not* talking to that witch Gabrielle!'

'I'll make it up to you, I promise,' he replied, kissing her.

You're going to have a lot of making up to do, she thought bitterly.

Usually when she watched Cal playing football Angel was an enthusiastic supporter, her attention entirely held by the game, but the following day her mind was on everything but the pitch. Her close friends couldn't have been sweeter, all rallying round her and trying to protect her from the curious and superior glances she was getting from some of the other WAGs. Angel felt awful because she had missed Candy's wedding, as it had been impossible to go with the press pack on her heels, but Candy had been so wrapped up in her big day that she hadn't time to question Angel's reason for not being there. Now that she knew all about what Angel had been through she totally understood. Thank God Simone wasn't there, after Jamie had dumped her, but Gabrielle was and Angel was aware several times of the icy stares being directed at her by the Captain's wife and Lauren, her sidekick. And after every stare the two of them would whisper and giggle together, obviously bitching about Angel.

'Just ignore them,' Madison told her. 'They're not worth it. And it's not like Gabrielle has a perfect marriage, is it?'

'No,' Angel replied sadly, 'but I thought I did once.'

'Oh, I didn't mean you to take it that way!' Madison explained. 'No one has a perfect marriage, but yours is a strong one. You will get through this.'

Angel could only mutter, 'I hope so.'

England were thrashed by France. Usually Angel would have been gutted for Cal, but this time she barely registered the defeat. She had done her duty and now all she wanted to do was go home, but she had promised Cal she would stay for one drink so made her way to the players' lounge along with the other wives. Her friends stayed close to her but that didn't deter Gabrielle from coming over to their table.

'Gabrielle, how nice to see you,' Candy said insincerely. Gabrielle ignored her and looked at Angel, saying snidely, 'Not much fun reading about what your husband's been up to in the press, is it?'

'Well, I'm not as used to it as you are,' Angel snapped back. 'It must be a weekly event for you.'

'Shut up!' Gabrielle hissed, her composure cracking. 'And don't go near my husband.'

'I wouldn't go near him if you paid me!' she replied.

Gabrielle was visibly shaking with anger and was clearly about to reply when her huge bodyguard walked over to the table.

'Everything all right, Mrs Carter?' he asked, giving Angel a menacing look.

'I think Gabrielle was just leaving,' Suki put in, and though Gabrielle looked as if she had plenty more to say she turned and walked away, with her bodyguard closely behind her.

'What a bitch!' Candy exclaimed when Gabrielle was out of earshot, while Angel put her head in her hands and said, 'I've had it with that woman!

Maybe it would be better if Cal was dropped from the team and then I wouldn't have to meet her or her vile husband ever again!' She looked up to see the shocked expressions on her friends' faces. 'Okay, I take that back, of course I don't want him to be dropped, but you know what I mean?'

'We do, babe,' Madison agreed grimly.

At that moment the players walked into the lounge and Angel couldn't believe it when she saw Cal laughing and joking with Connor as he walked over to them. So much for him being angry about Connor's pervy little invitation! She was expecting Connor to go straight over to Gabrielle, sitting at the opposite side of the room, but instead he stayed at Cal's side and came over to Angel's table.

'I don't know what you two are smiling about,' she couldn't stop herself from saying, 'that was a shit game.' Usually she would never be that critical, but Cal had just made her very angry.

'Now you can tell us what you really think!' Connor joked back, then he said to Cal, 'I wouldn't take that attitude from my missus!'

Angel glared at Cal, thinking that if he said anything to piss her off then she was out of here, but she didn't hear his reply as they were joined then by Liam, Reece and Bradley.

Connor hung around a little longer, chatting to his team mates, and made sure that he was standing where he could keep staring at Angel, something that only increased her fury at her husband who seemed completely oblivious. Finally, to her relief, Connor said his goodbyes, but his parting comment left her reeling.

'By the way, Cal's up for that dinner we never got round to arranging so I'll see you soon, Angel.'

That did it! Angel abruptly got up and said, 'Cal, I want to go. Now.'

'Oh, come on, babe,' he replied. 'Liam's just got the drinks in. Let's stay for one more round.'

She couldn't believe he was behaving like this, after everything that had happened and after what they had agreed. He seemed more interested in looking good in front of his team mates than he was in her feelings.

'I'll meet you in the car then,' she said, quickly made her goodbyes to her friends and marched out of the lounge. In the players' car park Angel headed for Cal's Bentley and then did a horrified double take when she saw what she was convinced was the same 4x4 that had pursued her so dangerously on the motorway. She walked towards the vehicle, determined to get a closer look, but just as she did Gabrielle's bodyguard opened the door and stepped out of it.

Shit! It was the Carters' car!

Angel walked swiftly to the Bentley and got in, activating the central locking system so that no one could get in. She was really shaken but made herself watch the bodyguard's every move as he lit a cigarette and stood by the car smoking. Then she almost jumped out of her skin when Cal rapped on the window and she had to let him in.

'You didn't have to walk out like that, I felt a right idiot,' he said, sounding pissed off.

Like she cared about that now!

'Cal,' she said urgently, 'I think I've seen the car that chased me.'

'What!' he exclaimed. 'Are you sure?'

Angel nodded. 'I'm pretty certain it's that 4x4 over there.' She pointed out the Carters' car.

Cal shook his head. 'No way! That's Connor's car. You can't seriously think he would do something like that?'

'Not him!' Angel replied angrily. 'His wife, or more likely her bodyguard. You should have seen the look he gave me in the lounge, and he practically assaulted me that time in Portugal. I reckon he'd do anything Gabrielle asked him.'

Cal shook his head in disbelief. 'Angel, I can't believe Gabrielle would have anything to do with something like this.'

'You don't know anything of the sort!' Angel was raising her voice now, furious that Cal wouldn't take her accusations seriously. 'She's been funny with me ever since her pervy old bastard of a husband wanted me to have a threesome with them – and *he's* been chasing me. She's really jealous. She could be the one who took that picture of you and Alessia. Or if she didn't, I bet she knows who did.'

'Come on! I don't believe it,' Cal replied.

'Don't or won't? Because you can't upset your precious team mate!' Angel shot back.

'Well, it wouldn't do me any favours if I went around shooting my mouth off about the team captain,' he answered. 'I'd probably be dropped from the squad, for Christ's sake.'

'And we can't have that, can we?' she said bitterly.

'Look, babe,' Cal said, 'this has been a really stressful week for both of us, and I know you didn't want to come today either. I think you're just really over-sensitive at the moment. You need to put this all behind you. Whoever it was has got what they want. It's over now. Let's get home.'

Angel had to drive as he had been drinking and neither of them spoke during the two-hour journey. She was deeply hurt by Cal's attitude. And there was still no escape from the press. When she drove up to the gate, they were still camped out there in force.

'Why won't they leave us alone?' she said despairingly. 'How much longer can this go on for? I don't want Honey seeing all this – it's not good for her!'

'I know,' Cal told her, 'but it will burn itself out soon, I'm sure. The worst is over.'

But he was wrong; there was worse to come. At one a.m. they were both woken by a call from his agent. Angel sat up in bed, clutching the duvet to her as she studied her husband's drawn expression, heard him say, 'Are you sure it's going to come out tomorrow? And there's nothing we can do to stop it?' while the all too familiar sick feeling of dread grew inside her.

'What is it now?' she asked as soon as the call ended.

Cal's face had turned ashen. He couldn't look at her.

'There's another story coming out about Alessia and me tomorrow,' he said quietly.

'See!' Angel exclaimed. 'I knew she'd sell her story.'

Cal shook his head. 'She hasn't, but the paper have found out that . . .' He hesitated, clearly reluctant to carry on.

'Cal, just tell me!' Angel cried out.

He sighed heavily and said quietly, 'We didn't just have a one night stand.'

'Oh my God! You lied to me!' She sprang out of bed. 'How long did you see each other for?' she shouted.

'Three months.' Cal's voice was barely above a whisper. 'I thought you'd leave me if I told you the whole truth,' he said, hanging his head in shame.

Angel felt as if she'd been struck. She stood rooted to the spot, twisting her wedding ring around her finger.

'I know how bad it looks,' he continued. 'All I can say is that it was a terrible mistake and I will never be unfaithful again, never. I swear.'

'I can't believe you lied about it!' Angel shouted. 'Were you ever going to tell me?'

'I don't know,' he replied. 'I just didn't want to hurt you.'

'It's too late for that, isn't it!' Angel finally pulled the wedding ring off her finger and threw it at Cal. It struck him on the cheek, leaving an angry red mark. Then she turned and ran out of the bedroom, locking herself in the guestroom. Cal came after her and begged her to listen to him, but she refused and curled up on the bed sobbing, her hands over her ears to block out his voice.

When she walked into the kitchen the following morning Cal was already reading the paper. He looked as if he had aged ten years overnight.

'Let me see it,' she demanded.

'Please don't read it, Angel.'

'Give it to me,' she repeated, holding out her hand. Reluctantly Cal gave her the paper. Alessia was plastered across the front page, looking sensational in a black evening dress, with a smaller picture of Angel, taken recently, looking less than hot in a baseball cap and shades, under the headline: '*Cal Plays Away!*' The paper went on to reveal that Cal and Alessia had met secretly for three months to carry on their affair. The paper had details of the hotel suite the couple had met in, with photographs of the bed where they were said to have enjoyed all night 'romps'. Alessia's 'friend' gave more details: this time of Cal's prowess in bed, how he was a 'three times' a night lover; how he had lavished on Alessia gifts of expensive jewellery and sexy lingerie; how he'd been infatuated with the beautiful Italian model.

'I'm really sorry,' Cal said quietly. 'They're making it out to be something it wasn't. We probably only saw each other seven or eight times.'

'Perhaps I should phone Alessia for some tips,' Angel said bitterly. 'It's been a while since you've been a three times a night lover with me.'

'I'm so sorry, Angel . . .'

'Will you stop fucking saying sorry!' she shouted. 'It's not enough, don't you understand? It's not going to make everything better.'

'I know, but it's the only thing I can say.'

Suddenly she realised that she just couldn't go on living like this. 'I've got to get away,' she said, all the fight gone from her.

'Please, Angel, I love you more than anything else in the world,' Cal cried passionately, trying to hold her, but Angel backed away.

'I believe you love me, but I just can't be with you at the moment, I really can't.'

She was crying now and so was Cal. He was

begging her, 'Please, Angel, stay. I can't live without you.' She had never seen him so desperate.

'I can't think straight at the moment, so please, Cal, go back to Italy. I can't see what else we can do at the moment,' she said through her tears. 'I thought I was strong enough to give you a second chance, but now I don't know. I just need to be on my own for a while.'

And as she said the words she felt as if her heart was breaking.

Chapter 14

Escape To LA

'Darling, I think at last we've got your big break in the States!' It was Carrie on the phone and she sounded beside herself with excitement.

'Go on,' Angel said, not caring what her agent came out with. It had been three days since Cal had left for Italy, three long days of crying and misery. Carrie's phone call found her still in her pyjamas at eleven o'clock in the morning, mindlessly eating cereal straight from the packet.

'You've got a part in film! They start shooting in two weeks' time!'

'Really? How did that come about?' Angel asked, still not sharing Carrie's excitement.

'Because of my contacts, darling, and your good looks!'

'So what's the part?' Angel asked. 'You know I've never acted before.'

'Never say never!' Carrie said perkily. 'You can

be an MTA just like all the others. Think of Kelly Brook!'

'Yeah, but I don't want to make a complete tit of myself. Shouldn't I have some acting lessons or something?'

'Don't be silly! You're a natural in front of the camera. They just want you to look pretty. You haven't got to say very much, just a couple of lines. You're playing the girlfriend of some kind of megalomaniac in an action film,' Carrie continued. 'Doesn't it sound fantastic?'

Totally predictable, Angel felt like answering. Instead she said stubbornly, 'I'm not doing any nudity. I want that written into my contract.'

'Oh, Angel,' Carrie sighed, 'when did you get to be such a prude? No, there is no nudity. I think you have to wear a bikini and parade around a bit. Do you think you can manage that?'

There was a pause while Angel weighed up her options. *She had nothing to lose and maybe it would be good to be out of the country for a while. At least she would be free from the media scrum and might be able to think more clearly about what she should do next.*

'Okay, Carrie,' she said finally.

And her agent gave her more details. She would be out in LA for just under three weeks. At the mention of the city Angel thought of Ethan and almost changed her mind; she didn't think she could ever face him again. Then she reasoned that surely LA was such a big place there was no way she would run into him.

'Are you sure you'll be okay?' Angel asked Lucy for the twentieth time. She was getting ready to go out to one of Larry T. Chance's legendary pool parties, leaving Honey and her nanny in the luxurious house they were renting in Bel Air.

'We'll be fine,' Lucy reassured her, used to Angel's worrying. 'Just go and enjoy yourself.'

Angel shrugged, thinking that it was unlikely. They had been in LA three days now and Carrie had pretty much ordered her to socialise, telling her it would be good for her profile out here. She had hoped that being away from home would help clear her head, help her decide what she wanted to do, but she felt more confused and conflicted than ever – and on top of that had to put on a brave face and show the world that she couldn't have been happier.

The limo arrived to take her to the party and she gave her appearance one last check. Knowing that there would be eye-popping amounts of female flesh on display at the party, and knowing too that as one of the former centrefolds of Larry T. Chance's magazine *LA Dreams* she would be expected to bare some flesh herself, Angel had found what she thought was the middle ground.

She'd put on a black bikini and over it wore a loose black tee-shirt, which hung off one shoulder, pulled in at the waist with a silver belt, which just about covered her bum and a pair of killer-heel black ankle boots.

She knew the LA models would all be in girly colours and usually Angel would be the first to go for pink, but she also liked to be unpredictable and anyway black suited her mood right now. Without Gemma to do her make up, Angel kept things simple but dramatic with thick black eyeliner and several layers of mascara and wore just a dab of sheer lip gloss, so the look said 'just got out of bed sexy'.

As she sat back in the limo, Angel wondered what to expect from the party and whether she would know anyone at all. Maybe she'd see one of Larry's girlfriends whom she'd met before? And she meant 'one' because he had seven girlfriends who shared his pink mansion. Angel had posed for his magazine – a mix of sports features and naked models – several years earlier, in what had been her most revealing shots ever. She had bared everything. Since then Larry had wanted her to do another shoot, but so far she had resisted. She knew that while Cal might just about accept her going topless for the occasional glamour shot, if she went any further he wouldn't be happy. But a voice inside her said that maybe it didn't matter what Cal thought anymore . . .

*

'Angel! How lovely to see you again, and how gorgeous you look!' Larry kissed her hand while his babes looked on. He owned up to being sixty-five though Angel was sure he was way older, but the fake tan and dyed black hair, and no doubt regular face lifts, did a pretty good job of disguising his real age. She smiled and took the compliment graciously.

'Why don't you take Angel round the party?' he said to Cindy, one of the babes who was sitting next to him, sucking a lollipop.

'Cool,' she answered, slipping off the bar stool and taking Angel's hand. Cindy looked like the stereotypical LA girl, all bleached blonde hair, silicone implants and perfect tan. She was wearing a silver bikini top which left little to the imagination and bottoms which made a Hollywood wax absolutely essential. They walked round the party, Cindy smiling and fluttering her false eyelashes at any famous men and Angel taking in the sights – and there were many – topless girls playing volley ball in the pool; topless waitresses circulating with trays of exotic-looking cocktails; topless jugglers, fire eaters and acrobats performing; topless girls pole dancing on a stage on one of the lawns. Cindy chatted away, asking Angel the usual questions about how long she was out for, had she been here before and what she was doing, to which Angel gave fairly short answers – she didn't exactly see Cindy as her future soul-mate.

The other girl was seriously impressed that Angel was going to star in a movie and said that she had been in several herself, though she was very cagey when Angel asked what they were, saying that she couldn't remember the titles. *Or didn't like to,* Angel thought to herself, convinced that Cindy was talking about starring in porno flicks. The girl then asked her if she wanted to check out the games cottage which was hidden away in a small wooded area. Angel remembered it from her last visit – one of the rooms was devoted to a pool table and fruit machines, while the other was for more adult entertainment. All it had in it were cushions, a luxuriously thick carpet, a mirrored ceiling and a wide-sceen TV occupying an entire wall. But people didn't go in there to watch TV . . . Angel shook her head.

'What about the Jacuzzi?' Cindy asked. 'There are some really big stars hanging out there.' And she whispered the name of a famous movie star. Angel shook her head, knowing perfectly well that when guests weren't being naughty in the games room, they were playing sex games in the Jacuzzi. Cindy shrugged and gave her a look as if to say 'Loser' and Angel suddenly thought that she would rather be on her own.

'Cindy, I'll be fine if you want to go,' Angel told her. Cindy perked up, and after saying she would hook up with her later, tottered off in the direction of the Jacuzzi.

Angel made her way to the poolside and took a cocktail from a tray offered to her by a topless waitress then sat down at one of the many candlelit tables. Carrie had told her to go to the party and see Larry, which she'd done, and the way Angel saw it she would have her cocktail then slink off. She just wasn't in the mood for making small talk and no doubt every man she met would think that as one of Larry's former models she would be sexually available to them. There was someone heading towards her right now, a tall good-looking African-American. Angel frowned, trying to work out where she'd seen him before, and then she remembered: it was Logan, Ethan's friend and fellow baseball player. Her heart suddenly skipped a beat. Did that mean Ethan was here too?

'It's Angel, isn't it?' Logan asked. 'We met last summer.' He reached out his hand and Angel shook it. 'Hi, Logan,' she replied and couldn't help checking over his shoulder to see if Ethan was there too. But there was no sign of him.

'So what are you doing here, Angel?' Logan asked, and she gave a very edited version of why she was out in LA.

'Ethan's here somewhere,' he said, scanning the partygoers around them. 'I'm sure he'd like to see you again.'

'See who again?' Suddenly Ethan was at his friend's side, but the look of complete surprise on his face revealed that he hadn't been expecting to see him with Angel.

'Hi,' she said quietly, feeling very shy and self-conscious in his presence and remembering all too clearly how they had parted.

'Hi,' Ethan replied, and the initial shock had been replaced by his usual cool knowing look. *He wasn't going to let her in again,* Angel thought, and despite herself she felt regret.

'So who's this?' A blonde in a bright yellow bikini top and thong appeared at Ethan's side, wrapping her arms possessively round him.

'She's a model, just like you, Kasey,' Ethan said, in a way which Angel was sure was supposed to antagonise her. And Angel was sorely tempted to say that no way would she parade around in public with her arse cheeks on display, but she zipped it. She probably deserved that dig from Ethan.

'Oh,' replied Kasey, clearly not liking to see any competition near her man. 'Shall we go to the cottage?'

Angel couldn't stop her mouth from twitching into a smile which Ethan saw. 'We're playing pool, if you must know, Angel.'

'Oh, right,' she said sarcastically. 'I'll bet Kasey's got very good ball control.'

'You could always come along and watch,' he

replied, and his blue eyes which had looked so full of warmth all those months ago were now as cold as ice. *She had seriously pissed him off.*

Angel shook her head. 'I'm fine here, thanks.' Ethan gave her a barely perceptible nod, did that super-cool hand touching thing with Logan and left, with Kasey clinging on to him.

Logan was staring at Angel, almost open-mouthed in surprise. 'I had no idea he was going to be so rude to you. Are you okay?'

'Believe me, Logan, worse things have happened to me than that,' Angel said ruefully, hoping she could sneak out of the party right away.

'Well, I'm sorry he was like that. Listen, you should come and meet my wife and family while you are here, can I take your number?' Angel hurriedly gave it to him. Seeing Ethan again had unsettled her more than she could ever have anticipated. But just then a young woman in her twenties who was wearing a dress, a real novelty as nearly all the other female guests were in bikinis or thongs, came over and introduced herself. She was Camilla, assistant director on the film Angel was going to appear in. So instead of leaving Angel found herself spending much of the evening with her.

Camilla was English which was both welcome and unwelcome news to Angel. On the plus side it meant she didn't feel like quite such an alien talking to her; on the downside Camilla knew all about what had happened between her and Cal. Fortunately she only asked how things were and Angel simply replied 'fine'. Camilla seemed perfectly nice but that didn't mean Angel could trust her and she didn't want anything she said to come out in the press. Camilla knew quite a few other people at the party, several of whom were actors who were going to be in the film with Angel, including Parker, a quirky-looking young actor who was playing Angel's brother. He was funny and flirtatious and she instantly hit it off with him.

'Do you think it's okay if I fancy you? Seeing as you're my sister?' Parker asked after a couple of cocktails. 'Couldn't she be my adopted sister?' he added, turning to Camilla, who shook her head and laughed.

'Don't worry,' Angel put in, 'I'm only in for a couple of scenes and then I die, so you won't have to suffer for long.'

'Maybe we could add a scene where I get to do mouth-to-mouth resuscitation?' Parker persisted hopefully. Camilla and Angel laughed and at that moment Ethan walked past. He turned and looked at Angel and their eyes locked for a fleeting second before he walked swiftly away.

Whatever! Angel thought. She had way too many other complications in her life to worry about Ethan, didn't she? But that night when she lay in bed, unable to sleep, she did think about him. She remembered that connection between them, remembered the undeniable sexual chemistry. *He hates me now,* she told herself sternly, recalling the way Ethan had looked at her so coldly, and tried to silence the voice inside her which said she wished it wasn't so . . . And then almost immediately she felt guilty for even thinking about another man in that way.

The following morning as she was relaxing in the house with Honey, Parker called her to invite her to his birthday party that night, which was being held at Tropicana. Angel's first reaction was to say no, but Parker was so sweet and she realised it would be good to know a few more people in LA.

She spent the rest of the day with her daughter and Lucy. First of all they strolled down Rodeo Drive, one of the most exclusive shopping streets in the world, as Lucy was desperate to do some celeb-spotting. She was over the moon when she saw Lindsay Lohan and Paris Hilton. Then Angel took her to the Beverly Center, a trendy indoor mall. But her own heart really wasn't in shopping, she was just doing it for Lucy who had been so brilliant during the nightmare with the press in the UK. Angel ended up buying her several hundred dollars worth of clothes as a thank you, plus a few things for Honey, but nothing for herself. New clothes were not going to make her feel any better about her marriage. And even in LA she was followed by the paps – news of Cal's affair was still hot in the British press, with daily speculation about whether Angel would stand by her man or dump him – which made the shopping trip more of an ordeal than a treat.

Back at the Bel Air house she phoned Gemma who still sounded very down. Angel longed to say something that would make her friend feel better, but knew the grief was something Gemma was going to have to work through on her own. When she ended the call she felt so sad for her friend, and also lonely because she hadn't felt able to tell Gemma anything about how she was feeling. Angel had always relied on her friend in the past to help her through a crisis. Now she didn't feel that she had anyone she could confide in. She also had several messages from Cal. She really didn't want to speak to him but knew she had to eventually.

'Hi, it's me,' she said when Cal answered.

'It's so good to hear you! I've been thinking about you all the time. How are you? How's Honey?' The words were pouring out of the usually restrained Cal. She almost felt sorry for him; then stopped herself.

'We're fine,' she replied coolly. And as Cal went on to bombard her with more questions about what she'd been doing, gave only monosyllabic answers, keeping him at arm's length.

'I hate you and Honey being so far away from me. You will come back as soon as you finish filming, won't you? I've got to see you,' he said urgently.

'You'll see us soon,' Angel said abruptly, then made some excuse about needing to talk to Lucy. She sighed heavily as she ended the call. *She really didn't know what she wanted to do. Didn't know if she had a future with Cal.*

She checked on Honey who was fast asleep in her cot and then padded into her bedroom trying to decide what to wear for her night out. Carrie had told her to make a big effort when she was seen out in public, but right now Angel didn't really give a shit what she looked like. In the end she went for black skinny jeans and a black silk top worn with black satin Christian Louboutin stilettos.

'Angel!' Parker exclaimed. 'I'm so glad you could make it. Come on, let me introduce you to everyone.' She dutifully smiled at the tableful of his friends, who were lounging by the pool. Maybe it hadn't been such a good idea to come here. She felt her usual mixture of self-consciousness and nerves at being with people she didn't know. And to add to her unease she was at the same bar she'd been to with Ethan nearly a year ago. She remembered him saying that he often turned up there on Thursdays which were DJ nights. But maybe that was why she had come. Deep down she wanted to see him again.

Fortunately Parker's friends were as nice as him – mostly actors plus a couple of models who were all fascinated by Angel because of her beauty and her accent, which they all thought was 'so cute'. Their comments made her smile. To think how she was slated by some people back home for having a Brighton accent! She very quickly drank a glass of champagne, to give her confidence.

Parker sat next to her and always made sure that Angel's glass was topped up and that she was involved in the conversation. He was very sweet, but Angel hoped he didn't think he could be anything more than her friend. After a while a track came on that was one of her favourites.

'Do you want to dance?' Parker asked, seeing her tapping her fingers in rhythm on the table. 'Oh, come on,' he continued as she shook her head, and Angel thought, *Why the hell not?* Parker grabbed her hand and as she went to pull away, said, 'Angel, we're just friends, right? But it's my birthday. For one night, can't I be the envy of all these other men who think that you might, just might, be my girlfriend? Think of it as my birthday present.'

She laughed and kissed him on the cheek, saying, 'Okay!' then willingly took his hand and headed off for the dance area.

She had the shock of her life, though, when the

two of them wove their way through the clubbers and she noticed Ethan, chatting to a group of girls who seemed to be hanging on his every word. *How typical,* she thought dismissively. He hadn't seen her. Angel put her head down and practically legged it to the dance floor. Once there she made sure that she was looking in the opposite direction from where Ethan was standing but couldn't stay focused for long as Parker danced outrageously, deliberately camping it up to the music, dancing suggestively close to her or twirling her round and round, causing her to laugh out loud.

So it was that a dishevelled, out-of-breath Angel was leaving the dance area, hand in hand with Parker, when Ethan walked right in front of her. There was no escape from his intense blue eyes this time. Angel defiantly shook back her hair and tilted her chin up, as if to say, Come and have a go then.

'We really must stop meeting like this,' he said dryly. 'One more time and I'll think you're stalking me.'

'I'm just here with some friends,' she said quickly. 'I had no idea you would be here, but don't worry, I'm just leaving.'

'Heading off with your new boyfriend?' Ethan asked sarcastically.

She remembered with a pang their easy conversations in the past.

'He's not my boyfriend, he's in a film I'm in,' she

said hotly. Then she turned to her dance partner and said, 'Parker, this is Ethan Taylor.'

Parker was looking totally starstruck, and stuttered, 'Oh, I know who he is.' He reached out a hand to shake Ethan's and said, 'It's awesome to meet you. It's my birthday and it would be so cool if you could join us for a drink? I had no idea you were a friend of Angel's.' He looked at her as if to say, Why the hell didn't you tell me!

Angel was expecting Ethan to politely decline the invitation, but to her surprise he replied, 'Sure, I can stay for one drink before my date gets here.'

He was no doubt referring to cling-on Kasey. The three of them made their way back to the table, Parker leading the way with Ethan and Angel trailing along behind. *God, this was so embarrassing.* She just prayed no one asked how she knew Ethan.

She had imagined that he would play his cool offhand public persona with Parker's friends. Instead he was charm itself when they arrived at the table, shaking all the men's hands, kissing all the women, signing autographs. Everyone was in total awe of him and bombarded him with questions about how he thought the season was going and what he thought the Dodgers' chances of winning were. His replies were friendly and self-deprecating. Angel had forgotten what a truly nice guy he was, or at least she had willed herself to forget . . . She felt so awkward sitting with him, wondering what on earth he must think of her. Every now and then he would glance over at her and Angel would quickly look away, unable to meet his eye. She was just wondering how she could sneak away when Parker asked the question she'd been dreading: 'So, how do you two guys know each other?'

'We met briefly last year, when Angel's husband was over here playing soccer in the World Cup,' Ethan replied. He didn't mention her last visit. He was staring right at her while she did her best not to squirm in her seat with embarrassment. But she knew she was blushing, there were just too many memories.

'Anyway,' she said abruptly, making a big show of looking at her watch, 'I've really got to go, I'm still feeling pretty jet-lagged.' And she quickly got up and made as if to leave.

Ethan got up as well, saying, 'I'll walk you out,' then lowered his voice so that only she could hear. 'There are things you and I need to talk about, Angel.'

Oh, God. Angel's stomach plummeted at least twenty floors.

''Bye!' she said brightly to the group, giving Parker a quick kiss and waving to everyone else.

As she and Ethan walked away, she said, 'Thanks for coming over, it must have made Parker's birthday.'

Ethan put his hand on her shoulder and Angel could feel the heat of his touch through her thin silk top, which sent her stomach into another free fall. 'I didn't do it for Parker,' he said, and when Angel looked up at him his eyes had become warm again.

She was just wondering what to reply when Kasey appeared in front of them. She was wearing a few more clothes than at Larry's party, but only just – a pair of tiny white shorts and a white cropped halterneck top – and a very sulky expression. 'There you are!' she said petulantly. 'I've been looking all over for you, Ethan.' He abruptly removed his hand from Angel's shoulder.

'Angel, you remember Kasey?'

Angel nodded and, feeling Kasey's eyes boring holes into her, said, 'I'll see you then, Ethan.' Before he could stop her, she quickly wove her way through the clubbers to the exit, feeling simultaneously relieved and disappointed that she hadn't been able to hear what he had to say to her.

Angel had had no idea how knackering and boring it could be, appearing in a film. She'd naively thought she would breeze in, spend a bit of time in make up, rehearse her scene a couple of times, do a take and then go. Two days after that chance meeting, two long days during which she had tried and failed not to obsess about Ethan or Cal, she was on the film set at five a.m. and in make up. She felt more like a thing than a person as the make-up artist covered her in body paint to ensure that her skin looked absolutely flawlessly tanned. Her long hair wasn't deemed long enough and she had to be fitted with a blonde wig, which practically came down to her bum and instantly made Angel feel so hot she was sure she could feel the make up sliding off her. Then she was presented with her costume – a tiny red bikini top with a matching thong – and a full-scale row erupted because Angel drew the line at the thong.

'My agent said there would be no nudity,' she told the dresser.

'You won't be nude, you'll be wearing this,' the dresser insisted, sounding very pissed off, holding up the tiny garment in her hand.

'I count having my arse cheeks hanging out as being practically nude, I'm not doing it,' Angel said stubbornly. *She might have guessed something like this would happen.* Eventually a self-important-looking woman showed up wearing a headset and gripping a clipboard, to try and solve Thong Gate. After trying and failing to persuade Angel to change her mind, they agreed that she didn't have to wear the offending item.

After that she was left waiting in a robe for three hours before she went anywhere near the camera. Parker popped by to see her so at least she had him to talk to. As the time dragged by Angel grew increasingly nervous. She had learned her lines by heart but she also knew she was no actress and didn't want to make a complete idiot of herself. Parker was very sweet and gave her some pointers but Angel still didn't feel at all confident.

'And how come you're my brother when you've got an American accent and I've got an English one?' she asked.

'Oh, don't worry about it, no one will notice,' he said casually. Angel could only hope that he was right. 'So have you seen Ethan Taylor again?' he asked.

'I've no plans to,' Angel replied, somewhat abruptly as she was unsettled by the question. 'And I don't know him very well at all.'

'Pity, he's such a cool guy and you two would make a great couple. Oops, sorry, I forgot. You're married, aren't you?' Parker replied.

'Yes, I'm married,' Angel answered, turning away so he wouldn't see the look of pain in her eyes.

Her first scene was being shot at the poolside of her boyfriend's mansion. Her 'hard man' Russian boyfriend (oh, yes, this film really had left no cliché unused) was lying by the pool, on the phone to one of his henchmen, and all Angel had to do was hand him a drink, say, 'There you are, baby,' and then recline on the lounger next to him. Simple, or so Angel had thought, but it took over twenty takes before the director was satisfied, by which time she felt she would scream with frustration.

She was definitely not cut out for the acting world, she thought as she wearily returned to make up to get changed. By the time she returned home it was nearly six and Lucy was giving Honey her tea. It was so good to see her daughter. After hugging her, Angel collapsed into a chair at the kitchen table. 'I'll take over now, Lucy,' she told her. 'Go and have a swim or go shopping, I'll pay for the cab.'

She watched her daughter contentedly eating her yoghurt, spooning most of it over her tee-shirt but refusing all offers of help from Angel. 'You're so stubborn,' she told her, 'just like your dad!'

'Dada!' Honey said happily, looking round the room expectantly.

'Oh, Honey, Daddy's not here! But you'll see him soon, I promise,' Angel exclaimed, feeling that she was somehow keeping the little girl from her father.

She sighed and reached for her mobile to phone Cal. It went straight to voicemail so she simply left a message telling him that everything was fine, Honey had asked for him, and that she'd be going to bed soon as she was knackered from filming so there was no point in him calling her back.

It was true that she was exhausted but she could have spoken to him, just didn't want to. She was wiping off the yoghurt from Honey's face and right ear when her phone rang. She frowned when she saw it was not a number she recognised.

'Hello,' she said, instantly wary, dreading that it would be a journalist. But it was Logan, inviting her to a barbecue at his house. She was all set to refuse him but he managed to persuade her, telling her that his wife really wanted to meet her and that they had a little boy the same age as Honey. She wanted to ask if Ethan was going to be there as well, but couldn't bring herself to mention his name.

As soon as she put the phone down she wondered if she had done the right thing. What if Ethan was there? She felt so awkward in his company, and although she didn't want to admit it to herself there was still an attraction between them.

But then she had no more time to brood as the rest of the evening was taken up with trying to settle Honey. Angel ended up lying by her daughter's cot and holding her hand to comfort her and then must have fallen asleep herself. She woke up at midnight with a stiff neck, tiptoed out of the room and collapsed into her bed. She only had four hours before she was due to be picked up again for the second day's filming.

This time her scene was being shot in a casino and she was relieved that she'd get to wear a dress, though when she put on the jade green slinky gown she realised it was only slightly less revealing than the bikini as it had cutaways at the side, revealing most of her stomach, cleavage and back. Most of her body, come to think of it. A fact which she was quick to point out to Parker.

'Well, Angel, I don't mean to be rude, but I think that's kind of why you got the part, wasn't it?' he teased her.

'Okay, I know,' she replied; he was right, she shouldn't take herself so seriously. She didn't even have any lines to say in the next scene, she just had to sit there looking sexy and sultry, which took far fewer takes. Angel realised her gut feeling that she couldn't act was spot on, but at least she was under no illusions – unlike some stars who thought that just because they had excelled in one area they could shine in another, even with no discernible talent whatsoever. She made a vow to herself there and then to stick to glamour modelling.

A day later and she and Honey were being dropped off at Logan's mansion in Santa Monica. She took a moment to take in the view of stunning sandy beaches, palm trees, and the diamond glint of the Pacific Ocean. It was quite breathtaking. Two boys – one around ten, one eight – opened the door to them and with impeccable manners introduced themselves as Logan's sons, Jermaine and Roscoe. They then led the guests through the beautiful house to the vast garden. Angel had been expecting to see lots of people and was slightly taken aback to discover that it seemed to be just Logan's family. She also couldn't help feeling disappointed that there was no sign of Ethan . . . However she soon felt more relaxed when Logan introduced her to his wife Alisha, who was lovely and welcoming to Angel and Honey.

'What a beautiful daughter you have, Angel!' she exclaimed, reaching out and touching Honey's cheek. 'But then, I wouldn't have expected anything else with looks like yours.'

'Actually she looks exactly like her dad,' Angel replied.

'Dada!' Honey exclaimed again. It was lovely that she kept saying it, but every time she did it was like a punch in the stomach to Angel.

'Well, he must be one good-looking man,' Alisha continued.

'He is,' Angel replied, desperately wanting to change the subject. She was saved from further questions as Alisha's two-year-old, cute as a button son, Cody, toddled up, wrapped his arms round his mum's leg and started chanting, 'Swim, swim, Cody want to swim!'

Alisha laughed and scooped him up in her arms. 'How about it, Angel? Do you and Honey want to go in the pool before lunch?'

'Honey would love that, wouldn't you?' she replied.

412

For the next half-hour Angel played in the pool with Honey, Alisha and the boys while Logan busied himself with the barbecue. Seeing her daughter's blissful expression as she splashed about in the water, in her favourite Little Mermaid armbands and costume, helped lift Angel's spirits no end. *This is what matters,* she thought to herself, *that Honey is so happy.* And then she thought of Cal and how much he would have loved to have been here with his daughter. *Was she being selfish? Was she hurting Honey, by wanting to have some time to herself?* Angel didn't know; she just knew that she couldn't blindly stand by her man and appear to accept everything that had happened.

Suddenly Jermaine shouted out, 'Hey, he's here at last! Come on, Ethan, get in the water!' And when Angel turned round she was confronted by the sight of Ethan standing by the pool looking achingly cool and sexy in combats, a vest and Aviator Ray-Bans.

'No way am I getting in the water, guys!' he replied, sipping his beer. 'Hi, Angel,' he added, raising the bottle to her.

'Hi,' she replied, suddenly feeling self-conscious in front of him and turning her attention to Honey to avoid further conversation.

'Is Kasey with you?' Alisha called out.

'Nope, and she won't be again. We broke up,' Ethan replied, sounding perfectly happy about it.

At that moment the two boys crept up behind him and shoved him with all their strength, and because he was standing right on the edge of the pool, he lost his balance and went in with a huge splash, much to the boys' delight. They stood on the side giving each other high fives. Ethan emerged spluttering from the water.

'You, you – monkeys!' he exclaimed in mock anger. 'I'm going to pay you back. Maybe not this afternoon, maybe not tomorrow, but one day . . .'

Angel and Alisha burst out laughing. 'You don't really mind, do you, Ethan?' Alisha asked. 'I'll get Logan to find you some fresh clothes.'

'No, I'm used to it,' he replied ruefully, wiping the water from his eyes.

'Ethan is Jermaine's godfather,' Alisha explained, 'and Jermaine sees it as his mission to make him suffer for it! Fortunately for Jermaine, Ethan's just about the most laidback guy around kids that I've ever met.'

More praise for Ethan! To avoid replying, Angel dived underwater, retrieved Ethan's shades and handed them to him.

'Thanks,' he replied, smiling, and while Angel was relieved to see that he no longer looked at her so coldly, she was completely wrongfooted by the new look in his eyes – of warmth, and unless she was mistaken desire . . . But it only lasted a few seconds because then his attention was taken up by Honey and he spent the next few minutes entertaining her, making her giggle by swimming underwater and then popping up to the surface when she least expected it. And then he got involved in a chasing game with Jermaine and Roscoe. Angel was completely disarmed by this side of him; she hadn't expected him to be so good with kids.

'Food's up!' Logan called from the barbecue, and everyone exited the pool. Angel tried not to look at Ethan, tried not to notice how his wet clothes clung to his body, but when she thought she was safe she sneaked an appraising glance only to be caught out when he looked right at her.

She quickly got Honey dried and changed and dressed, just slipping a long white tee-shirt over her own bikini. Logan and Ethan disappeared inside to find him some dry clothes, and while Alisha got the children settled round the outside table she chatted away to Angel about her husband's team mate. In the space of five minutes Angel discovered that he was one of their oldest and closest friends and that he was an all round great guy. Angel couldn't help feeling that Alisha was trying to sell him to her.

'Has Ethan paid you to be so complimentary?' she asked. 'I hope my friends are as nice about me as you are about him!'

Alisha shook her head and smiled. 'No! It's just, I wouldn't want you to be put off by his reputation in the press – he's really not like that. I mean, sure, he's gone out with a few women. I mean, a lot of women,' she added, seeing Angel's sceptical expression, 'but I think he's just waiting for "the one", if you know what I mean?'

At that moment the two men returned and Logan enveloped his wife in a huge hug. Angel looked on, envying their closeness, thinking back to the good times between her and Cal.

Over lunch she found herself sitting opposite Ethan and had to steel herself to stay calm. In contrast to the last two occasions they had met, he was charming, almost back to how he had been last year – almost, but not quite. It was as if he was holding something back. *And who could blame him?* Angel thought. Now he was asking her how long she was over in LA for.

'Just another week,' she replied. 'I've only got one more scene to shoot.' At this she rolled her eyes. 'It may well be my one and only film role.'

'I'm sure you're great,' Ethan replied.

Angel laughed dismissively. 'I won't be picking up an Oscar any time soon, more likely to be a Razzie!'

He smiled. 'You should stay out in LA a little longer, you'd soon learn not to be so down on yourself. By the way,' he added, lowering his voice, 'I was sorry to hear about what has been going on back home with the press. It must be hard.'

'I suppose that's partly why I took the film, it was

a chance to get away,' she answered, turning to check on Honey's progress with her bowl of pasta so she wouldn't have to look at Ethan.

'Well, in spite of how it must have seemed, it's good to see you again, Angel,' he said softly.

And when she looked up at him he was staring at her. She felt his gaze on her like a caress and suddenly remembered what it felt like to kiss him . . . so damn' good . . . and was only too aware that her nipples had hardened in response to the memory and were clearly visible through her thin tee-shirt. *Damn him for being so gorgeous! She didn't need this complication.*

After lunch, as Honey was clearly exhausted from all the swimming, Alisha kindly suggested that Angel put her in Cody's cot for a nap, assuring her that they could have the baby monitor on outside. Angel gratefully took her up on the offer and spent a while settling her daughter before she returned outside.

She checked her appearance in the mirror in the hallway. Her cheeks were flushed and there was a sparkle in her eyes that hadn't been there for a while. *Get a grip,* she told herself sternly. She quickly brushed her hair, still wet from the pool, and tried to regain her composure. *Maybe she should have taken this opportunity to leave; Ethan was dangerous to be around. He aroused such strong feelings in her.*

'Still the most beautiful woman I've ever seen.' Ethan appeared from nowhere and leaned against the wall, staring at her.

Angel shrugged dismissively, but oh, how she wanted it to be true.

He moved towards her. 'I told you how I felt last time we met, Angel, and my feelings haven't changed. In spite of your best efforts to break my heart.' Now he was standing so close to her that their bodies were almost touching. He moved closer so his mouth was practically brushing against hers.

'I still want you, Angel,' he murmured, moving even closer so that now his lips were on hers, lightly at first as if he was expecting her to pull away at any second.

But Angel didn't pull away this time; she kissed him back, teasingly at first, then with deeper, hungrier kisses, wrapping her arms round his neck and pressing her body against his. *God, he felt so good*. She wanted him with an intensity that she hadn't realised was within her. She felt lost in her desire for him.

Suddenly it was Ethan who was pulling away. 'I'm sorry, that should never have happened,' he said, head bowed, not looking at her. 'I must go.'

And before Angel had the chance to say anything to stop him, he was walking away. As if in a daze she heard the front door open and close. He had really gone.

Angel was in turmoil. She didn't know what to think, what to do. As soon as she got back to the rented house she called Gemma, desperate for her friend's advice, but again she sounded so down that Angel realised she couldn't talk about her own feelings. She called Jez but he was still in the grip of wedding planning meltdown, ranting because the florists were unable to provide him with flowers that exactly matched the pale lilac suit he was going to wear.

'Honestly! It's not rocket science, is it?' he exclaimed 'I just want everything to co-ordinate, is it too much to ask?'

'I'm sure everything will look fine,' Angel said wearily.

'Fine!' Jez spat back. 'Fine won't fucking cut it! I want *divine*!'

Realising there was no chance of getting a sensible word out of him, she said goodbye, promising that she would be back in time for his stag night. And then it was just her and her thoughts, tumbling round her head like some insane merry-go-round that Angel longed to get off.

What were her feelings for Ethan? Was it just lust because he was so gorgeous? Or was she looking for revenge because of Cal's infidelity? No, there was more to it than that. It felt so right when she was with Ethan. And it was more than a physical attraction, though that was powerful; she felt connected to him, felt that he understood her. Over and over the questions went round in her head, and she felt a sudden surge of rage against Cal for putting her in this unbearable situation. It never would have come to this if he hadn't betrayed her. He had made their marriage, which she had thought was a beautiful, unbreakable thing, into something tarnished and she couldn't forgive him for it.

'Okay, that's a wrap, everybody!' Camilla shouted out.

Thank God for that! Angel thought. She'd finished shooting her final scene, where she was shot by the hero of the film who was trying to shoot her megalomaniac boyfriend. It had taken just the fifty takes to get it right. She walked wearily back to her dressing room, desperate to take off the costume which was now stiff with fake blood. As she walked into the room her heart skipped a beat because there was Ethan.

'I wanted to apologise again,' he said quietly, his face serious.

'There's nothing to apologise for,' she said warmly. 'Nothing at all.'

'Yes, there is!' he said passionately. 'You're going through all this shit with your marriage, you don't need me complicating things for you.'

'No,' Angel replied, equally passionately, '*I'm* the one who's sorry – for the way I treated you. I didn't mean to lead you on like that. It was wrong of me.'

'But understandable,' he said ruefully. 'Anyway, Angel, I just wanted to say good luck. And in another life maybe we could have . . . well, you know.' And then he left.

What was it with him, walking out on her the whole time? Angel paced feverishly round the dressing room. He'd sounded as if he never wanted to see her again. Was that really what *she* wanted? She couldn't deny her feelings for Ethan. Suddenly the thought of never seeing him again was unbearable to her. She knew what she had to do.

Her heart seemed to be beating so wildly that she thought the limo driver must be able to hear it. The closer they got to Ethan's beach house the more nervous she grew. *He probably won't even be there,* she told herself, trying to hang on to the last scrap of rational thought she had left. *But he had to be! She had to see him. She couldn't wait another second.*

When they drew up to the house, the limo driver announced her arrival in the intercom. As soon as the gates were opened, Angel was out of the car and running to the front door. She was about to ring the bell when the door was opened by Ethan. He looked stunned to see her and was about to speak when she burst out, 'What if I want us to be together in *this* life?'

His eyes searched hers for a second as if he was trying to read the truth. And then they were in each other's arms and all Angel could think was that she wanted him so badly, nothing else mattered.

They kissed – feverish, hungry kisses that left Angel wanting more. She ran her hands over his body, slipped them under his tee-shirt and touched his smooth hard skin as he unbuttoned her dress and caressed her breasts. And then he was picking her up and carrying her upstairs to his bedroom, where he laid her on the bed. For a moment he looked at her as if he was unable to believe that she was really there, and then they were tearing off each other's clothes. Angel gasped in pleasure as he explored her body with his hands, with his tongue, and inside she felt as if she had turned to liquid fire. Then she was pushing him back on the bed, caressing his hard muscular body, and it was as beautiful and sexy as she had imagined. And there was no guilty voice in her head telling her to stop, just her need to carry on making love with this beautiful man . . .

'Beautiful Angel,' Ethan murmured afterwards, tracing her mouth with his finger. 'Are you sure I haven't died and gone to heaven? Can you be real?'

She smiled. 'Oh, I'm real.' And she kissed his finger, then gently sucked it.

Ethan groaned. 'I know I told you once I had stamina, but even I need a bit longer!'

Angel only sucked his finger harder. It had been good the first time, but she just knew it would be even better the second . . .

It was early-evening by the time she left him; they'd spent the whole afternoon in bed. Part of Angel didn't want to leave, wanted to stay with him – where everything seemed clear, where everything was about their desire for each other. But she had to get back to Honey. Ethan had wanted to come with her but Angel wasn't ready for that, not yet anyway.

There were several messages from Cal but she didn't return them. She had once thought that she and Cal would be even if she slept with Ethan and that then she could pick up the pieces of her marriage. But Cal had hurt her so deeply she no longer felt like that, she just thought about Ethan. She was completely intoxicated by him. She spent the next two days in a lust-fuelled dream, longing for the nights when she could be with him. Lucy obviously knew something was going on but was too discreet to say anything. And when Honey was finally asleep at night, Angel would get straight into the limo Ethan had sent over for her.

On her final night in LA talk between the two of them turned serious. They'd just made love and it was even sweeter than before. Now they were outside, lying on a blanket together, staring at the stars.

'I can't bear the thought of you leaving tomorrow,' he said, gently kissing her.

'I'll be back soon,' Angel replied, 'I promise. I just have to go to my friend's wedding, sort some things out.'

'What about –' Ethan hesitated before saying '– Cal?'

'I'll tell him I've met someone else,' Angel replied. Lying here with Ethan, everything seemed so simple.

'He won't want to let you go,' Ethan replied, holding her tight in his arms. 'If I was him, I would never let you go.'

'He's lost me,' she replied, 'I want to be with you.' And now she was kissing him back, wishing that she didn't have to leave.

'I have to tell you something, Angel.' He paused, and for a moment she feared that he was going to say that there was someone else. Instead he continued, 'You probably think it's too soon to be saying this, but I can't stop myself. I love you, Angel. Love you more than I have ever loved anyone.' He was gazing at her intently and she felt as if he was looking into her soul.

'I love you too, Ethan,' she whispered back.

'You will come back to me, won't you?' he asked.

'I will,' she replied, pulling him back down to her again.

Chapter 15

Angel's Choice

During her three-week stay in LA, Angel had largely managed to avoid the attention of the press. There had been the odd paparazzo snap, but she thought she'd managed to keep a low enough profile and had not been seen anywhere in public with Ethan. But she had underestimated the British tabloids' hunger for a story and arrived back home to a media storm. The first she knew of it was when she landed at Gatwick and was surrounded by a scrum of photographers, but this time the name they were shouting out wasn't Cal's, it was Ethan's.

'What's going on with you and Ethan Taylor? You're having an affair with him, aren't you?' She put her head down and didn't say a word.

Thank God Ray appeared with two of his lads, and helped clear a path through the crowds for her and Honey. 'I told Cal it would be better if he stayed in the car with this lot around,' he said quietly.

Angel bit her lip and nodded. She had known all along that she would have to tell her husband the truth, but in her worst nightmares she had never dreamed it would be like this. She was expecting him to be angry when he saw her but he was subdued, simply giving her a kiss on the cheek and making a big fuss of Honey, who was overjoyed at seeing her daddy again.

'I understand why you did what you did, Angel. I know I deserved something like this,' Cal said as he drove them out of the airport. 'But now we can start again, can't we?' He looked so hopeful that Angel didn't think she could bear it.

'Let's not talk now,' she replied, staring out of the window to avoid seeing his hurt expression.

Back home she pleaded jet-lag and went to bed while Cal looked after Honey. When he finally came up, she pretended to be asleep. She knew it was cowardly of her but she wasn't up to talking. Cal put his arm round her and whispered, 'Love you, Angel,' and her eyes filled with tears, but she didn't reply.

Everything had seemed so simple and clear-cut when she was out in LA with Ethan. She would tell Cal it was over, and that she wanted to be with Ethan. But seeing her husband again had shaken everything up and now she just didn't know what she wanted. Nor did they get a chance to talk the following day as Cal had to rush off to Rufus's stag night which was being held in Manchester, while Angel had to go to Jez's which was in London.

Angel had been dreading that Jez was going to want to throw a wild stag do in the style of one of Kate Moss's parties. But Jez in fact had remarkably restrained plans – they were to start with a cream tea at Brown's Hotel in Mayfair; have cocktails at the Sanderson, followed by dinner at Nobu. Despite being in LA, Angel had called all Jez's friends who were going and asked them to buy him a small gift and write something for a book of photographs and memories she was compiling for him. She was really looking forward to showing the resulting scrapbook to Gemma as the two girls were going to travel up to London together. She was also hoping for a heart to heart with her best friend.

But Gemma had other things on her agenda. As soon as the driver picked her up she started on Angel.

'What the fuck do you think you're doing getting involved with that Ethan? Have you gone mad? Do you know what it's been doing to Cal?'

Angel could hardly believe her ears. 'Why are you having a go at me! If it hadn't been for Cal, I never would have got close to Ethan! You're my best friend, you're supposed to be on *my* side!'

But Gemma wasn't going to stop at that, she was in full flow. 'I think you've turned into one of those LA air heads. You have no idea how upset Cal has been, have you? On top of worrying about losing you, he's been beside himself thinking that you're going to leave him and take Honey. You should have seen him the other night. He came round to ours, and honest to God, I've never seen Cal in that state before. He was crying, Angel. I don't suppose you thought of that while you were busy shagging your baseball star – who, by the way, has the worst reputation with women ever. He's a dog! He's shagged everyone!'

'Oh, and Cal's perfect, isn't he!' Angel shot back. 'He had a three-month affair, Gemma, have you forgotten that? And anyway, Ethan's different with me. He told me he loved me, and I think I'm in love with him.'

'Oh, please! You just think you are. And he only said that to get into your knickers.'

'Really, Gemma, he's not like that,' Angel said again.

Gemma looked at her in disgust. 'I think you'll be making a big mistake if you leave Cal for him.'

'Okay, well, *I* think you've said enough, don't you?' Angel answered abruptly. She couldn't believe that her best friend was turning against her like this. It was a total nightmare. The girls were silent for the next twenty minutes, ignoring each other until Angel could bear it no longer and said, 'Anyway, how are you feeling, Gemma?'

'I'm fine,' came the brittle reply, making it clear that this was not a conversation she wanted to pursue. And much as Angel wanted to make things up with her she realised it would have to wait – today was about Jez.

As they drew up at Brown's, Angel took a deep breath and steeled herself. She was going to start pretending everything was great in her life. She'd got used to doing that lately . . .

Fortunately it was wonderful to see Jez who was on fine form, loving being the centre of attention. 'Angel!' he cried as soon as he saw her, kissing her and giving her a hug. 'It's so *fantastico* to see you! I've missed you! And there's so much gossip to catch up on.'

Angel whispered so that only he could hear, 'I'll tell you later, Jez, but not today, because today is all about you.'

He put his hand on his heart and assumed a mock Texan drawl. 'Well, being as how I'm so shy and retiring, I don't know if I can cope with that, Miss Summer.'

'Oh, give over!' she exclaimed. 'We've got presents!'

Jez's eyes gleamed. 'Well, why didn't you say?' And the whole group laughed.

Angel did her best to smile and seem light-hearted, but her heart felt so heavy, and she was devastated by Gemma's comments. Her best friend spent the rest of the party ignoring her.

Ethan texted her halfway through the evening. Angel's heart flipped when she read, *Miss you, Angel, miss your body, miss your kiss, miss you. Love you x*. She wanted to reply but saw Gemma looking at her and couldn't. Cal also texted her. *I love you, Angel, never forget that. Let's talk tomorrow x*.

Angel had always thought it ridiculous when people said they were in love with two people, but right now she felt torn . . . Instead of travelling back with Angel to Brighton, Gemma said she was staying in London so Angel went home alone. It was two in the morning. In LA it would be eleven. She wondered what Ethan was doing. She longed to hear his voice, but didn't know what to say if he asked her when she was coming back.

She spent Sunday at her parents' with Honey. They both made a huge fuss of their grand-daughter. They had obviously read the story about Angel and Ethan because practically the first thing her dad said was, 'That's a lot of nonsense, isn't it, about you and that baseball player? You and Cal are back together now, aren't you?'

'I don't want to talk about it,' Angel replied, surly as a teenager. The last person she wanted to discuss her love life with was her dad.

And all day she was dreading Cal coming back,

dreading that they would have to talk. He finally returned home around eight. Angel was sitting in the lounge staring blankly at the TV. She had no idea what was on.

'How was Rufus's stag night?' she asked, falsely cheerful.

'It was good, quite restrained, though I did get propositioned in a gay club.'

'Great,' Angel replied, not listening to him. 'Do you want something to eat?'

'No,' he replied, sitting down next to her. 'I want you to tell me what happened between you and Ethan?'

Angel shook her head. 'I really don't want to, Cal.'

'Don't want to because it didn't mean anything and doesn't matter, or don't want to because it meant something?' Cal's voice faltered here. Angel turned to him and saw the look of hurt and pain in his brown eyes.

'It did mean something, Cal. It does mean something,' she said quietly.

'But we can get through this, can't we?' he said. 'It's just because of what I did, but we can get over it. It doesn't matter about Ethan, I don't care that you were lovers, so long as you stay with me. I know I really messed up, but please, Angel, don't leave me.'

His eyes were full of tears. Angel felt as if her

heart was being ripped apart, she just hadn't expected such anguish from him. She couldn't do this to Cal. She put her arms round him and for a while they held each other tight.

'Why haven't you returned any of my calls?' Ethan was on the phone to her. Angel was standing at the kitchen window, watching Cal push Honey on the swing in the garden.

'I'm sorry, it's been impossible,' she replied.

'So have you told him you're leaving?' Ethan persisted.

Angel hesitated.

'I'll take that as a no then,' Ethan replied, sounding hurt, then added, 'Angel, please tell me what's going on? I miss you.' And this time his voice was low and intimate, and stirred up strong feelings in her.

'I miss you too,' she whispered back, staring out at Honey laughing in delight as Cal pushed her higher and higher in the swing. Then, summoning all her strength, and knowing she had to make this sacrifice, she went on, 'But I'm married.'

There was a long exhalation of breath from Ethan. 'Don't do this,' he implored her. 'You can't act as if our time meant nothing to you. Angel, we are meant to be together. I love you and I know you love me.'

'Goodbye, Ethan,' she said in a cold, hard voice

that she didn't recognise as being her own, and switched off her phone.

Somehow she got through the next couple of days, but she felt as if she was sleepwalking. She longed for Ethan, ached for him so badly. No, she told herself sternly, over and over, she would not allow those thoughts in, she would get through this, and soon he would be a distant memory. She wouldn't think about him. Cal was clearly relieved that she was staying and was acting as if nothing had happened, desperate for them both to put the past behind them.

'We should really think about renewing our vows soon,' he said as they lay in bed together, the night before Jez's wedding.

'Mmm,' Angel replied, her heart sinking. She didn't know if she was ready to do that yet. And there was something else. Since she'd returned home, she hadn't wanted to make love with Cal, and every time he went to touch her she pulled away, made some excuse. When he kissed her she felt as if she was betraying Ethan, which was mad because she had told him it was over, hadn't she?

She had barely spoken to Gemma since Jez's stag night and so when it came to the wedding day Angel was fully expecting to do her own make up. But on the morning of the wedding Gemma finally called her.

'Do you want me to do your make up then?' she asked, still not sounding particularly friendly.

'It's okay, I can do it myself if it's a problem,' Angel replied, feeling sad that Gemma was being so distant with her.

'I'll do it,' she insisted. 'Jez would never forgive us if you didn't look perfect for his day. I'm sure he'd have you airbrushed out of the pictures if you didn't look fabulous!' Finally she was back to sounding like the old Gemma.

'If you're sure?' Angel answered.

'Yes,' Gemma insisted. 'And I'm sorry I had such a go at you. I completely understand why you got involved with Ethan. I had no right to be so judgemental. It's just, I was still feeling so upset after the miscarriage that I took it out on you.'

They ended the call by agreeing that Angel would drive over to Gemma's flat and meet Cal at the wedding.

'Jez, you look amazing!' Angel exclaimed as she walked into the hotel room where he was getting ready. Lack of finances had caused Jez and Rufus to scale down their wedding plans, and instead of the stately home Jez had dreamed of they had booked out a boutique hotel in Brighton.

'Really? Are you sure?' an uncharacteristically nervous Jez asked as he fiddled with his hair. 'Do you think Rufus will like the suit?' He was wearing a beautifully cut pinstripe suit with a lilac shirt – he had ditched his plans to wear a lilac suit, saying it made him look too queenie.

'He'll love it! You look so handsome . . . and so masculine!' Angel replied, walking across the room and giving him a reassuring hug.

'You sound surprised,' he answered. 'Didn't you think I could pull it off?'

'Of course I did!' Angel assured him, giving herself a mental smack on the head because Jez was hyper-sensitive to any comments about his appearance.

'Shall I walk you downstairs?' she asked.

Jez nodded and as he took her arm said emotionally, 'I can't believe that I'm actually doing this! It sounds like such a cliché but this really is the happiest day of my life.'

'I'm so happy for you, Jez,' she told him, willing herself not to think about Ethan.

Jez and Rufus were getting married in the hotel's garden. The trees had been hung with red and pink lanterns, and an arch decorated with flowers had been set up on the lawn. They would say their vows beneath it. Guests sat on cushions on the grass – Jez had a horror of rows of chairs, saying they reminded him of school – and music was provided by a harpist. Rufus was already waiting under the arch with Cal standing to one side as Angel and Jez walked slowly towards them. Cal was looking at his wife with such a look of love Angel forced herself to smile back.

She had tears in her eyes throughout the ceremony. She was very happy for Jez but at the same time remembered her own wedding vows. They had promised to be faithful to each other, and now look at them. They had both been unfaithful, had broken these very vows, and now there were Jez and Rufus embarking on their own marriage, full of hope. Angel felt as if her own store of it had been used up. Something had been broken in her marriage and could never be repaired.

After the ceremony handsome young men, stripped to the waist and wearing wide-legged purple silk trousers, circulated with trays of champagne and pale pink cocktails.

Cal sought Angel out. 'That was great wasn't it?' he said, putting his arm round her.

Angel nodded. She just didn't want to be with him right now. She was haunted by thoughts of Ethan, fearful that she had made a mistake by telling him she didn't want him. So she slipped away from Cal when he got talking to one of the guests. She went inside the hotel and locked herself into one of the bathrooms where she sat on the edge of the bath and took out her mobile to start typing a text to Ethan, saying that she was sorry and she really needed to talk to him. Then she sighed and deleted it all. There was no way he was ever going to want to have anything to do with her again, after the way she'd treated him.

She returned to the reception and tried to appear as upbeat and carefree as the other guests while her heart felt so heavy. Cal stayed close to her and again put his arm round her. Angel had to fight the urge to tell him to take it off her, tell him that she didn't belong to him. It was a relief when it was time to go inside for the wedding breakfast.

After the main course, which she picked her way through, it was time for the speeches. Angel gave hers first. As she loathed public speaking it was short, sweet and to the point. She just recounted a couple of funny anecdotes about Jez and wished the couple every happiness. Then it was Cal's turn. In contrast, he was extremely good at public speaking and his speech was entertaining and funny. Angel remembered him giving the best man's speech at Gemma and Tony's wedding when he had ended up proposing to her out of the blue. It had been the most romantic moment of her life . . .

Then she tuned back into this speech and was shocked to hear Cal making it personal again. 'I've been married to Angel for nearly two years and I'm sure you all know something of what we've been through. There were times when it looked like we might not last but we've pulled through . . . we're pulling through.' He was staring right at her, as if willing her to feel the same. 'I can't marry Angel a second time, but I do want to declare my love for her again – sorry, Jez, I know it's your day, but being at a wedding, thinking about love, has made everything clear to me. Angel, what do you say? Will you renew your vows with me?'

Cal looked at her expectantly; the whole roomful of guests looked at her expectantly. It was too much. Angel tried to keep things light, but felt herself trembling under the pressure when she replied, 'Oh, Cal, it *is* Jez and Rufus's day, and I don't think Jez would ever forgive me if I upstaged him. Can we talk about this later, please?'

Cal looked momentarily shocked but quickly recovered himself and proposed a toast to Jez and Rufus before making his way back to her.

While Jez and Rufus worked the room he said quietly to Angel, 'I don't feel totally humiliated then.'

'Cal, I'm sorry, but we've been through so much. I just need more time.'

'That's exactly why we need to make this commitment again. Then, as well as telling each other of our love, we could get the press off our backs.'

'I don't fucking care about the press!' Angel exclaimed, suddenly furious with her husband. 'And, remember, *you* were the one who got us into this!'

She got up and abruptly walked away. She was just making a beeline for Gemma when the hotel receptionist came up and informed her that a gentleman was waiting to see her in reception.

'Well, who is it?' Angel demanded, automatically assuming it would be a journalist.

'He didn't leave his name but assured me that he wasn't from the press.'

Sighing, Angel turned and followed the receptionist.

When she walked into the hotel lobby she got the shock of her life. There, sitting in an armchair and looking more wickedly handsome than ever, was Ethan. For a second she was almost speechless then she managed to stutter, 'Wh-what are you doing here?'

He got up and walked towards her. 'I just had to see you again, Angel.'

She was about to speak when Cal marched up behind her and said angrily, 'What the fuck's *he* doing here? She made it clear she wanted nothing more to do with you, so get out.'

'I don't think that's true,' Ethan said quietly. 'And I think it's Angel's turn to speak, don't you?'

'Well, you know what she's going to say, don't you? She's already made up her mind – she's staying with me,' Cal said, though his voice had started to falter.

Angel took a deep breath. It was now or never.

She had to make a choice . . . and then she knew with absolute certainty who she wanted to be with. If she didn't go with him, she would regret it for the rest of her life. So she turned to the man she knew she had to be with, looked him in the eye, and said, 'Ethan, take me, I'm yours.'

Sapphire

Katie Price

Sapphire Jones doesn't believe in relationships any more – not since she caught her husband in bed with another woman. Now Sapphire only sees men on her terms, which is why her current lover is younger than her, good-looking, doesn't place any emotional demands on her (so far, fingers crossed) and is great in bed. What more does a girl need?

Sapphire puts all her passion into running her own business – a high-end lingerie and hen-weekend company. She is doing well and life seems pretty good until she meets a very handsome, charming businessman who seems more than a match for Sapphire. Then things go badly wrong at the hen party she has planned for a soap star and tabloid darling. The evening is one that everyone will be talking about for all the wrong reasons, and Sapphire faces front-page headlines all of her own . . .

Suddenly her business is in jeopardy, her well-controlled private life is falling apart, and in the middle of all this Sapphire realises that she is not immune to love after all, but has she left it too late?

'An incredibly addictive read' *heat*

'Fun and full of excitement. A feisty tale of friendship, love and fame that's bound to be a bestseller' *Woman*

arrow books

ALSO AVAILABLE IN ARROW

Paradise

Katie Price

It's six months since beautiful model Angel Summer found herself having to choose between a life with Ethan Turner, the laid-back Californian baseball player, or giving her marriage to football star Cal Bailey another go. Her friends and family were stunned when she picked Ethan, but it looks like Angel made the right decision: Ethan loves her and she loves him.

But nothing is perfect. Ethan has secrets in his past that could threaten their relationship and when he faces financial ruin the couple are forced to star in a reality TV show about their life together. Despite everything, though, Angel is convinced that Ethan is the man for her. So why can't she stop thinking about Cal?

As the tabloids have always been quick to point out, the path of true love has never run smoothly for our sexy celebrity, and when her dad falls dangerously ill Angel rushes back to England to be by his bedside, throwing her and Cal back together. But Ethan loves her, Cal has a girlfriend, and Angel has made her choice. It's too late to go back now . . . isn't it?

'A fabulous guilty holiday pleasure' *Heat*

'Peppered with cutting asides and a directness you can only imagine coming from Katie Price, it's a fun, blisteringly paced yet fluffy novel.' *Cosmopolitan*

arrow books

THE POWER OF READING

Visit the Random House website and get connected with information on all our books and authors

EXTRACTS from our recently published books and selected backlist titles

COMPETITIONS AND PRIZE DRAWS Win signed books, audiobooks and more

AUTHOR EVENTS Find out which of our authors are on tour and where you can meet them

LATEST NEWS on bestsellers, awards and new publications

MINISITES with exclusive special features dedicated to our authors and their titles

READING GROUPS Reading guides, special features and all the information you need for your reading group

LISTEN to extracts from the latest audiobook publications

WATCH video clips of interviews and readings with our authors

RANDOM HOUSE INFORMATION including advice for writers, job vacancies and all your general queries answered

Come home to Random House

www.rbooks.co.uk